D0386878

THE DRAGON
OF HANDALE

THE DRAGON OF HANDALE

CASSANDRA CLARK

MINOTAUR BOOKS
NEW YORK

THE DRAGON OF HANDALE. Copyright © 2015 by Cassandra Clark. All rights reserved. Printed in the United States of America. For information, address St. Martin's Press, 175 Fifth Avenue, New York, N.Y. 10010.

www.minotaurbooks.com

Designed by Omar Chapa

The Library of Congress Cataloging-in-Publication Data is available upon request.

ISBN 978-1-250-05886-7 (hardcover)
ISBN 978-1-4668-6338-5 (e-book)

Minotaur books may be purchased for educational, business, or promotional use. For information on bulk purchases, please contact the Macmillan Corporate and Premium Sales Department at 1-800-221-7945, extension 5442, or write to specialmarkets@macmillan.com.

First Edition: March 2015

10 9 8 7 6 5 4 3 2 1

To my dear white hart

ACKNOWLEDGMENTS

Many thanks to Bill, Marshall, John, and the sturdy walkers of Loftus who, with the help of the magnificent Sustrans, accompanied me along the pannier way to Handale.

THE DRAGON OF HANDALE

Chapter 1

The blade plunged gently between the man's buttocks, then pushed its full length in one slow movement to the hilt. The action was perfectly controlled. The stiletto was withdrawn and the assassin wiped the blade on his surcoat. His accomplice, pressing the man's face into the bedclothes, felt the shudder run through him.

Replacing the stiletto in its sheath, the assassin picked up the leather document bag from beside the bed, fingered through it, then threw it to the floor, grunting, "Untie him. Let's get out."

They had picked up the courier's trail outside York after he left the archbishop's palace, taking over from the previous riders, who had followed him all the way from Westminster. For sure he became aware of them fairly soon. The flat November light could conceal no one. The roads were deserted, apart from a few peasants walking to the fields.

Autumn rains had churned the track through the forest to mud, and even the well-maintained king's highway made hellish going. Horses up to their bellies in mud. Slipping, stumbling, near enough breaking their legs to keep up. He was riding at a desperate speed. To make it worse, the rivers were in spate, and many fords were impassable. He gave them a run for their money all right, doubling back on himself, even turning off the road and striking out into dense woodland when the opportunity arose, and generally making life difficult for them. They cursed when they lost him somewhere near Knaresborough but rejoiced when they picked up his trail—more by chance than from their own skill, as they admitted—when he started out across the moors.

"He's going the wrong away about it if he thinks he's heading for Alnwick Castle," observed the elder of the two. His accent was northern but not Scottish. The man with him gave a growl of assent. Like a lymer, he hunted in silence. And he didn't care where the man was going. He wouldn't get there.

On the high moor, the trail led towards the coast, Whitby the only town of note unless he decided to strike north to the Tees. He was perfectly visible now, with nowhere to hide in the oppressive desolation. It was made worse by bellied clouds full of sleet. The load was scattered now and then, driving hard fragments of ice into their muffled faces. They allowed him to keep a mile or so ahead, as if running free. He was a dot in the landscape, the only moving thing. A speck of colour hardly brighter than the winter moors, comical really, riding hard down one side of the undulating moorland and equally hard up the other. All that effort.

They saw him disappear over a far ridge, and when they reached the top themselves, there he was again, still kicking up the mud, horse racing as gallantly as ever, with mane flying, across the wide dale below. But even the best courier has to stop sometime.

He chose an inn conspicuously in the middle of nowhere. Perhaps he thought nothing could happen to him with so few travellers on the road. A stranger highly visible in such a place. Anything that happened would be noticed at once, the perpetrators seen and remembered.

Maybe that's how his pursuers thought about it, as well. His disappearance would be an event in this godforsaken place. His lord and master would be informed as soon as ever. His missive still-born, as it were. And maybe that's how they wanted it.

They closed in.

"Has a companion of ours just ridden up, master?" They knew he had.

The aleman gave them a sharp look. "He might have."

"Wanting to get his head down for an hour or so, I shouldn't wonder. We noticed his horse in your yard. He rides like the devil. We have a message for him, but it's taken us a hell of a ride to catch up with him." Squat, mongrel-featured, his local accent making him acceptable, and he gave what passed for a smile to add to it.

The alemaster nodded. "He's bested you, all right. He's taken t' chamber up aloft." He thumbed the air above his head. "Nobody else in this day. The weather. Who's travelling in this but for thieves and gentlemen such as yourselves?" He lifted an eyebrow. A big man. Veteran of the Scottish wars. A cleaver on the trestle in front of him. He could afford to say what he liked.

"We'll go and disturb him from his slumber, beggin' your leave." The man nudged his companion.

Unchecked, the two went out.

The alemaster was suddenly uneasy. He glanced at his companion, a Saxon blonde, breasts jutting out of her shift the way he liked, and frowned. "What do you say, Mary dove?"

"Oh, let them be. They're covered in muck. They must have been on the road for hours. It's nowt to do with us. They can only be heading for Whitby, and what's there?"

He shook his head. Priests and fish merchants came and went. His regulars were shepherds. When the fair was on at Corpus Christi, it was different.

"Go up and see if you can hear owt."

Flouncing, but wary of disobeying in case he decided he could do without her, she climbed the wooden stairs and hovered outside the door. Came only the murmur of men's voices from within. Then a little silence. An exclamation following. Nothing much. When she heard footsteps crossing the floor, she hurriedly slipped back down the stairs, and the two men only caught up with her when she was at the bottom.

The shorter of the two gave her a lingering leer and his glance came to rest on her breasts with such intensity, it seemed he would never look away. "Time for a quick one, mistress?" he asked, his eyes never lifting. He moved closer. She could smell his breath.

"What's your will, master?"

He squeezed one of the swollen globes and sighed, then pressed himself against her, so she could feel the doorframe digging into her back and the links of his chain-mail hauberk crushing her breasts.

"You'd best ask"—she nodded towards the aleman—"and settle it with him."

He stepped back. "We'll eat first. Our friend does not want to be disturbed until morning. He gives you this." He held up a silver coin. "Later," he told her as she reached for it. "Don't be greedy."

Affronted by the man, she turned to the alemaster, but he pretended not to have heard and instead continued to pour the two guests long stoups of ale from a flagon, then chivvied her into going out back to bring bread and pottage for them.

When they left, the alemaster lifted Mary's skirt and gave a groan as he entered her and began to pound her against the counter. When he finished, he wiped himself on a cloth and said, "I thought those bastards would never leave. I didn't like them."

"They went back the way they came," she pointed out. "It must have been an important message to bring them all this way out." She rearranged her kirtle.

A few customers came in. The day progressed. The night. Morning came.

There was no sound from the guest chamber, and Mary went to stand outside the door to listen to the silence. When it continued and curiosity got the better of her, she pushed open the door and poked her head round.

Slanted light across a bed from between half-closed shutters. Three cloak hooks on the wall. His cloak where he had flung it. Stale straw underfoot. And the guest still in bed.

A cover was pulled up to his shoulders and he lay facedown, one arm trailing to the floor.

Above the ale room's clatter and stink, the air was fetid with the stench of butcher's blood.

She had the silver coin safe in the cleft between her breasts. The alemaster had laughed at her. "Think it's safe there, doxy?" He had proved it wasn't but, later, had given it back with interest.

Nothing to lose, she went over to the bed. "Master, it's morning now. He'll be docking another day's silver for your extra use of his chamber if you don't stir yourself."

The man did not move. Neither was there the rise and fall of breath of someone asleep. When she put out a hand to shake him, she felt the chill of dead flesh under her fingers. She screamed, long and loud.

When she found herself somehow at the bottom of the stairs, the aleman gawped. "What's up, dove? Your face is as white as a nun's thighs."

5

Chapter 2

Hildegard pushed open the door into the prioress's cell.

"Ah, there you are." The prioress of Swyne lifted her head from her missal.

Her tone of voice suggested that she had seen Hildegard only moments before. In fact, Hildegard had trudged back to the priory the previous night after more than a year's absence. She stepped inside the stone chamber and was met by the usual blast of cold air that came funnelling through a small unglazed aperture next to the altar.

"Safely back from Santiago de Compostela," the prioress commented. "So how was it?"

As no invitation to be seated was made and, indeed, the chamber contained only one small bench, where a cat resided, Hildegard remained standing, as did the prioress.

"The pilgrimage was not without its adventures," Hildegard began. "As you know, the duke of Lancaster, our ambitious John of Gaunt, had himself crowned king of Castile in the cathedral at Compostela. His militia was much in evidence in the surrounding countryside."

"I understand his Portuguese ally, King João, has proved more duplicitous than even Duke John could anticipate?"

"Be it so, I believe the duke will find a way to turn the situation to his advantage. He has already shown he means business by having a would-be assassin burned alive in the marketplace at Ourense."

The prioress raised her eyebrows. "Heaven forfend such barbaric practices do not take hold in the realm of England."

"I can hardly see King Richard wishing to burn anyone alive. Some say he is too lenient with his enemies."

The prioress nodded. "I believe it. And he is reaping the harvest of his softness already. But what about Compostela itself?"

"Bursting at the seams with pilgrims from all over Europe. A most feisty bunch. The cathedral custodians are forced to swing a great censer of incense above the nave to keep down the stink of unwashed bodies. Of course," she added generously, "most of them have walked from as far afield as Flanders, an immense distance. We English only had to walk the eighty miles or so from Coruña, and we had ample opportunity to wash. In fact, the friars at the refuges on the way make a point of bathing the feet of pilgrims in thyme soaked in sweet springwater as they arrive."

"No doubt for their own comfort," the prioress sniffed. "And you yourself?" She gave Hildegard a piercing glance.

"I—" Uncharacteristically, Hildegard faltered.

"Travelling as Mistress York without the protection of your Cistercian habit must have been an interesting experience?"

"It was, but I was fortunate enough to meet a helpful group of pilgrims on board the ship from Bordeaux and in particular a Bristol merchant who took everybody under his wing and made sure none of us was shortchanged."

"A widower?"

"As it happens. His pilgrimage was in order to light a candle for his wife at the shrine of Saint James."

The prioress gave her another piercing glance. "You would both have something in common, then?"

Hildegard lowered her head.

"And were you invited to become this merchant's wife?"

"I believe the idea crossed his mind."

"And you were tempted?"

Her head shot up. "Hardly so. Nor do I wish to be anybody's wife."

"After that no-good fellow you were involved with in London, I'm not surprised."

Hildegard gave the prioress a stare of such coldness even she faltered and added hurriedly, "I was led to believe that Rivera was a spy for Bolingbroke and therefore an enemy of our anointed king?"

"He saw his error."

"So, after Brother Rivera, as I said—"

"Nothing more would have been possible at that time," Hildegard said hoarsely. "Not between us. I was always aware of that. There was too much against us and—" She broke off, scarcely able to speak for the lump in her throat. At least his name was out in the open, and with the prioress observing her so closely, she felt little need to add anything else.

"If you feel like that," the prioress observed more softly after a considering pause, "you may as well rejoin the Order." She gave Hildegard a good long look. It was not without kindness. "But you're still undecided?"

She nodded, but before she could excuse her reluctance to make a decision, the prioress smiled. "I have an idea, Hildegard. If you're doubtful about us here at Swyne, and still see yourself as a lost soul—which the Church undoubtedly does—then why not stay as a guest at another priory? See things from another side?"

"How do you mean?"

"Stay at a different monastic house belonging to another Order, without the obligation of donning a habit."

"Somewhere like Watton?"

The prioress laughed. "With all the overprivileged ladies and their little dogs? Hardly! I can't see that appealing to you. I'll ask my brother about a congenial place in the north of the county." The brother she referred to was Alexander Neville, archbishop of York. The previous year, Hildegard had been his eyes and ears during the time of the Westminster Parliament. He fell foul of the king's enemies and his situation had become precarious.

"Is he back at his palace at York?" she asked now.

"He is." The prioress looked disconcerted for a moment but shrugged the matter aside. "He's likely to know somewhere that would suit you. This East Riding air is too mild for you at present."

Hildegard was already shuddering with cold in the chill cell.

The prioress, as ever, seemed oblivious to it. "I'm thinking of somewhere near Northumberland's territory." She smiled. "Let me think on it."

Suspecting her of an ulterior motive with her reference to the earl of Northumberland, whom some were calling the "king of the north," Hildegard was unsurprised when the prioress exclaimed, "I know just the place for you! Small, remote, bracing—and Benedictine. That should help you achieve clarity. It's called Handale Priory. Go there."

"Very well." Wondering what she would find to do in such a place except pray for Rivera's soul and her own, she went out into the cloister as soon as she was dismissed. The prioress, however, called her back.

"It may be as dull as you obviously imagine, but I've heard an interesting report that the serpent has been seen again."

"Serpent?"

"Oh, some faradiddle about a fire-breathing monster, a kind of dragon, they say. Feeds on virgins. Superstitious nonsense, of course, but it should be enough to take your mind off things. Oh, by the way," she added, "I permit you to take an extra cloak. You'll need it up there."

It was not in the prioress's power to permit or forbid anything at present, as Hildegard had not yet renewed her vows, but she merely nodded her head in thanks and left.

With her bag as yet unpacked after the long pilgrimage back across the sea from northern Spain, Hildegard had little to do but have her boots repaired and a horse readied for her onwards journey to Handale.

Attired in the garments of a townswoman, she felt out of place at Swyne among the familiar white-robed sisters who had been her companions in the past and she was now glad to have an excuse to leave. To their questions, she had no answers. She did not know whether she would rejoin the Order, having left it after discovering that her husband, believed dead, was alive. Much else had happened to send her on the long miles to Compostela, there to light candles for Rivera, the man for whom she would willingly have relinquished her soul into the flames of hell if it would have brought him back to life.

Now she knew that if the desire to achieve certainty about rejoining the Cistercians had been her aim, then it had failed. There was something to be said for living outside the Order as an ordinary woman in the thick of everyday events. Much to be said, also, for renewing her vows and returning to life in a nunnery, where she might do some good.

Maybe Handale Priory and its nuns would provide an answer to her dilemma.

She wondered if Abbot Hubert de Courcy shared the Church's view that she was a soul lost to God's grace.

Aware of the immense stretch of country from the River Humber, south of Swyne, and to the Tees in the north, and between the long and varied coastline to the east and the mysterious Pennines to the west, she contemplated the journey to Handale with misgivings. It was a bleak and largely unpeopled stretch of country once the city of York was left behind.

She set out.

Holderness, where the priory at Swyne lay, soon merged with the undulating hills and secret dales of the Wolds before the land turned savage as the moors were reached.

At their northerly point, near no great market town, and served only by the castle of Kilton—itself nothing more than a fort to hold the coast road between north and south—came the ridged-backed ironstone hills of Handale Forest, with the priory of the Benedictines at its heart.

Handale.

She arrived at Earl Roger de Hutton's castle north of York, halfway to her goal.

"Handale?" he shouted. "God's bollocks, Hildegard, why do you want to go there?"

Hildegard, feasted and somewhat feted, for Roger was fond of her, had told him straightaway the purpose of her journey and looked at him with renewed misgivings.

"What do you mean, Roger? It can't be as bad as that. My prioress suggested it. My onetime prioress, that is, at Swyne."

"I don't need to be told who you mean, and I'd like to know her motive," he said.

"I could think of nothing better to do now I'm back from pilgrimage. I feel unsettled. I don't know what to do. Whether to rejoin the Order if they'll have me back or to stay out. But if I stay out, then what? She seems to think time at Handale will persuade me to renew my vows."

"Or put you off for good," he grunted with satisfaction. "It's in the middle of nowhere. You'll hate it."

"Have you been?"

"No, of course not. Nobody has. Why would they? But strange stories are circulating. The previous prioress left in a hurry not long since. It's supposed to be a secret, dark, brutish place with nothing good to be said for it."

"I'm told she was offered a comfortable corrodiary in York and the new one came in to sort things out—whatever that means."

Roger indicated to his page to pour more wine. "You'll be there as Mistress York, will you?"

"I have no choice until I discuss my return to the Order with Abbot de Courcy."

"Hubert will want you back in the fold. He'll stop at nothing to get you back."

"It won't be his personal decision."

Roger dismissed this. "Stay with us," he coaxed. "I'll find a handsome knight for you." He regarded her with some sympathy. He knew what had happened last year down in Westminster when King Richard had called Parliament to plead for a war fund to defend the country against the French invasion. But the place had been full of spies. A vicious bloodletting had followed. Enmities at court and in the City of London had come to a head in a brutal clash of rival factions. The dukes had made their first open move against the young king, Richard II, and Hildegard had been caught up in it. The king's position was now even more precarious. The struggle for power was not over.

"King Dickon was in York while you were overseas," Roger told her. "His uncle Thomas Woodstock has been running the royal council to his own advantage while young Dickon kept away from London, trying to drum up support from the rest of the country."

"Was he successful?"

"Not very. People are sick of war. And he hasn't fully come round to the idea that he needs an army of his own. He'll soon learn words and promises come cheap. He seems to think verbal support is enough, without the backing of strong steel. The dukes rarely travel without their armed escorts and enough bowmen to frighten anybody. Dickon needs to do the same if he's to stand up for himself and protect the Crown." He gave a snort. "I'll definitely be turning out if he gives the summons."

"Is it likely?"

He looked grim. "You've been out of the country. You have no idea what's been going on. Those three traitors have raised armies, and the latest news is that the duke of Warwick is standing by at Waltham Cross, just outside London. Is that a threat or what? Thomas Woodstock and that snake Arundel are heading that way with their own musters. Meanwhile, we sit and wait for Dickon to call us to arms."

"I heard something like that was intended by Arundel when I arrived at Southampton. He was engaging men down there. He's done it now, has he? He's always been an ally of Thomas Woodstock. And they say the king is at Windsor?"

"Yes."

"What's their excuse for threatening him?"

"They say it's because they don't trust him. He's supposed to have been plotting to murder them in their beds—"

"Woodstock's been trying to ruin the king's name ever since he was made to look a fool at Smithfield."

"It's not Woodstock any longer. It's the duke of Gloucester." Roger snickered. "He's still a prickmaster, whatever his name. But let me tell you this: They're spreading a story that the king went on a pilgrimage to Canterbury, his real purpose being to barter Calais and Guînes for French help against his own countrymen!"

"That can't be true!"

"It's true that they say it, but I agree, it can't be true. He would never do any such thing. He knows the value of both places and would never give them away, let alone do a deal with the French. But folk are so dumb-skulled, they'll believe anything they're told. Where's their evidence for such lies, I ask!"

"So what are they going to do with their armies? They won't march against the king himself?" Hildegard looked shocked.

Roger scowled. "They will if they get an excuse they can pass off as a good one."

"Let's hope they don't manage it. But tell me, where does Bolingbroke stand in all this? Is he in with them?"

"He hasn't shown his hand yet. He'll wait until he sees which way the wind's blowing. He's got three men between himself and the Crown." Roger ticked them off on his hand. "He's got his father, the duke. His uncle Gloucester so-called. The fourth earl of March, the king's chosen heir. Bolingbroke can wait for his father to succumb to natural forces. But how can he get rid of Gloucester? He's in his prime. And the earl of March is a child, with years ahead of him, God willing. Bolingbroke's going to have a long wait before the Crown falls to him in any natural way. Make of it what you will. To me, it's as plain as a pike up the backside. He'll wait, and when his chance comes, he'll grab it with both hands."

"His father's still in Castile, crowned in St. James at Compostela, and doing deals left and right, so I heard."

"While everybody here is bowing and scraping to favourite son Bolingbroke. He's all but duke of Lancaster by now. Gaunt should get himself home, or he'll find he hasn't got a duchy to come home to. Do you realise, Hildegard"—Roger looked grim—"I'm one of the few magnates here to give the king outright support?"

"I hope you'll keep it that way."

"I will. And so will Ulf."

Hildegard's expression lightened. "How is dear Ulf?"

"Married and miserable."

"Surely—"

"Nothing more to be said, Hildegard. You'll go that way out when you leave here?"

"I need to get to Handale soon. I've been travelling for months. But I will see him. I want to. He's always in my thoughts. I'll settle at Handale first."

Earl Roger de Hutton, with his uncharacteristic gloom, worried Hildegard. It was over a year since she had been embroiled in affairs of the realm, albeit in a minor role, but now it seemed there was work to be done again. Handale would afford no opportunity to participate.

On a different level, it was saddening to hear that Ulf was unhappy with his new wife. No doubt things will shake down after the first few troubled months, she told herself. Ulf was probably too used to doing things his own way. She could scarcely imagine the sort of woman who would be able to tame Roger's wild northern henchman.

Turning her horse's head towards the north, she set out on the final leg of her journey.

CHAPTER 3

Kilton Castle. Midnight. So exhausted, she could only throw the reins of her horse to a stable lad, untie her bag, and follow the steward's servant blindly to a guest chamber. Barely able to kick off her boots, she sank down on a palliasse in her clothes and was asleep at once.

She awoke at dawn to the sound of rushing water. Dragging herself to the window loop, she peered out and saw that the castle was perched on a soaring crag that fell dramatically to a boulder-strewn beck below. Opposite, thick woods clothed the hillside.

When she arrived in the night, she had been too tired to notice much more than the towers jutting above the trees into the moonlit sky. Clattering under the arch of the gatehouse into the bailey, she had been aware only of shuttered buildings on all sides and a further arch leading into an inner yard. Now, coming out at the bottom of the tower steps, she saw a rough-hewn garrison, crowded with militia, the smoke from a blacksmith's brazier billowing across the yard. Birds of prey circled the summits of the towers. The clash of steel on stone filled the air as a detachment of men was drilled. Archers were firing at the butts. No one gave her a second glance from under their steel helmets.

She sought out the steward in his office. He grudgingly offered bread, cheese, and wine from his own table, then rose to grab a bunch of keys from a hook.

"You'll be wanting to be off. I'll get them to open up for you. You'll have to proceed on foot. We'll stable your horse with the others from the priory."

Before she could make any remark about this arrangement, he went to the door and barked at a passing servant. "Escort!"

When he returned, a heavy-looking fellow in a hauberk accompanied him. "Go with him," the steward told Hildegard. Grim-faced, he sat back down and began to add to a list scratched on a wax tablet.

Hildegard followed the man into the bailey. By the time she had brought down her bag from the turret room, the great wooden doors at the gatehouse were grinding open, and she followed him outside.

Thick woodland fringed the lane leading down to the coast road, and when they crossed the wooden drawbridge, Hildegard expected the man to set off down the lane the way she had come last night, but instead he led her along a narrow path skirting the moat until he came to an opening between the trees. It was little wider than a deer run. He set off at a brisk pace.

"Is this the road to Handale?" she asked in surprise as she hurried to keep up.

He grunted an assent. As he strode on, his only concession was to throw a glance back over his shoulder now and then to make sure she was still following.

The path was winding and barely perceptible. In moments, Hildegard felt lost. The trees were not yet in leaf. Even so, unpollarded, they grew thickly, poles of ash forming barricades on all sides, bramble roots weaving between the bars of saplings, a mix of hornbeam, hazel, and alder making passage difficult. The deeper they went into this thicket, the darker it became. The branches met overhead and they walked in a gloomy tunnel, downwards, as if into a pit. The only colour was now and then the dark green of juniper and holly, glossy and sinister. No birds sang.

Hildegard caught up with her escort. "How on earth do you find your way through this thicket?" she demanded. Her hand was already hovering over her knife, for she did not trust him.

"Keep following," he ordered.

I'm hardly likely not to, thought Hildegard, or I could be haunting Handale Forest forever. She peered up through the branches and tried to guess where the sun was to get her bearings, but the sky—what bits of it she could see—was overcast.

After some time, the Kilton man suddenly bent double and, pushing his way under some overhanging branches, burst out into daylight. When she followed, he was already marching across a clearing towards a wooden door set in a high stone wall. She saw him bang on it with the hilt of his sword.

The door had just begun to open when he turned, gave her another nod, and without a word disappeared back into the undergrowth.

The prioress, Basilda, red-faced, overweight, and perspiring, reclined before a blazing fire in a chamber that stank of bird droppings, incense, and sweat. She was enthroned in a cushioned chair, her feet in fur-lined slippers, an embroidered overmantle lined in the same stuff round her shoulders. She looked askance at Hildegard's plain woollen cloak, the extra one she had been instructed to bring with her.

Hildegard flung it over the back of her chair as she sat down. It's like a furnace in here, she was thinking. How different from Swyne.

Prioress Basilda inched a goblet of wine towards her, then fixed a beady eye on her over the rim of her own one of chased silver. A hawk sat behind her on its perch and eyed Hildegard with malevolent concentration. "So, Mistress York," began the prioress, "what skills can you bring to us in exchange for our hospitality?"

Hildegard replied with caution. "Some herbal lore, but not above the ordinary. Some skill in writing."

"A fair court hand?" Basilda raised her eyebrows. "Latin? French?"

Hildegard hesitated. "I make no great claims, my lady." She would not admit much until she saw how things lay. So far, she was unimpressed. If Prioress Basilda was typical, the priory was slack. Difficult to believe it was a religious house at all. Sweetmeats on a tray, she noticed. A luxury of gold and silver glinting everywhere in the soft light of beeswax candles. Furs thrown over cushioned benches. She would have been better off at Watton with the widows and their little lapdogs.

The prioress was considering matters with a furrowed brow. "Unlike the Cistercians, God take them, we only have our manors, mills, and churches to bring in revenue. Even so, I have much correspondence. It needs constant attention. You may have noticed our building works?"

Hildegard agreed that she had. It would have been difficult to miss them. Within the enclosure marked off by the high walls of the priory as well as an outer garth of farm buildings and storage sheds, there was an inner garth. This was dominated by a church at one end, with cloisters running down one side to link up with the refectory, the bakehouse, brewery, and kitchens supplying the domestic needs of the community.

On the opposite side was the thatched-roofed *dortoir* where the nuns had their cells. Farther off were two separate buildings for guests. Rearing up above the outer wall, the hoists and scaffolding of the masons were visible, evidence of the large new establishment being built.

Prioress Basilda gave a sigh of satisfaction. "My new chambers are being built by a master mason from Durham. This one is far too small for the dignity of my office. Divided, it should do nicely as cells for my nuns." She gestured to include the not overly large chamber, making Hildegard wonder just how little space her poor nuns would be obliged to enjoy. "Well, mistress, you know what builders are like," she continued. "Constant questions and resulting disagreements. I wish to have it all in writing in case of problems later. You can attend to that."

"I'm honoured, my lady," Hildegard replied. An effort was required to keep the note of irony out of her voice.

Basilda stared at her. Her eyes were like pebbles washed by the North Sea. "What made you choose us?"

"I desired somewhere remote from the world."

"Hm." Basilda sounded as if she rather resented her priory's being described as remote, as if there might be some criticism intended, but Hildegard's bland expression mollified her for the moment.

"You will, of course, dine with us and attend all offices."

"Certainly. And I wish to make myself useful in any other way I can."

"I'll bear that in mind." She picked up a small ceramic hand bell and gave it a shake. It made a musical tinkle. At once, a nun appeared. Black-robed, head bowed.

"Show our guest to her chamber, sister, and then return to your duties."

The nun fled ahead like a wraith along a corridor to the far end of the guesthouse and the moment she had shown Hildegard to the door of her chamber she turned to leave.

"Wait, sister," Hildegard put out a hand. "If we are to see each other over the next few weeks, we should at least exchange names. I am Mistress York—"

The nun looked no more than eighteen. She gave a hasty glance over one shoulder. "Forgive me. I am forbidden speech."

"Forbidden?"

The girl whispered in a frightened tone, "My penance, mistress. The prioress decrees it."

"Penance pays all debts," murmured Hildegard automatically. Without another word, the girl fled.

Speculating on the nature of the sin to warrant the punishment, Hildegard put the matter to one side for the moment and opened the door to her chamber.

It was certainly austere, even to Cistercian eyes. The prioress clearly had one view of her own comfort and another for her guests.

So this was to be the place where she would make one of the most momentous decisions of her life. She looked round with misgivings. Even on pilgrimage, the hospices had not been so bleak.

There was a wooden clothes chest in one corner, an aumbry for personal items, and a narrow bed with a thin coverlet across one wall. She dumped her travel bag onto it and began to unpack.

She took out her cures and put the scrip in the aumbry. Then she withdrew spare leggings, an undershift, a missal, a folding ivory case with a mirror in the lid, and a small comb that opened out, revealing a carved bone handle. She arranged them where she could find them. There was also a knife in a leather sheath, and she left that at the bottom of the bag.

She took off her head covering and combed her hair. It had grown during her sojourn in Spain and she had not bothered to cut it. Now it ran like molten metal through her fingers before she hid it under a clean white head scarf.

These Benedictines, she was thinking as she completed her few tasks, were somewhat different from the Cistercians. True, the latter had been set up specifically as an antidote to Benedictine love of luxury, and as a consequence their austerity attracted people of some principle, women such as the prioress at Swyne and men like Abbot Hubert de Courcy of Meaux. They would be scandalised by the luxury she had so far seen in the prioress's parlour at Handale.

Her thoughts snagged and came to a stop on the image of Hubert de Courcy. Handsome, austere, driven, with a steely intelligence, he was a man haunted by the sins of his past. His attraction, however, never failed to draw from her recognition of her own failings, ones of unmitigated physical desire and something more which she could not describe. Even when in the arms of the spy Rivera, she had been conscious of Hubert's existence, of his approval and disapproval. Every thought of him resulted in a feeling of guilt for the great wrong she had done him.

The bell began to toll for tierce.

Intending to take a shortcut from the one side of the garth to the other, she opened a studded door and ended up in a small stone cell. Crossing to the other side, she found herself in yet another small chamber.

It was in darkness.

About to turn on her heels and retrace her steps, she heard a scuffling sound inside, and thinking it was a rat, she began to back hurriedly out. Then something about the sound drew her attention. It was human. Peering into the shadows, she was astonished to see someone crouching there, shrouded in black.

"Who is this?" She stepped forward, the better to make the person out.

The door behind her groaned on its hinges and the cell was plunged into blackness.

The creature in the corner began to make snuffling noises. They resolved themselves into a defiant protest. Hildegard could distinguish only one or two words. "No! I won't!" and "Please, don't!" and then "No, no, no!"

She edged back to where the door had closed behind her, only to find it locked. This could not be so. She pushed her shoulder against it, but it did not yield. "Let me out!" She hammered with both fists. Behind her, the creature fell silent.

"Open this door, someone!"

Her shouts brought a response from the other side. "Keep quiet, curse you!"

"Open the door!"

"The prioress will blame me for your racket. And you know what'll happen then, you sinning bitch!"

A bang on the door with a hard implement reinforced this threat.

"I don't know who you are and you don't know me. But I assure you it'll be the worse for you, not me, if you don't open this door immediately. I'm a guest here and I demand to be released!"

A hush fell on the other side. Slowly, the door ring began to turn.

When the door opened, a wan face peered up at her from under a black cowl.

On seeing a respectable-looking townswoman confronting her, the woman fell to her knees. "My most gracious lady, I am deeply at fault."

Hildegard kept one hand on the door to allow light to be shed into the corner of the cell. She looked back, to see a creature crouching on the bare stone with her knees up to her chin. Two frightened eyes stared out of the darkness.

Worst of all was the bloody slash of a wounded mouth. It was a nun, a young woman of no more than twenty or so.

When she saw Hildegard standing in the light, she rubbed a hand over her face, smearing the blood across her cheeks, and began to rock back and forth, emitting a keening sound, halfway between a prayer and a curse, that sent chills up and down Hildegard's spine.

"My dear sister—" She went over and bent down beside her. A shadow loomed over them and the older nun stepped inside.

"She knows why she's here. Leave her to the contemplation of her sins, mistress. Come out now. I beg your pardon for my rough welcome."

Hildegard reluctantly rose to her feet. It was not her place to interfere with the running of the priory. Even so, she was disturbed by the poor girl's distress. "Does she eat?"

"She's on bread and water and she and her confessor know why." The woman held the door open.

It was too late to attend the service at tierce. It began to rain. She walked back and forth in the cloister until everybody came out. Strict silence seemed to be observed. In moments, the nuns walking two by two had disappeared into the nearby *dortoir*. Not sure what to do, she pulled up her hood and set off across the garth with the intention of exploring the rest of the enclosure, when she felt someone tug at her sleeve.

It was the young priest. Head bare, pimply-faced, a boil on his neck, he looked raw with cold. She wanted to offer a cure for the boil but did not want to patronise him. Rain hurled itself in gusts between them.

"M-mistress," he began nervously, "the prioress has asked me to warn you about leaving the precinct."

"Leaving?" a smile hovered round her lips. The woman must be a mind reader. "But I've only just arrived!"

"N-no, I mean, in a case you should decide to take a walk in the woods. If the weather improves," he added.

"A walk?"

"It is not safe."

She raised her eyebrows to encourage him to continue. He looked uncomfortable and seemed to be finding it difficult to be more forthright.

Hildegard took pity on him. "I should tell you, sir priest, I am very used to taking care of my own safety."

He drew back, a look of alarm on his face. "Not against the beast, *ma donna*," he gasped in a shocked tone. "No one is safe. A man has been killed. None of us now walk there. The masons have to work outside the precinct walls because of the prioress's new works, but even they go armed at all times."

"Beast?" she frowned. "What sort of beast?" She vaguely recalled the remark concerning a dragon before she left Swyne. "Is it a wild animal of some sort?"

He shook his head. "Human, we believe, or at least partly human."

"Walk with me." Hildegard put her arm in his, a freedom she would never have taken had she still been wearing her nun's habit.

Unresisting, he allowed her to lead him back into the empty cloister, at a distance from the busy domestic offices, close to the warming house, where they were sheltered from the rain by the ribbed vault that ran the length of it. "Now," she encouraged, "what do you mean by part human?"

"I may be trusted to speak the truth. Let me assure you of that. I'm a priest from the Abbey of Whitby. My ancestors owned Kilton Castle. I am here to wait on the lawyers to give judgement on our claim to ownership just as my father and his father waited on the law. Until then, I suffer and pray in this hellish place. I tell you this because you will understand that I know the woods of Handale as well as anyone living. It has long been a story told by the ignorant that a dragon has roamed here since the time of the Northmen." He hesitated.

"Please continue."

"They say the dragon was killed by a hero named Scaur. Until now, I regarded it with all the scepticism of an educated man"—he gave a deprecating smile—"but even I begin to fear there might be truth in the stories. Not the story of a dragon, of course, nor even a wild dog or wolf, but of something evil out there at least. Some monstrous thing with no name."

He gave a fearful glance towards the trees spearing above the precinct walls. They were black with rain. Tight-packed, they grew up to the walls themselves, except for the clearing near the main gate, and seemed to draw on the stones for sustenance. For a moment, he seemed in thrall to their menace, but eventually he dragged his glance away. "*Ma donna,* you should know that a man has been killed out there."

"Long ago?"

He shook his head. He seemed terrified. Hildegard asked, "So why does this suggest a dragon of some sort? Why not a more familiar danger?"

He gave her a steady stare. "Because of the nature of the dead man's wounds." His hands, she noticed, were trembling, although whether it was with cold or some emotion, she could not tell.

"The dragon makes its presence known at night with a terrible howling, like nothing you will ever hear again. It turns the blood to ice." His face twitched. "They say it's a nun and her devil helpmate from long ago, one who was turned out of the precinct for her sins and was left to die. It was only by means of a pact with the devil she saved herself and was turned into a dragon, and now she roams the woods, looking for human blood on which to gorge."

"Why does someone not find her and bring her in?" Hildegard suggested sensibly. "That would be the kindest deed."

"Because she is not of human form. They are in terror of meeting her. They say she has lived on human blood for over a hundred years."

He lowered his voice. "I am not a free man. I have no choice but to stay here until my family's inheritance is restored. But you, *ma donna,* have a choice. Find an escort to take you back to the outside world; then run for your life. Do not stay here when you have no reason to."

"I never run," replied Hildegard. She gave him a smile that for a split second was reciprocated.

Then his face twisted into a grimace and he pressed his raw red knuckles into his mouth. "This is a place of penitence, *ma donna.* It's where those nuns who have broken their vows are sent. They come from many different places, sent here as a last resort. Many come from Rosedale, and when that bleak moorland prison fails to tame them, they finish up here. They are the hardest souls, the most fierce in sin." He pointed across the rain-swept garth. "See that cell with the bars?"

Hildegard followed his shaking finger to a set of iron bars at ground level. Beyond them lay darkness. It was a prison cell belowground, she surmised with a shiver of revulsion.

The priest explained. "The worst are kept in there until they mend their ways."

"I came across a nun with a bloody mouth just before tierce, as if—I'm not sure—as if she had been hit across the face or—"

He gave a furtive glance round. "They say the monster in the woods may have infected one of the nuns within the precinct. To draw her down to the devil's wiles. This is only a story"—he gave a nervous laugh—"but how would we know it wasn't true until it was proved otherwise?"

Hildegard gazed at him in disbelief. "This nun—within—who is she?"

He pulled his hood closely over his head, face hidden. "I think you may find out to your cost, *ma donna* . . . if you stay."

Hildegard stifled a response. She bowed her head. "I thank you most cordially for your advice, sir priest, and shall take as much heed of your warning as common sense dictates." She stepped from out of the cloister into the rain-swept garth.

CHAPTER 4

The midday meal was being served when she entered the timbered refectory, where she found six or seven nuns seated at one long table and one or two novices attending them. Prioress Basilda was not in evidence. A nun she took to be the cellarer beckoned.

"Sit there, mistress." She indicated a place at the end of the table, then continued to eat with downcast eyes. The rest of the nuns scarcely looked up. They went on eating, the silence broken only by a nun reading from the works of Saint Benedict. A wooden bowl containing gruel was placed in front of Hildegard by a soft-footed novice. Soft-footed, she noticed, because barefoot. Her feet were blue with cold as she padded back and forth over the flagstone.

The entire meal continued in a heavy silence, broken only by the droning voice of the nun chosen to read that day. At last, one of the nuns rose, mumbled a short prayer of thanks, and then the rest rose in a group and filed out, leaving only the cellarer and her servant.

"I am instructed to have you conducted to the scriptorium," she told Hildegard, not looking at her. "Follow me."

The cheerless repast, the silence of the black-robed nuns, the chill in the atmosphere are burdens to be born, Hildegard told herself as she followed the cellarer up a flight of stone stairs to the first-floor level. This was maybe how outsiders first saw the Cistercian priory at Swyne, little knowing of the rich inner lives of the assembly or the general kindliness and compassion that prevailed. It was no doubt the same here and invisible to the eye of a casual guest such as herself.

Why she had been sent from Swyne to a house of correction was another question. One which would bear scrutiny later. Was it a covert message from her prioress that she needed, like the nuns here, to absolve herself from her own guilt? Impatiently, she dismissed the idea. It was too oblique. Her prioress was nothing if not forthright. She would tell her in plain Yorkshire fashion what she thought of her activities in Westminster the previous year if she thought Hildegard had done wrong. Of her own secret thoughts about Hubert de Courcy, the prioress could know nothing.

The priest's story, however, was simply outrageous. A man dead. Killed by a dragon or a ghostly nun? The penitent with the bloody mouth worried her. As did the half-underground cell. It was a species of refined cruelty, surely, to keep imprisoned in those cold, cramped quarters someone who could see others walking about freely in the open air. What sins were these nuns accused of to merit such punishment?

If anything was designed to keep her here, there was enough for now. She would not rest until she understood what was going on.

Feeling helpless, torn by the knowledge that none of this was her direct concern, she pulled out her beads from the embroidered pouch on her belt.

The cellarer turned at that moment. "Devout, I see." She eyed Hildegard suspiciously. "Always a virtue, of course."

"I have concerns about a nun with a bloody mouth," Hildegard offered. "Is it some kind of punishment, or has she been injured?"

"I know who you mean. She has had trouble with her teeth

for some time. She begged the barber to extract one and now suffers daily and with less stoicism than one would wish for." The cellaress avoided Hildegard's glance and, briskly, as if having no time for such trivialities, conducted her into the scriptorium.

It was a small chamber above the prioress's own chamber at the end of the building, abutting the church. It had a dusty, unused look, but when Hildegard glanced round, she saw that it was equipped well enough. She would have to make ink afresh, but there were unsharpened quills in a jug and a ream or so of vellum on a shelf.

The cellaress explained that they would be pleased if she would help order the correspondence with the master mason at work on the current extension. "Absent at present with other works across the county. Always on the move, these masons with their little armies of labourers. He's a great catch for us. His current work in Durham is with the cathedral there. Under the control of Walter Skirlaw. We're fortunate to have snared him."

" 'Snared'?"

"Such a catch for us. So much in demand, the good ones."

"And costly, no doubt?"

The cellarer was not to be drawn out on how such a small foundation such as hers could afford a man so much in demand. "For now, you can file those papers, if you will. Put the accounts in some sort of order."

"Do you expect me to do those, as well?"

"The subprioress will see to that."

I am to be a mere dogsbody of a filing clerk, then, thought Hildegard. Well, so be it. I'm here to help and to forget my own self.

The cellarer was staring at her. "Have you experience of greater responsibility, mistress?"

"I'm here for prayer and contemplation, sister, and to resolve certain doubts in my mind."

With a sideways glance, the cellarer left.

Hildegard moved over to the table. A horn blind covered an unglazed window looking out onto the outer garth, where a cow was stalled under a thatched lean-to. There was a swinecote next to it.

She sat down to read through the heap of receipts and demands.

And so the afternoon between sext and nones passed in her first day at Handale Priory.

When eventually the next bell began to toll, Hildegard got up with an exclamation of relief. Now, maybe, something would happen to give a more favourable impression of this grim place.

The scriptorium was in a chamber above that of the prioress. A stone stair led down past the door. As Hildegard descended, she was met by a waft of warm air and noticed that the door stood open. It briefly raised the temperature in the freezing stairwell. As she descended, she could not help casting a glance inside.

Prioress Basilda was heaving herself out of her chair. A man wearing a blue townsman's cloak over a brown houpelande was offering his arm to her. Intent on each other, they did not notice Hildegard. The prioress's expression as she looked up at her visitor made Hildegard miss a step. She recovered and opened the door into the cloister garth.

A file of black-clad nuns had been drawn from their cells by the tolling bell. They were processing two by two towards the open door of the church. Hildegard tagged onto the end of the line and was last to reach the door.

The same barefoot novice, wearing nothing but a thin shift, was standing just inside the door. She had her head bowed and the palms of both hands extended as if to receive alms.

But it was not a gift of coin or bread the nuns bestowed. It was a sharp lash with small whips of willow each of them carried. With every lash, tears seeped from between the girl's eyelids. Hildegard saw her flinch in anticipation of pain as she heard the whisper of Hildegard's approaching step.

"What is this?" Hildegard murmured. "Open your eyes. I'm a guest here and am not going to punish you."

Cautiously, as if fearing a trick, the girl lifted her lids. Hildegard stared into eyes full of such misery, she exclaimed at once, "My dear, what is this for?"

The novice drew back. "Show me no pity, mistress, or they'll punish me more than ever."

"This cannot be." Hildegard lowered her head to conceal her response.

Aware of the small congregation clustering near the altar, their heads turned in speculation, she walked down the nave to join them. She could not believe it. What sort of place was this? Her heart began to thump with rage.

Nones: the service conducted by the prioress's priest. As well as a fear of dragons, he demonstrated an imperfect rendering of the Latin texts. Hildegard ticked him off in her mind, then covertly observed the rest of the community.

Prioress Basilda herself sat on a sort of carved wooden throne, her flesh bulging through the frets of oak leaves and gargoyle faces. Her feet rested on a box containing enough burning charcoal to keep them warm. Hildegard thought of the novice, barefoot on the flagstones by the door and serving food in the refectory.

Next in precedence was the subprioress. Her face colourless, eyes of a washed-out grey, not a scrap of hair showing to betray its colour, as was correct, and pale fingers clasped over her stomach, with a dripping string of colourless beads between them.

Next to her was the cellarer, who had shown Hildegard into the scriptorium. Gaunt and yellow-faced, she allowed her hooded eyes continually to sweep the faces of her companions. Hildegard thought she saw obsequiousness in her posture, something that suggested support for her superior's harsh rule.

She recalled the priest's observation that the hardest souls were sent here for punishment.

My prioress at Swyne has seen fit to send me to a prison, she realised. Aware that the prioress of Swyne never did anything without forethought, Hildegard found her mind wandering from the priest's droning to the purpose in sending her to this particular place. Perambulating round the possibilities that opened up, she was unable to make sense of it. Was it to show her that Swyne was a place to be desired?

Add to the brew the distant presence of the earl of Northumberland, the rumour of a mysterious beast in the woods, the recent death of a man, and it was an even deeper mystery. From the desire to get out of the place at all costs, she found herself speculating on how, or if, any of these things were linked—and how long she would have to stay before she found the answer.

Novices, two of them, heads down, stood like shadows behind the nuns. Their wispy voices singing the responses to the priest's whinnying tones were swamped by the bellowing alto of Prioress Basilda.

The ritual was stumbling towards its conclusion when there was a sudden enraged shout from the cloisters. A man's bass tones echoed along the arcades, followed by the sound of a scuffle. A female voice cried out. And was abruptly cut short.

CHAPTER 5

Hildegard was first to cover the length of the nave and ran outside. At the far end of the cloister, the townsman she had glimpsed earlier through the open door of Basilda's chamber grasped the arm of one of the novices, the one who had been standing at the door of the church.

No more than fifteen or sixteen, she was slight of build, and now she shrieked as the man slapped her across the face with the flat of his hand. She tried to evade his grasp, but he would not let go, so she tried kicking out at him with her bare feet. It made no impression. As he raised his hand again, Hildegard grabbed his arm.

"Stop!" she shouted.

The man froze in astonishment. The girl was trying to say something, her words muffled, when her assailant wrested his arm from Hildegard's restraint and clamped it over the girl's mouth.

"She's mad!" he exclaimed. "Off her head. Lies! It's all lies!"

Hildegard tried to free the girl from his grip, but he shouldered her aside. "Keep out of this, mistress. It is no concern of yours!"

"Take your hands off her, you brute!"

Before he could reply, Prioress Basilda puffed up. Assisted by the cellarer and one or two others, she was close enough to call out,

"Alys, what on earth are you doing out here! You have duties to attend to!"

Hildegard turned in astonishment. "My lady, you fail to understand. This fellow here is behaving in a most brutal manner to—"

"Pray do not meddle in what does not concern you, Mistress York. She is a known sinner. That's why she's here. And this 'fellow,' as you are pleased to call him, is Master Fulke, our great benefactor. He is within his rights to chastise her." She gripped the girl by the scruff of the neck and pulled her away. "Get to your duties, chit!"

With the girl snivelling and making good her escape, the prioress turned smoothly to the benefactor of Handale. "My deepest apologies, master. You know how she is already."

"Indeed, my lady, to my cost."

A look was exchanged between them and as one they turned, smiling, to Hildegard, the man, Fulke, smoothing a hand over his beard and adjusting his capuchon.

Basilda's tone was placating. "I can understand your concern, mistress. It must be a shock to come across something like this. But believe me, your concern is quite misplaced."

"Is it?"

"Indeed. The unfortunate child was sent to us as the final straw in a long history of uncontrollable behaviour. Her poor mother was beside herself with grief. The girl was running wild, lured by the devil into many sinful and indecent acts. We took her in at her mother's request. She begged on her knees for us to take pity on her and rescue the poor child from the devil's clutches. And, of course, that is our purpose at all times, praise God." She crossed herself, then turned grandly to Master Fulke. "No doubt she was importuning you again, master?"

A look of surprise flashed across his face before he recovered enough to match the smooth manner of the prioress. One eye on

Hildegard, he gave an apologetic shrug. "Begged me to commit a most foul sin, my lady. But"—he pulled at his neatly clipped beard—"no harm done, as you see. I chastised her for it and no harm came of it."

The prioress turned to Hildegard, silky and self-confident. "All over now, mistress. My deepest apologies for such a distressing scene. Believe me, it will not happen again."

Hildegard could well believe it. She glanced across at the small prison, half underground on the other side of the garth, and wondered if the girl, Alys, would finish up in there.

Aware that she should not expect an honest answer from any of the questions that seemed most urgent, she nodded. "It was an unfortunate incident, my lady. My apologies for misunderstanding the master's purpose." She flashed him a glance and met his black stare full on. He turned away, still brushing himself down, as if the girl had in fact contaminated him.

The group broke up, the nuns back inside the church, the prioress and her benefactor towards the refectory in the wake of the novice.

Hildegard watched them go. This will not be the end of it, she vowed.

She paced the cloister for some time, but the prioress and Master Fulke did not reappear.

For the next few days, life within the precinct passed without incident. The Holy Offices succeeded one after the other in predictable succession.

In the time set aside for relaxation, the nuns gathered in the cloister under the beady eye of whichever of the prioress's inner circle was assigned to the task. There they were allowed some time to talk, or pray, or do whatever they fancied within the Rule. Except for the most innocuous of exchanges, mainly to do with the weather, they ignored Hildegard and kept to themselves. It was almost as if they were afraid to speak to her.

She did not come across the novice who had been struck by Master Fulke during this time. Nor was there any other penitent standing at the church door. No doubt Alys had learned to toe the line and was now going about her duties with sufficient obedience to satisfy the novice mistress and the prioress.

Master Fulke had disappeared as well after that first encounter. There was no one to answer any of the questions Hildegard wanted to ask. The nuns, in an aura of sanctity, were seen flitting from one office of the day to the next and attended their silent meal at midday. A few lay sisters went unobtrusively about the work of keeping the precinct clean and tending to the domestic duties demanded by their betters. The lay brothers kept in seemly fashion to the farm garth, and from the window in the scriptorium, Hildegard saw the cow taken from its stall and later, looking contented, with wisps of winter grass hanging from its mouth, returned by a ragged boy.

At least one creature is happy here, she told herself.

The hush that hung over the precinct whenever the tolling bell was stilled was not one of contentment, but of heaviness, as if the individuals living here had lost all hope. In fact, only the prioress and her inner circle seemed content with such an iron rule.

It was after watching the cow brought back to her stall several times that Hildegard decided to escape the seemingly endless task allotted to her and go in search of the meadow where the cow was taken to graze.

Pulling on her cloak, she tidied up her work, then descended the stairs to the outside. A pall of mist hung over the crucked roofs round the garth, and the top of the bell tower disappeared into the filmy air. There was no one around. The place seemed dead. And for once, she felt unwatched by the sidelong glances of the nuns.

With a lightening of her spirits, she went round the side of the guest quarters to the yard at the back, where the cow was kept. It had already been taken out to the meadow. Glad of her boots, she followed the river of mud churned up on its daily comings and goings and found it led to a wooden gate set in the wall of the enclosure. Stepping through, she came to a path that wound through a thicket and in a short time found the cow munching grass in a small meadow.

Her hope that she had discovered a way to the outside was dashed. The area was enclosed on all sides. Above the top of the high brick wall, the trees grew as closely together as elsewhere. Handale is nothing but an open prison, she thought, but there must be a way out other than by that narrow track from Kilton Castle.

The boy who tended the cow was nowhere to be seen. She leaned against a tree and watched the animal's peaceful munching for some time.

It was just as she was about to wend her way back towards the cloister garth that she saw something in one of the trees overhanging the wall. She went over to have a look.

"Good morning, little bird. How are you?"

The cowherd looked down. "I'm well, mistress, and yourself?"

"I would be more well if I knew how to get out into the woods."

"This'n here is one way." He grinned, indicating the tree in which he was sitting.

"My tree-climbing days are over, more's the pity. Is there a more regular way out into the woods?"

"You'll have to find the little door in the wall," he said with a mysterious smile. "But they say you can't go out there these days, for fear of the dragon."

"Have you seen it?"

"No, I ain't, praise God, but I've heard it all right."

"What does it sound like?"

"The devil in his death throes."

"To the good, then?"

He grinned and began to scramble out onto one of the branches to show her his tricks. When she tired of seeing him hang upside down, she bade him good day and followed the river of mud back to the gate.

The priory was set in a deceptively large enclosure. The outer court, where the conversi laboured, was made up of a muddy yard, with the swinecote at one end and a henhouse next to it, the latter surrounded by a scattering of hens, five plain white geese, and one gaudy cockerel lording it over all on a dung heap.

Moving on past this farmyard scene, she came to the fish ponds—two silent lakes of black water. In their placid depths, speckled fish innocently waited to be netted.

She reached the back of the main abbey buildings and the prioress's current living quarters. They adjoined the church, with its square Saxon tower and newer nave and apse, the domed roof of the latter gleaming through the mist, with new slate tiles on its roof.

Beyond that, across a scrubby stretch of grass, was another stone building, small, oblong, with a thatched roof. The enclosure wall rose behind it as high and solid as elsewhere. Hildegard made her way in that direction.

Here the ground sloped away and the main buildings had their backs towards this part of the grounds. Although it was open, no windows overlooked it and the sense of privacy allowed her to feel free of the sly, staring eyes of the priory inmates.

She reached the thatched building standing in an isolated position from all the rest and tried the door. It swung open at a single push. Dark inside. A strong scent of incense. Roof rafters yawned above her head and disappeared into the shadows. Many candles burned deep inside the building, shedding little light in the cavernous interior. It took a minute to adjust to the sudden gloom.

She saw a trestle with something white lying on it at the far end of the building. There were thin candles at each end. As her sight slowly adjusted to the fitful light, she realised she had entered the mortuary.

What she had noticed on the trestle, she realised, was a body in a winding-sheet. Reverentially, she made her way over to it. The light flickered over the folds of linen. It must be the mason lying here, the one allegedly killed by the dragon, she thought. There was no sound. Even the birds outside seemed stilled by the horror and solemnity of death. Cautiously, in order to witness for herself the nature of the man's wounds, she slowly pulled back the rough cloth.

The body of a young man was revealed, limbs so bloodless, they seemed to glow like opal through the dusky half-light. He was lying on his back, his chest horribly ripped and dark with gore, displaying the wounds that must have killed him.

She stared in horror. Many deep gashes ran from neck to groin; much blood, now black and hard, was not entirely washed away when the body had been laid out.

She felt sick.

His wounds were like the ravages inflicted by a deerhound. But she had never seen a hound with such huge claws. Horror slowly stole over her as the young priest's frightened words drifted back to her. Could it be true? Was there a monster of some kind haunting the woods?

She stepped back and automatically crossed herself.

Taking a moment or two to recover, she forced her revulsion to one side long enough to take a closer look. The dead man's face was unmarked. Silver pennies rested on his eyelids. She looked closely at his hands. They were rough and calloused. Scratches like ones sustained in a struggle covered the palms.

He must in life have had a pleasant, open face, given to laughter, judging by the lines around his mouth. Fair Saxon features, still ruddy from last summer's sun. Broad-shouldered, in keeping with his trade. He seemed altogether like a man who could have looked after himself in the ordinary way. But was his death ordinary? That was the question.

She remembered her prioress at Swyne and her humorous remark about the serpent, by which she meant dragon. The peasants called such creatures serpents or even worms or, if with two legs, wyverns. The creature was the same whatever its name. A figment of the imagination. There were many known by hearsay throughout the land. But who had ever seen one? No one she had ever met. They were stories for children to frighten them into good behaviour. Maybe now, here, a story for the nuns, and with the same purpose?

What they said about dragons was that they possessed teeth and talons and great enmity towards humans. Nonsense, of course. They were beasts imagined by old monks in their monasteries hundreds of years ago. The drawings they made in their illuminated bestiaries came entirely from their imaginations.

It was plain that this unfortunate youth must have had an accident while involved in some dangerous task, something to do with the building works Basilda had mentioned. Nothing to do with imaginary dragons.

But why the mystery? If he had fallen from the building, for instance, someone would know. His wounds, however, were not the sort to be caused by a fall.

She reached out and touched the pearl-like skin of his shoulder. The bulge of the muscle under her fingertips was cold. Impossible to believe this flesh had once throbbed with lifeblood.

The sight brought an unbidden memory of Rivera. For a moment, she felt a spasm of grief. She remembered how she had seen his decapitated corpse lying in his coffin in the Temple church in London. Tears sprang from her eyes before she could stop them.

For some time, she stood before the body with the words of a prayer on her lips. The ground seemed to open beneath her feet. She found it difficult to breathe. Time seemed to make no difference to the depth of her grief over Rivera's fate. Someone, somewhere, would be grieving for this young man, too.

A sound made her turn. The door had been opened and now it slammed shut. The mortuary was plunged into near darkness as the frail candle flames guttered in the draft.

She put up her hands and called out, "Who's there?"

"Who are you, more to the point?" came a man's voice out of the shadows.

"Open the door," she said.

"I said, who are you?"

"I'm a guest here."

There was a chuckle. "So you're that Mistress York, are you?"

"At least you know my name. Who are you?"

"You don't need to know that."

"I don't intend to continue this conversation in the dark." She began to move towards the door, but something loomed towards her out of the shadows.

The knife she usually carried was in her bag inside her chamber. She bunched her fists in readiness.

There was a swift sound of footsteps and light blazed into the mortuary as the door was opened and she saw the figure of a man silhouetted in the doorway. Blinking, she moved towards the figure, but before she could reach him, he slipped away. The door slammed behind him.

By the time she got outside, he had disappeared. The precinct wall lay behind the mortuary, across a stretch of grass, with a tangle of bushes growing against it. She was about to follow what she thought was a glimmer of footprints in the wet grass, when a voice stopped her.

"Mistress York! You! I absolutely forbid it!" The cellaress, with long strides, came hurrying towards her. Face like thunder, she was shouting, "This is hallowed ground. No one is allowed in this part of the precinct without permission."

When she reached Hildegard, she snaked out a hand to grasp her by the sleeve. "Get away from here! This is our mortuary. Get away from here!" Anger brought a flush to her sallow features. "Why are you poking round here? Return to your own domain, madam!"

It was raining. Ice-laden. Nasty. Gusts hurled the hail horizontally across the garth on a biting northeasterly wind. Hildegard was used to it. Even so, she was aware that she would need more protection than her winter cloak. She took out the waxed cape she had carried on her pilgrimage to Compostela and shook it out. It had stood her in good stead then and it would do so now.

Putting it on and making sure the hood was fastened on tightly, she went out into the hall and opened the outer door. The freezing blast swept into the entrance, wetting the tiles.

Peering out, she saw, as hoped, that the cloister garth was empty.

Nobody, she told herself as she hurried along in the shelter of the guesthouse, tells me where I may or may not go.

She reached the mortuary building again but did not go inside. Instead, she followed the faint footprints left by the man who had burst in on her earlier. They disappeared into the undergrowth. She pushed on through the stinging wetness of nettles and long grass until she came out next to what the little cowherd in the tree had mentioned: a door in the wall. Since it was concealed by the bushes behind the mortuary, she would never have guessed it was there. Smiling with satisfaction, she was even more pleased when she found it unbarred. She stepped through to the other side.

Chapter 6

An unexpected scene met her gaze. It struck her as domestic. Sheltered by the rising bulk of the abbey buildings on the other side of the wall was a single-storey thatched house.

When she looked more closely, she realised that it was a workshop first and foremost. The masons' place. Piles of cut stone slabs were stacked in some sort of order on the side nearest the wall. Farther off, on the edge of the woods, were heaps of small uncut stones. A stack of timbers were ready for the axe.

In the middle, under a thatch with deep overhanging eaves, was a spacious lodge of wattle and daub. A brazier was burning under the shelter, and four men in working clothes stood round it, warming their hands. A woman, singing a dirge to match the weather, could be heard from inside the lodge.

Hildegard, hood up, approached through the pelting rain.

One of the men exclaimed in surprise on catching sight of her. They all turned to stare. She pushed back her hood when she reached the shelter.

"Mistress York, I do declare!" exclaimed one of them in ironic tones. "So what brings you out from the comfort of Handale Priory?"

"As comfortable as an animal's cave," she replied. "I believe those nuns have ice in their veins."

A stoup of ale was offered.

"You must be the masons working on the prioress's new house?"

"We are indeed, more's the pity."

"Why so?"

"Fetched us far from home, it has. Except for our master with his nice little wife to keep him warm, we poor devils have to make do with this purgatory until the job's done."

There was an outbreak of chaffing laughter from his two companions.

"It's true!" protested the first speaker. "Why else is our master still safe and sound in Durham? Because his little wife is there, that's why."

"You ain't even wed, Dakin," objected one of the fellows round the brazier. "You ain't got nothing to complain about."

"Oh, haven't I? For what you know, I might have a nice little doxy in Durham city and be pining mightily for her right now."

"Aye, *might*'s the word. *Might not*'s a better'n."

"Let me explain who these rough fellows are," said the first man, Dakin, leaning towards Hildegard and giving her a close look. "Then you can entertain us with a story about who you are and what you were doing trespassing in the mortuary. This here"—he cuffed his neighbour on the shoulder—"is Matt. Apprentice stonemason."

"Aye and general dogsbody." He was a tough-looking lad of sixteen or so with rumpled mouse-coloured hair kept back from his brow by a band of coloured leather. He gave Hildegard a wide grin.

"This here'n is our strong man—"

"Chief stone carrier," explained an older man, red-whiskered and offering a toothy smile. "Will of Durham at your service."

"And if you've noticed the legs on this one, mistress, you'll guess he's our windlass man, Hamo of Easington." He nodded a silent greeting, then turned back to the brazier.

Replied Hildegard, "And you already seem to know who I am."

"They're telling us you be Prioress Basilda's guest?" Will eyed her with undisguised speculation.

"I am."

"Strange place to come guesting?"

She nodded. "As I'm beginning to discover."

"So you know her history, do you?" asked the windlass man.

"Does she have one?"

Glances were exchanged.

Dakin spoke up. "That's something we would all like to know. Blows in here, throws a few nuns out, or so we're told, brings in Master Fulke, hires us. We're not complaining. Just curious. We don't come cheap."

"The Benedictines are not an impoverished Order," Hildegard replied with caution. "They're well able to afford new buildings."

Dakin threw back his head with a jeering laugh. "Our master is one of the highest-paid masons in the north. We are, likewise, as his chosen men. We're not used to working in a back-of-beyond place like this. Cathedrals are more our line."

"You sound sorry you've been hired?" She was interested.

"We don't complain about the job. It's the strange obligations she puts us to that makes us curious."

"Such as?"

"No going off-site until we're finished? Working through the winter? Well, we can't do much in this weather and we told her, didn't we, fellas? We can't put the roof up until the weather improves. Still she wants us here. No visitors. No women. Maybe she thinks she can turn us into monks?"

There were raucous laughs. "We won't be out of here till Bartholomew's Day. Might as well be monks," added Will.

"And then there's Giles."

The men sobered at the name and crossed themselves with differing degrees of piety.

"Giles?" asked Hildegard, already guessing what they would say. "Was that his body in the mortuary? I saw him—his terrible wounds—"

"Aye, you saw him. I know that," said Dakin. "Having a good look like any old leech woman. I went to make sure the candle was still alight. I guessed who you were when you spoke. They'd warned us there would be an outsider living in for a while. And they warned us not to entice you from your meditations or speak with you."

"That's a strange rule to put on you. I see you're obedient types."

"It's one rule among many we're happy to flout." Dakin gave a grim smile.

"I heard a strange story from the priest back there about a dragon. Indeed, the whole priory seems to be in thrall to such nonsense, so may I ask how your workmate met such a gruesome death?"

"Whose story do you want, the official one or the one we believe?"

"Both, if you choose."

"Official—it was the dragon of Handale did for him. Unofficial—somebody attacked him with a grappling iron." He nodded over towards the half-finished building, where the scaffolding was hung with ropes and pulleys. It was festooned with hooks. For that matter, the masons' tools were lying around where they had evidently been using them shortly before she arrived.

"Do you have any idea who would attack him?"

"Your guess, mistress." Dakin shrugged. He had blue eyes of

a particularly icy hue. They were like a blizzard now. "Giles never harmed a soul in his life. Good worker. No reason for getting killed. Ain't that right?"

The others nodded. "Never got on the wrong side of anybody, Giles didn't."

"But don't you have any suspicions?" Hildegard asked in astonishment. "In such a remote place, who is likely to have done such a thing?"

"Ah, so you believe the unofficial version of events?"

"It's certainly more plausible than a wild beast roaming the woods and attacking people. Or a blood-drinking nun," she added, remembering what the priest had told her.

"That's all cock," agreed Hamo.

"Where did you find him?" She glanced round.

"In the woods," Dakin told her.

She was surprised. "So you did go in there?"

"Aye. Into dragon territory."

"All this fancy about dragons came up after that." Dakin explained.

"It's thick woodland out there. So how was it possible to find him?"

"It was the little novice Alys from the priory had the misfortune to stumble across him. Nearly sent her out of her wits. She came screaming back in here, white as a sheet."

"A novice? What on earth was she doing outside the precinct?"

"Trying to escape, if she'd any sense."

"When we first settled in here, the nuns used to walk about the woods for a while before vespers. Taking the air. It was forbidden for the novices, but Alys still used to sneak out, collecting leaves and that."

"And found the body."

Silent Will spoke up. "In a rare state of terror she was, poor pet."

Hamo took up the story. "We went to have a look ourselves and she led us to where he was lying. Already dead. In a mess. Nothing we could do for him. Stiff. Been there all night. We thought maybe he'd decided to make a run for it, to hell with his obligations to the guild. We couldn't make it out. He'd said nowt to us. Dakin took the little novice in to tell the prioress." Hamo turned to Dakin, who related what happened next.

"All she said was, 'I've warned my sisters of putting pleasure before duty. Why do they walk in the woods? For mere pleasure and frivolity. And this is what happens. But will they listen? This is always the result when disobedience is the rule.' The novice would get it in the neck, no doubt. They know how to punish, by all accounts."

Hildegard stifled her feelings. "I suppose the coroner has been summoned?"

"Eventually, aye. The bailiff from Kilton Castle was here not two days since. Had his clerk make a few notes. Muttered something about the bishop's having to throw his weight about. Then buggered off without another word. Meanwhile, we need to inform our master over in Durham. We sent for a courier, but he's not allowed to set foot in the enclosure. We have to send a message through the prioress herself."

"And whether it's reached its destination or not is anybody's guess," Hamo said.

"We daily wait on the appearance of our master to rescue us from limbo—"

"Fearing we'll have a long wait," Will muttered.

"But no blame to him. He'll have to tie things up in Durham and only after that set out for this godforsaken spot. It'll take days in this weather, roads like loam in the rains."

"No guessing when he'll get through." Hamo scowled. "And we're stuck here like lost souls until he arrives."

"Three days there and back, plus time dealing with the bishop?"

"Likely that, to look on the bright side, more likely longer," agreed Hamo. "And likely they'll turn up together."

The men spoke in turn, as if long used to thinking each other's thoughts. Their grief for their dead workmate was obvious.

Hildegard was confused. "Surely," she began, "there must be some clue as to how he was killed?"

"It was murder," replied Dakin. "Obviously. But not by any murdering dragon."

"But why?" she asked. "Who would want him dead?"

They shook their heads.

"We go out in pairs now."

"You weren't with anyone when you entered the mortuary," she pointed out, addressing Dakin.

"I reckon I'm safe enough in the enclosure, and if I'm not capable of seeing off a nun or two, I'm not worth saving anyway." He grinned for a moment, but then his expression turned bleak. "We want to get to the bottom of it, mistress, but we don't know where to start."

"You could begin by telling me something more about Giles himself. Where was he from? How long had he worked with you? Were there any circumstances in his life that brought him enemies?"

A few glances were covertly exchanged. So there was something, then.

Settling down round the freshly stoked charcoal brazier, the stonemasons told her what they wanted her to know about Giles.

It amounted to very little. He was second to Dakin. A journeyman mason. Employed, like Dakin, by their master for a year or more. They travelled from site to site. Never a cross word. What else to say? Dakin shrugged. "That's it, mistress. He was my right hand. A regular and blameless life. Now snuffed out like a candle."

Hearing the bell for the next office, Hildegard apologised for having to leave. She thanked them for their ale and promised she would do what she could to help from within the priory. Somebody must know the something that would lead to the killer. The priest, for a start. He seemed to have a good idea of what was going on within the precinct. She mentioned the warning he had issued, and they again mocked the idea of a dragon running loose.

She was about to leave, when a sound came from inside the lodge. She glanced across. A young woman was standing in the entrance, looking out. Dark-haired, with large hands and with a workman's leather apron over a russet kirtle, she wore a thick shawl pinned at the front by a pewter brooch. She surveyed the group round the brazier with a sour smile.

"And this is our imaginator," announced Dakin. "Mistress Carola, carver of stone devils."

She nodded briefly in Hildegard's direction, then turned to the men. "When you boys have finished yarning, you might decide to do some work today." She went back inside the lodge.

Hamo chuckled. "Come on, lads. Orders is orders."

"Back to the grindstone!" Will chuckled without rancour and began to head towards the shell of the new structure.

Dakin turned to Hildegard. "Come and visit us again. The prioress doesn't rule you. We'll show you the house we're building. You'll find she's doing well for herself. And maybe by then we'll have discovered something that will put Giles's killer in chains."

By the time Hildegard had crossed to the door of the enclosure, the men had returned to their work. One of them began to chip at a piece of stone. A chisel chimed regularly, echoing the regular and deeper tolling of the priory bell.

Master Fulke had honoured the priory by purchasing a trental from them—that is, he was paying in gold for thirty masses to be sung to ease his soul to heaven when the time came for him to depart to what he must assume would be an even better life.

Hildegard understood now where the money for the new building was coming from, but she couldn't help wondering what Fulke's sins were that he believed he needed so much help from the Great Measurer. Or was it something more to do with the earl of Northumberland? The priory had been his own family's endowment more than two hundred years ago, when one of his Percy ancestors had founded it for the greater glory of the Virgin Mary.

Was there something in it for Fulke in these days of shifting allegiances? Did it somehow help his dealings with the earl to be seen to support the Handale Benedictines?

Putting these matters aside for the moment, she made her way out of the church in the wake of the ever-silent nuns and trudged across the wet grass to her chamber.

The rain had stopped and the pale northern sun had made a fainthearted appearance. It was a blur of watery crimson behind the black skeletons of the branches hanging over the enclosure wall. Chilled, she let herself into the silent house.

A candle in a sconce was fixed just inside the doorway, and she lit it at once, using the tinder that always stood beside it in a niche in the wall. The entrance to the guest quarters was windowless, but the candlelight flared into the corners and dispersed the shadows. She was about to cross to her chamber, but then she thought she heard a sound like an aumbry door closing inside.

She froze. No other sound followed except for the *drip-drip* of a leak in a room above.

Her knife was still inside her bag on the floor by her bed. She looked round for something to defend herself with. Nothing was at hand. The words of the mason came back: "If I'm not capable of seeing off a nun or two . . ."

Emboldened, she doused the candle and stepping silently towards the door, gripped the metal ring, and, so it did not squeak on its hinge, turned it gently round until she felt the latch rise. Whoever was inside was in darkness, too, the shutters being closed, and with luck would not notice the movement.

Her shoulder against it, she inched the door ajar.

Silence within.

She pushed the door wider and stepped inside.

CHAPTER 7

Without warning, something came flying out of the darkness and hit her in the face. A brutal commotion of blows and flailing limbs followed and then the sense of a black cloak muffling her face, fingers clawing; then she grasped flesh, soft pouches of her assailant's face as she groped for the eyes in a reflex to defend herself.

As suddenly as it had occurred, the attack ended. All that remained was a black shape flying out of the door and, between Hildegard's fingers, a piece of torn fabric.

Her attacker hurled itself across the garth, with Hildegard speeding after, but the shape was immediately swallowed up among the shadows in the cloister. Sprinting over, she was in time to glimpse the hem of a cloak disappearing behind a pillar.

By the time she reached it, a line of nuns were processing towards the refectory. Two by two they came, cowls pulled half over their faces, crosses and beads swinging. Innocent as lambs.

But one of them was her attacker.

Enraged by her own stupidity, Hildegard poked her head inside the church. It was the nearest place for anyone to seek refuge. She was forced to peer through a fog of smoke and incense to make anything out. One or two nuns were pacing down the nave in front of her, one of them swinging a censer as if to block her progress.

She fingered the piece of fabric between her fingers. Someone at Handale must have a torn gown, she thought.

She moved closer to the two she had followed inside. They had gone to stand against the wall to her left, heads bowed, hoods casting deep wedges of shadow over their faces. In the flickering candlelight, it was impossible to tell one from another. Those in the inner circle were grouped round the prioress near the altar, discussing something in low voices. They were too far along the nave to have just come inside. She turned her attention back to the two by the wall. Was her assailant one of these?

She listened to try to detect anything in their breathing to show they had been running, but they were both as composed as stone. She cursed to herself, free of nunlike vows, and peered along the wall, but they were the only two here. A closer look showed how optimistic it was to expect to find a tear in their garments. Most were threadbare. And she didn't know whether it was a fragment of a sleeve or a hood or the edge of a cloak she held.

Prioress Basilda, as massive as usual in her wooden chair, was being helped out of it by the cellaress and the sacristan. The pimply priest was present. The nuns in attendance were speaking in wispy voices.

After this, supper.

She turned to go.

If the intruder was a nun and not one of the servants or lay sisters, which seemed most likely from her black garments, then she must have missed vespers in order to have had time to enter Hildegard's chamber while she was absent. Nothing told her who had failed to put in an appearance, and there was no way of finding out.

Only one course suggested itself. She would have to match the piece of fabric she held with a tear in one of the nun's habits. It was no use expecting to find a match here. She would have to find an opportunity in the refectory. One of these furtive, hooded figures knew she had been attacked, and had, in turn, been toughly resisted. Her face must be blotched with small wounds, thought Hildegard, smiling to herself. The culprit would have to do something out of the ordinary to get out of the trap she had set herself.

And so would Hildegard herself, to spring it.

The barefoot novice who brought the bread round to everyone was there again.

Thinly clad as usual, she held out a basket of wastel to each of the nuns in turn with her head bowed. She looked too cowed to do otherwise. Chewing on the fine white bread, Hildegard watched her scurry from one to the next, giving a little curtsy to each nun in turn. It was plain she lived in fear. This must be the one the masons had referred to as Alys, the one who had found the body of Giles in the woods. No wonder she looked frightened.

Her attention moved to the other diners. Four sat on each side of the long table, including herself. As usual, no one spoke. In order not to interrupt the reading from the lectern, they merely waved a hand for what they wanted, beckoning, dismissing, never looking the novice in the face. How old would she be? Younger than Hildegard had first assumed. Thirteen? Fourteen? Approaching marriageable age. Assigned to the monastic life by some guardian or a parent reluctant or unable to feed her? And by the look of her, profoundly unhappy.

Hildegard gestured for more bread. When the girl was near enough, she asked, "How long have you been at Handale, my child?"

The girl gave a darting glance at the nearby nuns and whispered, "Since Martinmas, mistress." She saw that nobody was bothering much, so she added in a whisper, "I was sent from Rosedale. I do not wish to be a nun."

Hildegard glanced at the dirty feet, the thin shift, the broken fingernails and tangled hair. "Come to my guest chamber before compline," she murmured. "I would like to know more about this."

The novice gave a slight nod and moved away.

No sign of a torn sleeve. It was difficult to inspect the hems of the cloaks tumbled onto the benches beside the sisters. Three or four still wore theirs, hoods up, faces concealed. One of those four, guessed Hildegard after looking at the smooth faces of those with their hoods thrown back. She rose to her feet.

There was a rustle of speculation. No one got up from her place before the prioress.

Hildegard moved behind the line of nuns sitting on the bench she had just vacated. She could not see their faces, but she could do something to make them turn. With a sudden loud scream, she pointed into the corner of the refectory. At once, heads swivelled. Three hooded nuns briefly turned to stare at her. Two of them had faces as smooth as alabaster. The third was covered in scratches and had a red mark under her left eye.

"Mistress York! What is the meaning of this?" The prioress was in a fury and started to heave herself out of her chair.

"There, my lady! In the corner! I think I see something moving!" she exclaimed. She lowered her hand. She had found out what she wanted. "Forgive me, my lady. I now see I was mistaken."

There was a rustling, not quite a murmur, from the nuns. The word *dragon* was heard.

"One of you go and have a look. Set our minds at rest," replied the prioress, giving Hildegard a hard glance as she sank back among her cushions.

The subprioress got up and peered cautiously into the corner, where she poked around for a moment. "Nothing here, my lady."

Hildegard dropped a curtsy. "My dear and reverend prioress, pray forgive me. It must have been a trick of the light. Or a mouse."

"Sit. Finish eating."

Hildegard returned to her place. Her assailant was only two places away. Out of the corner of her eye, she watched the nun pick up a piece of bread and begin to eat.

"A moment, sister!" The black shape was hurrying to be first out of the refectory as soon as the final amen was uttered, and when she didn't stop, Hildegard ran behind her and grasped her by the sleeve. "Sister, I believe I have something of yours!"

The nun was jerked to a stop. Slowly, she turned round. Her hood was over her face, but Hildegard pushed it back to reveal a long scratch down one side of her face and a series of small contusions under one eye.

Hildegard bobbed her head. "Forgive me."

"For what?"

"For causing injury, although I'm sure you'll realise it was in self-defence."

"I don't know what you mean."

"I think you do."

"What do you want?"

"I want you to look at this." Hildegard opened the palm of her hand, where the piece of torn fabric lay.

The nun's eyes darted from side to side when she saw it. "It's nothing to do with me!"

Hildegard still held her sleeve. "But how strange! It seems to match this tear exactly." She chanced on the exact place where the fabric had been ripped at the cuff.

The two women regarded each other for a moment. They were of the same height and build, evenly matched.

"So what do you have to say?" prompted Hildegard.

"There is an explanation."

"I'm sure there is."

A sudden voice boomed: "Who is that conversing in the cloister?" It was the cellarer. She strode swiftly over to the two women.

Hildegard turned with a smile. "I am at fault again, sister. I asked a question. Does the rule of silence prevail in the cloisters, too?"

"Get to your cell, Sister Mariana. Now!"

"I beg of you, don't chastise her," Hildegard broke in as the nun hurried away. "She did not speak. The fault was all mine." Putting on her most helpless expression, she said, "It is so very strange for me to find myself in a community with such strict adherence to Benedict's Rule. You and your prioress are to be commended for following the saint with such remarkable zeal."

The cellarer looked baffled for a moment, then decided to take it as a compliment. "We do our best," she replied with a tightening of her lips. "Now I suggest you retire to your quarters until compline and pass the time in the much-needed discipline of prayer."

"That is what I'm here for, sister. I do it with a glad heart." Inclining her head, Hildegard backed away.

Sister Mariana. So what was she up to? Had she been sent to poke around Hildegard's chamber by the prioress? Is that why the cellaress had prevented her from blurting anything out? But what did they hope to find? It was a mystery, but one she hoped would be solved very soon, because she did not doubt that the nun would try to explain away her actions before long.

Meanwhile, there was another visitor.

It was later that evening and already dark. The cloister lamp was lit, but its faint light did not go far, and the garth itself lay in darkness. Standing at her chamber window, Hildegard glimpsed a small shape materialise from the direction of the buttery, then vanish into the long shadows. A few moments later, there was a slight noise outside her door

She went to open it. "Come inside. Did anyone see you?"

The novice shook her head.

"Here," said Hildegard, noticing how she was shivering with cold. "Wrap yourself in this cloak for a while. You'll be going down with an ague next."

When she was snug inside the woollen cloak, she gave Hildegard a frightened glance. "I shouldn't be here. If they find out, they'll torture me."

"Torture?" Hildegard frowned.

"You've no idea. It's only because you're not one of them I dare risk speaking to you. Oh, mistress, I don't know what to do. Please help me!"

Hildegard leaned against the window embrasure and gave her an encouraging smile. "I will if I can. It's obvious you're unhappy. But now you are here tell me how you come to be here against your will?"

"I've got to get away. I'm so frightened. Please say you'll help?" She glanced nervously towards the door.

"You're quite safe here for now. Just tell me how you come to be here in the first place?" Hildegard prompted. "Begin at the beginning."

The girl took a deep breath. "My father was a vassal of the earl of Northumberland. We lived in a fortified manor in the Eastern Marches. Father was killed in a skirmish with the Scots when he was in the service of the earl. My mother had already died years ago from the plague. I scarcely knew her. I'm now completely alone." Tears began to trickle down her cheeks. "I don't want to be a nun. I just want to go home."

Hildegard went to sit beside her. "Who sent you here?"

"My guardian. A hateful man. He sits in my father's house as if he owns it. But it's still at law. It should come to me and my brother. My father willed it so. My little brother is only nine. He can't do anything."

"And where is he?"

"He's in the retinue of Sir Edward Umfraville, but it's miles away, in the west of the county. I'm sure he doesn't even know our father is dead. My guardian intends to wait until he has ownership of our property before he lets my brother know about Father. I'm so miserable, mistress. I think and think, but my thoughts run all over and I can find no way out."

"Isn't there anyone who'll support your claim?" Hildegard asked. "What about your father's steward?"

"He would help, but he was dismissed by my guardian on the day Father was buried. I have no idea where he is now."

"Then we must find out. The law, fortunately for us, often takes its time. Tell me where this manor is."

She named an unfamiliar place that was, Hildegard guessed, deep in Northumberland's most northerly territory. A border stronghold. First to exchange hands in the dangerous game of barter and attrition being played out in the lawless region between Scotland and England.

"We've got to be quick," the novice whispered. "They say they're going to send me to the dragon as punishment if I do anything wrong. That's where they send nuns and novices who need correction. None of them ever returns."

"The dragon? But that's just a story—"

"No, the novice who was here before me has been sent there. She'll be his prisoner until he devours her. I'm so afraid—"

"Who told you this nonsense?"

"That man, Master Fulke. He was the one who brought me here through the woods on the last stage of the journey."

"Be reassured. I won't let any dragon get hold of you. I don't believe in them. And as I'm used to fighting for what I do believe in, you can rest assured that will not happen. These days, the theft of an inheritance is a familiar one, unfortunately, but there's usually a way out for those who are determined to find one. Abduction is a crime punishable under the laws of England. No one should be forced to marry against her will. It cannot be allowed."

"They'll kill me if they find out I've been talking to you."

"It won't come to that. Believe me. Now, I want you to promise me you'll say nothing to anyone, not even to your best friend. Do as you're told by the nuns, as if nothing has changed, and if anything happens to alarm you, let me know at once." Hildegard stood up. "You'll be missed if you stay much longer. Let me make sure there's no one around to see you leave here."

She went over to the window and peered out through a corner of the blind. The garth was deserted. Trusting that no one was watching from the cloister, she doused the candle so that the girl could slip invisibly back through the shadows. "Go," she whispered. "Trust me."

Poor little creature, she thought as the girl slid nervously into the darkness. Hildegard paced the floor for some time after the novice left, until a plan began to form. She would need outside help, but how to obtain it was the question.

The doleful bell began its summons again. Compline. She let herself out and crossed the garth.

———

Next morning, she hurriedly broke her fast, then went to see the masons. Matt greeted her then blurted, "Giles probably died because of me. It's my fault. I was hankering after a really good-size piece of beech and he said he knew just where to find one. That's where it happened. By the great beech." Matt's ever-ready smile had faded and his eyes clouded over.

Before Hildegard could offer any remark, Carola put a hand on his shoulder. "That's a sot-witted thing to say and you know it." She turned to Hildegard.

"I'm sure Mistress York would like to see some of your work."

"I would indeed." The two women exchanged a look.

Matt, oblivious, stood up. "This chair"—he indicated the one he had been sitting in—"what do you think of it?"

"Did you make this?" Hildegard ran her hand over the silky wood. It was a fine piece of craftwork.

"Oh, he's that proud of it. You'd think nobody had ever made a chair before." Carola punched him teasingly on the shoulder.

"I haven't made one before, and that's a fact, so give me leave to strut in my achievement." He smiled faintly.

Carola said, "I hope that there fat prioress appreciates it."

"You don't think I'm leaving this for her to sit on and turn to matchwood, do you?"

"You'll be copping it, then. She'll have you up for stealing priory property."

"She owns all the wood God grows, does she?"

"All that on priory lands, yes."

"She'll get it returned in its former state, then, as a lump of wood. See what she does with that. My craft isn't for sale to any old barterer."

Despite the apparent good nature of their exchange, there was heaviness in their humour. It was apparent that the death of their fellow mason weighed on them all.

"Show Mistress York your little figures," suggested Dakin.

Matt went to a shelf and lifted down some pieces carved from wood: an angel, a grotesque, and a stag at bay, its antlers as graceful as the real thing but in delicate miniature.

"All wood from hereabouts," he explained.

"And this one?" asked Hildegard, noticing another one on the ledge.

They all looked at it in silence. Matt made no move to get it down.

It was a dragon, unfinished, but its claws and the scales on its back gave testimony to what it was.

Dakin broke in. "Mistress York, come and look at our edifice. If Matt can strut, so can we."

He led her outside. "He's taking Giles's death hard, both of 'em being of an age and mates, like," he confided. "We're all cut up, of course. It shouldn't have happened. We're still waiting to hear back from the master. He'll root out the culprit, sure as hellfire. It's the waiting for justice that's getting us down."

"I notice the coroner hasn't shown up yet," Hildegard said.

"It'll be the weather that's holding him up. Until he shows his face we're stuck here in this hellhole." His voice, though not much above a whisper as they stepped inside the shell of the building, echoed round the half-built stone walls with frustrated rage.

"It seems close to being finished," observed Hildegard, looking about. "When does the roof go on?"

"Not yet awhile. Foundations laid last summer. Walls half built before the bad weather set in. Two storeys. A spiral stair, half built. The whole to be roofed in slate. We're making use of the weather to construct the wooden centring to support the stonework. We can't get on with the rest of it until the weather improves. Too wet now. The mortar won't set. Then we have to bash a hole through the enclosure wall so the prioress can have her grand entrance. She wants a wall round her enclave so she can have the privacy of her own garden. And"—he grimaced—"to keep her safe from the wild beast of Handale, of course. It'll be a neat little setup."

"Plenty of work for you to be getting on with."

"Nice profit for our master. Carola's working on carvings for the corbels, along of me. Matt works in wood, as you saw. We tell him it's because he's soft. Riling him, like. He knows we mean it in jest, poor sot."

For all his attempt to be cheerful, he had a sad expression. He looked up at the opening above their heads. Rain was beginning to spot down. The stone pavers at their feet were soon wet. He gave an openly wistful smile. "Are things well with you inside that place?"

"Not well, no," she admitted. "I'm troubled by one or two matters, which is partly why I wanted to speak to you this morning." She told him about the young novice whose inheritance was at risk, although she made no reference to the intruder in her chamber. "I need to leave the priory for a few hours but have no wish to draw attention to the fact. There must be a way in, other than the main gate and that little track through the woods? How do the nuns obtain their necessities? That path I came by looked rarely used."

"There's the beck. They use a boat."

Hildegard frowned.

"It comes now and then with stuff they can't grow or provide. Not often, though. They seem to provide everything they need for themselves."

"Have you any idea what's going on in there?" she asked abruptly, gesturing towards the enclosure wall.

Dakin shook his head. "Is anything going on?" He eyed her closely.

"I think so."

"We're forbidden to enter—except now we're allowed to mourn for Giles in their mortuary. They're a secretive lot. They hate anybody from outside."

"I can see that."

"I'm amazed they allow guests."

"Maybe they had no choice?" She was ignorant of what strings might have been pulled from Swyne and from the archbishop's palace to get her in here. It was already dawning on her that until she found out why, she would have to stay.

She had another question for Dakin. "Do you think Giles's murder has anything to do with the priory?"

"I wondered that. But why? It doesn't make sense."

"Could he have stumbled on some secret?"

"He said nowt to me if he did."

"Can you tell me, have any of you been back to the place where he was found?"

He shook his head. "It may seem we're lackadaisical, but we work hard during daylight hours. They're short enough at this time of year and our lady prioress wants a deal of fancy decoration in her new house. It's exactly the sort of thing to keep us busy. At night, when our time's our own, I doubt any of us would dare set foot in such a thicket." He grimaced. "Not from fear of dragons. We're not lily-livered. It's just that none of us wants to be lost in those woods forevermore. You've seen how dense it is? It's like a maze."

"I know. I felt lost almost as soon as we set foot in there."

"Maybe there's something I ought to show you." He led her across to where the timbers, felled to make room for the prioress's new lodging, were stacked and waiting for the woodman's axe. He pointed to something behind them. Hildegard approached.

Under the sheltering trees waiting to be felled, she saw a print in the mud. Three claws.

She turned.

Dakin was watching her carefully.

"It would have to be a very large deerhound," she said. "I had a lymer like that once. When did it appear?"

"The morning after Giles disappeared. Almost," he added, "as if it was looking for another victim."

He turned and went back towards the lodge. With a glance into the woods, Hildegard followed.

Dakin stood under the eaves, out of the rain, which was falling faster now. "Why did you ask if we'd been back to where he was killed?"

"I'd like to have a look myself. Will you take me there?"

CHAPTER 8

They took some persuading. None of them wanted to accompany her. When they saw she was going to go anyway, they eventually agreed. Dakin refused to enter the woods alone, however; he wanted one of the men to accompany them. "Safety in numbers."

Matt gestured towards Carola. "She'll stay to guard the castle. I'll come because I'll recognise the tree my wood should have come from where they found him. Will can stay to guard Carola. And Hamo's staying to guard Will."

"What, from me?" Carola gave a faint smile.

"You're wrong on one count, young lad," said Hamo. "I'm going with you. I don't want to miss anything. And I have something you might need." He produced a short broadsword from under his cloak. Hildegard had already noticed that everyone, even Carola, carried daggers in their belts.

So it was that Hildegard and her three escorts set out just as the sun was starting to trickle between the trees to the east. The going was soft after the rain. Dakin went ahead on a path that was no more than a shadow in the undergrowth.

Hildegard asked, "Are we going to lose ourselves?"

But Dakin shook his head. He was breaking off the stems of

branches as they pushed their way through. "We know the general direction. If you listen, you can hear the beck over to our right. There's also a faint trail where folk have walked already."

Far away, from the direction of the ravine, came the distant roar of water being forced through the cleft in the rocks.

"That's Kilton Beck," Dakin told her.

"I could hear it clearly when I slept at the castle. It was way down at the bottom of an ironstone cliff. It runs quite fast and powerful, by the sound of it."

"It narrows when it leaves here, then widens out again at an old Norse settlement called Killing Grove on the coast. There was a pitched battle there, hundreds of years ago, when the Norsemen landed and met with more resistance than they reckoned on."

They walked in a sober silence, as if the ghosts of the dead invaders still haunted the woods.

"This is the place." Matt, pushing his way ahead, came to a stop under a large old beech. It had wide-spreading branches, making a sort of clearing round itself.

"Look at it! Isn't it a fine old fellow?" He ran his hands over the smooth grey trunk. A low branch stretched above his head and he put up his hand to pat it. "I can see this turning itself into something useful as I look." He turned to the others. "Poor old fellow." This time, it was clear he did not mean the tree.

Hildegard paced the open space under the branches. The ground was ankle-deep with last autumn's fall of leaves. There was a jumbled heap of them, scuffed and turned, so that the darker leaves that had lain all autumn underneath were now on top.

"Yes, this is the place where he had his struggle." Dakin stood beside her, eyes cast down.

Hildegard bent to peer more closely at something. She touched a leaf with the tip of one finger.

Dakin knelt beside her. "What is it?"

"Nothing much." She straightened. "A spot of blood?" The rains had washed the rest away. "It's sheltered here. Despite the rain, things can lie hidden for some time under the leaves."

Not quite sure what they were looking for, the rest of them began to tramp about.

"Maybe better not to do that." Hildegard, alone, began to trawl back and forth, being careful where she put her feet. After a while, she bent down again and lifted something from the mulch of leaves. She held it up. "Recognise it?"

"I do," said Matt, coming forward and taking it from her. It was a pewter badge. "He wore it on a lace round his neck." He held it in the palm of his hand. His lips twisted. For a moment, he was unable to speak. Then he gave Hildegard a sideways look. "To protect him from danger."

"It tells us nothing that we didn't already know," Dakin briskly pointed out, taking the badge and pushing it deep into his pouch.

Hildegard turned away. To give them time to recover themselves, she moved off to gaze down the slope towards the sound of the beck.

Here, as elsewhere in the wood, the trees pressed in close together, staves of ash and willow making a barrier as thick as any wicket fence. Now and then, there appeared small openings where animals had pushed through to force a path for themselves. The small ones had been made by rabbits, but the larger gaps would have been made by deer. Or men. Somewhere beyond the slope of woodland was the waterway that crossed the coast road that led north and south to the outside world.

She well knew what the pewter badge belonging to Giles represented.

When she rejoined them, she asked, "What lies upstream?"

"The water mill. A miller grinds wheat for the priory."

"Is he violent?"

Dakin half smiled. "Not that we know. I don't think any of us has ever clapped eyes on him."

They were itching to get back to work by now. The sun was already above the horizon, gleaming silkily through a haze of moisture between the boles of the trees.

"We'll cop it if master arrives and we're none of us at our benches," said Hamo, guiltily starting back. The rest of them trickled after him.

On the way, guided by his markers, Dakin asked, "Has that taken us any further, mistress?"

"I don't know yet. We need more time. We have to ask ourselves a few questions, don't we? Was it really a wild animal that attacked him? Or was it a man? If the latter, are we saying his murderer came from somewhere in the woods? Or did he come from the direction of the priory?" To herself, she added, Or from your own lodge?

When she arrived back inside the enclosure, she went straight up to the scriptorium. There must be a way of getting a message out, she thought.

She began to unfold the writing table where she had left it propped against the wall. As she pulled it open, a piece of vellum fell to the floor. Surprised to think she had left something in her desk when she had finished copying the previous day, she picked it up. In an unfamiliar hand was a line of writing.

"There is more to this than you know. Watch your step."

It was unsigned.

Whoever had written it had carefully wiped the quill and stoppered the inkhorn before putting them away.

———

The refectory. Rain was falling again. Whenever anyone opened the door, water could be heard sluicing through the stone gutters. The sun of early morning had failed to live up to its promise. The nuns shook their cloaks, scattering water everywhere before taking their seats at the long table. The nun with the swollen eye, Mariana, took her place farther along the bench. She did not look in Hildegard's direction.

A benediction was said. The reading began. Salt passed from hand to hand. Bread came round, offered by the same novice as before—Alys. She glanced once at Hildegard and her eyelids fluttered, but she quickly continued down the line.

Sister Mariana broke off a piece of bread, murmured thanks, and scooped up gruel with a small bone spoon. She finished quickly, wiped the spoon, and hooked it back onto her belt. She sat for a moment or two with her hands loosely clasped, as if offering up a prayer. Hildegard finished her own gruel and waited.

Alys returned with wine. She refilled Hildegard's beaker, then asked if she would like to refill the flask on her belt. Hildegard unstoppered it and a steady stream of wine was poured in, and then she heard the whisper: "They are taking me away tomorrow, when Master Fulke returns."

Hildegard exchanged a glance and mouthed, "Trust me."

A prayer of thanks was offered up. The prioress rose to her feet and processed out. Sister Mariana got up next and passed close by the end of the table, where Hildegard was sitting. She herself rose. She followed the nun outside.

In the cloister, Sister Mariana was dallying with her cape and hood before plunging out into the rain.

"Going to the scriptorium?" Hildegard murmured before setting off across the garth towards the building opposite. Without looking back, she heard the nun follow her.

When they reached the door that opened into the shared entrance with Basilda's parlour, Hildegard gave it a quick survey to make sure the coast was clear, then nodded to the nun to follow. They climbed the stairs and reached the top not a moment too soon. The door below creaked open and Prioress Basilda stood there, looking up.

"Mistress York? Is that you?"

The nun found herself pushed into the scriptorium and Hildegard went back to look down the stairs. "Who else would it be, my lady? Am I to have help?"

"No, no, not at all. Not that. I can't have people up and down these stairs all day. The sooner I have my own private quarters, the better." She went irritably back into her chamber.

Too fat to climb the stairs, thought Hildegard with relief.

When she went into the scriptorium, the nun was standing on the far side, a frightened look on her face. "Is she coming up?"

"Not a chance." She threw her cloak on its hook. "You left a note, I believe?"

"I had to. I'm at my wit's end." She paced backwards and forwards across the small room. Thought Hildegard, I've heard this already. The nun swivelled suddenly and stared into Hildegard's face, a nerve jumping at the corner of her mouth. "Something horrible is going on here, mistress. I don't know which way to turn. I have to talk to someone. That's why I came to your chamber yesterday, but when you crept in like that, I mistook you for someone else and panicked."

"I'm at fault, then. But please go on, tell me what you mean. What do you think is going on?"

"You must have noticed the harsh penance meted out to the sinners brought here? Some of the girls stay for no more than a week or so; then they disappear. We're told the novices are making up their minds whether to join the Order, but I fear something worse happens to them."

"What do you fear?"

"That they're abducted and kept prisoner until their family pays a ransom. If they're orphans, they can be sold in marriage. Their husbands make a profit from their inheritance."

"What makes you think this?"

"That man Fulke. I don't trust him. Why is he always here when someone goes missing?"

"Is he?"

She nodded.

"Could it be coincidence?"

The nun shook her head. Her raw knuckles ground into her eye sockets, making her eyes redder than ever. When she blinked back her tears, she said, "They treat them brutally enough while they are here, but no doubt far worse when Fulke gets his hands on them."

"He's supposed to be a benefactor of the priory. Just because he's often here doesn't mean he's involved in criminal activities."

"But the girls, so many of them. Why here? If they're interested in becoming nuns, they can go to any house near a town where they have family. These girls come from far afield. I fear for them."

A sound from outside prompted Hildegard to go to the door and fling it open. The prioress was halfway up the stairs.

"I want to bring you this," she puffed. In the hand that wasn't hanging on to the rail was a sheaf of vellum.

Hildegard said loudly, so that Sister Mariana would have time to conceal herself, "That is most kind, my lady. I see I'm to be kept busy during my sojourn here. Praise be to God. Let me take it from you."

She descended in such a way that the prioress could not have got past even if her great bulk would have allowed it. They stood facing each other, Hildegard looking down and the prioress, wedged, looking up.

Conceding the fact that she would not be able to reach the top with Hildegard in the way, she forced a smile. "Most kind, mistress. You've saved me from this terrible climb." She backed down heavily, step by step, breathing audibly. Hildegard watched until the prioress entered her chamber and closed the door.

When she turned back into the scriptorium, the nun was nowhere to be seen. Going over to the large store cupboard, she pulled open the door. Mariana came tumbling out.

"What did she want?" she gasped. She was trembling with fear. "She must know I'm here! Oh, God, save me!"

She was cowering against the wall, scarcely able to catch her breath.

"Don't be alarmed. She's gone back down to her chamber." Hildegard peered closely at the nun. Despite Sister Mariana's apparent strength when she had attacked Hildegarde in her chamber the previous day, she was wasted to skin and bone, frail wrists poking out of threadbare sleeves, thumbprints of fatigue beneath her eyes. She could be no more than twenty-four. She looked truly terrified.

"What would she do if she found you?" Hildegard asked, unable to hide her concern.

"Flagellation. It takes place in front of everybody in the chapter house. Other unspeakable cruelties. Nothing to eat or drink but bread and water. Eating meals from the floor. Isolation for weeks on end. They did this." She lifted a finger to show where the nail had been ripped out. The wound had healed, but it was red and swollen. "This is the priory where we're sent to be punished according to the Rule. Nobody dare talk about it. I can't tell you how terrible it is. We live in daily fear." She crumpled to her knees and began to sob.

"And what brought you here?" Hildegard asked as gently as she could after a few moments.

"My own folly." The nun's lips tightened. When Hildegard said nothing, she got up and tried to pull herself together. She paced the chamber once or twice, then blurted, "I was a nun at Rosedale. Sent against my will when I was no more than a child. I sinned." She faltered, then said in a rush, "I was sent here and imprisoned for two years in a cell. Beaten. Scourged. Other cruelties. They know how to cause pain, these nuns. Then the old prioress left and I thought it might be different. But it's not. It's just as bad."

"Why do you stay?"

"How can I escape? I did try running away but I got lost in the woods. I spent a night in utter terror, fearing they would track me down. The lay brothers found me next day and dragged me back—" Her words were cut off by another sob. She went to Hildegard and gripped her by both hands in desperation. "Mistress, you must understand, most of us have no kin. Whom can we turn to for help? Elsewhere, it might be to our prioress. Here, there is no one to turn to and nowhere to run."

It seemed she could not stop shaking.

"Have other nuns gone through all this? Is that why they're here?"

"Them! The sheep! The prioress's favourites—" Her eyes were full of bitterness. "They glory in the power they're given. They love pain. They inflict it with as much malice as they can. They see it as a holy rite. Punishing sinners for the glory of God. How they relish it!"

"Not all, surely?"

"The inner circle, the subprioress, the cellaress, one or two cronies of theirs. They say they're only doing God's will. The rest of them enjoy having pain inflicted on them. They rejoice in it. The worse, the better! It's their ecstasy. They imagine they're divinely blessed by it. Look closely at the studded collars under their robes, the private pain they enjoy. Is that not the sin of vanity?"

"What about you?"

"Me?" She looked at Hildegard in amazement. "Can't you see how much I long to get away? And how deeply I fear it? I hate being here! I hate it all! As do those who understand what is happening to them." Her face was suffused with blood, eyes glittering, the wound above her eye standing out. "But what can I do, mistress? Tell me!" Her voice fell to an impassioned whisper. "I have been alone ever since I came here. I am alone now. That is unless—" She gave a desperate glance at Hildegard, then bowed her head and began to sob again. "I am truly near my end, mistress. I shall never escape. But if others can get away, then something good will come of my own agony. Help them!"

Hildegard felt remorse for inflicting pain on such a sad creature. Her cheek was quite swollen where Hildegard had fought her off. "I believe this place is under the jurisdiction of the deaconry of the archbishop of York," she said slowly. "I'm sure he has no idea how harshly the Rule is administered here. It looks to me as if he should be told. I don't wish to make things worse for you. How we proceed needs careful thought so that you don't suffer retribution later."

"Fulke returns tomorrow. He's coming for one of the novices. I fear for her, for the fate that awaits her."

"What do you mean?"

Mariana gave her a wild, staring look. Her mouth worked. When she could speak, she blurted, "I mean he brings girls here who have been abducted. He sells them on."

She turned hastily towards the door. "If they know I've been talking to you, I'll be sent to the punishment cell again. I can't stand much more of that. Look." She opened both palms. They were covered in scars. Then she pushed up her sleeves to reveal what looked like recent burn marks. "I told you they know how to inflict punishment on those they hate."

"Is there an apothecary to tend your wounds?"

"Yes, down by the herb garden near the enclosure wall. She helps when she's allowed to. The rest of my body is much the same. You see, I'm no use to them. I'm too impoverished to be married off and too old for the stews. I'm kept here to be tortured for their pleasure, having no other use and refusing to be one of their sheep. I fear they will break my limbs next time they fault me. Then I'm finished."

She reached the door. "I must go before they find my cell empty."

Hildegard put out a hand. "Don't go yet. I need to make sure Basilda won't see you leave. I also need to know names and dates of these others, the ones you say have gone missing. Once I have them, I vow you shall have justice."

CHAPTER 9

So Fulke was coming back. Hildegard recalled that complicit look she had witnessed on her first day here, between Basilda and the man in her chamber, before she knew his name.

Was Sister Mariana telling the truth about him, or was it the raving of someone cooped up for too long in a desolate and desperate place? The atmosphere was enough to crush the spirit of anyone with a spark of life in her—and if not crush her, send her mad.

Her wounds were real enough, however, even though it was a possibility that they were self-inflicted. Hildegard, feeling a pang of guilt at not believing entirely in what she had been told—it was far removed from her own experience at Swyne—knew that here was yet another reason to keep her at Handale for longer than she would like.

She went down into the garth and headed slowly towards the buildings that housed the kitchen, the bakery, and the brewery. The door leading into these offices had a lay sister in attendance. She was a short, thickset, blunt-faced woman with her sleeves rolled up.

"Yes?" she demanded when Hildegard put in an appearance.

"Our lady prioress has requested a cure. I have but little knowledge beyond the ordinary but intend to avail myself of your facilities." She swept past before the woman had taken in what she had said. Evidently, the name of the prioress was enough to make her give way, but she was eyeing Hildegard with misgivings as she walked through the kitchen and out into the bakehouse on the other side.

A swift glance showed that the little novice, Alys, was not present. Nor was she in the malthouse. A couple of lay sisters were idly stirring the barley mash with long wooden paddles.

"I seek a novice, as I bear a message from our lady prioress," Hildegard said, surprising herself at how easy it was to lie when the cause was sufficient.

"You mean Alys." One of the women nodded. "Out back, slicing turnips. Next to the dairy."

Hildegard sauntered through the far door, as if her appearance was of no consequence. There in a wooden lean-to sat the girl, surrounded by a mound of turnips fresh from the field and holding a bowl of amber-skinned slices on her lap.

She looks, thought Hildegard, for a moment recalling her own daughter at this age, just like a child bespelled by a wicked witch. "Alys," she called quietly, casting a glance back into the brewhouse, "when is that man arriving?"

"He usually comes in the middle of the day, just as we're starting to eat. Then he stays for his own mass and leaves before nightfall."

That suggests he lives no more than a comfortable ride away, Hildegard decided. "Have you been told where they're taking you?"

Alys shook her head. "To another house, they said."

"A religious house?"

"They didn't exactly say that. Why? What other sort of house would it be?" A look of alarm suddenly ran across her face. She put a hand to her mouth in horror at the alternative. Plainly a worse place had never occurred to her till now.

"I shall ask the prioress to allow you to help me with a few tasks. If you're sure about wanting to avoid being taken away, then you must trust me."

"I do. I will," Alys said, half rising.

"Get ready, just as if you're leaving with him." Swiftly, fearing someone was approaching, she picked up one of the turnips. Bending close, she whispered, "Come to me secretly after matins tonight. We'll leave then, when everybody has gone back to bed."

She returned through the brewhouse, holding the turnip aloft so the brewers could see it, not that they took much notice. When she reached the kitchen, she asked for one or two herbs and proceeded to make a decoction, as if she had indeed been set such a task by Prioress Basilda. No one spoke to her. For that matter, they did not speak to one another, either.

In midafternoon, when the place was quiet, she went to her chamber to fetch her thick cloak, then took the now-familiar path to the door in the wall behind the mortuary. Before she was halfway across the rough grass that separated the building from the rest, she heard voices.

Ahead appeared the cellaress and four or five nuns carrying lighted candles. They were walking round the outside of the mortuary, singing a hymn for the dead.

When they reached the door, two of them went inside, leaving the door open, while the others continued to go in procession round the outside. It was plain there was no way past them without being seen.

For the rest of the day, the nuns attended the dead man, praying, singing, keeping the candles alight for Giles in the belief they could help his soul wing its way to heaven. Whenever two of them began to make their way back to the priory, two more appeared.

It seemed to Hildegard, waiting impatiently in the lee of one of the buildings, that a deliberate watch over the door to the outside had been set. She gave up after a while and, hoping to put the time to better use, visited the kitchen gardens, pretending to look round for a few suitable herbs.

There had to be another way to get in and out of the enclosure. If not, she was as much a prisoner as Sister Mariana, Alys, and the rest of them.

She walked slowly past the main gate, where she had entered on her first day. It was in full view of anyone in the cloister garth. After that, she strolled down to the orchard, as if to have a look at the fruit trees, sauntering between the clipped branches until she reached the bottom of an avenue of pears.

When she turned to look back, the orchard appeared to be empty, until she noticed a distant figure shamble behind a tree. Or was it just a shadow? she asked herself. A trick of the light?

At any rate, there was no way out of the enclosure down here, either. She began to wander slowly round the enclosure wall.

On the way, she came across several wooden barns standing in plots of their own in what was the outer garth. One of them was evidently a grain store. A lay brother, one of the conversi, was methodically shovelling winter wheat into a sack.

A small stone-built tower with a window loop high up stood nearby. It had a lock with a key sticking out of it. In the opening at the top, a fluttering of wings drew her attention. A couple of birds flew out. The dovecote.

When the conversi had his back turned, she went over to the door and turned the key. The door swung open with a groan. A blast of foul-smelling bird droppings nearly knocked her back. There was nothing else of note. The inside walls stretched up to the window loop she had seen from outside. Some doves were crowded on a perch, softly cooing in the gloom.

She closed the door and turned the key.

Farther on, she came to a lopsided cottage. Its thatch needed replacing and its window openings were roughly made, but it had a pretty symmetry, with honeysuckle growing raggedly round the door. Dead now, it would give off a heavenly perfume in summer.

No one appeared even when she went right up to the door and stood gazing at the upper window for a few moments. When she turned, the main buildings were hidden behind a row of hawthorns. It gave the whole place a secluded air, separate from the priory and yet a part of it.

By the time she found herself back where she had started, she knew she must have covered every inch of the enclosure. She felt she had seen every building and both entrances. There was no other way through the high walls, and they looked impossible to breach. It must be as Dakin had told her. Anything from outside that had to be brought in must come by boat along the beck or be carried in over the tortuous woodland path.

Her only recourse was to get the girl out past the nuns in vigil at the mortuary. If they were to seek safety at the masons' lodge, there was no other way.

Fulke arrived. One minute, only women's voices could be heard from the choir; the next minute, a male voice was booming along the cloister. Where had he come from? And why a day earlier than expected?

Alarmed, Hildegard went to sit in a niche with her beads in her hands and her hood up. No doubt of it, here he was, as large as life.

It was a superficially innocent scene. Suspicion could not be derived from it: the lady prioress, Basilda, sailing in front of the merchant benefactor through the wide-open doors of the priory church; obedient nuns following two by two; barefoot penitents trailing after them. And the priory guest getting up from her niche, the last to enter. The doors closing, the service beginning.

Hildegard observed the scene with increasing anxiety: the

nuns, with Sister Mariana among them, almost indistinguishable in the black garments designed to erase any quirk of individuality; the penitents in rough woollen shifts, heads bowed, one snuffling, perhaps with cold; a group of lay sisters in grey; the cooks and gardeners and other labouring members of the community, and even the boy, no more than six or seven, whom she recognised as the keeper of the cow.

And Master Fulke.

Strutting, more vibrantly coloured than any one of them except perhaps Basilda in her gleaming gold-thread cope, he established his preeminent place nearest the altar—this, a gaudy, glittering edifice, was vibrant itself, and seemed to mirror Fulke's power and glory. Today, it was ablaze with beeswax candles, mirrors reflecting their light back to themselves in myriad winking images; only the tortured body, agonising on the cross, was black with the threat of the end days.

Strange how candle flame means one thing and hell flame another, mused Hildegard, looking sideways at the scene before bringing her attention back to Fulke.

He made her feel uneasy. A provincial merchant. A nobody in the scale of things. But a man with that overweening pride in his own righteous actions. Was this true, or just her imagination? She watched him and tried to gauge the truth of him.

A man of mature years but not yet old. A man of whom it might be said, "He is in the prime of life." A man seemingly given to many pleasures, full-lipped, high-coloured, dapper in his deep red capuchon, vibrant blue cloak, ermine-trimmed to flout the sumptuary laws, and not averse to a good gold ring or two. Was that a balas ruby? That one a sapphire? Unlikely, Hildegard corrected herself. More likely cornelian. Large, though. Well set. As indeed was everything about Master Fulke. Well set. Well set up.

As the service proceeded, she wondered where his wealth came from, living here, near the sea—a trader perhaps? An importer of goods from the northern countries, from the Baltic? Furs, maybe, timber, hawks, to be sold on, north and south, to Scotland maybe. Arms?

Why not. Big money.

For some reason, she remembered the garrison at Kilton Castle. It would be one of Northumberland's southernmost strongholds, a protection for the coast road and the traffic on it. Tolls, maybe. Intelligence: who was travelling, where they were going, why.

She thought of King Richard. His attempts to rouse an army in his own defence. And the dukes, his uncles, determined to stop him.

Back to Fulke. *The strong man is bound so that his lands may be plundered.* Why had he chosen that psalm in particular?

The weedy-looking priest lifted the chalice above his head so that everyone could witness the miracle. Hildegard waited for something to happen. Nothing did. Not then. The priest lowered the chalice and took a sip. His eyes widened.

He glanced up towards the cruck-beamed roof.

Something had alarmed him.

Then his face twisted into a grimace.

He bent double.

One hand stretched forward, the chalice tipped from his grasp, and the consecrated wine spilled in a bloody flow over the altar cloth. He lurched and fell with a terrible shriek.

For a moment, he writhed in pain, half lying across the altar; then he gave another convulsion and slowly slipped to the floor, dragging the embroidered cloth with him.

Everyone gaped in silence. Then the cellarer staggered forward. She fell to her knees beside the priest and lifted his head, let it loll in her lap. She pushed up his eyelids, sniffed his breath. She opened his mouth and pulled out his tongue. A horrified glance upwards as the prioress loomed from her chair.

Gripping onto the wooden arms, she bent forward. "Dead?" Her tone was aghast.

The cellarer nodded. "So it seems." She got up from beside the inert body of the priest and reached for the chalice. Nothing remained in it, its contents now seeping into the altar cloth like blood. Worse than blood. It was plain what she suspected.

Hildegard stepped forward. But the priest was clearly dead. She could do nothing by revealing her own small knowledge of such matters. No antidote would restore him. She stepped back.

She watched to see what Master Fulke would do. He was standing in a bull-like pose, his face reddening, his fists bunched. His glance flickered over the circle of faces staring from under their black cowls. He turned towards the prioress. Moved like a man in a nightmare towards her.

"Come away, my lady. The shock. Do not upset yourself. Come away to your chamber. Let your nuns deal with this."

He took her by the arm, ushered her from the scene. They plodded together towards the prioress's own private door behind the altar. Hildegard slipped after them in time to catch the end of a phrase.

". . . today of all days." Fulke continued: "I must leave at vespers."

Reassessing her plan to rescue little Alys from Fulke's clutches, Hildegard decided she could not wait in her chamber for the girl's knock on the door. If Fulke was leaving while everyone was at prayer, she would have to act now. Suddenly, everything had changed.

Chapter 10

"There are nettles hereabouts. We must get some boots for you. Maybe the masons will have a spare pair."

"I have some pattens."

"No time to fetch them now. We must hurry."

"They said tomorrow. They told me he was coming for me tomorrow. Why has he come now? What was wrong with the priest? I don't understand."

Hildegard had rushed the girl from out of the back of the church while everyone else was milling round the body. She hurried her across the garth just as Fulke and two henchmen appeared outside the door to the prioress's chamber. When someone called to him from inside, it enabled Hildegard and Alys to get away before he saw them.

Her plans had gone awry. The hunt had started sooner than she'd expected. As soon as the girl's absence was noticed, the nuns were encouraged to ransack the priory in an attempt to find her.

Luckily, the ones on vigil at the mortuary had gone to see what the commotion was about. Like two wraiths, Hildegard and Alys fled to the door in the wall and pushed through. The lodge lay in silence.

"Dakin!"

Under the wide eaves, a half-finished gargoyle leered at them from its stone block. It was a grey afternoon already drawing to its wintry close. At her call, a light flared within.

"Who is it?" Dakin, knife in hand, stumbled from the shadowed depths of the lodge.

"We are in great danger, Dakin. I beg you, help me. I would have asked you, begged your help before now, but was unable to approach earlier without being seen—"

"Come in." He ushered her inside, then gave a hiss of astonishment when he saw the novice. "Should she be out of her enclosure?"

"Her prison, you mean." Hurriedly, she explained about Fulke's unexpectedly early arrival and the death of the priest. "And now at this very moment, they're searching the precinct for her."

"Leave her with us. I have a hiding place should they dare to come to us. Go. You can trust us."

Hildegard played hide-and-seek on her way back to her chamber. The nuns, like hounds searching for a scent, were hallooing across the garth with little purpose other than to look busy. What alarmed her was what she heard as they swept back and forth. It seemed they had already chosen their culprit without the inconvenience of a trial.

"A poisoner!" she heard. "How could she learn such devilish arts!"

"To think we've been harbouring a witch in our midst!"

"They burn witches. And rightly so."

Praying that Dakin's hiding place would be as safe as he claimed should the search spread outside the enclosure, Hildegard took off her boots and pretended to be asleep in her bed when they eventually came knocking at her door.

"What?" she asked sleepily.

"The novice, have you seen her?"

A light shone in her eyes.

"Who? What? Which one?"

They opened the aumbry, peered under the bed, knocked on the walls in hope of finding a secret cavity, then left.

She heard them do the same in the empty chamber across the hall. Lights bobbed back and forth in the garth. Eventually, the bell tolled, beckoning them all for the next office. What was it? Blearily, she realised it must be no later than compline. Silence fell.

A little while after this, she heard men's voices and the sound of footsteps as someone entered the building; next came the clank of a sword, a curse or two, and complaints about being stuck here in a priory all night when there was his woman's bed waiting for him, followed by some coarseness about nuns.

Two voices.

Fulke's henchmen. Bedding down for the night in the chamber opposite. So where was Fulke?

At least it meant they were taking a rest from the hunt and Alys was safe for now. Did it mean the search would continue the next day? It looked like it. Maybe it would only cease when they found her. But how long could the masons keep her hidden?

More bells. Hildegard lost count. It was pitch-black outside. She remained sleepless through the hours. Lauds came. She dragged herself out to see what she could glean.

A hurried service, no more than a prayer, a psalm, a hymn. The sacristan, unused to authority, stood in for the priest. Fulke and the prioress were absent.

Sister Mariana came brushing close as she filed out after the others, a hectic flush adding to the swelling wound Hildegard had inflicted, her eyes darting, dilating in terror in the trembling candlelight. Or was it triumph? It could look much the same. Was it possible that in her febrile state of mind she had poisoned the priest for some twisted purpose of her own? It was certainly true someone here must have done it. Her glance rested blankly on Hildegard as she passed.

The rest of the night was furtive with shadows, doors slyly opening and closing on voices echoing from hollow rooms, dawn bringing with it no relief from the passion of the hunt.

Emerging with pretended innocence at prime, Hildegard, a knife now on her belt underneath the townswoman's shawl, the second cloak pinned, asked, "What was the disturbance last night? People came to my chamber, asking questions. Is the priest really dead? How did it happen?"

Downcast eyes. More singing and garbled prayers. Rain. Daylight slowly seeping inside the enclosure. Like water, greying everything.

The night's rain will have washed away any trace of our footprints in the mud, she thought as she followed a fluttering group headed by Fulke in his blue cloak as they crossed the grass to the mortuary. He went inside ahead of everybody else.

Four lay sisters came up, staggering under the weight of a stretcher on which lay the body of the priest, shrouded, a rosary twined between his lifeless fingers.

Prioress Basilda was carried in her chair across the wet grass by Fulke's two roughneck henchmen. A servant ran alongside, holding a waxed canopy above her sacred head.

The thickset lay sister Hildegard had seen guarding the entrance to the kitchens followed with a handful of conversi. More singing round the body in the echoing, windowless house of death.

Then Fulke, poised in the doorway, gazed outside with a wrinkled forehead, trying to work something out.

The cellarer appeared behind him and pointed to the barricade of bushes growing at the foot of the wall. Fulke and his followers swarmed in the direction she pointed out. They found the wall door behind the bushes. When Fulke raised his hand, they came to a stop and milled about like a small pack of hounds.

Hildegard took the opportunity to mingle on the fringes of the group, suspecting that the presence of this door into the dragon-infested wood held something of horror for most of the nuns by now.

Then she went cold.

Fulke was bending forward to peer at something. He reached out and plucked a woollen thread from between the wood of the door and the rough brick surrounding it. "This—" He held it up.

The answer came from one of the nuns. "I'll warrant it's a thread from that witch's shift!"

Murmurs of agreement followed. The cellarer glanced at this infringement of the rule of silence, but the prioress, transported in her chair to the centre of the group, was by now less concerned with rules. "Let me see it!"

Fulke placed the wisp of fabric into her outstretched fingers.

"So she condemns herself by flight! The little witch must have come this way. But we've caught her. She won't get far in Handale Woods!"

To gasps of horror, everyone watched as Fulke pulled open the door.

Despite their fear, they craned to see what lay beyond. He and his two henchmen, burdened by the prioress, closely followed by the cellarer and the kitchen guard, stepped through. The rest of the nuns drew back.

"My lady prioress—beware of the dragon!" one of them called.

The nuns clustered at the door, but none dare step through.

Hildegard felt her breath stop. Dakin, she thought. She crossed herself.

CHAPTER 11

The rain stopped as abruptly as a pump switching off. It struck everyone as magical. The wood must be enchanted. It lay mist-wreathed and glittering in the dawn light.

The two men struggled with the chaired prioress across the stretch of wet grass in front of the masons' lodge. They dropped it down as soon as they got a chance. Dakin and Matt were so intent on their work that at first they did not look up, not even when Fulke strode up to the entrance and poked his head under the eaves.

His shadow must have fallen over the stone block Dakin was working. Only then did he raise his head. "Master!" he exclaimed, smiling pleasantly. "Have you come to see how well we're getting on with the embellishments for the prioress's new house?"

Instructions shouted from the unfinished structure echoed across the grove. "Down a bit, Will. No, up a bit. That's it. Hold it!"

Fulke looked towards the sound. Will, working the windlass, was on top of the building, looking down. He was raising a block of stone to the top of the wall while Hamo stood patiently below guiding the holding rope. At his feet was a bucket of mortar, already mixed and quite contrary to what Dakin had told Hildegard about their procedure.

Fulke turned his head to look back at Dakin. "What's that?"

He indicated the stone on the bench in front of the mason. It had only just begun to be worked, by the look of it.

"This," announced Dakin with apparent pride, "is a rendition of the dragon of Handale."

"You've seen it, then, have you?" Fulke queried, glancing over his shoulder into the woods.

Dakin said nothing but resumed his work with the chisel.

Fulke went over to Prioress Basilda.

Furious, red-faced, and helpless in the prison of her chair, she was peering impatiently into the lodge. "Ask him about the girl, Fulke."

There was a crunch from above as the stone block was dropped into place on top of the outer wall, and she glanced up as if fearing the whole edifice, the dream house befitting her grandeur, should come toppling down on top of them. Then she turned back to Fulke. "Go on, ask him! What are you waiting for?"

Fulke gave a disparaging look at Dakin. "Well?"

"Well what, master?"

"Have you seen a novice from the priory?"

"I've seen several about the place."

"You have?"

"When I came in yesterday to pay my respects to my work-mate, Giles of—"

"Not then. Now. Last night." Fulke looked exasperated. He gestured to his two men. "Go in and search."

When he heard this, Dakin rose to his feet. The claw-hammer in his hands took on a more menacing appearance.

"I mean"—Fulke smiled, showing his teeth in the nest of his beard—"when we have most humbly begged your permission . . . master," he added, as if to make less of the noise of rapidly drawn swords behind him.

Dakin smiled most affably. "By all means. It will be an honour to show you and the lady prioress our workplace." He made a wide gesture of welcome and stepped to one side.

The prioress grunted irritably. "You go, Fulke. Give it a good going-over."

Dakin moved forward to bar the way to Fulke and the two men at his shoulder. He addressed the prioress directly. "Of course, should any damage occur, it will be charged to your ladyship's account."

"Of course," agreed Fulke with a scowl. To his men, he said, "Hear that? You know who'll be settling the final bill."

The men nodded, sheepish, now thwarted in what they might have regarded as a bit of fun, turning over somebody else's possessions and trampling them a bit.

Hildegard, heart in mouth, watched the three of them enter the lodge.

At once, a female voice was heard from within. It was raised in protest, and the three men slunk back out again.

Dakin bowed in what could only have been humility at his mistake. "I beg forgiveness, master. The daughter of the master mason of Durham Cathedral is within."

Carola appeared. She put on a fair performance of outraged dignity. "This intrusion shall be reported to my father, Mason Schockwynde. He will demand recompense for such gross impertinence. My lady"—she looked across to the prioress as if just having noticed her—"I beg you, be my witness. These men must be called off. My father will not countenance such trespass. These are the guild's private quarters."

Before the prioress could think of a reply, Dakin laid a restraining hand on Carola's arm. "Mistress, I fear it is I to blame for the intrusion. It is I who gave these visitors permission to inspect our lodge. I humbly beg your forgiveness."

She brushed him aside. "It is against all the rules of our guild," she replied shortly. "Only those admitted to our mystery are allowed to set foot in the precinct."

Dakin became a supplicant. "That may be so and I know it right well, but as you have the power to interpret the rules in the absence of our master, I pray you oblige the benefactor of Handale Priory in his request. A novice has gone missing and he fears for her safety." He paused. "She may have been abducted. Such heinous crimes are not without precedent in these dark days."

Carola turned to Fulke with all the authority of her position. "Then pray enter, master." She glanced at the two henchmen with drawn swords. "However, our guild is not a military one. The two men-at-arms must remain outside."

Fulke by now was storming with impatience. Without a word, he ducked under the eaves and strode into the lodge. For a few minutes, he could be heard banging about inside.

The group in the grove, kitcheners and the like and the frightened nuns staring out through the open door in the enclosure wall, waited to see what he would find. The prioress, already convinced that the girl could not be here and must have escaped into the woods, gestured to Fulke's men to hoist up her chair again.

Before they could do so, Fulke emerged, scowling. "Let's get off after her." He nodded towards the trees.

His men began to follow but the prioress shrieked after them, "Who's to carry me back, you dolts! Don't leave me here!"

Fulke frowned. "Convey her to her chamber and be quick about it."

The two hoisted the chair and, staggering, carved a path through the onlookers. When they reached the door in the wall, there was a delay because somehow, this time, the chair would not fit, and the prioress was almost pitched out as they tried to manhandle it through the gap. Nuns scattered on the other side, and the kitcheners, disconsolate because no capture had been made, followed as soon as the gap was unplugged.

Fulke fumed in the interim.

Hildegard went up to him, the better to distract him from further thoughts about the novice's hiding place. A glance at the path into the woods showed no sign of its having recently been walked. "Master Fulke," she began, "dare you risk entering the wild wood with the fire-breathing dragon at large?"

"Who said it was a dragon?"

"So I've heard. Am I misinformed?"

"It may be a dragon, mistress. It may be a fire-breathing stallion, a story I've heard," he countered, "but, yes, I dare risk entering the wood. My duty obliges me." He was about to turn back to the lodge.

"But master,"—she put a hand on his arm—"how will you defend yourself against such a great danger? Look what it did to the poor apprentice."

"My safety is my concern, mistress, not yours." He was evidently not completely satisfied with his search inside the lodge and was still staring towards it, but then another thought struck him, or maybe it was something about Hildegard herself, a comely townswoman, softly spoken, her hand on his arm, because he turned back with a sort of smile on his face. "So, what brings you to Handale, mistress?"

"I am a widow, master. I am in mourning." The latter was true. She felt she would never be out of mourning for Rivera.

"I see." He cleared his throat.

"I am here to consider where and how I might best bestow my fortune."

Fulke looked thoughtful. He bowed. "I trust you will feel free to avail yourself of my experience in such matters, widow."

"I am most grateful for your kindness, master. It is a welcome offer in a time of much confusion. Will you stay long here?"

"I have business elsewhere after this little matter is sorted out, but I shall return within the next day or two and trust that we may converse more deeply on your dilemma?"

"I shall deem it an honour and indeed I look forward with great eagerness to your return. It's quite a marvel to me that you should be able to give so freely of your time to this little community and to we helpless women. The prioress must ever be in your debt out of gratitude and obligation."

"More like I myself am in debt to the prioress and her nuns for their piety, widow. God be praised for their devout ministrations on my behalf in easing my way to heaven."

Hildegard inclined her head and slowly withdrew a string of beads from the embroidered bag on her belt. She saw Fulke glance at them, assess the worth of coral, amber, and French ivory.

He gave a complacent smile.

"I shall return, widow."

By now, the two men-at-arms were marching across the grass towards them. Fulke, still smiling, threw a glance over his shoulder to make sure they were following, then began to shove his way through the trees.

Dakin had been intent on chipping at the stone block through all this. Will was still sitting on top of the wall, where he must have had a good view of things on both sides of the enclosure wall, and Hamo was attaching the bucket of mortar onto a pulley with half an eye on what was going on behind him. Carola and Matt had gone back inside the lodge.

Hildegard saw Fulke and his men disappear from sight before turning to Dakin and pointing into the woods to indicate that she would follow them. Dakin put down the chisel for a second and clenched his fist in a salute. Hildegard set off quietly in the steps of the three bloodhounds in their futile chase.

That gesture of Dakin's interested her. It was made without forethought and was the usual sign of comradeship between the White Hart rebels. The pewter badge lost by Giles when he had been attacked was also a sign of allegiance. It was an enchained hart, seated, the emblem of King Richard.

Hildegard made sure she kept out of sight, allowing Fulke and his men to get far enough ahead so that if they turned, they would not see her. It was easy to follow them by sound alone. They made no attempt at stealth, confident that the difficulty of forcing a path through the thicket would prevent the runaway from finding an alternative route and making good her escape. Indeed, it would have been difficult for anyone to force a way through, let alone a barefoot girl, because there was no break in the barrier of uncoppiced saplings.

Mounds of brambles, fruit withered on the spiky stems, formed an additional barrier. Ivy trailed haphazardly on all sides. Fallen trees sometimes barred the way. The path, recently trodden by Dakin and his fellows, and Giles before that, and at least one other, showed up clearly.

The sound of the beck, in spate after the rains, was loud from below the hill.

The men were slashing at the undergrowth with their swords and, unbeknownst to them, making Hildegard's path easier than before. Even so, she was careful not to gain on them.

She reached the glade where the body of Giles had been found. The men, walking ahead, did not pause, however, but continued, to all intents as if they knew where they were going. Now and then, she heard Fulke's voice, giving instructions, the grunt of a response, then again the slash of their swords. Suddenly, the sound stopped. Hildegard crept forward.

They had come to a halt in a open stretch where deer had nibbled the undergrowth and clipped the grass short. In the middle stood a stone tower. It was too large to be a dovecote.

Fulke looked at it for some time. There was a chain across the door. No windows.

He began to fumble in the leather pouch on his belt. He drew forth a jangling bunch of keys. "I'm going in. Just to be sure. You two stay out here and keep a look out for that little bitch."

The men stood with their hands on their hips, staring in opposite directions into the woods.

As soon as Fulke had opened the lock and pushed on into the tower, they relaxed, sitting on the ground, one of them unstopping the costrel on his belt and tipping ale down his throat. He handed the flask to his companion, who shook his head and reached for his own. "Will he be long?"

"What do you reckon?" Both men laughed nastily.

Hildegard was afraid that when Fulke emerged, the three of them would start down the path and she would be discovered, but it was difficult to know how to force a way through the undergrowth without making a noise.

A cloud came over while they were waiting for Fulke to do what he had come for, and soon rain began to patter through the branches. Hoping the noise would disguise her attempts to get off the path, Hildegard began to part the saplings so she could squeeze through. As suddenly as it started, the rain stopped. In the sudden hush, she heard the branches behind her snap noisily together.

A voice floated from the glade. Silence followed. When she turned to look back, she could see the dark shape of a man standing motionless in among the trees, ears cocked for the next giveaway sound. She froze as she watched the shape began to move stealthily down the avenue she had made. He was trailing her with the silence of a staghound.

She could not wait until he caught sight of her. He would move faster than she could, wielding his sword to carve a path to where she was hiding. She could only push a way through the undergrowth in the hope that he would not realise it was anything more than a deer.

But he kept coming on.

In her favour was the astonishing fact that he had not seen her. Soon, though, she was scratched and bleeding. The undergrowth was thicker than ever. Brambles tore her clothes. Her feet slipped over roots and into puddles. Her head scarf was torn off and she had to turn back to retrieve it.

With a sudden shout, the man caught sight of her. She glimpsed him through the branches, sword raised to slash at the barrier that lay between them.

Then, with no warning, her feet disappeared from under her and she was falling, plunging down in a confusion of earth and stones, uprooted plants, and saplings flying down the side of the cliff. She reached out wildly for anything to hold on to, clutched at air, was hit on the head by a stone, then felt something under her fingertips, grabbed on to it, felt it slip, hung on tighter, and found herself lying breathless on a ledge of crumbling chalk with the rest of the woodland cascading past her ears.

The pause before the debris hit the ground seemed to continue for some time. She imagined the broken bones should the ledge give way.

A shout came from above her head. The second man-at-arms must have followed the first, because she heard two voices, snatches of conversation discussing the rockfall.

"I tell you I did! It was just there, right in front of me."

"It must have been a deer. Nobody daresn't come out here. Shit-scared they are now, with the dragon story an' that."

"Do you think it was?"

"Was what?"

"You know."

"Sot wit."

There was a pause, then the first voice again.

"Shall we tell him?"

"You can. I'm telling him nowt."

"Bloody hell. It gave me a right turn. What do you think it was?"

"I've told you."

"It looked like a woman."

"Women on the brain, you."

"It might have been that bloodsucking nun they keep talking about."

"Come on, you dolt. It was a deer. Let's go back before he comes looking. Whatever it was, it'll have broken its bloody neck in a fall like that."

"It was a deer, then. That's what we'll say."

The sound of trampling feet. Silence. The peace of the woodland returned.

A single stone fell past the ledge into a vast silence. Grains of red earth trickled between Hildegard's fingers and vanished from sight over the edge.

CHAPTER 12

She did not dare breath too deeply. The slightest movement would dislodge her and send her toppling down into Kilton Beck.

Her heart stopped its hammering after a while. For the moment, she was secure enough. When she took stock, she had to assume the ledge whereon she sat was solid enough. A matted growth of roots and ivy stems sprouted from the cliff face. Saplings grew in the crevices. A previous rockfall had left a red scar in the ironstone about ten yards away, leaving a scree-covered slope from the top of the bank to the bottom.

None of these—roots, saplings, rockfall—were close enough to reach. Directly below the ledge that had stopped her fall, the beck roared and thundered on its course.

Time passed. The sun began to tilt through the boles of the trees, striping the cliff with bands of light and shade.

Hildegard lifted one hand to test the strength of the roots above her head. A tug brought more loose stone scattering down. Gingerly, she shifted her position so she could see over the edge. Vines snaked to a few feet above a rubble of boulders heaped on the bank above the rushing water.

There was no sound from above now that Fulke's men had gone.

An occasional glitter of melody from a blackbird broke the silence now and then. She felt defeated.

Reassessing the possibility of climbing upwards, she wriggled onto her knees and put out a tentative hand to grasp the nearest root. She tested it, prayed that it was strong enough to take her weight, then began to pull herself up inch by inch until she was standing.

She had to lean out over the edge of the rock shelf and hoist herself up over the overhang. Her feet scrabbled for something to support her weight, found a fissure in the rock, steadied her. She dared not look down. Pressing herself against the cliff face, she clawed amid the foliage to find another handhold. Bit by bit, she began to drag herself upwards.

It was a temptation to rush, to make a grab for any handhold, but she forced herself to test each one before trusting herself to it. At one point she had to rest because the muscles in her legs were trembling so much under the strain, but after a pause she was able to continue a slow, frightened crawl to the top.

There was an added alarm when she was within reach of the summit. The broken lip of the cliff jutted out, and when she felt the edge, it crumbled under her touch. Lumps of ironstone flew past her head. She kept her nerve and eventually found a secure hand-hold. Feet kicking in empty space, she somehow managed to haul herself up over the edge.

She lay at the top in the long grass, panting with fear and exultation. She had done it. Relief swept through her like a flood. She wanted to weep.

Shaking herself, she scrambled to her feet, found the path Fulke's man had cleared with his sword, and set off towards the tower.

She approached the grove with caution but the men had gone. More boldly, she broke from between the trees and walked over to the tower. When she was close enough, she saw that the door was securely locked again. There was no clue to what was behind that lock and chain.

She circled the walls, looking for a way in. It was stoutly built of smoothly worked local stone, reddish gold in colour, but without a single opening unless you counted the window slit high up. Prompted by the suspicion voiced by Sister Mariana that girls were being kept prisoner until their ransoms could be paid, she called out and was unsurprised when there was no response.

It was a far-fetched idea. One or two, like Alys, might be found husbands if they were clearly not cut out for the monastic life, but to run an entire business of bartered girls was too much to believe. Mariana scarcely seemed in her right mind.

If Fulke was up to something, and it certainly looked as if he was, then it was more likely to be stolen goods being kept in a place like this. Few people would know about the tower, and even if they did, few would dare think of trespassing in the priory's woods to satisfy their curiosity.

It was commonplace these days for gangs to be maintained by small local landowners in self-defence. Their activities often degenerated into nothing less than robbery with violence. Such gangs were rife in every part of the country. It was often men like Fulke who ran them. Men with a respectable veneer to hide the illegal side of their activities.

It would be trade that had enriched Fulke, as she had first imagined. He probably augmented his profit by avoiding import duty on certain goods. There were so many places along the coast where a ship carrying imports from the Baltic or the Scandinavian regions could dock. Anything could be slipped ashore. The tower was an obvious and safe hideaway to those who knew the woods.

If he was a local man, as it seemed, Fulke would be well aware of the places he could store his goods without drawing attention to them.

The more she thought about it, the more likely it seemed.

The proximity of the garrison at Kilton Castle might make things difficult. Maybe that was why he found the priory useful. His activities could be confined to the isolated moors road.

Traffic between York and Newcastle. Rich pickings.

Satisfied that this was the answer and eager to return to the lodge and get Alys to safety, she turned to leave.

She stopped and drew in a breath. She was being watched.

On the far side of the clearing, half hidden behind a tree, stood a man. It was a stray shaft of sunlight shining on a leather jerkin that gave him away. Her hand shifted to her knife.

Then the light changed and she smiled. It was only Dakin.

At first, he seemed to be frowning, but as he walked towards her, he began to smile.

"Will was right!" he greeted her. "You didn't come back. We were worried. He was keeping an eye out from the top of the wall and said he saw Fulke and his cronies heading back, but he swore there was no sign of you."

"He was right. I thought I'd have a look round."

How long had Dakin been watching her? Why hadn't he made his presence known at once? Despite his friendly manner, she had the uncomfortable feeling he had been there for some time.

Now all he said was, "I thought you might have fallen foul of the dragon of Handale."

"More likely of Fulke's bloodhounds," she replied.

He laughed. "It's a dangerous place, this. Doesn't look it, does it?" He threw a glance into the glistening woodland, the autumn gold deep beneath the trees and soft underfoot. "At least they didn't find little Alys." He gave a confident chuckle. "And you, what about you? You've been some time. Did you find anything out?"

"Such as?"

"What did they do when they got here?"

She shrugged. "They didn't seem to make much of a search. Fulke was more interested in something inside the tower. His two men waited outside. Then he came out and they left. Do you think he's given up looking for Alys so easily?"

"What else can he do? He'll assume she's still somewhere close to the priory. I expect they've turned their attention to the track you came in by. They'll think she's tried to get back to the main road leading to the castle."

He made no comment about her dishevelled appearance.

A bell began to toll deep in the thicket. "Tierce," he remarked. "Are you coming back?"

"I am. And with no danger of getting lost. They've made a clear path for us."

"Fortunate," replied Dakin as he followed her. "No sign of the dragon, either." He glanced over his shoulder. She noticed he had taken out his knife.

"What was the tower for?" she asked when they reached the lodge.

"No idea," he admitted. "I expect it was an old hunting lodge from years ago when Kilton Castle was busier than it is now. There's nobody in residence because the lawyers can't make up their minds who owns it."

Hildegard remembered the priest and his claim, but before she could say anything, Dakin had ducked his head under the thatch, calling back, "You'd better come inside for a moment."

She followed him in. The men were there, busy as usual.

"That was a close thing this morning when Fulke came clumping in here looking for the girl," Dakin began. "I wouldn't like to think what could have happened if he'd found her."

"Is she safe?"

"She is. Scared out of her wits at what she's done but even more scared at what might have befallen her—or might yet—if Master Fulke gets his hands on her. Come."

He led her through into a neat little chamber at the back. Carola was bending over a drawing on a piece of stretched vellum. When she saw Dakin and Hildegard, she put her finger to her lips. Moving quietly, she went over to a screen and pulled it to one side. Alys lay curled up under a rug. She was fast asleep.

"I must get her away as soon as possible. I can't thank you enough for your help," Hildegard said.

"You'll have to avoid the priory. They're still hallooing all over the place for her," Carola told her. "How do you propose to get out?"

"While I was in the woods, I noticed a way along the beck. You mentioned it, Dakin. It's strewn with boulders, but it should be possible to pick our way round them to the road. We'll just have to make sure Fulke's men have given up and gone."

Dakin was watching her closely. "What will you do when you reach the road?"

"Trust to God."

He offered no alternative. Instead, he looked faintly relieved. She put it down to his anxiety about being found harbouring a runaway. The sooner she was off his hands, the happier he would feel. That was the impression.

She said, "I'll come back when it's dark. That will be safest. Will you make sure she's ready to leave?" Before she left she asked, "Where was she hidden so that Fulke didn't find her?"

Dakin smiled and pointed his finger up towards the thatch. "She said she could have touched his bald patch by stretching out one little finger." He was amused by this. "What a blind, sot-witted prick he is."

The rest of the day dragged. Hildegard went to her chamber and spent the rest of the morning tidying herself up, bathing her scratches, enjoying the brief luxury of brushing her hair and putting on a clean head scarf.

She made an appearance at the daily offices: sext, nones, vespers.

No one seemed to notice she had been missing. A subdued hysteria seemed to reign. No further sightings of the witch had been made. The nuns were quivering with the expectation of seeing her dragged back from the dragon's lair by Fulke's hard-faced men. It was clear they hoped the men would have made her pay the price.

Later in the day, a mass was sung for the two corpses in the mortuary chapel. Hildegard went along with most of the others to pay her respects. Sister Mariana, who avoided her, kept her head down, her face shadowed under her hood, lips mumbling rapidly without a pause.

The prioress was not present as, with her two chair men off with Fulke, she had no way of getting out to the chapel. The nuns were too frail to carry her the distance.

The subprioress stood in for her and left before everyone else. Hildegard followed after the cellaress when the last amen faded. "That poor young priest," she began. "Was it really poison, as the nuns are saying?"

"That's nonsense. You should close your ears to rumourmongers, mistress. He had a falling fit. It happens."

"But he looked so young. To have a falling fit at his age? It seems scarcely credible."

"These things happen where God wills." The cellarer was curt.

"Even so," murmured Hildegard, refusing to be brushed aside. "Had he complained of sickness previously?"

"I'm led to believe he complained of an ague. And of course, we must not forget that the plague takes many forms and strikes with swiftness where it finds weakness." She increased her pace, as if to leave Hildegard behind.

"Oh dear," exclaimed Hildegard, keeping up. "Is it likely that those here will also succumb?"

The cellarer sniffed at such qualms. "We must hope we are made of truer stuff, mistress, and put our faith in God. As He wills, so be it."

"Indeed. And I'm relieved to note you do not subscribe to a rumour I've heard about the place."

The cellaress lifted her head.

"I mean this story about the novice being a witch. I'm sure her running away will be found to have nothing to do with the priest's death."

"We should hope so for her sake. If it were discovered that she had used witchcraft, she would face the full punishment of the Church. And no one would want to be excommunicated, would they?" She stopped and turned to look fully into Hildegard's face.

"I should think not. But I wonder, sister, has her family been informed of her disappearance?"

"She has no family." This was a flat contradiction of Basilda's story. The cellarer was eager to be on her way, however, and by now they had reached the cloister. Before going inside, she added, almost as an afterthought, "Mistress York, I cannot help noticing that you have good knowledge of our rites."

It was stated as a mere observation, a shot in the dark, but said in such a way as to leave a threat hanging in the air. Hildegard bowed her head. "One tries," she murmured.

She would have to watch her step. Were there spies here as well as in Westminster? The dukes played a hard game. It was easy to forget that this was Gaunt's territory, not part of the duchy of the House of Lancaster, but close enough to the many establishments that owed their existence to the patronage of Lancastrian gold.

Knaresborough, Scarborough, Malton, Ripon. And, keeping an eye on the archbishop himself, St. Mary's in York. In fact most, if not all, the minor castles and Benedictine houses were scattered like chess pieces across the north.

I'll have to make a liturgical error of some kind, like the ordinary townswoman I'm supposed to be if this is the view they hold of me. She smiled to herself. Anything to put them off the scent. No point in arousing suspicion now she was convinced there was something afoot.

The day could not move swiftly enough, but eventually the final repast of the day was taken, compline prayer was said, and the priory fell into the black silence that would last until the midnight office dragged everyone out again. It was in this space of time that Hildegard had to take her chance.

Still aching in every muscle after her climb up the cliff, she let herself out of her chamber as soon as the cloister garth fell silent and stood for a moment with her back against the door of the guesthouse.

On the opposite side of the square formed by the main buildings, the shadows yawned, black and silent. She could imagine a hundred eyes peering out of the darkness. Not until she was sure there was no movement did she begin to feel her way along the wall as far as the corner. Now out of sight of anyone watching, she hastened across the grass towards the humped shape of the mortuary.

The moon was faintly visible behind a gauze of cloud.

It made the slate roof little more than a shadow against a star-filled sky. The tops of the trees on the other side of the enclosure wall were stiff, skeletal-like fingers groping blackly upwards.

Tonight there was a light frost. Hildegard's footsteps showed up as dark prints in the grass. All she could hope was that if anyone saw them, that person would imagine they were left by a nun intent on offering night prayers for the dead youths.

Moving swiftly to the door in the wall, she let herself out into the deeper night of the woods.

A velvet blackness enveloped her. Imagination might suggest a nightmare of trees inching closer to the priory walls, pressing in against them, swarming in the pitch-black depths of the night to overrun the habitation of the nuns. A lone bird screeched as it flew overhead, followed by a clatter of wings as it broke into the undergrowth.

A light shone round the edges of the masons' door. Hildegard edged past the stack of felled trees, round the half-finished stone building, across the yawning void of the interior, and, with a strange breathlessness, gained the safety of the lodge.

A figure loomed from the darkness, but before she could retreat, a man's voice whispered, "She's ready, mistress. Here."

A small hand was pressed into her own. It was Alys's.

"She has some boots, a cloak lent by Carola, and small parcel of bread and cheese. Is that all you possess, Alys?"

Hildegard felt the girl nod, then a tug on her arm. "I'm frightened, mistress."

"Trust me."

She thanked Dakin for his help.

He had a question for her, one he had already asked: "And where are you heading once you reach the coast road?"

"Across the moors to York," she replied firmly.

"Very well. God be with you."

He melted back inside the lodge.

Intensely aware of their surroundings and of who might have been awake under the eaves to watch them leave, Hildegard led Alys swiftly outside.

"I know the path through the woods by now. There's a way down to the beck not far from here. We'll tread carefully."

She led the way along the path tramped several times now and then found the way down towards the sound of running water. Dakin had already mentioned the corn mill farther upstream, the one owned by the priory. It was what was called an overshot, because the water ran over the top of the wheel to turn it. He had also mentioned a landing stage where goods and supplies were brought in.

They had to turn right some way before reaching the mill, he had told her. If they found the mill, they had gone too far. Once she found the path that led down to the beck, the going would be easy. One section would be difficult, he'd warned, and they would have to scramble over rocks along the bank to reach the main road.

"We'll find a way along the bottom of the ravine, below the castle," she began to explain, but Alys suddenly froze in alarm.

"There's something ahead, mistress!" She clung hard to Hildegard's arm.

"It's nothing but the shadow of a tree," Hildegard murmured after she had had a good look at where Alys directed her gaze. "Come on, don't be fainthearted. We'll soon be away from here."

Alys began to cry. "I can't! I daren't! What about the dragon?"

"Come now. We have no choice."

"I daren't go any farther," whimpered the girl, gazing into the thicket with dread.

"Would you rather return to the priory?" Hildegard asked sharply.

"No! Not that! Please don't make me go back!" She clung to Hildegard like a limpet and made it difficult to go on.

"Shush, Alys, you'll have the prioress out here in her chair and two of those nuns will have to carry her all this way. They'll be sweating and cursing and the prioress will be tangled in the thicket and waving her stick and bringing down the wrath of God on their heads, and you wouldn't want that, would you?"

At the thought of the prioress in her chair caught in the thicket, Alys began to giggle nervously.

"That's better." Hildegard tugged at her arm. Reluctantly, stifling sobs and giggles by turn, the girl allowed herself to be hurried along.

Branches scratched their faces and tugged at their hoods. Alys squealed and said she thought they were fingers, but Hildegard did not allow her to slacken her pace. They were soon at the rockfall and began to pick their way down over the scree of ironstone.

They were about halfway down when suddenly from somewhere behind them came an unearthly sound between a shriek and a howl. They stopped in their tracks, transfixed.

"Save us, oh merciful Lord!" whimpered Alys.

The sound came again, just as bloodcurdling—and somehow nearer.

Alys dropped to her knees and began to pray.

"Get up! Get up at once, you silly child!" whispered Hildegard impatiently. "It's only a fox or a stag."

"I'm frightened!"

"It has as much right to be here as we do." Hildegard pulled her to her feet.

Before they took two steps, the sound came again. It was like nothing she had ever heard before, but she had to get Alys on the move as fast as possible.

Then it came again. From the very top of the cliff.

CHAPTER 13

Alys was subdued by the fact that she had been so childishly frightened by one of the many commonplace sounds of nature. "Are you sure it was a stag, mistress?"

"Yes," replied Hildegard shortly.

By now, they had reached the road after a precarious scramble over the boulders that littered the edge of the beck. At one point, they had been forced to enter the water under the cliff below Kilton Castle, where the current flowed violently through a narrow neck of rock. They held each other by the hand so that if one slipped, the other would save her—though how Alys could have saved Hildegard was unclear—and then they made their way up to the road that wound through the pass.

It lay empty and mysterious under the stars, but at last they were free from the purlieu of Handale and were out on the open road.

A period of hard walking up a steep hill followed, with Hildegard determinedly leading the way, and when they came to a small vill, they managed to skirt it without waking any dogs and walked on until they came to a road leading off across the top of the moor. Hildegard ignored it and kept on walking.

After a while, Alys, looking back, said, "You told Dakin we were going to York."

"I know I did."

"We've passed the road end. I know because that's the way I was brought to Handale."

"Yes, but I know a place nearer than that where the lord will give you all the help you need."

They were climbing up to the high cliffs overlooking the sea by now. It could be heard, though not seen, beyond the brow of the hill. Behind them, where the road came snaking up from Kilton Beck, they could look down on the track across the moors.

Hildegard allowed them to stop for a moment while she looked back. Her eyes were adjusted to the varied shades of darkness, the black clumps of a group of trees, the lighter shade of the open hillside, the shade, lighter still, of the road.

Far below them, in a black smudge of shadow that must have been a copse, a little way along the road to York, she thought she saw a moving shape. She put a hand on Alys's shoulder. "Listen."

In the still night air came the unmistakable metallic sound of horsemen, the clink of a bridle, the slither of steel, a brief murmur of men's voices.

It might mean nothing, she told herself. The garrison from Kilton going about their duties. A merchant and his entourage travelling late. Or it might mean Dakin cannot be trusted.

"Let's not talk for a while," she suggested in a whisper. "Sound carries clearly on a night as still as this." She gripped the girl's hand more tightly in her own.

Once over the brow of the hill, Alys risked a question. "Who is this lord you say will help me?"

"It's the lord of Langbrough."

"Langbrough?" repeated Alys. "Where on earth's that?"

"It's farther down the coast. He's a vassal of Earl Roger de Hutton and a man I would trust with my life."

After a pause, Alys asked, "Does that mean you wouldn't trust Master Dakin?"

"I suppose it might."

"I see." After another pause while she took this in, Alys remarked, "You may be right. He was worried about something and that's why he came out to search for you. Hamo was keeping a lookout."

"They were making sure no one came back from the priory to search the lodge again, I expect."

"No, I heard Dakin say, 'I'll find her. Can't be too careful.'"

"Did he say this to all of them?"

"No, just secretly to Hamo. They thought I was asleep behind the screen."

"What do you think it was about?"

As expected, Alys did not know. They were out of earshot of the horsemen by now and Hildegard allowed her to chatter on. "They're worried about their master and the way he suddenly appears when they least expect it," Alys told her. "Checking up on them. Dakin thinks he tries to catch them out. He makes a joke of it in front of Carola, but I think it really bothers him."

"Maybe he believes his master thinks he's not working hard enough."

"Maybe that's it. And he fears to get a shouting if the master finds him wasting time. Or worse. He could get a fine from his guild master. He's funny, Dakin, but I like him," she continued without a break. "Do you know what I think? I think he's secretly enamoured of Carola. He's always wary around her, as if he's afraid of saying something to upset her. He acts all strange in front of her. Do you think he wants to marry her, mistress?"

Hildegard frowned. "He won't find it easy. He's only a journeyman. When work at the priory is finished, he'll have to seek employment elsewhere, and his master may not decide to keep him on. Carola is the master's stepdaughter, I understand. She'll be looking to have a husband who's a master mason himself."

"Poor Dakin."

"He may find the resources to become a master eventually."

"But by then Carola may have met someone else."

"That sometimes happens," said Hildegard. "But it won't matter if he's not her beloved, will it?"

It was as she had hoped. The sun was not quite up by the time they came within sight of the moated manor house that was their destination, and it was just beginning to stir into life.

It looked serene in the winter light. A thatched house, lowlying within a curve of the hills, with a moat as protection from attack. They could see through the gates into a yard where geese and hens were roaming, and from a milking shed came the lowing of cows. They crossed a wooden drawbridge and entered through the open gates. A horse or two were tossing their heads in their stalls and the whole place looked prosperous and inviting. When a cockerel roused the alarm, a stable hand appeared at a side door.

"Is your lord at home?" called Hildegard.

The servant came out into the yard. "Aye, he is. I'll fetch him."

Before he reached the house, the main doors opened and a figure familiar to Hildegard, though a year older than when she had last seen him, came out onto the step. His face was a picture when he caught sight of Hildegard accompanied by a ragged girl.

"Hildegard! Do my eyes deceive me? I thought you were in Compostela."

"See? I have returned." She spread out her arms as if to demonstrate her reappearance.

"Praise Saint Benet and all the angels!" By now he was across the yard and had taken in the fact that she still wore her towns-woman's garments. He swept her into his arms and hugged her warmly, and she felt an unexpected sense of homecoming. Tears prickled behind her lids.

"It's been so long. So much has happened," Hildegard said. The same long, untidy sun-bleached hair pressed against her cheek. The same sea blue eyes looked into her own. "You haven't changed, Ulf!"

"Older and wiser." He sounded grim. His eyes briefly clouded. "Did you fill the cathedral with candles for Rivera as you vowed?"

"Let's go in."

"And where's your nun's habit? Discarded forever, I hope?"

Hildegard noticed Alys give her a swift, startled glance. "Let's talk properly later, my dearest. We've been walking most of the night. I have here a young woman rescued from abductors, to our great joy and relief. Alys, this is Sir Ulf, the lord of Langbrough."

Ulf bowed as if to a great lady. "My entire domain is open to you, young mistress. First, I think, the kitchens for a bowl of warm milk and oats. Agreed?"

All at once, the fear seemed to lift from Alys and she smiled trustingly up at Ulf and followed him like a lamb into the house.

Ulf, with his new wife, whom Hildegard had yet to meet, was flourishing, she observed. Her heart was filled with gladness. Everywhere she looked, she noticed signs of industry and wealth.

Under the low beams of the kitchen, a comfortable-looking cook was singing as she stirred something in a large pot over the fire. She glanced up when Ulf conducted the newcomers inside and then began to bustle about. Soon they were eating hot porridge and warming their toes on the hearth. Ulf pushed the flagon containing small beer close to Alys and poured Hildegard a beaker of wine. Then, while the cook fussed over the girl after they finished eating, he indicated that Hildegard should follow him.

"So what's all this?" he asked when they were seated in a small chamber crammed with rolls relating to the running of the estate, where they could talk in private.

Quickly, Hildegard told him what had happened since she had arrived at Swyne, how the prioress had suggested Handale so she could find peace and solitude to make up her mind about reaffirming her vows—or turning her back on the Order for once and all.

Ulf raised his eyebrows at this, murmuring, "With no other motive for her suggestion?"

Hildegard acknowledged this with a knowing grimace but continued with the rest of it.

Ulf was grim-faced by the time she finished. "So it looks as if they're using the place as a way point on the journey of those girls into either marriage, if they're heiresses, or the stews if they're poor and landless?" He frowned. "And the story Alys tells seems to prove it. Well, we can check that. I'll contact my good friend the sheriff at Durham. He'll be able to tell us more about Alys's brother and Sir Thomas Umfraville. Then we'll find out what the law says about her father's will." He paused for a moment's reflection. "This tower you mention? What do you imagine the Handale benefactor stores in there?"

"Stolen goods of some sort. Arms, perhaps? Or smuggled items, maybe. Imports from overseas?"

He nodded. "That would be likely, a local merchant, one throwing his money about. And you say he's called Fulke? It's a name I've heard before."

He ran a hand through his hair, making it even more untidy. Hildegard smiled. It was such a dear and familiar gesture.

"What are you grinning for?" His blue eyes pierced.

"Just you. I think I've missed you."

"Only think so? You're not sure?"

She nodded. "I am sure. Very sure. It's about all I am sure of at this moment." She drew back from dangerous ground. "But about Fulke. What have you heard?"

"He's alleged to be a pillar of piety. Has a tannery at a place called Ruswarp. Other interests—importing furs from the Baltic through Whitby. Sells them on in York and Durham. Made quite a packet for himself." He looked thoughtful.

"That's not all, Ulf. Our old friend Master Sueno de Schockwynde—you remember he was the mason employed a few years ago by Roger de Hutton when you were steward at Castle Hutton?"

"Ha! Indeed I do remember him! What's old Sueno been up to?"

"He's the mason in charge of the building work at Handale."

"No? I'd heard he was at Durham on some prestigious long-term work for the bishop?"

"So he is. But this must have been a commission he could not refuse. It's small compared to the cathedral, but its patron, Fulke, seems to have deep pockets. Schockwynde, apparently, has a stepdaughter—"

"Yes, so I've heard. A talented imaginator, by all accounts. She's in charge of Sueno's drawings for the decorations at Durham. Very much sought after, I've heard."

Hildegard noticed his expression change. She leaned forward. "And what else?"

"Nothing really. She's a bit of a mystery, that's all. Nobody seems to know where she sprang from. How does Sueno come to have a stepdaughter? Did he marry? I never heard of it. And knowing him, it would all be done in magnificent style. He'd want a great show of it. And it wouldn't be to any mason's widow, either. Sueno's wife would have to be a lady at least."

"So who is she?"

Ulf got up. "I'm in the mood for action. This quiet life doesn't suit me. Let me go back with you and find the answers to all our questions."

Hildegard didn't move. "Your wife, Ulf. You haven't mentioned her."

His blue eyes darkened. "I'm surprised Roger didn't say anything. She's away at present. Her family are over the other side of York. She's visiting them."

Recalling what Ulf had told her in London over a year ago, she asked, "So which one did you choose, the older woman with lands of her own, or the younger one with nothing but beauty?"

He gave a rueful smile. "You'll call me a fool when you find out, and you'll be right." He did not enlighten her further. As he opened the door, he had a question of his own. "You haven't mentioned Meaux. I trust everything is well at the abbey?"

She knew what he meant. It wasn't the abbey he was curious about. It was his rival, Abbot de Courcy. She turned to face him. "I don't know. I haven't seen him."

He looked gratified. "You mean you've been in the country for all of six weeks and haven't yet had an audience with Hubert de Courcy?"

Now that Alys was safe under the immediate care of Ulf's cook and the rest of his household servants, Hildegard was eager to return to Handale as soon as possible. She explained to Alys that Ulf would send somebody with a message to her brother and his lord and that a serjeant-at-law would be appointed to look at her father's will. Her guardian would be called to account for his actions and everything would be sorted out for the best.

Alys seemed quite content to stay in the company of Ulf's

kindhearted cook, and when she came to the door to wish Hildegard a safe journey, she was profuse in her thanks for helping her escape from Handale.

Ulf walked with Hildegard to his stables. "What will you say when you get back?"

"I doubt whether I'll need to say anything. They leave me pretty much alone. I've been warned not to go into the wood, but that's about all. I do a little work in the scriptorium in return for my keep. At present, they seem to hope they're in the running to receive a chunk of my widow's inheritance, although one or two little things have made the cellaress look at me rather suspiciously."

"Be careful."

"I will be. I'm beginning to believe that my lady prioress of Swyne knew exactly what she was doing when she suggested Handale. Word of something nefarious must have reached her ears."

"But surely she wouldn't involve herself in anything as commonplace as smuggled goods or abduction?"

"The latter might depend on the identity of the girls being abducted." She frowned. "But I do agree with you. It's not her usual style and it's also right out of the Riding, not her fiefdom at all."

"It's probably just as she says, a place remote enough for you to think things through." He gripped her arm. "Even so, my dearest, be careful when you get back there. Tread carefully."

"If I'm back before midday, I can talk my way out of it should anyone question me. For all anyone knows, I could have been meditating in solitude somewhere about the priory. Minding my own business!"

"That'll be the day!"

They had reached the stables and Ulf made to usher her through. "Go on in. I'm riding as far as Kilton with you."

Before she could object, he added, "Then I can bring back the horse I'm going to lend you. We need a plan and we can stitch one together on our way."

By the time Ulf and his page were turning back to Langbrough, a plan of sorts had been agreed upon.

First, Hildegard would try to find out what was in the tower and whether Dakin was complicit. If he was involved with Fulke's shady dealings, it might implicate Master Schockwynde. They agreed they thought him honest. Even so, they both knew of his overinflated view of himself. Gold would help to bolster his high claims and ambition can turn even an honest man to crime.

Second, there was the death of the journeyman Giles to consider. So far, the coroner had not put in an appearance, and until he did so, there was no one to conduct the investigation demanded by law. Every day that passed made it more likely that his attacker would get away with it. The whole thing was turning into a shambles.

As for the priest, his death needed an explanation, too. Hildegard was not satisfied with the opinion expressed by the cellaress. Everyone suspected he had been poisoned. It was only the cellaress who had tried to brush it off as a kind of apoplexy.

To be fair, it was possible, of course, that he might have succumbed to sudden illness. But the way in which he had stared accusingly round the congregation as he grasped his stomach, as if trying to wrench something out of it, made it look like poison—and he knew it. As she pointed out to Ulf, it was more than likely he knew what Fulke was up to with regard to the novices. His knowledge might have made him dangerous.

She recalled his stammer when he spoke, his gentle nature, his hopes for the future. It was right that there should be a reckoning.

As for Alys, now she was free, due process would be followed.

Before they parted, Ulf reached out and put his hand over hers.

"I'm glad you're back. Glad you didn't go straight to Abbot de Courcy, damn his eyes. Maybe this can be a new start for us?"

"But your wife—"

"I feel she'll not be my wife for long."

"Ulf"—she gave him a soft look—"I wish you were happy with her. Be patient. Give it time."

"Time doesn't solve all problems. I wish I could be happy, too, but wishing doesn't help. I know that well enough—I've wished for us to be together longer than—" He broke off. "You know all this. I want only you, Hildegard. I always have."

"I can't give you any reason to hope, Ulf. I may rejoin the Order if they'll take me. My own wishes are a complete mystery to me at present. I simply don't know what to do."

"I'll wait. I've learned patience these last few months."

He turned his horse and spurred it onto the road back to Langbrough, followed by his page on a frisky pony, leading the one Hildegard had been riding. Soon they had both disappeared over the brow of the hill.

Hildegard made her way on foot along the Kilton Beck—an easier task in daylight, when she could see where she was going—then climbed up through the scree to the woods and followed the now-familiar path towards the enclosure.

As soon as she reached the lodge, she saw that something was wrong.

Chapter 14

Hamo was sitting astride the scaffolding high up, well out of what was happening below.

Half a dozen armed men were wrecking the lodge.

They were stabbing swords up through the thatch and strewing it around; they were slashing Matt's beautiful furniture and throwing blocks of painstakingly carved stone to the ground, where they kicked it with their metal boots and tramped over it.

Carola was screaming at them to leave her drawings alone. Matt was picking up pieces of wood and cradling them in his arms. Dakin was in chains.

Chains?

Hildegard gazed in astonishment.

From inside the lodge came more sounds of destruction and, above it all, a voice.

Prioress Basilda in her chair carried by two strong men was heaved outside and positioned under the eaves. "I will not have thieves working in my priory," she screeched, pointing a fat finger at Dakin. "Where is it, you lying toad!"

When Dakin didn't answer, she shrieked, "Brand him! Burn the truth from out of him. Do it!"

A gesture to the apparent leader of the forces summoned him to stand in front of her chair. "My lady Prioress, we have no authority to proceed further."

"Authority? What do you imagine I'm bestowing on you, sot wit? I'm handing you authority on a plate!"

"Beg leave, my lady, you are not my commander." The man went so far as to add, "I am not one of your monks."

"Then send me a monk! Send me the bishop! I will have the truth from this thief." She turned violently on Dakin. "Where is it hidden? Tell me that. Now! Or I promise I shall rip your tongue from your mouth with my own bare hands!"

Hildegard, unnoticed until now, stepped forward.

Basilda jerked her head round in surprise. "What are you doing outside the precinct, lady?"

"My gracious prioress, pray use more temperate language. This poor fellow must be allowed recourse to the law if accused of theft. Canon law does not apply here."

"What do you know about it? If the crime takes place within the purlieu of Handale Priory, then the trial and punishment take place here, as well."

She prodded an impatient hand at the nearer of the two men attending her chair to show that she wanted to be lifted up.

"There will be an investigation between sext and nones in my chapter house. And punishment will follow at once. On!" she ordered her porters, thrusted a pointing finger in the direction of the priory. "All convene at the appointed hour. You, captain, make sure this prisoner does not escape, or it will be your life for his!"

The men hoisted the chair off the ground and conveyed it rapidly away from the scene.

Hildegard went over to Dakin. "What happened?"

He refused to meet her glance. She saw his mouth tighten with suppressed rage. "Dakin, what is it?"

Matt spoke. "He's been put in the frame for theft, when we all know he's innocent and it's just a ploy to—" He broke off.

Carola, holding a piece of vellum rescued from her workroom, had gripped Matt by the sleeve to silence him.

Hildegard turned to her. "You explain, Carola. Why this?" She swept an arm to include the havoc created by the armed men.

Three or four others were emerging from their rampage of destruction and hung around their captain, as if eager for more orders along the same lines.

Carola glared at them. "They believe the runaway novice stole a gold chalice from the mortuary and that Dakin knows something about it. As proof, they allege they found a trinket from her belt beside the bodies and her belt here inside the lodge. One of the nuns claims that the belt belonged to the novice. Certainly none of us have ever seen it before."

She turned to stare hard-eyed at the cellaress, who had appeared silently from inside. "That is right, madam, is it not?"

"I have no obligation to answer such impertinence."

"I think you'll find you have," Hildegard said. "The guild woman here has every right to question you. Prioress Basilda is wrong when she claims that a crime has been committed within her domain. For the length of time the master mason sets up his lodge here, that place is his own by the laws of his guild and he can be tried by no one else."

The cellaress replied, "You seem extremely well versed in both monastic rites and the law, widow. May we be permitted to know by what means a mere townswoman such as yourself can claim such knowledge?"

"By my own private means," retorted Hildegard. She turned to the captain. "Where do you intend to hold your prisoner?"

He had clearly given the matter no thought and his mouth sagged.

"I suggest you order your men to clean up this place and allow the prisoner back into the lodge, where you can set a guard on him until the appropriate authorities have been informed of the prioress's intentions. Send a man to Durham to demand Master Sueno de Schockwynde's immediate attendance, and tell him to bring his clerk at law."

"Our lady prioress has already done that," the cellaress informed her.

"A reminder in case the first message went astray will not be unhelpful," replied Hildegard. She turned back to the captain. "Also send to the bishop. We seek clarification of the rights and limitations of canon law as it applies here. Is that clear?"

The captain nodded. "Who's to write all this down?"

"I will."

He glanced once towards the enclosure, as if seeking help. "To Master Schockwynde and to the bishop," he repeated, dragging his glance back to Hildegard.

She gave him a cold look. "We will not have arbitrary and unlawful punishment here. Who is your commander?"

By now, she had realised that the men Basilda had called in came from Kilton Castle. On their tunics they wore a strange device—three exotic green birds, parrots or popinjays, as they were called—the emblem of the lord de Thweng, whose family had owned the castle for many generations, along with much land in the East Riding, long before the current dispute arose.

The captain, thickset, bearded, unremarkable but clearly not happy, replied, "We have no commander but me and the steward at present. Our constable was recalled by the earl of Northumberland and his replacement has not reached us yet."

"All the more reason for not making a massive mistake at the prioress's behest and calling down retribution upon yourself and your men by acting without the earl's authority."

The captain evidently saw the sense in this and gave the appropriate orders.

"And see that the prisoner is fed and given ale," Hildegard reminded him.

"We'll remain here until our master arrives," Carola told them. "There'll be a reckoning, you can be sure of that. And make sure the guard does not set foot within the lodge when carrying arms."

"Stay outside, you hear?" grunted the captain. He settled down on an upturned stump and watched with a bitter glance as his men began to put the place to rights.

The cellaress surveyed the scene through narrowed eyes—the men busy; Dakin, wrists chained, sitting on a block of stone next to the captain; Carola and Hildegard going inside to find writing materials—then without another word, she strode back through the wall door into the enclosure.

Hamo swung down from the scaffolding and trudged towards the lodge, frowning.

After handing the letters she had written to the captain so he could send them on, Hildegard went over to Matt, who was still busy trying to reestablish some sort of order, and asked if she might have a word.

When they were out of earshot of the guards, she asked, "What were you about to say just now when Carola prevented you?"

He gave her a dark look. "It's obvious what they're up to. This so-called theft is just a ploy so they can hold somebody for that novice's disappearance. Now we're all in it up to our necks."

"I am at fault. I should never have brought her here."

Hildegard was surprised to find that Carola had followed them out.

"Nonsense." Carola gave Matt a sharp glance. "Would you have let that poor child be taken as a whore by scum like Fulke? Talk sense! If she was your sister, would you be so agreeable?"

Matt looked shame-faced. "You know I wouldn't. Even so, what's going to happen next? I could lose my apprenticeship. And then what? A life of beggary. You're safe, Carola. Nobody can touch you. What about everybody else?"

"Do you imagine I'd stand by and allow you to be thrown out on your ear by the guild? I despair, Matt. I really do. You have such a black opinion of us all." She turned to Hildegard. "I'll give him a good talking to later, mistress." She lowered her voice to a whisper. "I hope Alys reached safety?"

"She did. She's with a trusted friend of mine. She'll come to no harm with him." Hildegard paused. Was it Dakin who had tipped off those horsemen they had seen on the York road last night? She was about to tell Carola of her suspicions, when she stopped herself. She had no idea what the relationship was between Dakin and the imaginator. Alys believed they were sweethearts. If that was the case, it could place a burden of divided loyalty on Carola if her suspicions were correct.

She took her leave with a final promise that the prioress would find no grounds for holding Dakin and that soon their guild master and his law clerk would be here to lend the weight of reason to the situation. Meanwhile, Dakin would be safe enough.

As she crossed the cloister garth to the guest wing, she saw the two Kilton henchmen leaving Basilda's chamber. She decided to take the bull by the horns and changed direction.

She made her appearance in the doorway just as the prioress was reaching for her hawk. It was hooded. Its tinkling bells sounded incongruously cheerful. Basilda wore a leather gauntlet on her right wrist and held it out for the bird to step onto as she slipped off its hood. Beside her stood the cellaress.

Basilda jerked her head up when she noticed Hildegard. "So, widow, my orders have been countermanded?"

The cellaress had been quick, Hildegard thought, flashing her a glance. She stared back, brazen and glassy-eyed.

"I'm sure, my lady prioress, you understand the law as well as I do. The guild lodge, though temporarily within the purlieu of the priory is, in fact, deemed by law to be separate for as long as it is in use by the guildsmen. If you feel this is a misreading of the law, the clerk will be able to tease the matter out to the satisfaction of all concerned. Meanwhile, the fate of the mason in question cannot be determined. We must all be patient. It is, I believe, a virtue?"

Prioress Basilda sniffed. "You're taking advantage of me because of my incapacity." She slapped the side of her chair with her free hand. "But we shall have satisfaction. That chalice will be found. He will pay the price for his treachery. And we shall no doubt uncover his part in the abduction of one of our novices. Doubtless she has been defiled by that miscreant. He will pay the full price for that in our own court. But wait until Master Fulke arrives. He'll fetch my attorney and then we'll see what's what!"

"Where is the master?" asked Hildegard, surprised that he had not been recalled at once.

"He is dealing with other business." Prioress Basilda looked disillusioned for a moment but then her eyes became shrewd. "As for you, widow, if indeed that is what you are, I'll thank you to cease prying into our affairs. They do not concern you. I order my priory as I see fit. You are unaware of the currents of dissent which run here. A firm hand is needed. It may appear harsh to an outsider such as yourself but events make it necessary to deal strongly with the women sent to me." A sardonic smile curled her lip. "You may imagine they are as pious as yourself, but I can tell you stories about them that would make you weep at the evil of womankind and quake with fear at the sins committed. The worst offenders are sent here to be punished," she added, echoing the words of the priest shortly before he died. "Murder is nothing to them." Her eyes stared. "It would be as well to watch your step."

After this threat—there was no other way of viewing it—Hildegard made her way outside.

She sat down on the hard truckle bed that had given her such restless nights. It was difficult to know what to do for the best. It was a hard ride from Durham with the roads as they were. Schockwynde could not arrive for several days. Fulke, on the other hand, might only have to come from his tannery in Ruswarp and would be here the sooner. If he had any sense, he would remove whatever was hidden in the tower at the earliest opportunity.

The look that had crossed the prioress's face when his name was mentioned puzzled her. She had looked disappointed in her benefactor. Was there a crack in their complicity?

Was it connected to that "other business" Fulke was engaged in? Maybe something irrelevant to the loss of a novice? She could not believe he would give in so easily. Yet he would never find her. He would eventually realise that the effort he might be putting in was wasted when the law came after him.

This "other business," however—did it have anything to do with his activities at the tower, something that concerned Basilda, or was it nothing to do with the disappearance of the novice, maybe a private matter that simply involved making use of the tower? Was this what was worrying the prioress?

The entire matter was a mystery.

It was as puzzling as the presence of armed men waiting on the moors road the previous night. Dakin had asked twice which route she and Alys intended to take. His interest might have been prompted by mere curiosity, or it could have been because he needed to pass the information on to someone else—someone who wanted to abduct the girl a second time? Someone like Fulke himself, maybe?

She considered the possible reasons Dakin might have for getting involved with Fulke. Money was the obvious one, the love of it being the root of much evil. But what if Alys was right when she thought Dakin was in love with Carola? It was certain that the imaginator treated him with condescension bordering on scorn. If his emotions had been reciprocated, then he would need money, plenty of it, to put forth his suit. Only time would tell. Those night riders might have had nothing to do with events at Handale. Or with Dakin. Or Fulke.

It was all guesswork.

Even so.

She changed out of her clothes into clean ones—first a linen undershift, then an overgown in a different colour. As she pulled the green fabric over her head, she felt some pleasure. It would be hard to go back to wearing a plain Cistercian habit after this.

Her thoughts returned to the present.

The best thing about the whole business was the promise Ulf had made before leaving her at Kilton Beck this morning. He would find out more about the manor Alys believed she had inherited with her brother, then give Hildegard time to find out what she could from inside the priory. Then he would return with three or four men.

They had arranged to meet the day after tomorrow near the ford where the beck crossed the coast road and flowed on to Killingbeck and the sea. From there, it was a scramble back along the beck into the woods and a short climb to the tower.

She retied her head scarf, shook out the folds of her cloak, pulled it on, and refastened it with a silver brooch. The day was colder than ever. The frost remained. It powdered the gargoyles jutting from the priory walls and made their grotesque features stand out in livid detail.

The hut leaned against the farthest wall of the herb garden. To reach it, she had to find a way through the kitchen gardens between the beds of kale and winter cabbage. Frost put a silver patina over the fleshy leaves. Even the stalks of grass at the edge of the path were silvered by the cold. A path wound through a wicket gate and approached the herberer's hut between beds of rosemary and thyme. It would be difficult to approach without being seen.

When she reached the door, it was open, and she found the herberer sitting inside with her feet in a wooden bucket. Aromatic steam rose into the cold air.

"Greetings, sister." Hildegard stood on the threshold.

"Come for a bit of peace and quiet, mistress?" Eyes like green glass beads stared up at her.

Hildegard chuckled. "Something like that. May I enter?"

The herb woman nodded towards a bench against the wall. She was the oldest person Hildegard had seen at the priory. A stick was propped against the wall, within reach of the old woman.

"I'm not surprised you want to escape from them. They're moon-mad, at the full like the tide. Three days they'll foam and fret. As above, so below."

"Heaven must be in disarray at present, sister."

"So it be and so be this realm of ours, and I do not mean only Handale. The king is in danger and nobody heeds it. Least of all these women here with their clacking over sin and punishment."

"How do you know the king is at risk?"

"Aren't all kings, at all times, the focus of men's ambition?"

"That's probably true—"

"Probably?" The old nun rocked back and forth in amusement.

"There's nothing probable about it. It's as certain as the stars in their courses. And when the king is a young man with no friends, it cannot be changed—except as with any disease of the body. By rooting the contagion out. The realm is but a living thing, prone to sickness, to the actions of the planets and eventual decay."

"Sister, this may be true. Those who support the king must arm themselves and go to his aid. But these nuns can do nothing."

"They do what they do. The tanner is not as clever as he thinks. Let's hope he chooses customers who favour the king."

Sighing with relief, the old nun lifted her feet from the bucket of water scented with lavender and other herbs. She dried them on a piece of clean linen, wrapped them in a woollen cloth, then squinted up at Hildegard. "You're here to ask me whether it's the plague or the action of some evildoer?"

Taken off guard, Hildegard blurted, "The priest—"

"Of course, the priest! Who did you think I meant? He chose his own destiny. God grants free will. It's the planets try to set us on the wrong course and lay traps to test us."

Afraid that the conversation would turn into a theological discussion which would get them nowhere, Hildegard asked, "How did he choose, sister?"

"By the roving of his eye, that's how."

She unwrapped her feet, gave them a rub, and pushed them into a pair of pattens. Taking her time, she hung the damp linen on a peg above the brazier, where a weak flame gave off a little heat. She got up in a fluid movement, reached for a poker, and riddled the coals; then she lifted a pot off the gridiron, shook it to raise the sediment, and began to stir. When she replaced the spoon, she turned as if in surprise.

"Still here, mistress? What more do you need to know?"

"I need to know who would poison him for a roving eye."

"The moon will soon be at the full. That's the whole of it. The only answer is to pray." She turned her back, and it was clear she had ended their meeting.

Hildegard had an impression of the sort of cures the old nun used from what she saw hanging from the roof beams, but before she left, she asked, "Do you grow all the herbs they use in the kitchens here?"

She received a sharp glance. "All."

"And do the nuns come to fetch them themselves?"

The old woman jerked up her head. "They do."

"There are many here that might kill a man."

"Over time."

"Unless made into an elixir?"

"True." The old woman gazed out past Hildegard to where the garden lay in a sudden shaft of winter sunlight. "Beware the moon at its full."

Chapter 15

The list of poison plants was long. Some, of course, had dual properties and were only lethal in large doses. The ones that could kill instantly were rare. Hildegard could find no sign of any such as that growing in the gardens. Her knowledge was no more than any village herbalist; she was no apothecary. Even so, she was sure there was nothing here that could kill a man as suddenly as the one that must have been given to the priest.

Except if it were made up into a strengthened dose, she reminded herself. But who, apart from the herberer, would know how to do that?

She made her way to the priory church. The sacristan appeared as soon as she heard the door creak open. If she was always so prompt to appear, anyone would have found it impossible to approach the wine or the chalice, let alone slip a lethal dose into them.

Hildegard's voice echoed down the nave under the high vault. "Sister, forgive this intrusion. I seek your help."

"I'll help if I can," the sacristan replied directly. The hostility shown by prioress Basilda did not extend to everyone. She raised her head from her task of polishing one of the holy vessels she held as Hildegard approached. "What is it, mistress?"

"I'm greatly perplexed by the young priest's death."

"As are we all. But I can reassure you on one thing. It was not the plague. Rest easy on that. We're not going to be digging plague pits yet. These sisters may be frightening themselves with talk of witchcraft, but they're not far wrong when they say he must have been poisoned. There is no other explanation for so sudden an attack."

"The cellaress suggested apoplexy."

"Aye, she would."

"What do you mean?"

"That's enough now. How else may I help you?"

"I can't work out how it could have happened. I mean, could it have been self-inflicted?"

She saw the horror on the sacristan's face. "That would damn him to hell for eternity. No, he must have been dosed by someone."

"Did he have enemies?"

She shook her head. "That boy? How would he find enemies, living here so blamelessly?"

Remembering the words of the herberer, she was going to ask if the priest had liaisons with the sisters, but before she could put the question, the nun said, "Whoever did it must have flitted in here like a shadow once the holy vessels were in place. Those nuns are saying she wore a magic cloak. Can you credit the nonsense they have in their heads?"

"So you believe he died from poison administered by human agency?"

"Exactly so."

"And the next question is how."

"I can't help you. I'm as perplexed as everyone else. No one has anything to do with the vessels but for me and my assistant, and I'd vouch for her with my life."

"Do you lock the doors when you're not in attendance?"

The sacristan shook her head again. "There is always someone in attendance. Me or my servant. Night and day."

"So how could it have been achieved?" She went over to the altar, where the chalice was displayed. "Is this ready for mass?"

"No," the sacristan replied, "but that's how it is once the wine is poured in."

"Where is the wine kept?"

"Under the altar in this flagon." She reached down and pulled a brocade cloth to one side to reveal a stone flagon, some spills, a tinderbox and spare candles, and one or two other oddments. She let the cloth fall back into place.

"So anyone wanting to add poison to the wine could come up here when nobody was watching, unstop the flagon, and drop something in it?"

"They could if nobody was watching. Unlikely, as I've explained. But why? That's the question. Why would anybody want to do a thing like that? He was harmless enough."

"I'm told he had a roving eye—" Hildegard began.

The sacristan gripped her by the arm. "Do you realise what you're saying, mistress? This is a house of correction. It is the last place on earth where looseness of any kind would be tolerated."

"But if—" Hildegard persisted.

"Never, never."

"Do you have an alternative explanation other than jealousy for someone wanting him dead?"

"I don't. But it's not what you suggest. Never."

Hildegard tried another approach. "Can you remember who was here the day he died?"

"You have a strong interest in this matter—"

"I feel I owe it to his dear mother to find out what happened."

"He had no mother."

"You mean he was an orphan?"

"I mean he had no mother. He was the devil's own and working his way out of shame to his ultimate salvation."

"I don't understand."

"You wouldn't, not being of a monastic order. Life is more than buying and selling and being the grand wife of a merchant." She gave Hildegard's garments an up-and-down look.

"I'm hardly grand," Hildegard murmured as she caught her meaning.

"True, but you have no understanding of the teachings if you believe that all there is is this world of physical presences." She extended an arm to embrace the church with its trappings of gold and gilded wood. "There are other forces at work."

The wall paintings showed lurid scenes of martyrdom. Hildegard averted her glance. Unbidden, the memory of Rivera rose before her. She would never be free of him. "The force of destiny, I suppose you mean?"

The sacristan folded her arms. "And the force of divine will." She gave Hildegard a grim smile. "Since you ask who was here, let me offer the courtesy of a reply. That day, only yesterday, was the feast of Saint Thomas, was it not?"

"Indeed it was."

"And my servant was in here with me. She was polishing the sacramental ornaments and had replaced the chalice where it is now, just as you see it." She indicated the gold and wrought-silver vessel. "It was never out of my sight. As we were busy, two sisters came in to ask if everything was ready. I started to light the candles—"

"But in doing so, you could not have been watching the others."

"By then my servant was standing beside me, holding the tinderbox and some spills."

"And the two sisters?"

"Yes," the sacristan responded with a thoughtful frown. "One of them came to ask me some trivial question or other while the other one remained by the altar. I did not pay heed to her. They often come in to pray and to gaze on the cross."

"But on that particular day, only those two came in?"

"Let me think." Slowly, the sacristan began to sniff out a trail. "Yes. I'm sure of it. Only those two at that time, although earlier, before we started to make our preparations, there were several in and out."

"What happened next?"

"Before lighting the candles, I'd poured the new wine into the flagon. It came up from the general cask in the kitchen, ready for the priest, who would consecrate it after pouring it from the flagon into the chalice."

"So poison could have been added to the wine in the kitchen, or after it was poured into the flagon, or even," she added, "after the priest poured it into the chalice?"

The sacristan was reluctant to agree. The reason became clear when she admitted that she had tasted a sip when it first came up from the kitchen. "To make sure it was not sour," she added.

"So it was when the wine was in the flagon that someone could have poisoned it, or after it was transferred to the chalice?"

"More likely the former. After the priest had poured it into the chalice, there would have been too many people around." She was still frowning. "I still fail to see how anyone could have got at the flagon. It was kept underneath the altar until it was needed. I would have noticed if anyone had pushed back the cloth under the altar."

"And the sister standing at the altar while the other one engaged you in conversation, who was she?"

"Let me think. She had her hood up. It was the other one, Sister Desiderata, who sticks in my mind."

"Why is that?"

"Always putting her nose into matters that don't concern her. If you want to find out more, she'll no doubt have an opinion. And yes, I remember now. She was giving me advice on how to light the candles. As if I haven't been doing it these last ten years without her guidance."

"Desiderata and an unknown companion. Do they always go around in twos?"

"The prioress decrees it. They are safer that way. And she fears absconders. They watch each other."

Sleet was beginning to drive across the yard. It forced the nuns to take shelter in the cloisters. Black robes concealed identities, and only by looking closely could Hildegard see the differences between one and another. Sister Mariana stood out a little by reason of her height, which was slightly above the average.

At this moment, she was the centre of a discussion on the subject of whether animals had souls. Hildegard felt a yawn coming on. She lingered on the fringes and, with no wish to draw attention to her interest, tried to make a guess as to which one was Desiderata.

A sallow-faced nun stood on the edge of the group, twisting a rosary between her fingers while one of the others harangued her over her views. Her opponent was a short woman, young and rosy-cheeked, with a wisp of fair hair escaping from her coif.

She was mocking the other's ideas, and suddenly, for no reason Hildegard could discern, the argument became heated. The two women began to shout each other down. Mariana looked on with a troubled expression. The fourth member of the group stood by, head down, face obscured by her hood, and did not join in.

Two and two, watching each other. Four spies. She turned her attention to the other groups.

One nun was talking about the weather, a look of dismay on

her face as the sleet slashed across the garth. She stepped hurriedly back as it billowed into the cloisters. Her companion gazed bleakly at this scene without a word. The other two were standing talking together in voices so quiet, it was impossible to hear what they were saying. Nothing much to mark them out from the others. One tall, one short. Faces obscured.

Hildegard went to sit in a niche where she had a view of them all. Mariana's group was the most animated. They were still discussing the existence of animal souls. The fair-haired nun had raised her voice. "Once and for all, Tiffany, an animal is a mere beast. Of course they don't have souls. It's nonsense to make such a claim. I doubt whether some people have souls. And we cannot tell, because we have no test available."

"Except for common sense," the sallow-faced one retorted, identifying herself as Tiffany.

"Common sense? That's hardly a test for anything. What you call common sense might seem the most arrant nonsense to someone else."

"Are you accusing me of spouting nonsense?" demanded Tiffany in an aggrieved tone.

"I'm sure she didn't mean that," interjected the fourth member of the group, roused from her silence. "We are all enjoined to see the other person's point of view, are we not?"

"Enjoined to see it but not necessarily to accept it," Tiffany retorted.

"Certainly not to accept heresy," the rosy-faced nun pointed out. "Remember what the Cistercians say."

Hildegard pricked up her ears.

"What do they say?" demanded Mariana.

"That the heretic must be hunted down and killed like a fox among chickens." She crossed herself. "Bernard of Clairvaux was rightly made a saint for saying that. Don't you agree, Mariana?"

Before Mariana could reply, the sallow nun jeered. "Desiderata, I despair." She put her hands to her face and walked away.

So it was the talkative fair-haired nun who had entered the church and spoken to the sacristan while her companion stood by the altar, within reach of the chalice. So who had been her companion?

At that moment, the subprioress appeared from the far end of the cloister and rapped on the ground with a stick. "Enough of all this racket! Back to your cells!"

Sentences were left hanging in midair as everyone instantly obeyed. Mariana's lips tightened and she glared round, but if she considered rebelling, she quickly rejected the idea. Hildegard watched as she walked back beside Desiderata towards the *dortoir*. Mariana with Desiderata.

She waited until they had all dispersed. When she was sure she was unobserved, she made her way to the corner stair and followed them up to the floor above the low hall. She would find Desiderata and have a quiet word with her.

Two bleak lines of cell doors faced onto a straight corridor, with a further stair at the far end. It was an easy matter to glance into each cell through the small aperture in the door as she made her way along the corridor.

The occupants knelt on the bare flint floor, some on wooden prie-dieux that cut into the flesh. A mutter of prayer rose on both sides—regular, monotonous, hypnotic. In their identical robes and with hoods pulled over to veil their features in shadow, it was impossible to tell one from another. By the time Hildegard reached the end of the corridor, she was none the wiser. Wondering if it would be reasonable to knock on one of the doors and ask where she might find Desiderata, she hesitated. It would be best to keep her interest to herself. They were a close bunch. Nothing was more likely than that they would protect one another if need be.

On impulse, she ascended the nearby tower stairs.

The same arrangement of cells as below existed here. The occupants of the cells were less fortunate, their doors barred from the outside by means of wooden beams that dropped into slots on each side. She realised that these must be the cells of the penitents, then. The worst of sinners. The ones Basilda claimed could commit murder—and perhaps had already done so.

Hildegard glanced inside each cell as she paced the corridor to the far end. Astonished at what she saw, she was unable to tear her glance away.

In the first cell, a black cowled figure knelt on the bare boards. She was doubled over, rocking backwards and forwards with sobs and muttered curses interspersed with Latin phrases. Unaware of Hildegard at the spy hole, she did not look up or pause. Next, the occupant paced rapidly back and forth in the confined space. Her robe gaped as she beat her uncovered breasts with a strap. The spikes on it drew forth prickles of blood. From another cell issued an unearthly and intermittent wail, like someone in physical pain, as indeed may well have been the case.

Shouts came from elsewhere, the banging of fists against a wall. Screams to be let free, promises to do the devil's will.

Hildegard met the furious glance of another one of the inmates as the woman sprawled on the floor with robes rucked up, legs apart, blood from a spiked cuff round her thigh staining her flesh as she pressed the spikes deeper and fingered the oozing blood. Another stood naked, the folds of her habit at her feet, and lashed herself with a leather whip until her back was streaming with blood. Her eyes were fixed on the wooden cross on the wall as she cried out in convulsions of pain.

The noise was tumultuous, sobs and cries and breathless, desperate pleadings mingling with prayers beseeching help or begging for release from the constant agony of hellfire.

Hildegard felt her heart begin to race. Religious ecstasy on this scale had always puzzled her. It was as unlike the calm reasonableness of the priory at Swyne as could be imagined. A mixture of anger and compassion vied with contempt as she saw more horrors: spiked implements inserted into the tender flesh, blood and bruising, torn-out hair, pale limbs turning blue after self-inflicted punishment.

Witnessing the half-healed wounds on the women's limbs, she did not doubt that some of them were taken out for beatings under the eye of the prioress. It prompted an unpleasant memory of Abbot Hubert de Courcy undergoing ritual flagellation because of his confession of thoughts of venery. She remembered with a shudder how he had ordered his brother monks not to stop their punishment, and it was only when his prior called a halt that his penance was ended. By then, his back was a mass of bloody weals caused by the studded whips they used.

These women were guilty of greater sin than forbidden feelings. As the prioress would have her believe, they had acted out their sins to the deepest extent and thus deserved to suffer the penalty.

Only wishing she had not witnessed such desperate scenes, she hurried back down the stairs to the lower corridor, where the cries became fainter. Soon they were no louder than the wind in the eaves.

At the end of the corridor, a still figure was watching her. The face tightly bound in a wimple and the black head covering was familiar. It was Sister Mariana.

She drew level, but Mariana went on staring at her without moving. "Are you going to let me pass?" Hildegard demanded.

The woman seemed to come out of a dream. "Certainly." She

began to step to one side, then changed her mind. "Wait. You should not have gone up there. What are you doing here?"

"I was looking for one of the nuns. My private business."

"I hope you found satisfaction in looking in on the agony of our penitents?"

"*Satisfaction* is not the word I would use, no."

"Do you think they should go unpunished?"

"And put their souls at risk?"

Mariana's lips tightened. "Precisely so."

"I wonder at the sins they might have committed and who decrees them to be sins, after all."

"Our father Pope, of course," replied Mariana with a bitter smile. "Our convocations of abbots and other important men set the rules. Our Saint Bernard of Clairvaux." Her tone, though harsh, gave no sign of approval or criticism of this arrangement.

"Such young women being punished," Hildegard remarked, watching her carefully, "I hardly dare believe they're so wicked."

"More wicked than you can imagine." She lowered her head and moved to one side.

"Did worse happen to you?" asked Hildegard with sudden understanding.

Mariana nodded. "But it was in another time."

"What was your alleged sin?"

The form of her words seemed to open some spirit of confession in her because she turned, and looking straight at Hildegard said, "I lay with a man."

"By your own desire or despite it?"

"Despite it. But I got with child. And paid the penalty."

"And the man?"

"No doubt he still sits in his abbot's chair sipping wine, as was always his pleasure." She stepped aside to allow Hildegard to pass.

Outside in the garth, Hildegard breathed in the fresh clear air with a gulp of relief. Her intention to question Desiderata had failed. Instead, she had lifted a stone and found something horrible under it.

With time to spare, until the next office brought everyone crawling forth again, Hildegard walked away from the claustrophobic atmosphere of the cloister garth. Finding herself near the mortuary, she peered inside. A nun sat between the corpses.

She did not look up from her vigil when the door opened. Her hood was partly pulled down over her face. She could have been sleeping. She could have been praying. Whichever it was, her identity was concealed. Evidently, she was someone Prioress Basilda trusted enough to leave unchaperoned.

While Hildegard had been in the *dortoir,* the rain had turned to hail. Now it had stopped and was lying in freezing drifts at the foot of the enclosure wall. Glancing over her shoulder to make sure she was not being followed, she went to the outer door and gave it a push. Then she stepped once more into the rain-drenched menace of Handale Woods.

CHAPTER 16

She was confronted by one of the guards from Kilton Castle.

"No visiting the prisoner," he barked as she approached.

"I do not wish to."

"No visiting anybody."

"I'm sure I'm within my rights to speak to Mistress Carola. She's not under arrest, is she?"

He begrudged allowing her to stand at the eaves even to call inside and, to her chagrin, remained stolidly at her shoulder. Dakin was sitting in the doorway, wrists still chained, an expression of bleak resignation on his face. A stoup of ale and a hunk of bread were by his side, untouched.

The other masons seemed to be having their midday break. When she called to them, Carola appeared with a lump of black bread in one hand.

"Have the messages to your master and to the bishop of Durham been despatched?" Hildegard asked after a brief greeting.

"They have. We're waiting now for a reply. Assuming this time, despite the weather, the message gets through. But as you see"— she waved an arm—"we're beginning to pack our things, ready to leave. Nothing will induce us to stay here a moment longer than necessary under these conditions. We're counting every minute until the master arrives."

The guard was still hanging at Hildegard's shoulder, listening in, and it was obvious he was not going to allow her out of his sight.

She tried to spin out her visit, in the hope he would get bored and move off.

"This dragon," she said to Carola, "I haven't heard it, but I'm told it keeps everybody in the priory awake some nights. What trick is it, do you think?"

"One real enough to claw poor Giles to death."

After a pause Hildegard said, "I suppose you know the old story about the dragon of Handale?"

"What's that?"

The guard was still standing by, ears flapping, when Hildegard began. "It was long ago, when the Northmen ruled. Kilton Castle was a bustling place owned by a good family called de Thweng. Over the years, though, stories about a rapacious dragon began to spread, and soon people became too scared to hunt in the woods even with hound and hawk. The castle fell into disuse. Eventually, it was inherited by a young maiden, who lived here alone. One day, a passing knight heard about the dragon and resolved to slay it."

"Much like Giles. He used the excuse of getting wood for Matt, as it seemed less foolish than to admit to a belief in a dragon, but it was his curiosity about it that led him into the woods." Carola frowned.

"The old story has a different outcome. The beast was slain. The knight married the maiden. When he eventually died, he was buried in the woods in a stone coffin with the sword he had killed it with. On the lid of his coffin somebody had carved the words *snake killer*." She had Ulf to thank for filling in the details on their ride from Langbrough.

Carola had a melancholy look on her face by the time Hildegard had finished. "Poor Giles. I've never seen a stone coffin in the woods."

"Have you explored far?"

Abruptly, Carola turned away. "I haven't time for this. I have to get ready to leave." She went back inside.

The captain was still hanging over Hildegard's shoulder. It was obvious she would not be able to escape his watchful eye. To put him to the test, she told him she intended to walk awhile in the woods, where it was sheltered from the falling sleet.

"Oh no you're not. I've got my orders. Nobody goes in there without Master Fulke's permission."

"I fail to see what power your master has over the prioress's domain."

"She'll say the same."

Hildegard peered at the blazon on the man's hauberk under his cloak. "You're one of the men-at-arms from the castle."

"I may be."

"You are."

"So what if I am?"

"And yet you're taking orders from a merchant?"

"It was Fulke informed the steward at Kilton that there were poachers in the woods. Hunting game where they shouldn't. String 'em up when we catch 'em, he said. That's what."

"You're not likely to catch them while guarding the mason, are you?"

"He might be the poacher we're looking for."

"Have you found venison in his makeshift kitchen here?"

The captain turned away in disgust. "I'm not bandying words with you, mistress. Be off with you."

"Or?"

His hand came to rest on the hilt of his sword. "Try me."

Hildegard gave him a stony look. She went to the entrance to the lodge and called inside. "Will you send someone to the priory to let me know when Master Schockwynde arrives?"

Carola reappeared. "If you so desire."

"I know him of old," Hildegard explained.

Carola gave her a sharp glance.

"When he was mason at Earl Roger's castle near York," she explained.

Carola nodded.

Hildegard knew Sueno de Schockwynde would have mentioned a stepdaughter if he had had one. He was very much a confirmed bachelor in those days, driven by ambition and status, conscious of his Roman blood, a claim most people took with a pinch of salt, mocking his airs and graces behind his back.

Aware of all this, Hildegard could not resist asking, "The master must have taken a wife?"

"My mother. He married her a year ago." Carola seemed reluctant to add more, but then, apparently seeing no harm in the admission, she muttered, "My father was a master mason, but he was killed. He and my stepfather were great rivals. Sueno has taken over my father's greatest project, the work on Durham Cathedral. He boasts that his name will go down in history."

"And because of your father, you're a member of the guild. You have great talent yourself. I've already seen that."

Carola made some noncommittal remark and, turning back into the lodge, said, "I'll let you know when he arrives. It can't be too soon for us."

Seeing how anxious she looked, Hildegard called after her, "I'm sure Dakin will not be convicted when it comes to it. No one can prove that the emblem or the belt belonged to Alys. They're commonplace things. All the nuns wear similar ones."

As indeed do I, she said to herself, running her fingers over the little silver emblem of the shell of Saint James she wore as a memento of her recent pilgrimage.

Frustrated in her attempt to inspect the tower, she slipped back inside the enclave and decided she would have to return later. She would get back into the woods unobserved. She was determined to discover the secret of the tower, and no man-at-arms or anyone else was going to stop her.

During mixtum, while gnawing on a piece of hard cheese, Hildegard considered the options. There was, in fact, only one. She would have to return to the tower by night. The guard, presumably, would sleep sometime, and even if he was the wakeful type, it would be easier to slip past under cover of darkness than in broad daylight. With this intention, she made certain preparations throughout the rest of the day. By evening, there was just one thing more she needed.

"Yes, I'm back again, Captain, as you see." With her head swathed under a scarf and her waterproof cloak over her shoulders, he would have been forgiven for not recognising her straight away.

He gave a grunt when he realised who it was. "Go in, then."

Hildegard edged in under the shelter of the eaves. The sleet had turned to rain. No sign of Schockwynde. The state of the road across the moor from Durham could be imagined.

The masons had stacked their equipment against one wall, along with some personal bags and carriers. From inside the lodge came the sounds of a game, cheers alternating with a chorus of groans. Dice, she guessed.

The guard went over to a keg under the shelter to fill his mug with ale. His back was turned while he fiddled with the spigot. Unable to believe her luck, she edged over to the pile of equipment and, concealed by her cloak, closed her fingers round the implement she judged best for her purpose. Then she presented herself in the doorway to the inner chamber, where the game was in progress.

"Greetings. Still no message from the outside world?"

Carola glanced up from a drawing she was making on a piece of stretched vellum. "The moors will be impassable in this weather. We're stuck for the time being."

"Which means we're forced to the arduous task of dicing," Hamo cut in. He got up and stretched like a cat. He was a very muscular, barrel-chested young man, well suited to the hard physical work he did, maybe honed by it, too. "Come and join us, mistress. Give us chance to take some money off you."

Aware of what was concealed under her cloak, she shook her head. "I don't want to try the patience of the guard," she said, using this as her excuse. "How is he treating you, Dakin?"

Dakin lifted his chained wrists. "He took your dragon story to heart. Now he reckons he may have to rely on us if it shows up. He's turning as smooth as butter. Next thing, he'll be inviting himself in to play dice."

"And drinking us dry." Matt concentrated on his throw. It was a one and a three, and he gave a groan under his breath and pushed some coins across the floor with the toe of his boot. "Here, Carola." He held out the dice and cup. She shook her head.

"Is the cellarer keeping you supplied with vittels?" Hildegard asked.

"She is and she had better keep on doing so." Hamo sounded tough.

"Who brings it to you?"

"That cellaress and her shadow. The one we believe came up with those lies about the theft of the chalice from the mortuary."

"Not afraid of the dragon themselves, then?"

"She'd scare any dragon, that cellaress."

———

When Hildegard ducked out under the eaves into the pelting rain, there was a lull from inside, followed by the rattle of the dice in the cup before the rushing of the rain on the frozen ground drowned everything else out.

So the cellaress was keeping an eye on the masons, as well. Handale was full of spying eyes. She shivered and looked up into the trees. Nobody was watching from the branches. Not even a little cowherd hanging upside down.

The endless vista of tree trunks went on as far as the eye could see. Hildegard splashed her way back towards the enclosure.

Night fell, early at this time of year, sending the sacristan and her assistant round the cloisters to light the cressets well before compline. For a short time, the long northern night was kept at bay.

By the time the service was done, the frail lights scarcely penetrated the shadows. Fluttering in and out of the light like black crows, the nuns went from the candlelit church into the deepest night. They became indistinguishable except when the door to the *dortoir* opened and the light from within bathed them briefly in its radiance.

Hildegard crossed to the guesthouse. Prioress Basilda was confined to her chamber by the weather, they were told. The cellarer had taken her place and, grim as usual, had afterwards appointed one of the nuns to go and read to her in her chamber. Desiderata had been chosen.

Cursing again at another missed opportunity to speak to her, Hildegard let herself into her shadowy chamber and sat to one side of the window, where she could observe the garth from between the slats of the shutter. For a long time, no one appeared, nor did Desiderata come out of Basilda's chamber. The entire place lay in silence. One by one, the lighted windows of the nuns' cells went dark.

After a time, Hildegard was alerted by a change in the shadows across the garth as someone passed along the cloister. A light briefly appeared and was snuffed out. Desiderata, chore completed? She considered going out after her but stopped herself. It might be the cellaress or the subprioress or any one of Basilda's inner circle, fulfilling the role of circator. The garth, the cloisters, the entire priory fell back into silence.

When she was confident she would be unobserved, she let herself out, inched her way to the corner of the building, then turned and hurried across towards the mortuary chapel. The thin light of a vigil candle trickled round the edges of the door, enough to guide her in the right direction

When she reached the enclosure wall, she felt her way along it until she found the door to the woods. Earlier she had taken the precaution of wedging a stone in the opening, no more than a finger's breadth, but enough to avoid the giveaway sound as she pushed it open.

There was a weird stillness on the other side. The trees seemed frozen. Not a branch stirred. The lodge lay in a black silence.

From where she stood, she could sense rather than see the guard, a frail wisp of light captured by the steel links of his mail shirt revealing where he slouched at his post under the eaves. A snore broke the silence and there was a creak as he shifted position.

Treading as softly as she could, she glided into the thicket. Thoughts of the so-called dragon flooded her mind. It was a stag, obviously, rutting out of season. Common sense told her that. No such thing as a dragon haunted the woods. Even so, she found herself starting at every cracking twig, at the sudden flapping of a bird overhead, at the scuttering of nocturnal creatures underfoot.

As she broke through the undergrowth into the clearing where Giles's body had been found, there was a distant rush of sound. It approached rapidly, shaking the treetops, until she was drenched as a shower of sleet passed overhead. It drowned out the sounds she made as she pushed on, and then, brushing the last screen of branches aside, she came out at last near the foot of the tower.

It was a ghostly shape rising up against the black trees. It contained a secret. And she was going to find out what it was.

She took the leather bag from under her cloak, where what she had borrowed from the masons was concealed. Then she started to work on the padlock with Dakin's claw-hammer.

The shower stopped as suddenly as it had started, leaving only the sound of metal scraping on metal. It rang out for a moment, loud enough to wake the devil. She stopped abruptly and cast a hasty glance behind her, but nothing moved. With a final twist of the gouge, the padlock came off in her hands. The door groaned open on its hinges.

When she stepped into the darkness, the air trapped within the stone walls slapped like ice. There wasn't a glimmer of light from anywhere. Darkness deeper than the moonless woods outside seemed to have a physical weight. She brushed a hand across her face and shut the door.

Fumbling around in her bag for tinder, she managed to locate and light a taper. She blinked through the sudden dazzle of light. The inside of the tower swarmed into view.

Directly ahead was a spiral staircase ascending into the darkness of the upper floor. More interesting was what was piled on every side.

About fifty or so linen bales were stacked against the walls.

She went over to have a look and pressed one, expecting to hear the clink of steel. She was surprised when it turned to be soft to the touch. Her fingers sank into it. Inside the bale was something with an almost fleshy resilience.

Hildegard considered things for a moment, then took out her knife.

Carefully, the shaky yellow light in one hand, she dug the knife into one of the bales. When a hole had been ripped in the fabric, she replaced her knife in her belt and pushed her fingers in through the slit.

She felt around inside. Astonished, she fingered something soft. Under that she felt a thing that was hard, like bone. She drew out her fingers, and as she did so, the taper light picked out something that came out at the same time.

She caught it as it floated to the floor. A tuft from the quill of a feather.

She lifted it to the taper to have a better look. Inserting her fingers into the bale again, she searched around for more and pulled them out. They were long and white. Goose feathers. She reached inside again. More feathers.

She made slits in the rest of the bales. They all contained the same thing.

They were all packed with feathers. What on earth was Fulke's game?

More than ever curious to know what he kept in the rest of the tower, she went to the bottom of the stairs and looked up into the darkness. Guided by the wavering light from the taper, she began to make her ascent.

CHAPTER 17

At the top, two doors. One was locked in the same manner as the main door to the outside—with a padlock and chain. The other stood ajar. Holding her breath, she stepped silently to the threshold and looked inside.

Empty. On the outer wall was one of the window slits she had noticed when first having a look round outside. What she had not been able to see, now illuminated in the pool of light, was the lifting tackle attached to the inside ledge. She went over to have a closer look.

It was what was called a lewis, a shackle and wedge contraption, able to lift loads of several tons. It was arranged with workmanlike care, as if recently used and prepared for use again. It explained why the chamber had a swept-clean look. Something had been hauled up here for storage and then removed by the same method.

She peered out at the black woods below but then narrowed her eyes in alarm. The woods were not black, not entirely. She looked more closely. Alarmed, she realised a pinprick of light was glinting in the undergrowth. As she watched, it grew in size. Something was approaching the tower.

It was soon close enough for her to see that it was a lantern swinging from side to side as it was carried along by a shadowy form. Only the cuff of one arm was visible. Before she could think of escape, the figure emerged from the path into the clearing. The light continued to swing back and forth on its pole, and in the swaying, lurid glow she saw the man who carried it: Fulke.

He was not alone.

In addition to his usual three or four bodyguards, he was accompanied by a stranger. They stood for a moment in the cone of light. It gave Hildegard time to observe the newcomer. He was dressed in velvet, with a thick cloak over his shoulders and an elaborate capuchon on his head.

The capuchon overshadowed his face, but she could hear him saying something to Fulke and glancing nervously back into the woods. Fulke muttered something in reply and the group headed for the gaping door of the tower.

An enraged exclamation followed as Fulke realised the padlock had been smashed. She saw him turn to the man beside him. He was not a military man by the look of him and his capuchon made him look like a cockerel with its comb erect. His shadow danced grotesquely in the light from the lantern as the two men conferred then, drawing their swords, entered the tower.

In moments, she would be discovered.

Metal boots ascended the stone stair, the sound growing louder with every second. One small knife would be nothing against so many.

The sound increased until they were at the door. Hildegard swung up onto the roof beam and lay along it then waited for them to come inside.

The light from the approaching lantern burst like the sun over the horizon. It flooded into every corner of the chamber. Fulke stood directly beneath her, his velvet-clad companion by his side, the guards clattering in behind him. The shadows leaped.

She watched Fulke glower round, his features distorted by the light. With a roar, he went to the door and yanked it back on its hinges, then gave a curse when he discovered no one hiding behind it.

"Gone!" he shouted. "Who the devil was it? Is it that godshite mason? What in God's balls is he after?"

The man with the coxcomb hood said in a querulous tone, "I hope you haven't dragged me out to this godforsaken place on a wild-goose chase, Fulke."

"Rest easy. Your goods are in the other chamber, with the lock intact. I checked that as we came up."

"For your sake, I pray it is so."

With a snarl, Fulke shouldered his way past his guards and crossed to the other side. Everyone crushed out after him, taking the lantern with them.

In the blessed darkness that followed, Hildegard kept still in her hiding place. She heard the sound of the padlock being unlocked, the door flying back, the sound of the men as they jostled inside.

For a few moments, she had a chance to decide what to do next. Make a run for it? Best to stay where she was until she knew what Fulke was going to do.

She heard him snarl at his men to get out and search the woods in case the would-be thief was still lurking around. He must have turned to his companion then, because she heard him mutter, "I'm getting rid of them so we can talk. Nothing's been touched. We'll find the culprit. He'll rue his prying."

The echo of the men leaving the tower faded. Fulke raised his voice now they were out of earshot, and it came hollowly from the other side. "This makes no difference to our agreement, my lord. What do you think to the goods?"

A pause followed, as if the man being addressed was inspecting something. After a moment, he replied, "I'm well pleased, Fulke. This is more than I dreamed of."

"You know I only handle the best."

"I see that now. Forgive my doubts. When can I take possession?"

"As soon as I feel the weight of your gold in my hands."

"Tomorrow, then?"

"Can't wait, eh?" Fulke chuckled.

"I can't. I tell you the honest truth." A gloating tone entered the stranger's voice. "What about a little taster?"

"Get away with you! Gold first, bliss to follow."

"You're a hard man, Fulke."

"That's why I'm successful."

"I shall return tomorrow after dark. That's my promise."

Hildegard heard the door slam, the key turn in the lock.

"And you'll be at Kilton Castle, where I can find you?" asked Fulke as the two men began to descend.

"Certainly, for my sins. Don't keep me waiting. The big day is coming up. I want to be ready for it with all my weapons in place."

"I'll send men to escort you back through the woods."

Their voices faded and the light went with them.

For Hildegard, the immediate danger was over. She could scarcely believe her luck. No one had thought to shine the light above their heads onto the crossbeams that held up the roof. She gave silent thanks to Dakin for prompting such a hiding place when he found a hiding place for Alys.

Swinging easily down to the floor, she went to the door. It was all very well to have escaped notice for now, but there would be a guard set, and she would probably find she was trapped.

As she passed the locked door at the top of the stairs, she wondered what kind of goods Fulke had in there. It must be worth a lot. If she could find a way out without being seen, and keep her tryst with Ulf tomorrow at the ford, they could return and catch Fulke and his purchaser in the act and get a haul of contraband in the process. Weapons, the coxcomb had said. He wanted to get all his weapons in place.

Soft-footed, she was descending the spiral staircase when she heard shouts from outside. There was the unmistakable sound of a sword being drawn right outside the door. Then came a throat-wrenching roar of pain. A clash of steel followed—the grind of a blade slithering down a shirt of chain mail.

Then came the full-blooded shouts of man against man in a sudden ambush.

She ran to the door and peered through a crack. The clearing was alive with turbulent figures, swords thrusting, bellows of rage, a mayhem of bloodlust, with helmets ringing to the battering of steel. Of Fulke and his companion, there was nothing to be seen. They had melted into the darkness of the woods, leaving the men to their work.

To Hildegard, the two sides seemed equally matched. Who the attackers were was a mystery. She waited for an opportunity to escape. The fight raged this way and that, staying close to the tower. One of Fulke's guards fell against the door. He was so close, she could see the glistening of his eyes as he stared up at the swordsman looming over him, arm raised to strike. The guard kicked him in the bollocks and scrambled free.

In the moment when his opponent raised his own arm to bring his sword down, a blazon was revealed on his surcoat. She blinked. It was the lion of the Percy family, the Marcher lords, the emblem of the earl of Northumberland.

The two men locked and began grappling at each other's throats. They rolled on the ground until one of them managed to free himself. It was Fulke's man. He made off towards the woods with the earl's henchman in pursuit.

Hildegard took the opportunity to slip out of the tower and throw herself into the safety of the thicket. From there, she watched the fight until Fulke's guards were chased off in the direction of the priory.

"Leave them to scarper. Let's get this stuff out and down to the boats." Wiping blood from his nose, the captain pushed his men hurriedly towards the tower.

By the light of half a dozen cressets, the entire scene was illuminated in brilliant detail: men dragging the bales of feathers into the open, loading them one by one onto stretchers already concealed in the woods, hauling them away.

When she judged it safe to follow, Hildegard was guided by the lighted torches down the path forced through the undergrowth by the convoy. She guessed they were heading towards the landing stage on the beck side. Sure enough, they soon dipped out of sight down the slope and were shortly assembled on the bank below.

From her vantage point at the top of the cliff, she watched them load the bales onto two barges and eventually, torches still shedding a fitful light over the scene, push out onto the water and disappear downstream.

Their lights faded. Silence fell.

The moon appeared. It was ovoid. Not quite yet at the full. Nature silently regained her dominion.

But for the trampled and bloodied grass, there was no sign that a fight between two violent opponents had taken place. No one remained. The wounded had been carried away by their comrades.

Hildegard made her way cautiously onto the path to the priory. As she went, she picked up a stray feather from the grass.

Of course.

Now she knew what it meant: arrows.

She put the feather inside her leather bag, along with the mason's claw-hammer.

CHAPTER 18

Maybe the nuns are kept in such ignorance that they do not know what is afoot within their own purlieu? Hildegard thought. The atmosphere in the church when she returned, however, was febrile and it was evidence of some repressed knowledge. Even the subprioress, usually so colourless and self-effacing, had a flush of colour on her cheeks. The cellaress, hard-faced and authoritarian, swept the congregation of nuns with an excited glitter in her eyes.

Prioress Basilda herself, in something like high spirits, signalled for her servants to carry her out. Their triumphal procession was halfway down the nave when the prioress spotted Hildegard standing against the wall. She ordered her bearers to a halt.

Now what? thought Hildegard, bracing herself.

The prioress eyed her. When she spoke, her words were unexpected. "I beg to ask you to forgive us, Mistress York. As you may realise, the priory has been under some strain from those with ill intentions towards us. We are small and powerless"—her flesh bulged over the edges of her wooden chair, folds of fat shaking on her jowls as she spoke—"and being so weak, it behoves us to guard our interests as best we may. These ways may seem harsh to outsiders. I trust you are not incommoded by our regulations. The woods are now open. The dragon is dead."

Hildegard gazed at her in silent astonishment.

"Be so kind as to attend me in my chamber before Chapter. I wish to speak to you in private." A fat hand waved her bearers onwards and she was carried out in a waft of incense.

Hildegard's gaze followed and she waited a full minute until the prioress and her entourage had left the scene before allowing herself to consider this change of heart. It had to be something to do with last night's events at the tower.

The church had emptied by the time Hildegard reached the altar, where the sacristan was snuffing out candles. "Sister, you showed me the secrets of your work the other day. Is it possible for you to show me again the things kept under the altar?"

"No problem there, mistress. Here, have a look yourself. Nothing has changed."

As Hildegard remembered, there was a stone flagon for the Communion wine, a richly engraved ciborium, a tinderbox, tapers and so forth, and, behind them, something she had scarcely glanced at. Despite this, it had stayed in her memory, unexplained.

The sacristan handed everything out.

"No, that last thing, there at the back of the shelf." Hildegarde pointed to a small phial with a waxed-rag stopper in its slender neck. "What is that?"

The sacristan reached down. "It was his own. He suffered so."

"What does it contain?"

"His own elixir, specially mixed for him."

"By whom?"

"By our own sister apothecary. Why do you ask?"

"What was it for?"

The sacristan avoided her glance. "It was just some harmless thing he used, the better to fulfil his duties to us."

Hildegard took the phial. "May I?"

"Take it. Do. He has no use for it now."

Assuming it would be an elixir against headaches, Hildegard unstoppered it and sniffed. "I don't recognise the contents," she murmured.

"I believe it to be an old Saxon remedy. Best ask sister herberer herself."

When Prioress Basilda's servant opened the door into her chamber a few minutes later, it was obvious the prioress had been waiting for Hildegard to appear.

"My dear lady, pray be seated. Here, give her a cushion"—she tapped her servant on the arm—"then pour wine and leave us."

When they were alone, she gave Hildegard a winsome smile. "You must know by now that there were events in the woods before matins last night? The whole priory is seething with it."

"I was aware of a certain excitement, but maybe you can tell me more?"

"I will, gladly. It's connected to our benefactor, merchant Fulke. Unbeknownst to us"—she frowned—"he was secretly storing untaxed imports in a tower in Handale Woods!" She sat back. "What do you think of that?"

Hildegard adopted an appropriate expression.

"Yes, I can see you're shocked that someone should so impose on our goodwill to make use of us in such a way. Fortunately, the earl of Northumberland, master of the tolls, was informed and took immediate steps to repossess what is rightly his."

"What sort of goods was he smuggling? Was it Baltic furs?"

"Something like that." The prioress was lying—or was she in ignorance of the truth?

Hildegard watched her carefully, but she gave nothing away.

"We will not be bothered by him again, my dear," she continued. "I need not tell you that the rumour of a dragon which has so frightened everyone was nothing but a fabrication put about by

himself to deter anyone catching him in his deceit. Now, my dear"—
she resettled herself massively and poured more wine—"you are
to stay with us in peace and solitude until you have resolved the
problems of widowhood, and I need not tell you that you may avail
yourself of everything we have to offer."

The prioress, belatedly fulfilling her duty, had tipped off the earl's
officials. And the dragon had dissolved into air. Now, ever conscious
of her priory's needs, Basilda was softening up her widowed guest
in the hope of a bequest to swell the priory's coffers.

That's how it goes, Hildegard decided, philosophically enough.
The Benedictines depended on rents and tithes and had to pay the
king's exchequer a goodly whack in taxes on their agricultural land.

The Cistercians, on the other hand, paid no land tax and had
rents, too, as well as their massively lucrative Continental wool trade
to support them. She would have felt some sympathy for the prioress if only she had not witnessed the cruelty inflicted on her dor-
mitory of penitents.

No doubt, in her defence, Basilda would claim she was only
obeying orders from the Pope.

Hildegard's few belongings lay spread out on the lumpy truckle bed
while she considered the problem of meeting Ulf at the ford, as arranged, without being followed.

Why did it matter? She was free to come and go as she pleased.
The prioress, for whatever reason, had acted properly in the end.

There were strict regulations on imported goods and on sub-
mitting taxes to the king. Only last autumn, Chancellor de la Pole
had been impeached by Parliament for alleged breaches of the tax
laws. It was a trumped-up charge by the king's enemies, of course,
in that instance. It was their way of undermining the king's authority, the better to defeat him. Even so, Northumberland held the toll

rights in this region, so why keep quiet about the raid on the tower? His seizure of the bales was justified. Hildegard's feeling of unease persisted.

Fulke himself was probably in chains by now. On the other hand, he had disappeared quickly enough when Northumberland's men appeared, so maybe he had got away. Indeed, he might escape completely if no one came forward to accuse him. The prioress might be wary of doing such a thing. The nuns were vulnerable out here, despite the high walls, and it was not unknown for witnesses to be kidnapped, or worse, to save a criminal from the weight of the law.

The question remaining was whether Fulke would be able to return this night as planned. The promise of gold might be enough to make him take the risk.

What surprised her was that Northumberland's men had not ransacked the entire building.

The old herb woman was mixing something over the brazier when Hildegard arrived at the door of her thatched hut.

She jerked round when she heard Hildegard's step. "Another question, mistress?"

"Yes. This." Hildegard held up the phial belonging to the priest.

"Ah, I see. Come inside." Wiping her hands on her apron, she took the phial from Hildegard and unstopped it. "Who gave you this?"

"I asked the sacristan what it was. She said you would know and that I might take it away with me."

Without a word, the herberer took down a book from a shelf and began to leaf through it until she came to what she wanted. She held out the book to Hildegard. "Read?"

"Yes, I can." She took it in both hands. It was a Saxon leech book.

The page it was opened at was headed "A Remedy to Ease Manly

Temptations." Underneath was a long list of ingredients, including wormwood, betony, lupin, vervain, henbane, dittander, viper's bugloss, and cropleek. She scanned them to the end, noticed the lethal effects of several of them without careful dosage, and, farther down the page, read the instructions on what to do with the resulting salve.

It involved mixing it in with sheep fat and holy salt, straining it through a cloth, then placing it under an altar and having nine masses sung over it.

In conclusion, the text claimed that when evil temptations came over a man, he should anoint his face and wherever his body most troubled him, then sign him with the cross, cense him, and his condition would soon improve.

She looked up. "Did it work?"

"Well, let's put it this way, mistress, he's not troubled now, is he?" She cackled with stony-hearted mirth.

Hildegard handed the book back to her. "Did you mix this for him?"

"Surely. It did him no harm. He seemed content with it. The prioress should have been prepared for it, cooping him up here with a lot of women in the back of beyond. A cock among hens. What else did she expect?"

"How can you be sure it did him no harm? He died, after all, and it was most certainly poison."

"This was a salve. He wouldn't be soft-witted enough to eat it."

"But if he did swallow some—?"

The pale eyes blinked twice. "It would have killed him. Instantly."

It was when the entire convent were consorting in the cloisters during their recreation period, some to read, others to pray or gossip, that

Hildegard sauntered unobtrusively towards the gate leading out of the enclosure and let herself through. Hurrying past the closed door of the lodge, she soon found her way down to the beck and began the difficult scramble over the rocks towards the trysting place with Ulf.

As far as she could tell, no one followed her.

She arrived without a sound to a point overlooking the ford.

The water ran deeper than usual. It flooded the road and swirled on between the banks towards the coast less than half a mile away. There was no one in sight. She peered into the half-light under the trees. A clink of metal alerted her, and at the same moment Ulf appeared astride his horse, accompanied by a couple of men and his little servant lad.

She went down to meet him.

He looked anxious. "Hildegard! Have you heard the news?"

"About Northumberland?"

"No, about the king?"

"Tell me." She could see it was serious by his tone of voice.

"It's his uncle, Thomas Woodstock, earl of Buckingham, duke of Gloucester so-called, and his brother Warwick, with their ally the earl of Arundel."

"What's happened?"

"They refused to meet the king at Westminster when he summoned them, and now they're mustering their armies against him. Warwick is already standing by at Waltham Cross."

"Yes. I know. Roger told me. Do they seriously intend to march against the king?"

"There's no other interpretation."

"But that means civil war!"

"They're putting out a rumour that King Richard was plotting to murder all three. They're saying Richard's pilgrimage to Canterbury the other week was to have a secret meeting with the French king's ambassadors. He wanted to offer Calais and Guînes to the French. In return, King Charles would invade England in order to rout Richard's enemies, the dukes."

"But that's ridiculous! Surely nobody believes such nonsense?"

"They're only too willing to believe it."

"But it's clearly a campaign of lies to undermine King Richard."

"They'll pretend to believe it for their own ends." Ulf was boiling with rage.

"What on earth is the king doing?"

"He's in London, trying to ensure that the Londoners stay on his side. Robert de Vere is supposed to be raising levies, if he can tear himself away from Agnes de Lancekrona's bed long enough."

"That says it all about de Vere. Where is he now?"

"They say he's in Lancashire, intending to raise forces as he makes his way through Cheshire and into North Wales. But we don't call him the earl of Oxford anymore. He's the marquess of Ireland."

"Such nonsense. Why did the king put Robert de Vere, of all men, in charge?"

Ulf gave a snort. "Because he knows he's loyal."

"But he hasn't an ounce of military experience."

"I know. It's madness—"

"What about Bolingbroke?"

"He hasn't shown his hand, but they say he intends to lead his own army down to face de Vere head-on."

Hildegard shuddered. King Richard's cousin, Henry Bolingbroke, was coldly ambitious. Clutching at straws, she said, "Surely Bolingbroke will find it difficult to raise a levy with his father's militia already in Spain?"

"Gaunt sent most of his men back; he's using mercenaries to help him hang on to his Castilian crown. Bolingbroke'll be able to call on everyone who owes allegiance to his father. His access to the

Lancastrian fortune will make it easy to buy mercenaries. His patronage will ensure the barons and every shire knight will rally to his cause. The king has no war chest. He can't finance an army of his own—thanks to the royal council running his affairs over the past year."

Hildegard felt ill at the thought. "Poor Dickon." She frowned. "He looked so isolated at Westminster last autumn when Woodstock and Arundel showed their contempt for him. They know they're the stronger and they've deliberately run the council to keep him short of funds so he can't arm himself. The prioress at Swyne told me he has a loyal following of Welsh archers but that elsewhere the magnates closed their doors against him."

"There's been no call to muster an array up here. Northumberland is sitting on his hands, waiting."

"But why?"

"There's a big argument going on about a swath of land between him and the southern counties."

"What do you mean?"

Ulf got down from his horse. "This concerns Handale. The lord de Thweng held Kilton Castle from the old king, but he died without a suitable male heir. His eldest son died in childhood and his two remaining sons were already dedicated to the Church. His lands, including the castle, have been passed down the line and have now reached a bastard son and a remaining grandchild, a girl. Whoever marries her gets his hands on a swath of the North Riding large enough to hand him the balance of power between Northumberland and the king. For anybody with ambition, it's an irresistible prize. They say Northumberland is holding fire until the matter comes to settlement, because the last thing he wants is another enemy on his doorstep. He's got enough of those over the border in Scotland."

"So if the new lord of Kilton turns out to be an ally of Boling-broke and a traitor to the king, Northumberland will dance to his tune?"

"Exactly. He won't want to be on the losing side."

"Poor Dickon," she repeated.

"I don't need to tell you that Roger de Hutton is straining at the leash. He'll call us out for the king as soon as he can. Knowing him, he'd fight Richard's enemies single-handed if it came to it."

"When he raises his army, will you go?"

"You have to ask?" He suddenly reached down to her. "My dearest, this is no greeting. Is everything well so far?"

She gripped the hand he held out. "Northumberland's men were here last night. I recognised their lion badges. They raided the tower and took away Fulke's bounty but didn't bother with whatever goods are in the upper chamber." Her expression was bleak. "It's beginning to make sense. Can you guess what Fulke had in store?"

He shook his head.

"Feathers for war arrows." Her grip tightened. "But that's nothing to what you've just told me. I can't believe it. Surely the earl will support the king? He has to!"

Ulf looked disgusted. "His present excuse is that he can't leave the northern border unguarded, for fear of the Scots."

"Wise enough," she pointed out. "We know they're still smarting after their defeat at the battle of Neville's Cross. And there are rumours that they're rearming, not," she added, "that there's anything new in that. They're always rearming. The sale of arms is what keeps this part of the country out of poverty."

"Be it so, he's waiting to see which way the wind blows. Then he'll come out in support of the victors, whoever they are. Richard has no one except de Vere, with no experience of military matters, and Sir Simon Burley, poor old devil, who might be an acclaimed war hero but is well into his sixties, fighting days over, and can't be expected to command an army on the move."

"Ulf, the mystery at Handale, the deaths of the mason and the priest, terrible though they are, seem small beer in the shadow of King Richard's predicament. I'm frightened. Do you really believe the coalition of Woodstock, Arundel, and Bolingbroke will attack the king?"

"I'm afraid I do. This is just the opportunity Woodstock has been waiting for. There's another thing. This is top secret." He looked guarded and in a lowered tone told her, "Northumberland has convened a secret meeting of all the northern chivalry. They arrive at Kilton within the week."

"To discuss the latest from the dukes?"

He nodded.

"Let's pray they come out for the king," she said.

"That may depend on the allegiance of the next lord of Kilton Castle."

Ulf's men hobbled the horses behind a screen of trees above the beck, then followed Ulf and Hildegard into the darkening woods.

As they scrambled alongside the beck, Ulf said, "I wonder how Northumberland came to discover Fulke's illegal imports?"

"This is an ideal coastline for smuggling goods in from the Baltic and Norway, as well as from the south of England."

"Goose feathers from the port at Lynn? Yes, I can see that. It's rocky, with a hundred inlets and sea caves round here. Perfect for smugglers."

"I believe they knew exactly what they were looking for," she told him. "They were fully prepared when they turned up, with several barges ready to convey the cargo out to the coast. They'll be on their way to Alnwick Castle by now." The earl of Northumberland's stronghold at Alnwick lay several hours up the coast, near Bamburgh.

"So it looks as if somebody informed on this merchant Fulke?"

She nodded. "I believe it was Prioress Basilda."

"What? I thought he was her benefactor?"

"I believe she fell out with him for some reason and decided to ditch him."

"Maybe things were getting too hot for her?"

"She's certainly bitten the hand that feeds her. Something changed. But maybe you're right that things became too much for her, with an absconding novice and the death of the priest. Have you learned anything from Alys, by the way?"

Ulf shook his head. "She seems to know nothing, neither the name of her abductor who brought her to Fulke nor the destiny planned for her. She is merely grateful to have escaped his clutches. Her chatter mainly concerned the dragon stalking the woods, how it howls through the night and terrorises the nuns."

"Well, that's all over now." Hildegard gave him a warm smile.

He said, "Hildegard, talking about the ease by which smugglers can bring in their goods along this coast reminds me of something." He smiled fondly. "Do you remember that time everybody at Hutton Castle came out to the coast on some holy day or other when my father was head huntsman? How we found a sea cave among the rocks that was only visible at low tide?"

"And how you and some other boys hid inside it and we all believed you were drowned?" She chuckled. "How could I forget! The entire household stood on the cliff top, wailing and praying for a miracle."

"My father gave us hell when we reappeared at low tide."

"I was so releaved to see you safe and sound."

"What bad boys we were!"

By now, they were approaching the clearing where the tower stood. A chill wind had sprung up and was sweeping round the grove.

"According to the weather prophets, a blizzard is on its way," he murmured as they came to a stop to survey the scene.

"That won't please the masons. They're desperate to get away. They want to leave as soon as Sueno de Schockwynde arrives from Durham. If there's a blizzard, do you think there's a chance he might not get through?"

Ulf shrugged. "If it snows hard, he won't have a chance up there on the moors. But come on. We have things to do." He unsheathed his sword. "And this is the tower. It's almost dark now. Let's break open its secret once and for all."

Chapter 19

The door gaped just as it had when Hildegard last saw it. The padlock hung loose, rattling now and then as it swung in the wind.

While they had been making their way through the woods, the tops of the trees had started to thrash in a rising wind. The air became suddenly warmer and the clouds were distended and looked ready to burst. A silvery light stole over everything.

"How strange it is," whispered Hildegard as they reached the grey stone edifice. Ulf's men seemed subdued by the weird atmosphere and the moaning wind.

"I can understand country folk believing the woods are bewitched," Ulf murmured. "The trees seem to sense something's afoot. Come on, there's nobody here," he continued in a louder tone. "Let's go in and wait." He gave instructions to his men, then led the way inside.

One or two feathers lay on the threshold and Hildegard picked one up. Ulf took it. "Feathers for war arrows. That's what this is. Northumberland must be rearming. He'll be delighted with his haul."

"Except for the fact that it was probably his own consignment that was waylaid."

"And you believe it was being held here until it could be resold to a higher bidder?"

"Don't you?"

Ulf chuckled. "He must be pleased he'll be able to keep his fletchers in work."

He took the lead up the stairs to the top of the tower. Nothing had changed since Hildegard had last been here. The padlock remained on the door of the second chamber, untouched, and the other chamber was empty. Ulf resheathed his sword.

She showed him where she had hidden from Fulke, and his teeth gleamed from out of the shadows in a brief smile. "We might as well do that again. It's likely to be fully dark by the time Fulke arrives. After one surprise raid, he'll not expect another."

"We can't be sure he'll come back."

"It'll depend on the value he attaches to the goods. If he doesn't show up, we'll break the door open and see for ourselves what's in there."

They clambered in among the crossbeams, where the shadows were darkest, and settled down to wait.

In the silence that fell once they were comfortable, Ulf reached out across the gap for Hildegard's hand and gave it a squeeze.

As Ulf had predicted, it was fully dark before they heard stealthy footsteps coming up the stairs. They approached the door of the chamber opposite and came to a stop. Hildegard's hair prickled. It was as if a ghost had silently climbed the stairs.

There was the chink of metal as somebody fumbled with the lock.

Suddenly, a light flared.

Two shapes loomed in the doorway, then disappeared as the light went out.

The door to the second chamber had been left wide open to invite Fulke to believe that there was no one inside. Now they heard footsteps shuffle. Fulke was not alone.

The light flared again.

From her vantage point high up, Hildegard saw the velvet cox-comb capuchon she had seen before. A brief glint from the hilt of a sword. Again the clink of the padlock. A short pause. Then the creaking of the door as it was pushed open.

Ulf, indistinguishable from the upright beam where he stood, was leaning forward to get a better look. The light disappeared inside the chamber. The voices of two men came, low and intimate.

Fulke said more sharply, "Shut up!"

Hildegard gripped tightly onto the beam where she was hiding. "What have they got in there?"

"So there's your gold," came a voice she recognised as the coxcomb's. Then Fulke again, smug: "And your goods, my dear fellow. Much joy to you. Now let's get out. This place is giving me the creeps."

"Afeared of the dragon, are you?" The coxcomb sniggered.

The wind was moaning around the tower with greater force. Anything could be imagined.

A shadow within the chamber doorway lengthened briefly across the floor below their hiding place, followed by another more confused shape; then the light went out as the figures began their descent.

Evidently, something heavy was being carried, as there was a scraping sound and one or two grunted instructions from Fulke. After the sound faded, Ulf reached out and tapped her on the arm. "Let's go."

He swung to the floor and lifted up his arms for Hildegard.

"We'll let them lead us back through the woods, then stop them before they reach the ford."

"What if they have a barge, like the others?"

"We'll have to take a chance."

———

"Who is that overdressed fellow with Fulke?" Ulf whispered as he and Hildegard stayed inside the tower until their quarry moved off. The grove was lit by three or four blazing torches. The customer, they observed, had brought two men with him as well as a horse. The goods he had purchased were being loaded onto the back of the horse with some difficulty.

"I've no idea who he is," she replied. "I've only ever seen him here. He arrives and departs by stealth and never shows his face at the priory."

"He looks better suited to bowing and scraping at court than in the wilds of the north."

The buyer, swathed from head to foot in a thick cloak and pulling up his hood as he went, led the horse with its load deeper into the undergrowth after Fulke. His two men followed.

When the clearing had slipped back into darkness, Ulf went to where his men were stationed. Hildegard heard a muttered exchange. When he came back, she could tell he was grinning by the tone of his voice.

"My lad crept round to have a closer look at the horse. He took one of these off its bridle as a possible means of identifying the owner."

He held something out on his palm. She tested it between her fingers. It felt like one of the small studs used to decorate belts and bridles. "It might be an emblem or it might be decorative," she suggested.

"We'll see when we get it into the light." He slipped it into the pouch on his belt. "Now it's time to follow the trail before they get too far ahead."

Giving a whistle, he summoned his men and the resourceful little servant lad, and without needing to remind them to be quiet, Ulf led the way through the woods in the steps of Fulke and his companion.

The place echoed with strange sounds like ghostly voices calling to each other as the wind continued to howl and whine through the treetops. The branches seemed to lash the clouds, and the moon had disappeared.

After some time, Ulf whispered, "Where the devil does this path lead? I feel lost already."

"It goes back towards the priory," she told him. "The way down to the beck where we came up isn't far from here."

The sound of breaking branches and the occasional snort of the horse with its burden came from ahead.

The ground began to slope. There were sudden lulls in the wind, when every sound became audible. Fulke was crashing about with no attempt at stealth. They could hear him cursing at the inconvenience of the branches that impeded his way.

Eventually, he reached the clearing where the body of the mason had been found, because they heard him call back, "This is where I leave you, my lord."

There was a grunted response; then a querulous voice said, "I'm going to break my horse's legs going back down there. Isn't there another way to the road?"

"You'll be all right if you keep to the trail I marked out for you."

"It's that steep bank that bothers me. How am I expected to lead the brute through an avalanche of rocks?"

"By necromancy, my dear fellow, that's how." Fulke was sounding extremely pleased with himself.

When the wind dropped again, Hildegard was convinced she could hear the clink of gold. "I wonder how much this coxcomb paid for his illegal goods?" she whispered. "Fulke seems to be staggering a bit."

"We'll find out soon. We'll wait until his buyer negotiates the boulders and reaches the ford; then we'll do our bit. May as well let him do the brunt of the work himself."

Hildegard was trying to catch a glimpse of the men through the constantly moving branches of the trees, which were thrashed by the wind, but it was difficult to make anything out. A few flurries of snow began a descent.

A moment later, she clutched Ulf by the arm. "See that? Is there someone ahead? Can you—" She broke off.

Fulke was saying, "Fare thee well, my lord. You know where to find me if you need anything else."

A reply from farther down the bank floated up to them. "I know where to find you, Fulke. Don't you worry about that."

And at that moment, something came rushing through the undergrowth like a wild boar, followed by a sudden hideous scream that went on and on and on.

Fulke was shouting, "What the fuck—?" And then his words were cut off in a howl of pain. Something trumpeted a call, loud enough to make the woods ring with the sound. It battered the eardrums, savage and unearthly. Hildegard put both hands over her ears for a moment. Fulke himself was bellowing like a wild bull.

From the cliff path, his purchaser made not a sound.

As unexpectedly as it had started, the parched, rasping scream stopped. The rapidly fading sound of whatever it was as it fought its way through the bushes left the grove in an unearthly silence.

Hildegard was about to step forward, the better to see what had happened to Fulke, when Ulf laid a hand on her arm. "Leave him. We're off after that other fellow with his goods. We'll catch him red-handed."

"Is Fulke hurt?" she asked, shaking off his hand.

"I don't care if he is. Wait, Hildegard," he added as she began to push through the undergrowth. "He's not our concern."

She ignored him and parted the last of the branches just in time to hear a groan that must have been Fulke, followed by the crashing of someone making off towards the priory.

She turned back.

"Well?" asked Ulf.

"He's not wounded enough to stop him from getting away. What do you think that thing was?"

She glanced nervously into the darkness. The trees seemed to be thicker here, likely to conceal anything among their twisted roots and hanging vines.

"It certainly gave Fulke a shock," he replied, his hand still gripping the hilt of his sword.

"But what was it?" she insisted, staring into the darkness. It had not been Fulke himself then, scaring the nuns into keeping out of the woods. She was shaking.

Ulf's voice came reassuringly out of the darkness. "It was probably a wounded boar or a stag. It stopped too soon to get a fix on it." Turning, he called in a low voice, "Come on, men! Let's get after this thieving, whoreson of a coxcomb, whoever he is. We'll deal with the dragon of Handale Woods later."

They followed at a good safe distance along the bank of Kilton Beck without being observed. The waters roared over the rocks so loudly as to make conversation impossible. When they neared the ford, however, there was a surprise waiting.

Unexpectedly, the woods were swarming with armed men. Ulf's little servant had gone scouting on ahead and came dashing back with a warning, breathless and agog with the sense of danger.

"Who the hell are they?" demanded Ulf under his breath as he drew his small force to a halt under cover of the trees that edged the road. "How many are there?"

"It's too dark to tell," one of the men murmured.

"Make a guess."

"No more than seven or eight, not including the old coxcomb with the packhorse."

"Does that suit you?"

"It does. Eight of them to three of us—"

"Four," protested the boy.

"Keep out of this, Pippin. It's man's work. You go and get our horses back. From what I see, they've unhobbled them. That makes them horse thieves. And you know what we do to them." He drew his sword. "Hildegard," he muttered. "Can you go back and find out what happened to Fulke?"

Aware that he wanted her out of the way if there was going to be a fight, she nodded. She had no intention of leaving yet, however, not while Ulf's life was in danger. She shivered as she watched him pull up the hood of his mail shirt. His two men and the boy followed suit. And then, on a sudden command, they swooped.

She saw the boy, quick as lightning, slip through the bushes to the horses and begin to hack through the leather rein that held them together, and then her attention flew back to Ulf, one arm raised, the sword glittering in the light of the flares his opponents carried. Then it began.

Ulf and his men had the element of surprise and put it to good use. There was a moment of stunned immobility from their opponents before they grasped what was happening; then they recovered, swords were drawn, oaths roared out, blades slashed, and the horses, caught between the two groups, reared and whinnied.

Observing the plunging melee, Hildegard saw Ulf knock two fellows to the ground. One stumbled after his fleeing horse; the other rose up with his sword pointing, but Ulf swiped it from his hand, and he, too, grabbed at a passing horse and made off into the darkness of the night.

Ulf's men fought off the rest of the detachment, which was

putting up little resistance, and apart from one fellow left groping around in the bushes for his sword, the skirmish was over almost before it began.

By now, the snow had become a blizzard.

Ulf stamped out the flames from a fallen torch, took off his
gauntlets, and wiped blood on the back of his hand. "Everybody
still standing?"

The snow was beating down in a fury, a driving storm that
blinded them all. In almost no time, they were wrapped in a white
world without directions. Only one thing was clear. During the skirmish the man and his goods had disappeared. That wasn't all.

Ulf's little servant ran up, covered in snow. He was sobbing.

"What are you blubbing for?" demanded Ulf. "It's we should
be blubbing. We made a real hash of that. We've lost our quarry."

"I couldn't help it, my lord. It's my fault." He fell to his knees
in the snow. "Pray forgive me, for I never shall forgive myself. I
shall grieve forevermore."

"Get up, you young sot wit. It's not your fault. It's mine."

"I mean your horse, my lord. Dear Petronel. He's been stolen
before my very eyes. That man, that foul lord in the velvet cloak,
he took your horse. I fear we'll never see Petronel more."

Ulf uttered a curse. He looked as if he was about to strike the
boy, but instead he turned on his heel and walked away into the
blizzard. After a moment, he reemerged.

Noticing Hildegard standing by, huddled inside her cloak,
he snapped, "I thought I told you to get off after Fulke?"

"So you did, my dearest lord," she replied with a touch of sar-
casm, "but have you ever known me to take orders other than from
my prioress in the days of my obedience at Swyne?"

She could not see his expression in the driving snow, but she
was well aware of his scowl.

He admitted he was at fault for having the temerity to suggest she do anything to help.

Aware that it was the loss of his horse that was making him ill-tempered, she suggested that he and his men set off in pursuit at once and she would now do as he'd suggested and try to follow Fulke wherever he had gone. Ulf had the grace to suggest that one of his men should go with her, but she pointed out that when he finally caught up with his quarry, he would probably need both men by his side.

"How shall we meet up again?" she asked.

"We'll get Petronel back, sort out this horse-thieving fellow, then beg a night's stay from the constable of Kilton Castle."

"He's not at home. It's his steward you'll deal with. Don't expect lavish fare. I'll see you there sometime tomorrow. Godspeed."

Ulf glanced into the depths of the woods and hesitated, but then, seeing the sense in what she said, turned to pick a horse from the ones running loose.

She stayed to watch as the men hastily mounted. The boy roped a spare they found rooting for grass under the snow. Then all four were swallowed up by the blizzard.

Underneath the protective canopy of the trees, Hildegard trod with caution. She was conscious that the beast—the wild boar or whatever it was—might suddenly charge from the undergrowth. She kept looking back over her shoulder. What light there was seemed to linger in the snow, giving it an unearthly glow. Nothing moved except for stray snowflakes slipping through the black branches overhead.

It was like walking through a tunnel after the savagery of the blizzard out in the open, but where the branches thinned, the flakes swarmed like bees in a hive. They threw themselves into her face with a stinging attack, settled on her eyelids and in her mouth. They made the ground underfoot treacherous.

Slipping and sliding, she climbed steadily back up the bank. Fulke should have reached the priory by now. He might be badly wounded. He had made enough noise during the attack.

At the summit of the cliff, she paused and peered about for a moment to detect any sign of either Fulke or the dragon. Nothing stirred. More confidently, she made her way through the silent and continually falling snow onto the path into the woods.

The gnarled trunks of hundreds of ancient trees loomed out of the darkness. They were becoming outlined in snow. It made them look like human shapes bending into the storm. The wind dropped. It left the sound of water tumbling down from the moors among the rocks. She was aware of the crimping of her own footsteps.

As she went, she wondered what sort of thing the beast was, whether something real and recognisable in the light of day, or whether the old stories were true and it was a monstrous spirit from another realm. Could there really be a dragon at Handale, a descendant of the one killed many years ago?

One thing was certain: its rasping, leathery, unmelodic howl was like nothing she had ever heard before.

Senses pricked, she moved from the protection of one tree to another. Snow was beginning to pile up under gaps in the branches overhead. She approached these mounds with caution, eyes staring to detect the slightest imprint, relieved when there was no sign of the monster's presence.

At first, she had imagined it to be deer, as Ulf had suggested, or a fox, rutting in the deep midwinter to the usual deafening screams, but now, having heard it at close quarters, she was not so sure. No fox could emit sounds so loud and with such a drone and screech.

Eager for the safety of the priory, she pushed through the undergrowth as quickly as she could, casting nervous glances from left to right.

Snow was beginning to hiss through the branches with the force of its descent. As it fell, it loaded the gaps between the trees with dead heaps like so many burial mounds. Still nothing moved in all the weird glow except for the torrent of flakes hurtling from out of the void. They settled over the ridges and ravines of Handale Woods, concealing everything under a shroud of unearthly white.

The blizzard stopped as suddenly as it started. The sky began to clear. She knew where the lodge should be, but before it came into view, she noticed something standing not far from the path that led to it through the last of the trees. Something straight, like a tree, but it was not a tree. She stopped. It was nothing to do with the lodge, either. It was moving. There was a faint dragging sound as it made its way through the snow. Was it Fulke?

She froze as the shape came nearer. Then it seemed to notice her. Its head lifted. It swayed indistinctly from side to side, as if scenting something.

It wasn't Fulke at all.

She rummaged under her cloak for her knife.

The thing was still pale, shadowy. She could not quite make it out. It started to shuffle through the snow towards her. Slowly, and with deliberation, it was drawing closer.

The moon, now almost at the full, slipped from behind a cloud.

"Heaven forfend!" Hildegard gripped her knife in horror as the thing was revealed in the metallic light.

It possessed a long snout. Leathery and unreal, it glistened in the moonlight. It was a monstrous protuberance, inhuman, a shape of nightmare. She watched, transfixed, as it swayed from side to side, sniffing with a hoarse, throaty rattling, lifting to the moon.

During one of its head swings, it paused, lowered. She saw its glance fix on her. For an endless moment, neither of them moved. Then the creature opened its maw wide in total and awful silence. Two rows of fangs shone in its black gullet. Its mouth lolled open.

Hildegard was rooted to the spot. Questions teemed through her mind. She could only gape.

CHAPTER 20

Somehow, the will to survive brought life flowing back into her limbs. Gathering up the hem of her skirts, she started to run. Heart thudding, she simply ran with only one intention, to put as much space between herself and the monster that had stared at her with such malevolence as she could. All the irrational beliefs of childhood, the nightmares, the pictures of devils on every church wall raced through her mind in a turmoil of fear.

Without knowing where she was going, she tore through the bushes, hearing twigs snap, feeling them nearly rip her cloak from her shoulders, the whiplash branches stinging her cheeks, clawing at her, trying to drag her back. She ran from the undergrowth towards a belt of trees, through barriers of saplings and over bushes. Vines clung to her ankles; roots tripped her. Breath rasping, she ran on.

There was a steep slope ahead and she scrambled up it in a shower of loose stones, mud, and snow.

When she was far enough away, she found a wide oak, came to a shuddering halt, and risked a glance back into the trees. The wood was as silent as a catacomb. Branches laden with snow drooped to the ground. There was no sound from within the entire dark maze but her own laboured and panicked breathing.

She held her breath for longer than seemed possible. Still nothing. The thing had not pursued her. Or if it had, it was standing as still as she was herself.

As she brought her senses to some kind of order, she looked about, her glance fixing nervously on an odd-shaped bush lower down the slope. It was the same height as the thing. It did not move. It seemed only to be watching her.

A weight of snow slid off overburdened leaves. She stared harder. Snow dropped again, as if a hand was surreptitiously parting the branches.

There is no hand, she told herself after a few moments. There is no dragon. There may be someone, some human force out there. But it is of this world. There is no world of ghosts.

Despite this conviction, she stood for a long time under the oak. If the thing was waiting for her to show herself, she would outwait it. Or him.

Snow began to melt inside her boots. The cold began to rise up her legs. She shifted soundlessly. Still nothing. Eventually, she decided she would have to risk revealing her hiding place or freeze to death. She would get back to the safety of the lodge. Warn the masons something was out here. Watch what effect her words had on them.

The masons.

When she looked round to choose a route back, she forgot them. She was lost.

The stars shone in their thousands. She fixed her position and began to walk. Keeping to the ridge with the trees stretched in ominous darkness below as she went, she reminded herself that there were no dragons in Handale Woods. There were no dragons anywhere except on the escutcheons of some noble houses. There were no devils, no hobgoblins, no danger other than that which came from mankind.

But the vision of that long protuberance, the widening orifice—this was no trick of the light; it was real. The thing had stared at her with a sort of astonished hatred. And then it had vanished. It had simply melted away. She had somehow outpaced it. If she had not done so, it would have caught her. And then what? She shivered.

Despite the moon, the light filtered dimly through the thick canopy of the trees. When she followed a route downhill it was like entering a tunnel. She groped her way along from tree to tree. What had looked like a fiend with a long snout had been a deer, nothing more. It had been as startled by her appearance as she had by it. Prickles of some kind of primeval fear still fingered up and down her spine. It's nonsense to keep thinking about it, she told herself. Walk.

Keep walking.

And don't look back.

It was an immense relief when she eventually saw the humped shape of the lodge some distance below. It was just a short scramble to safety. Dropping down into the undergrowth that grew around the clearing where the lodge was situated took a final steeling of her nerves. Then she was pushing her way through and running towards it.

She ducked under the eaves with a gasp of relief.

Only then did she realise that the place was in darkness.

Odd, she thought, no lights.

The guard had gone. There was the stump he'd sat on, covered in snow. Gone, too, was the pile of masons' tools, their bags, and other equipment.

She fumbled at the door but discovered a wooden beam across it, holding it shut. When she tried to lift it, she found it was held in place by a padlock and chain. She rapped on the wooden panels, but without hope, and heard only the echo of empty rooms on the other side.

With a prickle of alarm, she glanced over her shoulder into the woods. Nothing moved.

Across the masons' yard was the gaping void of the unfinished building. On the other side were piles of cut stone, a stack of logs. A pool of darkness lay between the lodge and the enclosure wall.

Steeling herself yet again, she ran from the shrouded lodge across the blazing white expanse of snow to the door in the enclosure wall. Nothing broke from the trees in pursuit. If there was anything out there, it was doing nothing more than watch.

Now she was faced with the task of digging away nearly two feet of snow to get the door open. With her back to the woods, she began to scoop away the snow with her bare hands.

The celestial voices of the choir rang out over the precinct. Astonished to find that the regular offices of the priory had continued in her absence, she realised she was in time for lauds. As she entered the cloisters, the flakes drifted to a stop. Moonlight shone full and clear on the even levels of untrodden snow.

Approaching the church door, she could hear the choir, but there was something different about the sound. She put her head to one side.

If she was not mistaken, she could hear a tenor and a bass. Men's voices?

Astonished to think it might be Fulke and one of his henchmen, she pushed the heavy iron-studded door and stepped through into the nave.

A group of nuns, faceless under their black hoods, was standing against the wall, their heads bowed, hands clasped as usual. As the last note spiralled away into the vaults, she saw who had joined them. It wasn't Fulke after all.

The great bulk of the prioress in her chair was foursquare in front of the altar, the cellaress standing as usual beside her, but— Hildegard opened her eyes wide—next to her were Dakin and the guard from Kilton Castle.

She stared hard. Dakin's wrists were still in chains, but clasped across his chest, they looked natural, like something willingly worn. The guard, face red from singing, gave him a satisfied smirk as the sound rolled away to a whisper and vanished.

They must have been here most of the time she was lost in the woods, she realized. With the service nearing its end, presumably they had been here for some time.

Not Dakin in the woods, then. Not the mason playing some prank, thinking it a good laugh to scare the nuns who strayed outside the enclosure.

It was a thought that had helped to sustain her as she stood under the oak tree and considered the existence of ghosts and dragons.

Not Dakin.

One of the other masons perhaps?

Where were they?

Not here, that was for sure.

At a suitable moment and unobserved, she opened the door and went outside again. The moon shone brilliantly. It turned the garth into a silver lake, beautiful and sinister.

Then she stared hard.

There were not one but two sets of footprints cutting across the snow—one set her own, and a second pair that came side by side with hers to the very spot where she stood now.

In panic, she glanced along the unlighted arcade with its

arching vault and columnettes. A cresset flickered above the entrance to the prioress's lodging. It was enough to show that the footprints disappeared when they reached the cloister.

She groped cautiously along to the door, turned the ring, and inched it open. A lamp burned inside the entrance.

Then she noticed gouts of snow melting on the brown tiles.

It was hard to tell whether they went straight into the parlour or turned up the stairs to the scriptorium. Without hesitating, she crossed to the parlour door opposite. It opened into the prioress's private domain.

Now it was filled extravagantly with the glaring light of many candles. A book lay open on the reading stand. Next to it a wine goblet made of glass refracted a greenish light across a wall. The fire blazed. A log shifted. The prioress's fur slippers stood warming on the hearth.

Hearing the sound of the choir singing a last amen in the adjoining church, she guessed she just had time to open the farther door and glance inside before the prioress returned. She hastened across and pulled it open.

A figure was stooping over a small chest with its lid open.

It was the nun Mariana.

Hildegard recovered first. "Is the lady prioress still at lauds?"

Mariana straightened. Her eyes shone oddly in the light from the candles. "You must know she is, mistress. Could you not hear them singing?"

Not liking her tone, Hildegard moved farther into the chamber. "What are you looking for? Something she would not wish you to find?"

Mariana allowed the lid of the chest to drop and came to stand in front of Hildegard. Her long, thin fingers went to her mouth. She gnawed her knuckles. "You are a mystery woman and no mistake."

She moved closer, so that Hildegard was backed against the wall. "What's your trade, Mistress York?" she sneered. "Are you here to confess, or shall I find a way to force the truth from out of you?"

"By Saint Benet!" Hildegard exclaimed. "You're taking airs on yourself to speak to me in this manner. Move off."

Mariana's right hand snaked out and she grabbed Hildegard's head scarf. Just as quickly, Hildegard gripped her round the wrist and jerked her hand away. The nun clawed at Hildegard's cloak, got a firm hold of it with her other hand, and used it to bang her back, hard, against the stone wall.

Hildegard was just about to give Mariana a good push when a sound from outside caused the nun to gasp in alarm. She swivelled to the door. In a trice, she had vanished.

Voices echoed from outside the prioress's private entrance from the church. Basilda and her bearers. Her chair had evidently been dumped down and someone was starting to turn the door ring. On its perch, the prioress's hawk began to squawk at the sound.

Without thinking, Hildegard dashed through the door and flew up the stairs to the scriptorium. Almost before she reached the top, the downstairs door opened and Basilda could be heard scolding the servants for scraping her chair on the doorjamb.

Anticipating the presence of Mariana in the writing chamber, Hildegard steeled herself to enter. She was just in time. The door below slammed shut. She heard the two servants, grumbling, letting themselves outside into the garth.

She glanced round. The scriptorium was empty.

In all the haste and confusion, she had scarcely had time to cast a single glance at Mariana's footwear. It had been enough, however. Like all the nuns attending lauds and matins, she was wearing leather night boots. They were designed to be worn indoors. Puzzlingly, hers showed no sign of having been worn recently in the snow.

As she waited in the darkness for an opportunity to leave without being seen, she took stock of the last few minutes.

Someone had followed her across the garth to the cloister. There their footprints had disappeared. That meant they must have either gone into the prioress's private chamber or made their way farther down the cloister arcade.

Although Mariana's presence in the parlour begged an explanation, she could not have been the one whose prints Hildegard had observed next to her own. The nun's manner was extraordinary and her hostility demanded an explanation. That for later.

Meanwhile, it was clear that the person who had followed her had hidden in the cloister and had probably watched her enter Basilda's private rooms. Might, in fact, be waiting there in the shadows under the stone vault even now.

She reimagined what had happened after she had cleared the drifts to open the door.

Somebody might have been watching her from the woods and followed her in as soon as the door was cleared. Whoever it was would have been in the woods at the same time as she had. That person might have heard the dragon roar.

She arrived at the obvious conclusion that the person might have been so close to it as to have been one and the same.

The footprints following her own were slightly smaller, narrowish, and revealed that the person's shoe had a smooth sole. Ones like many others. It seemed to eliminate the masons, who were strapping fellows who went around in heavy boots. Not Carola, though. Slight and frail-looking despite her command over the men, she might wear soft-soled boots. Hildegard had never noticed. Nor had she noticed whether Carola had been one of the shrouded figures at lauds.

Apart from this, there was another possibility, and that was that no one had been watching her in the woods. It was simple coincidence that after she'd entered and crossed the garth someone had come out of one of the buildings, the mortuary perhaps, and just happened to walk in the same direction.

But for what purpose? she asked herself. Only the church was situated in that part of the priory, and no one had followed her inside.

The voices from below were louder. The cellaress seemed to be taking her leave. The outer door slammed shut. Waiting long enough for the place to fall silent, Hildegard eventually groped her way back down into the inky well at the bottom of the stairs. The cresset had been doused and she had to feel her way along the wall to the door, and when she found it, she had to locate the door ring by running her hands over the wood panels, then turn the metal ring without letting it make a sound.

When she stepped outside, the cloister yawned black and silent, but beyond it the snow was crisp, glittering in the moonlight.

The footprints of the cellaress were plain to see, large, square-toed, regular, to match the woman's familiar pace. Another set taking the outside path towards the *dortoir* she took to be those of Mariana. They were smaller but gouged deeply into the snow, as if the person had been running.

Hildegard hesitated, then plunged off, hand on her knife, towards the safety of the guest lodge. She turned quickly. Nothing had followed her. Imagination summoned a hooded figure standing beside one of the pillars. When she squeezed her eyes and looked again, it had gone.

The night was at its coldest in the hour before dawn. The regular congregation, those who had been absolved from their penitential bonds, were forced out prematurely by the cold to gather in the warming room before prime. After tossing and turning for an hour or two on the lumpy bed, Hildegard joined them for a hot drink to start the day.

It was a silent gathering. None of the masons was present. Everybody was yawning and shivering with cold. They soon drifted away towards the church. As soon as the singing started, Hildegard went outside. The jumble of footprints in the now-freezing snow were impossible to read. She gave up and sought the warmth of the scriptorium. It was kept warm by the continually burning log fire in the chamber below.

She had been in there only a minute when she heard someone go in.

"They all heard it," a voice called. It was the cellaress. It sounded to Hildegard as if she was standing in the doorway, and her words floated clearly up the stairs.

Basilda's voice replied from inside the parlour. "If you hear any of them prattling about dragons again, clap 'em in solitary for a day or two. That should stop their nonsense. Give the silly ninnies a dose of reality. Nothing like bread, water, and solitude," she added, "to send fantasies flying." There were three loud knocks. "This!" The knocks came again. "This is real. Not some faerie nonsense about dragons and elvish lore."

"What about angels, Basilda?" The cellaress, to Hildegard's astonishment, was laughing.

"All nonsense. Simply a way of picturing the virtues just as devils image the vices. Human qualities. Why do you ask? Are they still dreaming of handsome youths with golden wings?"

"I fear so. But then, some will preserve their dreams into dotage."

"Well, we can't. We're in charge. That's what we're here for. To knock some sense into them. To tell them what's what."

"Are we so empowered? You're edging towards heresy, my dear. Wyclif would be pleased with you."

Basilda said, "Are you going to stand there all morning, Josiana? Come inside."

"Can't. Just wanted to ask about that remedy from sister herberer. Is it working?"

"Like a charm." The prioress gave a ripe laugh. "I trust it is no charm?"

"If it is and you believe it works, I shall be pleased for you to be out of pain for once."

"So shall I. And I'll believe in it right well until the next twinge. What's in it? Did she tell you?"

"Not she. I've told her to write all her recipes down before too long. Her Saxon remedies are all very well, but it'd be a shame if her own knowledge died with her."

"So, on to other matters. About our guest, how much do you think she——" Their voices dropped, and Hildegard, straining to hear what was said, was thwarted.

It was a surprise to hear them conversing so amiably. Her fear during those hours in the woods paled into nothing. What a fool she was to allow morbid superstition to take such a hold. She was as bad as the nuns Basilda derided. For the first time, she had heard her as she truly was, and she did not sound like the monster she seemed. She was simply an old woman made angry by the pain she was in because of some physical ailment, nothing more.

The rough penance she exacted from her nuns, miscreants, as most of them were, was no harsher than usual in such an establishment. If the woman seemed to have forgotten the injunction to demonstrate compassion, it was nothing new. It was a tough regimen at Handale. But there was an explanation.

CHAPTER 21

By the time the cellaress—Josiana!—left, Hildegard had already begun to sort through the priory rolls and put them into date order.
Master Schockwynde's name appeared many times over the previous twelve months. His clerks had filed meticulous accounts. The
prioress was equally meticulous in the tardiness of her payments.

Fulke's name also appeared often, his donations generous and
regular. She wondered what it was that had made him fall out with
the prioress. Or, rather, the other way round, as it seemed he was
the one to be sent packing.

Basilda must have known about his activities at the tower.
Maybe now, with the earl breathing down his neck, she wanted to
dissociate herself from him.

Another possibility was that he had kept her in ignorance of
what was going on in the remote woodland, keeping her sweet with
his donations, and now that she had discovered the truth, she didn't
like it.

It would have been easy enough to keep his trade secret, as no
one from the priory had set foot in the woods since the rumour of
a dragon had started to spread. Fulke was probably at the back of
that, too. It had turned out to be a sure way of keeping a lid on
things.

The other view, that Basilda willingly connived at his secret trade, was a possibility not to be discounted. There would be a rich dividend in it for her. If that were the case, then why had she cut off this source of income?

As she worked steadily between prime and tierce, the snow fell softly without a pause. Now and then, she glanced out of the window. She saw the cow bier gradually being buried under a drift of snow. The little cowherd was nowhere to be seen.

It was so gloomy in the scriptorium that she kept the candle alight. Curse the expense. She would make an extra donation before she left. She was looking forward to meeting dear old Ulf later in the day. He might already have news about Alys and her guardian. He would also, surely, have got his horse back. And the identity of the coxcomb and the nature of his purchases would have been discovered.

All that remained to trouble her was her unease over the two recent deaths that had occurred. Giles and the priest.

The animal attack on Giles was not much of a mystery, as it was likely to have been a wolf or wild dog that had attacked him. The death of the priest was a different matter.

Either he had taken the poison accidentally, groping under the altar for the holy vessels used in the mass, his mind on other things, and had somehow contaminated the chalice before putting it to his lips—an unlikely explanation, Hildegard decided—or he had taken it deliberately, some deep sorrow or frustration driving him to self-hatred. It was a dramatic way to commit the sin of suicide, however, and it did not fit with the impression she had of a rather shy, retiring, and pious young man.

The third possibility—and the most likely in her opinion—was that he had been murdered. It was what the nuns thought, too, albeit they believed it was death by witchcraft.

Remembering what the priest had told her about the inmates

here, she gave an involuntary shudder. Someone, within the enclosure, was walking around under a cloud of guilt.

The puzzle was, how had he managed to fall foul of a murderess?

There seemed little more she could do to solve the mystery. Both the herberer and the sacristan seemed to have their suspicions, the latter made nervous by what might be uncovered. The coroner had been called, however—she had made sure of that—and when the weather cleared, both matters would be investigated by the appropriate authorities. The bodies would be buried. Mass said. The end.

Again she was haunted by a memory of the spy Rivera. His words came back to her and seemed now to be a portent of his own violent murder: *The purpose of life is death.* He had walked unflinchingly towards his own death at the hands of the London mob.

For a long while she gazed out of the window at the empty sky.

Snow was still seeping from between the clouds.

With an effort, she forced herself to the task in hand.

Working steadily for some time, she eventually had everything completed to her satisfaction. She replaced the neatly sorted rolls on the shelf in the aumbry where she had found them, then stood on tiptoe to fetch down a few others from the highest shelf. Obviously older than the ones below, they were covered in dust. Blowing it off, she took them over to the desk by the window and settled down again to put them in order.

What she unrolled onto the desk in the first one was a list of penitents, those who had been admitted to the priory since its foundation. They were names from many generations ago.

She scanned the Latin hurriedly, realising that this was not part of the work the prioress had asked her to do. She could not help being interested in the old names, however. They had an antique sameness, showing the Saxon origins of the early convent and the nuns who had chosen to settle in this remote place: Elfleda, Frea, Winifred, Agnetha, Gerda, the names of their vills an added means of identification. She could not help wondering about them.

She rapidly read through these rolls, and by the time she reached more recent rolls, she was already beginning to rewind them almost as soon as unrolled, because they were clearly not relevant to her task.

And then a name in one of the more recent ones caught her attention: Mariana of Stillingfleet.

So the nun was from a place near York. Not far from her own part of the world, as it happened. Her thoughts switched to the woman's hostility and apparent suspicion. Could she have recognised Hildegard as a nun of Swyne? No, she decided, it could not be that. And anyway, she would have said something by now. Given her evident anger, she would have gloried in revealing Hildegard's true identity if she had known it.

She read further. The reason for being sent here was added after the name and date of arrival, along with the date when her penance ended. It was as Mariana had told her. Her sin: venery. It did not say with whom. Nor was there anything about the fate of the child she had borne. Her punishment and two year's solitary confinement had ended a year ago. It would make her child about three years old if it had lived. So recent. No wonder she still raged.

Feeling that she was spying into what did not concern her, she was about to wind the roll up, when she caught sight of the name Desiderata. So she had arrived as a penitent as well, shortly after Mariana. Then a word leaped out that sent a shock through her, but before she could reread it, a surreptitious tread on the stairs disturbed her.

With an irrational desire not to be caught reading the document, she hastily rolled it up and swept the whole lot back onto the top shelf. She was just in time. The door opened.

It was the cellaress, Josiana.

Her glance flew round the room before it came to rest on Hildegard. "Mistress York. I wondered who was in here." She glanced at the still-burning candle on the desk near the window. "At work so early?"

"I felt desperately cold last night, and this was the warmest place I could think of."

"Disarmingly honest of you."

Hildegard gestured towards the completed files. "I also wanted to finish this little chore before I left. I'm now happy to say I have done so." She made up her mind in that instant. "If an escort through the woods can be arranged, I would like to leave today. I trust my work and the donation I intend to make will be adequate to show my gratitude for your hospitality?"

Josiana did not answer straightaway. A strange look of triumph entered her eyes.

"My gratitude for your work, mistress. However, I'm afraid an escort will be impossible. You will not be able to leave the priory."

"Will not? What do you mean?"

"I mean that we are snowed in. We are cut off entirely from the outside world. You are our prisoner. You must resign yourself to our hospitality until the thaw."

With a narrow-lipped smile of derision, Josiana went out.

Bone white. Desolate. The enclosure walls streaked and pitted with the stuff. The skeleton trees pressing close and overtopping the perimeter. All the odd angles of the roofs laden.

The thatch of the priest's house, separate in the outer garth, hidden under a mound of snow. Not a breath of wind. Icicles hanging from the gutters.

Hens in the yard not moving from their perches but merely

fluffing out their feathers and complaining. Pigeons absent, hidden in their cote. The pigs did not appear. The cows in the barn moaned at milking time but stayed within the byre.

The cloister garth was a desert, its silence broken only by the tolling of the bell and, minutes before the daily offices, by the stamping of boots in the doorway of the church. The barefoot novice was allowed a pair of scuffed pattens, which made a clicking sound on the tiles. But even the penitents were silent in their cells.

Wrapped tightly in two cloaks and a double pair of leggings, Hildegard paced the perimeter, making a complete circuit of the wall and finally reaching the priest's house again. No one had entered or left since the snows fell. Here, in the farm garth, the snow came up to her knees, and she imagined how much worse it would be on the unprotected moors road. Careless of her trail of footprints, she went up to the door of the house and pushed it open.

A dank gloom permeated the simple dwelling. A stale smell of unwashed garments hung in the air. No more than a single chamber on the ground floor, with a bed in one corner and wooden stairs to an upper room in the other. A crucifix on the wall above the bed. A cloak on a hook. Not even a rug to warm his feet when he rose in he middle of the night for matins.

She mounted the creaking wooden stairs, a short flight onto the plank floor of his reading chamber.

It was a bleak place. Enough to send into a spiral of despair anyone who lived here unless they possessed a deep faith in another, better world to come. An aumbry held a few books. A folding table he'd used as a desk was open, pushed against the window, with a chair aslant as it had been left. A quill or two. A sharpener. An inkhorn. And now the patina of a few days' dust.

His missal lay on the deep sill of the window opening. It was well thumbed. The usual thing. A few notes in the margins in a spidery, careful hand. She replaced it as she found it. No confession of self-harm had fluttered out. No last words to those he was leaving behind.

Frost drew leafy scrolls across the window blind. She pushed it to one side and looked out onto the herb garden.

Serried ranks of frozen leaves poking above the snow. At the far end, a curl of smoke over the thatched hovel where the herberer lived. She could almost smell the honeyed warmth inside of some potion designed to keep the chill at bay.

She went back down the stairs.

On the back of the door was something she had overlooked as she came in. Only now, on the way out, was her attention drawn to it. She reached to take it down. It was a belt. Thin, fine-grained leather, with a pattern of roses cut into it, designed to be wrapped several times round the hips over a cotehardie or a kirtle.

At one end was a silver emblem in the shape of a heart, and at the other a hand. There was an inscription, so small she had to hold it up to the light to read it. *Take my heart.*

A strange gift to give to a priest. Gifts of belts were commonplace between lovers, however. The words of the herberer returned with renewed meaning. *A cock among hens. What else did she expect?*

She replaced the belt on the back of the door and, deep in thought, let herself out.

Suicide? Was that it? Suicide for what he could not have? How tortured by carnality he would have had to be to take such a cure.

Recrossing the outer garth, she suddenly felt watched. Turning, Hildegard thought she caught sight of the hem of a black robe disappearing round a corner of the stores. It was a shadow. Nothing.

I've got to get out of here, she thought. With the snow as bad as this, Ulf would not have been able to get through. Penned, and furious that it was so, she joined everyone in the warming house before mixtum.

There was a feeling of something bubbling underneath the surface, like a kettle about to boil.

Hot bread at least, brought in by the cop-shod novice. Hands reached out to take a piece. Everyone made ravenous by the cold. Cheese going the rounds on a platter. Warm wine from a pot jug. Cinnamon floating in it. Nutmeg.

Hildegard sipped it. There was something else. It brought a flush to the cheeks of the nuns. One or two giggled over a joke. Another guiltily ran through her beads with downcast eyes. Carola came in.

She, too, was flushed, but more from a brisk walk than from the wine she had yet to taste. She caught Hildegard's eye and came over. "Still here, I see."

"You, too."

"Sueno will never get through in this. We're going to be trapped here forever."

"My feelings entirely. Is it really impassable down by the river?" she asked.

"Yes. Matt tried to get out that way this morning, but with no luck. It's in drifts waist-high. He came back blue with cold."

"It's a pity we have no boat."

"You'd risk a drowning if you tried that. Don't you think we've already considered it?"

"And then there'd be the problem of getting anywhere else, even if you did reach the road. Unless you wanted to go to Kilton Castle, of course."

Carola gave her a sharp glance. "Why would anyone want to go there?"

Hildegard shook her head.

The wine jug came round again. No one refused.

"How did you get permission to be allowed inside the enclosure?"

Carola looked pleased. "We persuaded the captain of the guard from Kilton to plead for us. He said he couldn't be held responsible if Dakin escaped while he—the guard, that is—slept. 'They cannot spare another man from Kilton at present,' he told the prioress. 'They're expecting important personages and need all the men they possess. Which ain't many,' he added to us." She brought a rueful smile to her face. "Dakin and the guard seem quite content to be bound to each other. We'll never let Dakin live it down." She frowned, adding, "Assuming he's ever freed."

"I'm sure Prioress Basilda will withdraw her charge when she realises he's going to fight back. After all, he has the guild behind him. I'm sure they'll need strong proof before they'll allow the accusation to stand." She paused. "Who is the important personage due to arrive up at Kilton? Do you know?"

Carola shook her head. "Some local knight, presumably. The guard was no doubt exaggerating his importance." She shook out her dark hair. "I'd no idea I'd be kicking my heels in this godforsaken place all winter. I'll never work outside Durham again."

Hildegard shared her dismay and as she did so, she chanced to glance up.

Desiderata was watching them both with an unfathomable intensity. When she noticed Hildegard look across, she turned away.

"Where are the men staying?" she asked Carola.

"In that guest wing with Fulke."

"Now he's gone."

"Gone? No, he's still here. He's got a cold and is having his meat and drink sent up to him."

"At the prioress's invitation?"

"I suppose so. Why?"

So after making his sale to the coxcomb, after his assault in the woods, he had come back and been welcomed in? She asked,

"Has he mentioned anything about the so-called dragon attacking him?"

Carola laughed aloud. "What? I'm sure he would have if—" She peered into Hildegard's face. "Are you serious? When was this supposed to have happened?"

"The other night," replied Hildegard, deliberately vague. "I'm astonished he didn't mention it. I thought he'd been injured." She stopped, realising that she had said more than she needed.

Carola gave her a strange look. "So you saw it yourself?"

"I heard something."

"We all heard something." Carola turned away. "We were inside the enclosure by then."

"All of you?"

"What is this? Has something happened?"

It was Hildegard who turned away this time, asking, "What is it? Or, more to the point, who is it? What is their purpose? Is it just a mean trick to frighten everybody? Or is there more to it?"

When she turned, Carola was biting her lip. "Do you think it's some prankster from the castle, mistress? Putting the wind up the nuns. You know what lads are like," she added.

"I thought it might be Fulke. Trying to keep everybody out of the woods so he can—" She broke off. "Something like that?"

She made an excuse to end the conversation by going to get more bread from the platter on the other side of the chamber, and by the time she had broken some off and returned to finish what she'd been saying, everyone was beginning to move off to the next office.

Feeling as if she was on a treadmill, Hildegard gulped it down and followed last of all.

CHAPTER 22

Time seemed to drag. It was the feeling of being cooped up against her will that was so hard to bear. Hildegard knew that. For the last year, she had been freer than at any time in her life. Free to walk the long pilgrim route to Santiago de Compostela. Free from the oath that bound her three times over. Of those, the vow of poverty was the least exacting.

She heard someone following her across the garth. It was Mariana. When they reached the shelter of the guest chamber, she called, "Mistress York?"

Hildegard turned. She eyed the nun warily. "What is it?"

Mariana dipped her head. "I have come to beg your forgiveness. Lord knows I don't deserve it. You caught me out in a place I should not have been in. I imagined you had been sent to spy on me." Her face puckered, eyes red-rimmed, the faint scar where Hildegard had defended herself showing up.

"Who would send me to do a thing like that?"

"Our most holy mother prioress, Basilda, of course."

"Why?"

"She does not trust me. Nor does Master Fulke. I thought you were one of his allies."

"Hardly likely—although I can see how you might have imagined it," she added, remembering that she was not wearing her nun's habit. "Why do they not trust you?"

"I shall always wear my sin like a brand on my forehead. They will never allow me to forget it."

"Mariana, may I ask you something?"

"What is it?"

"Where is your baby now?"

Sister Mariana gazed off into the distance, unseeing, eyes filling. "They won't tell me. I trust he's being cared for and loved."

"I'm sure he is. Can you not find out? Surely they won't withhold his whereabouts from you if you demand to be told?"

"They say it's part of my punishment for breaking my oath. That I deserve to live in this state of—this state of not living. In their eyes," she added bitterly, "my tears can never wash away my sins."

"I wish I could help."

Mariana's face bore a strange, ferocious look and her lips trembled. "There is no help. And as I'm condemned to hellfire, as they constantly tell me, then nothing matters much. Why should I care about anything?" Her head lowered and she pulled her hood up. "That's all I wanted to say. My rage was not meant for you."

As she was about to walk away, Hildegard put out a hand to detain her. "A moment. If I may ask, were you looking for anything special in the prioress's private belongings?"

Mariana nodded. "I thought there might be some clue as to where they had sent him. But it was just her store of gold."

"Perhaps there is a record elsewhere?" She took a risk and added, "Perhaps in the scriptorium, where the other records are kept?"

"Do you think so?" A brief flash of hope appeared in her eyes. Then she frowned. "I daren't go back up there. I've tried it before. They'd flay me if they found me there again."

"But not me."

Mariana looked at her in astonishment.

"No promises," Hildegard warned. "My time is my own at present. Let me try."

As Hildegard walked away towards the *dortoir,* she was aware of someone watching from just inside the guesthouse porch. It was a nun. One of the prioress's spies, she supposed. But when she saw who it was, she went cold. It was Desiderata. The woman was smiling. A few fair curls escaped from under her wimple. With hands clasped inside her trailing sleeves, she stepped into Hildegard's path.

"Dear Mistress York, this weather must be very trying for you?"

"Indeed. As it is for all of us."

The woman was all smiles and dimples. Hildegard wondered if there was another nun with the same name. It was difficult to believe what she had seen written in the roll.

"I noticed you earlier, chatting, so friendly to us, and as the rules are relaxed, I thought I would stroll over to have a chat, too. The guesthouse becomes quite a little haven of friendship at times like these. I love to hear news from the outside world. It reminds me how fortunate I am to be a sister at Handale."

"You are indeed," murmured Hildegard. "Clearly you don't find it harsh."

"Harsh?" She gave a peal of laughter. "If it is harsh, it is because we deserve it. But I am privileged. I am trusted, unlike some of the nuns here." Her small mouth pursed in distaste. "Shall we go inside, out of the cold, and continue our conversation?"

Hildegard spent a dull hour listening to Desiderata chat with all the vacuity of a provincial housewife. She would do well at Watton, she decided, remembering the nunnery not far from Meaux where the well-off widows of knights and the more distinguished kind of merchant ended their days.

It was no penitential Benedictine prison house. Quite the opposite. If Desiderata were as innocent as she appeared, she would enjoy the chattering company.

She risked broaching a question to see what answer she would get. "I wonder, did you ever consider living in a gentler part of the county, such as Watton?"

Desiderata looked shocked. "But they're followers of Giles of Sempringham. I could never follow him. He's an Englishman. I've heard they're quite licentious. They take their pet animals into mass and wear whatever they like and have a constant stream of male visitors." Her light tone belied the sneer that briefly flitted over her lips. "They appear to find their oath of chastity impossible to keep." She gave that sudden catlike smile again—so soft, she was almost purring. "But you don't have to bother about that, mistress," the nun blandly continued. "Your couplings are an accepted sin as long as you obey the Church's rules and fornicate only for the procreation of children and within the times and days decreed by our Holy Father, the Pope. Is your husband a York man?"

"Dead—" Something caught at her throat to prevent her from saying more. It was astonishment, either at her own ease in lying or grief at the deeper truth that lay beneath. "I must go," she added hurriedly.

But, with her mind still on the same topic, Desiderata had not heard her. "Women who behave in such a way deserve to be whipped, naked and in public, as fornicators, for flouting the Rule. Like that novice who disappeared. May she burn in hell. But burning is too good for them. She was a whore, hanging round the priest at every opportunity, driving him to sin. Those sort deserve to suffer cold steel—I've heard that in Spain they have a very special kind of torture for whores. It involves sewing their eyelids open and inserting—"

"No, I must go. I have something urgent to attend to." Hildegard backed away.

The guesthouse was crowded. Desiderata was not the only nun to have come in to take advantage of shelter from the bad weather and the relaxation of the rules. The masons were there, too, including Dakin and his guard, and Carola, of course. They were standing nearby and turned to stare at her as she made a clumsy exit into the open air.

It was a relief to escape such venomous prattle. With her promise to Mariana in mind, she made her way across to the scriptorium. There might be a reference in one of the rolls to the nun's baby and its whereabouts.

The task she had set herself was not as easy as she had supposed. The rolls referring to the running of the priory—the decretals, the copies of replies to a large number of official missives, and the copies of judgements taken on visitations by the bishop—were in no sort of order.

Unsure where to begin, she decided to order them by date. That way, she could narrow it down to the year when Mariana had been brought here.

The problem then was that many of the rolls were undated, so she had to open them, skim through the contents, deciphering the handwriting as well as the Latin and French as best she could while looking for clues to the date. Many different scribes had contributed to the records. Some had written in what the prioress would call a fair court hand; other documents were crabbed and blotted and almost illegible.

It took time.

The day drew on. She was forced to light the candle again, but it scarcely made an impression on the northern gloom.

At nones, she heard the nuns go down, the choir strengthened by Dakin and his guard. Heard returning footsteps, a door bang shut, silence again. Patiently, she continued the task. It was astonishing what was recorded here. With a sigh, she opened another undated roll and began to read.

With her back to the door to get the most of the light from the window, she was unaware of anyone having come in until she felt a cold draught tucker at the edges of her sleeve. It snuffed out the candle at once.

She made an exclamation and half rose.

Before she could turn, something caught round her neck and tightened. She began to struggle for breath. It was a ligature of some kind. Grappling at it as she fought for breath, she tried to get her fingers underneath it, but it was too tight. She kicked out at her assailant. It made little difference.

She was beginning to choke. It had happened quickly, the ligature thrown round her neck with such deftness, she had been taken completely by surprise. She fell against something. Tried to kick out again. Missed. Stumbled. Felt the noose tighten.

The blood was pounding in her eardrums. She felt as if her lungs would burst. She could not pull a single breath in.

She fell to her knees. Everything became black and swam away.

Matt was bending over her. His face was very close and illuminated by a taper.

Hildegard clawed at her neck and found something cutting deep into the flesh. She pulled at it and was able to take a deep, nurturing breath.

"What happened?" Her voice was hoarse.

"Take it easy, mistress. No hurry. Your attacker is gone."

"Who was it?"

"I've no idea. The culprit wore a hood."

"What are you doing here?" she asked, suspicion tinging her voice.

"Carola said you wanted to get away. I thought I'd come and ask you if you were game to try tomorrow morning—if there's no snow in the night and we go prepared, we should be able to dig our way through. Steady," he added when she tried to get up. "I thought you'd had it."

"My neck hurts." She rubbed it, winced, then massaged it where the ligature had bitten into the flesh. It was like a cord of fire round her neck.

After a moment or two, Matt was able to help her to her feet. "Come down when you feel you can walk. I'll get you a drink from the buttery. It's lucky I arrived when I did."

"Luckier still if you'd arrived before the person managed to get this thing round my neck," she croaked, trying to make a joke of it. The effort to laugh was too painful and she nearly choked as bile rose up. She unwound the noose completely, rolled it into a ball, and put it inside her sleeve. She would look at it later in a good light.

Matt held a taper and lifted it to show the way down the stairs. As he did so, her last memory before being attacked flooded back.

She recalled what she had just discovered among the priory rolls. It was so sensational, she imagined it must be a delusion brought on by being nearly choked to death. But she knew it wasn't. It had been there, written in an elegant hand. It was nothing to do with Mariana and was not what she had been looking for. It came from an earlier time and had been kept separately. The whole place would be rocked to its foundations when, or if, the truth came out.

CHAPTER 23

"And I noticed the door was open, so I went straight in, and whoever was in there heard me and nearly knocked me flat while rushing out, leaving Mistress York lying on the floor inside. My first thought was, Oh no, she's dead." Matt gave Hildegard a quick glance. "Then she gave a sort of choking sound. I was that glad."

Hildegard was shivering, despite a beaker of warm wine held between both hands. "I owe my life to you, Matt."

"I hope it's a debt I'll never have to call in." He grinned, and she realised he was still young enough to believe he was immortal.

"I hope you're right," she said. "But if, one day . . ."

"Morbid," clipped Carola. "I suppose it means you won't consider making an attempt on the outside now?"

Now, more than ever, Hildegard wanted to say. Instead, she shook her head. "It won't stop me."

"Straight after prime, then?"

"At prime, Matt, as far as I'm concerned," she replied. "Less chance of anyone seeing us, as they'll all be in church." She gave him a level glance. "I assume you feel discretion will be a good thing?"

He gave Carola a quick look, as if to find out how much he should tell her, then nodded.

Carola said, "We believe our messages to the master and the coroner did not get out."

"But the prioress said—"

"We know," said Matt, interrupting her. "But we're all of the same opinion."

Hildegard glanced round the warming room where Matt had taken her after obtaining wine from the buttery. The nuns had returned to their cells and only she and the masons were present, apart from one of the conversi, who was stoking the fire and intent on his job.

She asked in a low voice, "Do you have a reason for coming to such a conclusion?"

Hamo, silently stroking his red beard until now, spoke up. "Two deaths? She won't want coroners asking questions."

"Two very different deaths," Hildegard pointed out.

"And the rest," he added. "The comings and goings in the woods." He held her glance. She remembered what a good view he'd had from the top of the scaffolding and wondered now how much he knew.

"I don't mind telling you, I shall be glad to get away, especially after what has just happened." She fingered the welt on her neck "But before I leave, I would like to know who did this. I feel there should be some kind of reckoning."

"Best leave well enough alone," suggested Hamo unexpectedly. "You'll never win against the Church. They'll stick together, even when they know one of them's a bad apple. They'll want to deal with it in their own way. Best out of it altogether, say I."

"One question." Hildegard looked from one to the other and her glance lingered on Dakin. "Where was Master Fulke just now?"

"He's still moaning and groaning in his bed," volunteered Will. "I only hope what he's got isn't catching."

"That's settled, then. We leave at dawn." Matt was decisive.

"Carola will stay with Will to keep an eye on Dakin. It'll take three of us for safety's sake in the snow. We'll get to the nearest town and put the fate of Giles in the hands of the coroner. Then we'll let his people know what's happened."

A discussion of the condition of the roads followed, the difficulties of a courier's reaching Durham in such weather to inform Master Schockwynde of his journeyman's fate, and the possibility of hiring horses and so on, back and forth, until they arrived at the conclusion that they would know the answers for sure only when they got out and saw the state of the roads for themselves.

Only one thing was certain: Matt and Hamo would leave at prime and Hildegard was welcome to travel with them.

Eventually, she left them and returned to her chamber in the guesthouse. Every shadow alarmed her. She took out her knife before opening the door and held it ready under her cloak. When she got inside, she put a chair against the door. The sound of it scraping on the floorboards if somebody tried to get in would give her time to defend herself.

She sat down on the truckle bed and took out the noose from where she had put it inside her sleeve. When she held it up in the candlelight, she gave a gasp of recognition. The emblems at each end of the piece of leather, a hand and a heart, were unmistakable.

She was right to have felt she was being watched when she left the priest's house. Somebody had seen her go in. They had feared what she might have found. They had tried to stop her from taking the information elsewhere.

But she had found nothing of note. There was no one here she could offer information to even if she had found anything out. What was there to find out?

More puzzled than ever, she put the belt inside her scrip for safekeeping, packed the rest of her things, and lay down on the bed with the intention of getting a few hours' sleep before the bells summoned everyone to compline. She must have missed vespers. That was when her attacker had seen fit to enter the scriptorium. Despite what the masons had said, it suggested someone other than a nun had entered the scriptorium. The nuns would be loath to miss one of the holy offices and would no doubt fear having to explain themselves to the prioress.

But a guest other than herself was still within the enclosure: Fulke.

Unable to sleep when there were so many questions waiting to be answered, she eventually got up and went out, taking the cresset from its holder beside the door to light the way.

A breeze caught at the flame, making it dance through the metal bars, sending sparks spiralling into the already-darkening sky. Uncaring whether there was a watcher in the cloisters this time, she cut across the grass towards the priest's house in the farm garth.

She did not approach the front door. Instead, she held the lighted torch so that she could inspect the footprints in the snow leading to it.

Her own had been the first to mark the snow, but now there were others: one set going in and coming out, and one more on top of the others. Snow was sprinkled in two of the three sets of prints, in her own and in those of the person who had gone into the house after that. The third set were more recent and had been made after the last snowfall. That would put them at sometime after nones, when there had been a further brief flurry.

One of these two had taken down the belt from behind the door and later, during vespers, tried to throttle her with it.

It still made no sense. What could they believe she had seen in the priest's house that was so dangerous?

It was true that she had stumbled on a secret of life-and-death importance that afternoon, but it was a matter now for one person only.

The prints yielded very little in themselves. There was nothing to distinguish one from the other except size and length of stride, all quite average. If she saw them again, she doubted whether she would recognise them.

Still holding the cresset aloft, she made her way back into the garth with her eyes fixed on the ground. It would have been easier to find a pin in all the trampling to-ing and fro-ing that had gone on that day. Now the bite of frost was crisping them into uneven ridges.

She followed one promising-looking set but lost them near the warming room. She tried a different approach and made her way to the far side of the garth to the door that led from the frater of the conversi. Here again the snow was trampled into illegibility. Hamo was just coming out as she approached.

"You're brave being out and about in the dark," he said, greeting her.

She indicated the building. "Is this where you're being lodged?"

"It is, for my sins. Few creature comforts. We were better off in our cosy little den in the woods."

"Despite the dragon?"

He roared with laughter.

"Is Master Fulke still in residence, Hamo?"

"If he is, I haven't laid eyes on him. They say he's still suffering from an ague."

"He really hasn't set foot outside today?" She had already asked the masons as as group and wondered if Hamo would bear them out.

He puckered his face. "They're saying he daren't! Not since he came roaring in the other night shouting something about the dragon, or so I'm told. They all thought he'd been drinking."

"Who told you this?"

He grinned. "That buxom dairy woman you probably haven't noticed."

She smiled. "No, I hadn't."

"She's sent over to bring him milk and pottage every now and then. Should be here again soon."

Hamo went off round the corner, presumably for a piss against the wall, and Hildegard strolled back across the garth, still staring at the ground.

There was no reason for anybody to have attacked her. It made her wonder if she had been mistaken for someone else.

Imagine they had been after someone who used the scriptorium? Mariana was the only one Hildegard had seen in there. Why anyone should want to attack so pathetic a creature, she could not fathom. Whoever it was had known about the belt in the priest's house. That person had gone there, found it, and taken it. It was a pretty thing. It was clearly a love token. Maybe whoever had given it to the priest was frightened it would get into the wrong hands and lead back to the giver. Then, later, decided it was a useful instrument of murder, stupidly—or with a macabre sense of humour.

Did that mean there was more to the priest than that half-humorous remark about a cock among hens? The sacristan had been shocked to her shoes when Hildegard suggested he might be at fault. But maybe one of the nuns had taken a fancy to him? And driven by jealousy . . . She couldn't see it herself, but then, there was no accounting for taste.

If he had been unwise enough to succumb to the hothouse atmosphere and indulge in a liaison with one of the nuns, then the woman involved would have been punished horribly and, depending on who was making the judgement, the priest would have stood in danger of excommunication and any future in the Church would have been jeopardised. He'd been no abbot or bishop who could pull some weight to justify himself. This is no Watton Priory, either, where anything goes, she thought.

She remembered Mariana's fate and the penitents in the cells. The culprit, or lover, if there was one, was more likely to be one of the kitchen servants than a nun. That way, the priest would have been the one to be judged by canon law and the girl would simply have been thrown out.

If there was a girl, if the priest had been having an illicit affair, if, if, if.

Sighing, she turned into the porch of the guesthouse, drew her knife, and entered with the flaming cresset held in front of her. Apart from the leaping shadows the latter caused, a tomblike stillness hung over the place. She replaced the cresset, lit a taper, went to her chamber, and wedged the chair against the door.

Ulf would be at Kilton Castle. He would have accosted Fulke's customer and got his horse back. It was his horse that would have been uppermost in his mind.

Nothing to be done now but wait for morning.

She drifted off to sleep. But something terrifying woke her. At first, she didn't know where she was and she reached for her neck, as if fearing another attempt on her life. But then she woke up fully and realised that it was the same hideous roar they had heard in the woods a few nights ago. Now it seemed to be in the enclosure itself.

She threw back her covers and ran to the window. Others were coming out onto the garth. The moonlight picked out more than a dozen figures—nuns wrapped in cloaks, some barefoot from the *dortoir,* the conversi from the kitchen quarters, finally the cellaress, the sacristan, and the subprioress from the direction of the prioress's chamber.

They stood in the moonlight as the roar came again and again.

It was somewhere outside the walls.

One or two nuns fell to their knees and began to pray. The cellaress ordered lights to be fetched. Hildegard found her cloak and boots, remembered her knife, and went outside.

Carola came stumbling out after her a few moments later, but the lodgings on the other side of the garth remained in darkness.

"Can't those fellows of yours hear it?" asked Hildegard.

"They sleep like the dead," she replied. "Where is it coming from?"

"Outside, thank Saint Benet."

As quickly as it had started, the hideous sound ended. Everyone stood in silence to listen, and the praying nuns were shushed. No sound indicated whether the beast was still out there or not. Eventually, when it was clear it had gone away, they began to return to their beds, until the subprioress, as pale as paper, suggested they repair to the church to give thanks for their deliverance from yet another threat from the devil.

Hildegard trudged over to the frater above the stores, where the masons, the guard, and Fulke were sleeping. The door was open when she reached it and a bleary face poked out.

"What the devil was that row?"

"The dragon, we're to assume."

"Not that again."

It was Hamo and he made as if to go back inside, but Hildegard said, "Are the others with you?"

"Sleeping like the dead. Get some sleep. We're starting first thing, remember?" With this, the door closed.

Sighing with dissatisfaction, Hildegard went across to the church. At least she could find out how those in the priory were going to deal with it.

There was no sign of Basilda, either in her chair or out of it.

Her second in command, however, stood before them in the

gloomy cavern of the church, her face paste white, eyes staring with fear, and for the next half hour lambasted the nuns for their sinfulness, which had surely brought them to the attention of the devil.

"It can only be a demon of Beelzebub who torments us," she bawled. "His mission is to destroy this holy place and all in it. Confess and repent, or suffer in the eternal fires. Root out the sinners lest they bring us all to perdition. We are led astray and lost and it is the fault of those who sin and glory in their filth like swine in a bed of swill."

Her shrill voice continued its accusations, listing a variety of sins, all the seven deadly ones and many more that other folk outside the tight rule of the Order would regard as nothing. Groaning and self-beatings were aroused by this. Hildegard watched in horrified amazement. Only Mariana, cowed and miserable, sank down onto the tiles and kept silent.

Carola touched Hildegard on the sleeve. "Mistress, this is not for us. We'd best leave."

Outside in the cloister, she said, "Maybe they are better people than we are, but I fear they see the devil everywhere. If they looked for angels, maybe they would find a more natural joy in life."

"Why don't you come away with us in the morning?" Hildegard asked.

"I need to stay as witness for Dakin and because we've received no pay for our work. I daren't leave before we've come to some agreement with the prioress. I want to give her no excuse for withholding our commission fee. She'll cite the fact that the work isn't finished if we all leave." She looked as if she was about to say something else but stopped herself.

"What is it?"

She shook her head. "Only something to do with the nature of the work. It's something that goes beyond our usual remit." She turned away. "I fear we're in a web and I can't see a way out of it.

If I fail, the guild will claim it's because I'm a woman and should not have been entrusted with such responsibility." She glanced back at Hildegard as she took her leave and added mysteriously, "A man might not have my moral qualms about what is being asked of us."

CHAPTER 24

The two men put their shoulders to the door in the enclosure wall and pushed with all their might. It didn't budge.

"Something's keeping it shut on the other side."

"It must be a buildup of snow," suggested Hamo, puffing and taking a rest for a moment. "Mebbe one of us should climb over and clear it?"

Matt looked doubtfully up at the wall. "I reckon you mean me," he replied after a pause. He turned back to judge its height. "Likely I'll fall and break my neck," he said after a moment

"Come on, lad, don't be soft. You've plenty of snow to land in once you're over."

"I suppose—" Matt punched Hamo on the shoulder. "C'mon then, you bastard, give us a step up."

Hamo bent down with cupped hands, as if hoisting a master onto a horse, and Matt stepped up and began to claw at the wall. Somehow Hamo managed to hoist him onto his shoulders, and by reaching up, Matt was just able to lift himself onto the top of the wall. He heaved himself up and balanced there for a moment. He stared down without saying anything.

They saw his face go white.

The next moment, he was teetering on the brink; then with a sudden plunge he disappeared from sight.

"What the devil . . ." Hamo rammed with his shoulder against the door again but, of course, was unable to move it. "Matt?" he yelled.

There was no answer.

"Matt?" Hamo's voice had a note of alarm in it. He began to pound on the door with both fists. "Answer me, you dolt. What's up?"

There was a long silence. Hildegard was unable to make any sense of what had happened to make Matt fall like that. "Did he see something near the door? Is something keeping the door shut?"

It was dawn. The clouds were grey with unshed snow, but there was nothing sinister in the clarity of light; even so, an irrational fear gripped her. They had laughed at the idea of a dragon, but what if there really was something out there, some creature that defied reason, something with its own unexplained horror? They had heard it last night. And now maybe Matt had set eyes on it. And fallen to his doom.

"What has he seen?" shouted Hamo, helplessly turning to her, as if he had read her mind. "What is it?" He renewed his assault on the door, but it was immovable.

"Can you climb up there yourself if I help?" she asked. "Or should we go back and try to find a ladder?"

"You think you can give me a leg up?" He looked her up and down and made up his mind. "No, let's get the ladder. The lay brothers at the farm must have one."

The conversi, the lay brothers who worked the farm for the nuns, were found already at work around the animal pens. One of them was only too keen to drag a ladder from a store shed when he heard what had happened. With the help of another man, he carried it across the garth to the wall.

A nun who had been on vigil in the mortuary came out to see what the commotion was about. It was Desiderata. She looked washed-out, as if she had been awake all night, and Hildegard asked if she had been here when the dragon made its nighttime howl.

She nodded. "I stayed here and prayed. I thought it had got inside the precinct." She gave Hildegard a challenging look.

Hildegard explained when Desiderata asked what was happening, and they watched the conversi erect the ladder against the wall and hold it steady while Hamo climbed up. When he reached the top of the wall, they watched intently to see what he would do when he looked over.

He was certainly having a good look at something. Then he turned back to shout down to them. "Matt's knocked himself out. There's a body blocking the door. Plenty of blood. Looks like a large dog. Its throat's been ripped out and its belly's been cloven open. I'm going down to have a proper look."

He inched himself over the coping and, but for his fingertips grasping the top of the wall, vanished from sight. Then they vanished as well, to be followed by a cushioned thud as he dropped down into the snow.

After a moment, they heard two voices.

"That's Matt," exclaimed Hildegard with relief.

Slowly, the door was jerked open from the other side as the snow was cleared. The two labourers from the priory jostled forward with Hildegard to see what it was that had given Matt such a shock. Desiderata hung back.

It was as Hamo had told them. A large dog, a deerhound by the look of it, was lying on its side, its blood standing out against the snow, black and somehow shocking. Some thing had ripped the hound's throat out. Entrails oozed out beside it. It would not have suffered long. What had held the door shut was its deadweight, that and the drifts of snow blown against it as before, when Hildegard had had to dig her way inside.

A high-pitched wailing made them all turn. Desiderata was standing behind them, one quivering finger pointing into the woods. "The dragon!" she screamed when she saw they were all staring at her. "The dragon did this! I heard it in the night. It was coming for us! Pray to God, ye sinners. Pray and never stop!"

Hildegard went over to her. "It was more likely a wolf, sister. Please, control your fears."

Desiderata gave her a hostile glance and fell to her knees, muttering prayers.

The conversi offered to deal with the animal.

Hamo was brushing Matt down. He seemed concussed. He kept saying, "I'm all right. I'm really all right."

"Do you still want to leave?" Hamo asked him.

"Of course I want to leave. Come on. I'm off now. Come on." Matt swayed. Then, with an effort, he pulled himself together. "Let's go. I'm over it now. It was the shock. It looked like a woman lying there. It looked like one of the nuns."

While they were talking, Hildegard went outside and skirted the dead animal, keeping her eyes on the ground. A lot of footprints were scuffed into the snow where it lay, but a light step led away from the hound along the perimeter of the enclosure. Snow had fallen in the night and the indentations were almost obliterated. They reminded her of the footprints she had seen cutting across the garth the night she had entered the purlieu of the priory. Then, as now, they were too ordinary to connect to anybody in particular. What interested her was the way they continued along the wall until they disappeared into the undergrowth next to it. She would bet they could be picked up entering the priory through the main gate farther along.

She glanced back at the nun kneeling in the snow. Not Desiderata, then, not if she had been at vigil all night in the mortuary chapel.

They began to walk away. When Hildegard looked back, Desiderata was standing in the doorway watching them. She had an odd expression on her face. It sent shivers down Hildegard's spine. She knew it was because of what she had read in the priory roll about why the nun had been sent here. She had paid her penance, however; the slate was clean. She had been absolved.

They set off into the deep woods.

After the skirmish of snow around the door, the snow elsewhere was smooth in the open but pitted underneath the branches.

On the track down to the beck, it lay backed up against the rocks in deceptive drifts. It made for heavy going. They were slipping and sliding with every step as they descended the cliff and they kept falling knee-deep into random pockets of snow until, at length, breathless and stinging with cold, they reached the bank. It was sheltered enough in the lee of the crag for the going to be easier from then on.

Soon they reached the road. The ford was in spate and they had to wade through, emerging on the other side soaked to the thighs, their boots heavy with river water. They trudged on up the snow-covered hill towards the castle.

Hildegard had not been able to see what it was like when she had arrived there at midnight in what seemed, now, to be another world. It was built on a triangular promontory, towers marking the corners, its main gate approached across a ridge of moorland. It looked impregnable, sheer cliffs on two sides impossible to scale without being observed. Birds of prey circled and screamed around the three towers.

Now she understood that when she was escorted to Handale, they had left by a side entrance, following the rim of a half circle of moat in the castle's defences. The main gate was far more imposing and was reached along the peninsula on the landward side.

Today the battlements were decked with pennants. Red and gold, they cracked in the wind. Surprised, Hildegard saw that the standard above the main gate displayed the arms of Northumberland, a gold lion rampant on a red ground.

From the top of the gatehouse, a lookout in the earl's red and gold colours shouted down to ask their business. A door in the massive gatehouse was opened and someone poked his head out. He wore a basinet and chain mail with the Kilton emblem on his surcoat. Permission to enter was achieved with an amount of discussion that Hildegard, wet and cold from their walk, could have done without.

She was aware that Matt and Hamo were staring in astonishment as she parlayed with the guard, expressing more than a townswoman's confidence and showing a side of her they had not seen before.

Once inside, Matt, at sixteen, looked round with an open mouth. He had clearly never been anywhere like it. Hamo was more cynical, although even he, presumably, had never before witnessed such a concentration of military strength and the splendour that went with it. Both observed the armed militia and their gleaming weaponry with awe.

To judge by the emblems on show, several baronial households were present. It was clear there would be no stepping out of line with such tough-looking and well-equipped professional soldiers. A flotilla of servants followed them about. "Like gnats round a midden," grunted Hamo, striving to remain unimpressed.

They could see into a second courtyard through an arch on the other side of the yard. The colours of the earl hung from the battlements, and the clash of arms could be heard as the captains put their platoons through their daily drill.

Half a dozen guards were standing around the entrance and stopped them when they tried to walk through. They were quickly informed that only the earl's closest guests were allowed into the inner court. They were sent ignominiously back into the melee in the outer court.

"It wasn't like this when I arrived the other night," she told them both. "Something important is obviously going on." It was clearly no visit from a mere knight as she had assumed from Fulke's conversation with his mysterious customer. The harbingers of the earl had already arrived, as they soon discovered.

"Have we got a chance of hiring horses, then?" asked Hamo, looking round. "Somebody's got to get to Durham and let master know what's happened."

"A courier might be your best bet," Hildegard suggested. "Cheaper than hiring a horse anyway."

She stopped a passing servant and, after asking about couriers, she inquired where she might find Sir Ulf of Langbrough. He gestured towards the common hall. "Probably in there with the other knights."

"What's going on?" she asked.

He looked at her in astonishment. "What do you mean, mistress?"

"Why this gathering of militia?"

"His grace the earl," he replied, spacing the words as if talking to a country bumpkin, "will shortly be in residence? See his harbingers?" He hurried off, shaking his head.

"What earl's that, like?" asked Hamo when the servant was out of earshot.

"He'll mean the earl of Northumberland. Look at his colours." Matt pointed to the battlements. "But what's he doing here?"

"We'll soon find out. Follow me." Hildegard led the way to the great hall, and when they got inside, she asked the marshal to bring Ulf of Langbrough to them.

Over a hundred knights and their attendants were dining at tables of ten or so. Emerging from out of this crowd, Ulf greeted Hildegard with evident relief. Hildegard could not have been more glad to see him, either.

He took the three of them back to his table. He was sharing his place, as was the custom, with a knight of equal status. The man was a stranger to Hildegard and was eating as if food was a scarcity where he came from, and he merely glanced up, nodded, and carried on eating.

Ulf managed to attract the attention of one of the servers as he swept past with an armful of platters.

"You're late," he said, addressing Hildegard as he poured wine for them all. "I thought you were going to arrive yesterday. Was it the snow that delayed you?"

Hildegard nodded. "And much more than that. I'll tell you later. These two masons"—she introduced them—"wish to get a message out to their master in Durham and to call the coroner to register the death of one of their workmates. They fear that the prioress of Handale has not kept her word to them."

She explained further, interrupted now and then by Hamo and Matt as they told Ulf about Giles and what had befallen him.

Ulf was able to direct them to the steward's office, where they would be able to pay a courier to take a message for them. They went off looking slightly dazed by the noise and bustle of the place after months sequestered at Handale.

"Well," said Ulf when they left. "You look the worse for wear."

He refilled her beaker of wine. "So what's been happening? I expect there's more to it than you've just told me."

She gave a glance at the stranger still shovelling food into his mouth. Ulf caught her eye and got up. "Mistress"—he bowed—"will you do me the honour of walking with me in the courtyard?"

"Who was that?" she asked when they were outside.

"Just some passing knight from farther north. I don't think they know how to talk up there. So far, I've heard only grunts from him. As far as I can make out, he came down with Northumberland's retinue to prepare the place for his eventual arrival. I mentioned a secret convocation? This is it. Roger's around somewhere. The earl called all the barons of the north to discuss the latest with King Richard."

"Is there news?"

"It seems de Vere is marching his army along the banks of the River Severn as we speak."

"Under orders from the king?" she asked in astonishment.

Ulf frowned. "It looks like it. But it makes no sense. The news is that Richard is still in London. There's been no call from him to muster an army."

"So why has Northumberland decided to summon all the northern chivalry to this out-of-the-way place?"

"He expects to have to make a decision one way or another. To support the king when the call does actually come, as it must. Or to side with Gloucester, Warwick, and Arundel."

"And Bolingbroke?"

"He's yet to show his hand, but yes, I would imagine he'll fall in with them."

"God help King Richard." Her face expressed the depth of her concern. "Ulf, I'm afraid. Innocent people are going to die.

The barons are bringing the butchery of the *chevauchée* to England."

He touched her cheek with the back of one of his fingers and ran it tenderly to the corner of her mouth. "It won't come to that. Forget it for a while. Nothing can be decided until the earl arrives, and by then the situation may have changed for the better. Tell me what's been happening at Handale."

"Compared to your news, it's nothing much. Small events in the scale of things, even though they're matters of life and death to the individuals caught up in them."

She explained about the task Prioress Basilda had given her in exchange for the hospitality of the priory.

"It was while I was in the scriptorium that I discovered a secret hidden in the priory records. It is something that the prioress will want to keep quiet." She glanced round to make sure they would not be overheard. "You remember I mentioned the priest who died? I've now found out who his mother was." She hesitated. "Ulf, you won't believe this, but it was Prioress Basilda herself."

"Are you sure?" He sounded astonished. "When did it happen?"

"The boy was no more than twenty or so. He was born when she was a nun, during her first year, judging by the dates. The father must have been a wealthy man, someone who could afford to pay to keep the matter quiet and placate any retribution from the Church."

"He might have been a high-up churchman himself," Ulf pointed out realistically enough.

She did not agree. "Maybe it's something we shall never know, unless the prioress herself confesses. The reason I doubt it is this." Then she told him what the priest had said about his expectations. "He saw himself as one of the heirs to Kilton. There was a sister somewhere, although he had not seen her since she was a child of two. It was a matter that had been at law for some years. We must assume his father had waited in vain, in the expectation of having judgement made in his favour. But you know how these things go. The attorneys take their time. It's bread and butter to them, this sort of litigation. While they draw it out, they're spinning gold and the contesting parties are forced to live in a kind of limbo. This seems to be much what happened to the priest."

"So does it mean the prioress will inherit Kilton?"

"If her relationship was not regularised, she could not claim. And clearly it was not, or she would have left the Order. But don't you see?"

"What?"

"Fulke was making use of the priory to keep his goods out of sight until they could be sold on. Why did Basilda allow him to do so? She was getting an income from them to make it worth her while, as I saw from the accounts detailing Fulke's donations. But it's my guess Fulke must have known about her past mistake and used his knowledge to maintain a hold over her. It's not the sort of thing she would want shouted abroad. She was forced to accept his imposition."

"Blackmail, you mean?"

She nodded. "What else could account for her sudden change when her son died? Fulke was left with nothing to use as a threat. He had no hold over her after that. It would have been her word against his if he'd tried to reveal the truth. Without living proof, as it were."

"But how did you find out?"

"It's there, well hidden among the rolls in the scriptorium, and we must believe that is the only proof. I found a document naming the priest's birth mother and the agreement for him to be taken in as an oblate at Whitby Abbey. I also found copies of more recent letters from Basilda to Fulke complaining about the injustice of his demands on the priory. 'Do you not think I have suffered enough without you trying to rake up old mistakes?' she wrote. 'I have paid the price many times over for my foolishness. Do you want my blood, as well?' There was more, but something happened and—''

She put her fingers to her neck before she realised what she was doing.

Ulf bent his head. "What's happened, Hildegard? What is that?" He tenderly lifted her hair, revealing the weals from the noose. "You've been attacked?" He looked scandalised. "Who did this?"

"I don't know." She explained briefly what had happened.

Ulf was enraged, but he said very little. She could tell he was ready to do anything to discover the culprit.

"There's no point in getting into a rage over it. Something might happen to put us on his or her trail, but until then, there are other matters of far more importance." She put a hand on his arm. "Your dear Petronel, for instance. I trust you got your beloved horse back? And you haven't told me what happened to that coxcomb and his purchase."

He gave a curse. "I have not found my horse. We followed through the blizzard until we fetched up here. That thieving devil entered the castle and we were just behind him. We saw him ride through the blizzard onto the ridge and go up to the main gate. And then he disappeared. You can hardly credit it. But that's what happened. We haven't seen him or Petronel since."

"Did he come inside?"

Ulf nodded. "We saw him enter, all right. They opened the gates with more speed than when we approached. We were kept waiting an age while they checked our right to be here. A list had to be fetched. 'You're a day early,' they had the gall to tell me. 'I'm pursuing a stolen horse,' I replied. 'Who was that fellow who rode in before us?' They looked blank. Trained to look like that, deliberately to deceive. He must be someone of importance for them to behave so. Curse them."

"But Petronel must be in the stables."

"We've had a look but couldn't find him. And as for that thief in the capuchon, he's vanished completely."

"There are hundreds of strangers here, all with their mounts. It's not surprising you haven't found Petronel. We must start another, more thorough search. He's so distinctive, he won't go missing for long. If you saw him ridden into the castle, then he must be here. You're quite convinced the rider didn't turn off the road?"

"There's nowhere else he could have gone. We saw him cantering out along the ridge. We heard the portcullis rise and fall. Of course he came here."

"There'll be even more people thronging the place when Northumberland arrives. When is he due?"

"Imminently, we're told."

"I remember him from last year in London, when we had to accompany Mr. Medford of the Signet Office to Northumberland's town house."

"To seek out his secretary, Harry Summers? Yes, I well remember that. Dark days." He gave her a soft look, but she brushed it aside. Now was not the time to allow Rivera into her thoughts.

"Is Summers coming along here, do you know?"

"I haven't seen him. If he's still got his head on his shoulders, I expect he'll be travelling with the earl."

"There's an inner court over there, Ulf." She indicated the arch with the strong guard on duty outside. "We tried to go in before we met you, but they refused us entry."

"We lesser beings are not allowed inside."

"Do you think your man is in there?"

Ulf gazed gloomily across the busy yard. "He and my horse."

He nodded. "It's very likely that's exactly where they'll be. In a place barred to a mere shire knight such as myself."

"Barred, you say? In that case, we'll have to do something about it, won't we?"

On impulse, she stood on tiptoe and kissed him on the cheek. "I must go and sort out my lodgings and see how Matt and Hamo are getting on."

CHAPTER 25

To anybody not in the know, the two masons were absorbed in a game of dice. They were sitting over by the wall, not far from the entrance into the inner courtyard, when Hildegard went up to the guards. Hamo was looking up at the sky, as if asking for divine help for his next throw. Matt appeared to be inspecting his fingernails.

The better for her present purpose, Hildegard had taken off her head scarf, and her hair blazed like silver. It fell to her shoulders, uncut on the journey all the way to Compostela and back. Her undershift was unfastened at the neck and she trailed a cloak half off her shoulders. The guards jumped to attention at once when she greeted them.

"Well met, gentlemen. I'm here for a fellow who came in two nights ago. I was delayed by private matters. He told me you would know him by this and let me through."

They clustered round—closer than necessary, she felt. In her palm was a silver emblem. It was the one Ulf's page had so adroitly prized off the bridle of the coxcomb's horse in Handale Woods.

The captain of the guard picked it up and held it out to give it a good look. "Discretion the game, eh? By he's a lucky one." He turned to his companions. "The night before his wedding an' all!" He gave Hildegard an admiring up-and-down look that came to rest somewhere in the vee of her undershift. He smiled, as if he would like nothing more than to rip it aside. "What's he done to get you?" he asked. "Swart fellow like 'im."

The rest of them chuckled. One quipped, "Stay with us, mistress. We'll give you a better time of it than that squat toad could do in his wildest dreams."

"I can believe that, sir. Sadly for me, I have no choice in the matter. Is he within?"

"Third level up yon tower steps." The captain pointed across the inner courtyard to the opposite side. "When he's finished with you, come and see us." He handed back the emblem and deliberately entwined his fingers in hers. "Is it a promise, mistress?"

Agreeing to nothing and offering only a smile in reply, Hildegard allowed herself to be waved through.

She wished they had been indiscreet enough to mention the man's name. Squat toad. Swart. Wedding night. Maybe his purchase had been a costly wedding gift for his lucky bride, on which the duty would have been so punitive, it had been worth breaking the law to avoid it.

A couple of pages were lounging in green and blue at the top of the steps. They were about ten or eleven years old. Very smartly turned out.

"Your lord, is he in?" She pointed up the steps.

"In the feast hall, mistress," one of them piped up.

She dropped a small silver coin into his palm. "Then I'll just go up and deliver this gift." She indicated her cloak, as if there was something hidden in it.

"We'll take it up for you, mistress."

"That's kind, but I must take it myself. It's a secret for his wedding," she added mysteriously.

One of the pages was about to object. They clearly had their orders. But his friend, the silver coin in his little paw, gave him a dig in the ribs. Smiling, Hildegard distributed a coin to the objector. "I shall be no more than two minutes," she told them, walking briskly up the stairs before they could say anything else.

She reached a bend in the stairs, then picked up her skirts and hurried up to the third floor. A door opened onto a wide reception chamber looking onto the courtyard. A host of servants was scurrying back and forth. She whisked past them before she was noticed and climbed up another flight. She had no idea what she was looking for.

At the top, she came to other doors. One opened into a bedchamber with a four-poster draped in velvet. The other was locked. Some instinct told her that this was where the secret lay.

A sound below made her swivel. A man in the garments of a household steward was following her up. He had a small, well-kempt beard and wore a cold expression. "If you're looking for Earl Morcar, he's in the feast hall. Didn't they tell you that?"

"I'm at fault, sir. I misheard. I shall try there." She sidled past him on the narrow stair. As she did so, his hand lightly skimmed her breasts. She drew back in shock.

The steward gazed mournfully into her eyes. "He gets the cream. I often ask myself why that is." He squeezed one of her breasts before she could stop him. "Just a little feel, mistress. What do you lose?"

"What do I gain, more like," she replied cheekily, then took the stairs downwards two at a time before he could reply.

Breathlessly, she hurried past the two pages. She saw them gape at her hasty exit, and she slowed down as soon as she reached the yard so as not to draw attention to herself. It was the feast hall, then, but it would be a hazard too far if the licentiousness of those within matched that of their servants.

The Earl Morcar.

Piece by piece, the picture was beginning to take shape.

A pushing mob of servants obstructed the doors. Using her elbows, Hildegard forced her way through until she could grip the sleeve of a serving man in Morcar's colours of green and blue. "His grace, where is he sitting?"

The man looked at her strangely. "Something wrong with your eyesight, woman?" As he spoke, he automatically glanced over his shoulder. Hildegard followed his gaze to where a black-bearded fellow with a dark cloak over one shoulder was just beginning to get up from the table. He stood and tipped the contents of a wine goblet down his throat, then turned to one of his companions.

She heard him say, "I'll go up and get her." He began to stalk towards the doors.

The servant she had accosted stepped back to allow her through, but she did her best to melt out of sight and did not attempt to detain the earl. Better to find out how the land lay before she drew attention to herself. If he was marrying on the morrow, he might be off to fetch his betrothed.

He was uninterested in the mob round the doors and called for his path to be cleared. "Two or three attend me!" he barked, pushing his way through. A handful of servants in his colours scurried out in his wake.

Hildegard trailed along behind them. She had a head scarf over her hair now, to draw least attention to herself, and when Morcar disappeared inside the tower, she waited on the far side of the courtyard to see him reappear.

Her patience was rewarded. Not much later, he reappeared, not with his betrothed on his arm, but with a hooded hawk perched there. She. His hawk.

Accompanied by a small troop of attendants, he made off towards a corner of the yard and disappeared.

Following at a discreet pace, she found herself in the stable block. By now, Morcar and his companions were down at the far end, where the mews were situated. In a few moments, he reappeared with a couple of companions whose hawks must have been kept under the care of the Kilton falconer. In a determined bunch, they went out through a wooden door in the castle wall that she thought must lead into the ravine. She guessed that if they climbed to the other side, they would soon reach good hunting terrain.

This was the opportunity she wanted. He would be off for some time. She would risk getting up inside the tower to see for herself what treasure he was hiding in the locked chamber.

She hesitated. It might mean confronting the steward again. For the time being, she could think of no acceptable way of cozening the truth from him, even if he did know what was in there, which might not be the case at all.

First, there was something else to do. She would have a quick look for Petronel and bring a spark of joy to Ulf's heart.

The stables in this inner court were the place where the most important guests kept their mounts, expensive horses that cost a couple of years of an average freeman's wages. Petronel would not be out of place here, not because Ulf had paid through the nose for him, but because he had bred him and trained him, having noted the lineage of his dam and sire, and he was one of the best. Now was the opportunity to find him.

She began a casual stroll through the first open door into the stalls. A score or so of very fine horses were attended by a host of stable hands. In a haze of dust motes and sweetly smelling hay, she was making her way along the line of stalls and finding nothing like Ulf's favourite, when she was stopped by what was evidently the stable master.

He was rapping a whip against his boots in a hostile manner, and noting that she was not attired to go out riding, he looked at her with suspicion.

"Earl Morcar's horse," she began. "I've heard it's quite impressive."

"No idea where you heard that. It's nothing. What's it to do with you? Who are you?"

"Just a friend," she replied.

He picked up a broom and barked an order to one of the lads. The gesture was a clear threat to get out.

Thoughtfully, she made her way back outside. When she slipped through the inner gatehouse into the common yard again, the guard nodded and reminded her of the available delight of future assignations.

"I don't know how to get inside," she told Ulf. "It's a stout door. Oak. A heavy lock. Its on the side of the tower that looks over the ravine. There's no way in from that direction, as it's perched right up on top of the crag. I believe there's something important inside. Otherwise, why lock it?"

"I can get in anywhere you ask, mistress," said Ulf's page eagerly, turning to his master.

"Keep out of this, Pippin. I've told you already: Get along to the kitchens and fatten yourself up."

The boy bowed. "Very well, master." The grin in his voice belied his apparent disappointment. "I'll go and find Petronel for you when I've dined." He ran off.

"I''m sorry about Petronel, by the way. If he's anywhere, he'll be stabled in the inner court. I only had time to look at the horses nearest the door."

"I'll get in there and find him, if Pippin doesn't beat me to it," Ulf vowed.

Matt and Hamo had been told part of the story. The importance of Fulke's activities at the tower in Handale Woods was not lost on them.

"Giles must have guessed something was up," Matt admitted somewhat evasively when he was asked. "He turned silent after being out in the woods one day. There was something on his mind. We used to trap rabbits there, until he was killed. I asked him what was up, but he just shook his head."

"Did he see something being taken into the tower, do you think?"

Matt frowned. "He mentioned the way—" He bit his lip.

Remembering that thoughtless salute Dakin had given her one day, she aimed a shot in the dark. "If Giles or any others were sympathetic to the White Hart rebels, they would naturally be interested in the sale of arms, just in case it meant there was going to be a drive against any rebels from the Rising of '81 who are still at large. Many fled to the safety of the north when they were outlawed, as we all know. It would be worth warning them in advance so they could find somewhere safer to live—"

Matt was white-lipped. "What's that got to do with anything? It's a capital offence to belong to the White Hart Brotherhood."

"It may well be. It doesn't mean that people's sympathies cannot be with their cause."

She noticed him give a start of surprise and stare at her more keenly.

She continued. "There are many folk left who believe the rebels had a just cause and that they should be protected from the law. On the other hand, it would be useful for them to obtain arms, wouldn't it?"

He made no reply.

She went on. "Not only for the money that can be made from selling them on—which would ease the lot of anyone living outside the law—but also for the purpose of arming themselves against an attack by their enemies. It simply occurs to me," she continued when he still didn't say anything, "that they may be hiding arms in Handale Woods. It's private enough. Especially now there's supposed to be a dragon at large, keeping everybody away." That's spelling it out, she thought.

Matt considered the ramifications of what she was saying, weighed against the danger of admitting any knowledge about the rebels. But he was an apprentice. Even if he did not sympathise with them, he was of an age to be well informed of their activities.

Hamo looked away as if he could hear nothing of any of it.

Ulf eased his shoulders inside his mail shirt and stared at the ground.

She knew she was going too far. "Look," she said brusquely. "This is dangerous talk, but it won't go any further, Matt. You can trust me, and you can trust Ulf. Was Giles involved with the rebels?"

"He might have been. How would I know?" He gave Ulf a sulky stare.

Understanding the meaning of that look, Hildegard lowered her voice. "Ulf is no Norman overlord. You have only to look at him to see that. Nor am I unsympathetic to their cause. My own opinion is that the White Hart Brotherhood are loyal to the king. They have many reasonable demands, which will in time be met. The rebellion might be all but played out in the south. Up here, the remit of their enemies does not reach with any certainty. Their hopes and desires still flourish. Northumberland is against them, naturally, as he has a lot to lose. If their demands for a set price for land are met, for instance, he'll not be pleased. On the other hand, he's a pragmatist and would find a way of balancing his own demands with their own. If Giles thought he saw arms being taken to the tower, then somebody might have thought it necessary to silence him. We already know a little about what was stored there. There was heavy lifting tackle in one of the top rooms. It must surely have been used to hoist armaments up there for storage until they could be moved on." She gave Ulf a quick glance. "We saw something ourselves being moved on by Northumberland's men. Fulke was present. He's in it up to his neck. What interests us now is what else he had in that tower. Maybe Giles found out?"

Matt had tears in his eyes. "So was it Fulke who had him killed? I knew it was."

Hildegard shrugged. "It's beginning to look that way. He's certainly the chief suspect. Not that we can prove it."

"Giles was such a dear soul. He didn't deserve to die. All he lived for was his work. Of course he agreed with what the rebels wanted. Who wouldn't? But he never did anything about it. He hated violence."

"Let's find his murderer, then. Maybe we can do it by showing that Morcar is involved in Fulke's illicit trade."

He gave a slight nod.

"So, back to the main question: How are we to find out exactly what Earl Morcar bought from Fulke and now keeps in a locked chamber?"

"It can only be arms," said Ulf.

Hamo spoke up. "If it is, isn't it likely he's hoping to sell them to this earl of Northumberland?"

It was Hildegard's fear, too. But it was an assumption only and they had to take a risk. So far, too much depended on guesswork.

CHAPTER 26

Ulf had been all for marching in and demanding to have the door opened. "They'll respect a sword." He grimaced, touching the one on his belt. She knew he would not be so foolhardy and so willing to court certain failure. It needed something more subtle, and he knew it.

"What happens in the feast hall at night? Is there entertainment?"

He nodded. "Last night we could hear them out here. The monks at Whitby could no doubt hear them, too."

"It should be just as noisy tonight if Morcar has the intention of getting married tomorrow. He'll be celebrating, surely?"

Ulf twisted his lips in a humourless smile. "On his knees praying to find a way out, if he's any sense. But yes, you're right. It should be quite a night. Can you work your charm on the guards again and get us all inside while they're enjoying themselves?"

While they waited for night to fall, they split up. The intention was to find out what they could about Earl Morcar. He was new to all of them. They soon discovered the reason. His land was far up in the border country. Because of the continual war of attrition between the Scots and the English, he had lost his castle, regained it, lost it again, and then had his lands laid waste. He had taken it as a sign to get out and move south. The earl of Northumberland, who was his liege lord, had been unable or unwilling to find any other holding for him.

A rumour, corroborated by Matt in conversation with a couple of the earl's servants over several stoups of ale, was that he was a ruined man and was desperate to find a way of living in the manner he believed was his by right.

"Not that we minded his running arms across the border, but he's not going to be doing that down here, so where are we going to bed down? On the move from one man's kitchen to the next, the pauper guest and his retinue. It's degrading to us. But where can we go? What can we do with a landless lord?" The servants became ever more resentful at the ill fruits of their devotion the more they explained the situation to the mason.

Matt came back saying he was pleased he was his own man and had a trade that would always be needed.

"Did they give a clue about his bride?" asked Hildegard.

"Closed as oysters the moment I mentioned her."

"I wonder if she's arrived yet. Maybe she's travelling with Northumberland."

"Not our concern," remarked Ulf. "If he's dealing in arms, then this convocation here will be a convenient place to find a buyer. We know Northumberland is supplying his fletchers. Maybe this Morcar hopes to get a jump ahead of the earl with other armaments." He scowled.

"What is it?" asked Hildegard.

"Does it mean they're arming for King Richard? Or for his enemies?"

Snow was falling heavily again. It was what was causing Northumberland's delay. A rider managed to get through with the news that the cavalcade, having already set out from Alnwick Castle, was caught in a blizzard. Until the road was cleared in front of them, they intended to bed down along the route. No one was to leave Kilton before they arrived.

The fact that they had official news of the delay meant that as there was nothing to do but wait, they might as well enjoy themselves. It brought a festive mood to those trapped by the weather in a castle that was not their own.

The kitcheners were working overtime to feed everybody. Pippin attended Ulf now and then, always with his hands wrapped round a pasty or a hunk of cheese. Barrels of ale were rolled out into the outer court and wine casks were untapped for those fortunate enough to be lodged in the inner court.

Cressets flamed in every sconce. Music echoed within the walls. Servants threw snowballs at each other. They danced a farandole.

It was late by the time Hildegard made her approach to the guards at the inner gate. Even though their captain reminded Hildegard of his promise to give her a good time, he, like his subordinates, was too reeling drunk to have made good any promise in that line, and the presence of her three strapping escorts—Morcar's men, she affirmed—was enough to make them wave them all through with much ribaldry.

The four of them crossed the yard. Snow was falling in big fat flakes.

The feast hall was echoing to the rafters as they passed. Hildegard looked inside. Morcar and his men were there all right. Light spilled out across the snow and made the twirling flakes look like little moons.

"I could take a chance and go and search for Petronel," remarked Ulf with a longing glance towards the stables.

"Later," Hildegard told him. "Let's solve one problem at a time.

We may not get another chance like this. I know it may be nothing. The stash of feathers for the war arrows may be the most of it. At least let's find out."

"Did much gold change hands?" asked Hamo.

"So we imagine."

He exchanged a look with Matt that Hildegard noticed but could not decipher.

Her misgivings returned. She had often felt doubtful about the masons in the past. They were clannish. As was to be expected from a guild as important as theirs, they had their secrets, with severe penalties for anyone who betrayed them. Their secrecy made them notorious in some circles. It was said they were like a realm within the realm, with no law but their own and answerable to no one but the Grand Master.

At present there was little choice but to accept them at face value. After all, it was Giles's killer they hoped to apprehend, and Morcar and his secret dealings with Fulke seemed to hold a key to his death.

Ulf threw a few coins to the pages who were sleepily sitting on the steps, wrapped in their little cloaks. "Now then, young gentlemen," he said, affable in the way he knew well how to be. "We're here on important business on behalf of your master. Let us pass, like good fellows."

The two moved over and Ulf led the way inside.

"You and Hamo keep the steward busy if he's still around," whispered Hildegard to Matt, who was following closely at her heels.

Morcar's servants were out celebrating like everybody else. The apartment was empty except for an old woman asleep in a chair. They continued up to the next level.

"This is the door." Hildegard indicated the one opposite the earl's bedchamber.

Ulf took out a long, sharp-pointed knife. "Keep a lookout, you two," he said to the masons as he set to work.

It took a while. Hildegard was on tenterhooks lest someone should hear them and come up to investigate.

At last, the lock softly turned. Ulf put his hand on the door ring. "I'll go in first, just in case they've set a guard on the stuff."

They waited a moment until he reappeared. His expression was impossible to read. "Hildegard, you'd better step inside. Lads, keep watch."

Hildegard slipped through the half-open door, then came to a sudden halt. By the light of a single cresset, she saw a bed taking up most of the space in the small chamber. On it lay a girl. She appeared to be sleeping.

Hildegard glanced round. Not sure what she had expected—piles of bales as before, maybe sacks of body armour, or cases of steel weapons—she was confused.

She went over to have a closer look at the girl. "Do we have more light?" she whispered to Ulf.

He fumbled with tinder and a taper. The gold brilliance enveloped the sleeping form.

"She's beautiful," muttered Ulf. "Is this his betrothed?"

Hildegard was peering intently at the girl. When she did not stir, Hildegard reached forward and lifted one of her eyelids. She did not flinch. When Hildegard turned to Ulf, her expression was one of alarm.

Ulf understood at once.

"Drugged?"

"Is this how he intends to marry her?"

"But who is she? What is she?"

"We need not rack our brains to answer that one. She must be an heiress of some importance. Fulke up to his tricks. Morcar intent on ensuring his future."

CHAPTER 27

"If we do carry her outside, we'll surely be seen," muttered Ulf. He glanced back at the girl. "But we can't leave her here." He was talking to himself.

"Remember how Morcar carried her in a cloak out of the tower? Stupidly, we thought it was war goods."

"Are we sure about this, Hildegard? Is this what his purchase from Fulke amounts to? What if we're making a mistake? We'll pay a hefty penalty for abduction. Can't we just stop the ceremony tomorrow if it seems to be going the wrong way?"

She reminded him of what Alys had told them. "This is a bigger prize than merely selling girls on to the town whoremasters." She looked down at the girl again. "I wish she'd regain consciousness; then we could ask her where the marriage is to take place. If it's in the private chapel here, we'd never be allowed in. No," she said decisively. "We've got to take the risk. We must get her out."

"It may be aboveboard," he muttered doubtfully. "Maybe she takes regular sleeping draughts. Maybe Morcar was smuggling something quite different out of the tower in the bundle we saw." He spread his arms helplessly. "Don't you have anything with you to bring her round?"

Hildegard was still wearing her scrip on her belt. "I wonder if—maybe . . ." She went over to the cresset and by its light opened up her leather bag of cures and searched through it. "I can do nothing without water," she concluded.

"Let's send Matt to the kitchen."

"He'll never manage to get back without arousing notice."

"He has to."

Ulf went to the door and invited the two men inside. "Drugged," he told them. "We need water."

"I'll go," Matt replied at once.

Hildegard exclaimed, "No, don't bother! Look, just reach out to catch some snow. I can melt that in the palm of my hand and mix it with something I've got here. I just need to make a paste with it."

They clustered round when Hildegard was ready. She tried once more to wake the girl by shaking her, but when that failed and she merely moaned and turned over, Hildegard slipped her arm under the girl's head and lifted her so that she could wet her lips with the concoction she had made up. The girl gave a shudder.

Slowly, her eyelids began to flutter. "No—" She put out a hand to ward something off. As she regained consciousness, she began to lash out with both fists, screaming, "No! Don't—" Her breath became frantic and she struggled with an imaginary assailant until Hildegard, speaking as soothingly as she could, reassured her that she was with friends.

The girl opened her eyes and gazed round in confusion. When she saw four strangers staring down at her, she put her hand to her mouth in fear. "Don't hurt me!" She cowered back against the pile of silk pillows strewn across the bed.

Hildegard leaned forward. "Do you know where you are?"

"I am lost. I am lost forever. No one will ever find me."

"You're at a place called Kilton Castle. Do you know it?"

The girl shook her head.

"Do you know your name?"

"I'm—" She shook her head again, but this time in puzzlement. "My name, my real name, is Isabella. I live at Bowden Castle."

It meant nothing to any of them.

"Is it in the border country?" Hildegard asked gently.

She nodded and her pupils dilated. "So much bloodshed. The horror! My dear father—" Her eyes filled.

In a sudden movement, she slipped of the bed and ran towards the door. Ulf reached out and caught her. She cowered in his arms. Terror made her open her mouth, but something forced the scream to remain silent. Ulf released her and she backed across the chamber until she felt the wall behind her, then she slowly sank to the floor.

Hildegard said in a commonsense tone, "We're not here to harm you. We're here to help. We believe you've been abducted and Earl Morcar intends to take you as his wife. Is that so?"

The girl nodded. Sobs began to rake through her. "He's a monster." Her glance swept from side to side. "Where is he? Is he coming back? Don't let him take me—"

"We have to get her out of here," said Ulf decisively.

Matt took off his cloak. "Wrap her in this. Let's get out as quickly as we can."

He was too late. Before he could put the cloak round the girl's shoulders, a sound at the door made them all turn.

A short, fortyish, black-bearded man in an elaborate velvet capuchon sauntered in through the open door. He was smiling in triumph. "So what have we here? Four hanged persons and a ravished wife?"

His self-confidence came from the armed men in chain mail, wearing his colours, who followed him in. They had already drawn their swords.

The first man stepped forward with a pugilistic swagger. It turned to hesitation when Ulf drew his sword so quickly, it was no more than a blur of light.

"C'mon, fella, test my mettle!" called Ulf, beckoning with his left hand. Ignoring the other three men crowding into the chamber, Ulf lunged at the soldier, flicked his sword from his grasp, and gave a flashing smile. "Next?"

Needing no further invitation, the three men piled towards Ulf. Hildegard looked over at Hamo. She had already noticed his legs, muscular from working the windlass. Now he put them to magnificent use. Jumping up to grasp the rafter above his head, he swung forward and aimed both heels hard into the chest of the nearest attacker.

The man fell back, winded, cannoning into the man behind him. Before they could recover, Ulf had disarmed the fourth and Matt, gaping for a moment, pulled his wits together and drew a lethal-looking stiletto from his belt, threw his cloak over Morcar's head, and dragged him deeper into the chamber.

"Anybody make a move and your lord gets it in the neck!" he snarled, then added, "C'mon. Give me the pleasure!"

Aware of the cold steel pressed at his throat, Morcar made no effort to struggle.

The soldiers froze where they were.

Hamo dropped down from the beam but stood ready to swing up again. He, too, drew out a long, sharp-bladed knife.

Ulf prodded his sword into the chest of the nearest attacker. "Throw your weapons down!" he growled.

While there was a hiatus as the soldiers made up their minds what to do next, Hildegard grabbed hold of Isabella by the arm and pulled her towards the open door. At once seeing the means to escape, the girl fled down the steps, with Hildegard at her heels.

From behind them came several thumps as swords were thrown

to the floor. Matt and Hamo appeared at the top of the tower steps, closely followed by Ulf. The door slammed behind them, trapping Morcar and his men inside the chamber.

Glancing over her shoulder, Hildegard saw Ulf turn the big key in the lock and stuff it in his belt. "Get the hell out!" he shouted down to them.

Nobody needed to be told. With the fleet-footed girl in front, they descended the stairs at a run.

Just coming up at that moment, no doubt to find out what the noise was about, was the steward who had insulted Hildegard earlier. He had to flatten himself against the wall or be swept back down the steps as they raced past. His eyes darted from left to right as first one, then another went by. His jaw sagged.

Before he could protest, Ulf grabbed him by the front of his surcoat, lifting him off his feet before bringing his face up close to his own. "If you value your health, get along to the feast hall, keep your mouth shut, and don't come back until daybreak. Get it?"

The man stuttered an assent. With Ulf's encouragement, he stumbled backwards down the steps, then turned and followed the others. Ulf was right behind him. Glancing back, the steward set off at a shambling run across the yard, heading towards the feast hall, exactly as Ulf had recommended.

The others were by now streaking across the snow-covered court towards the inner gatehouse. Hildegard pushed ahead of the barefoot girl they had rescued and poked her head through the door into the guardroom. "All well, gentlemen?"

There were cheers at her appearance.

"Can't stop. We're playing catch with Morcar's men. Whatever you do, don't let them follow us!"

More cheers were aroused, with promises to keep the bastards penned where they belonged, and one of the guards staggered to the doorway, grabbing a pike as he did so. "They'll get this if they try, mistress. Trust us!" He gripped the doorpost to hold himself up. "Are you coming back to see us after?"

"Soon, handsome, very soon."

By now, the others had reached the shadows at the foot of the curtain wall opposite the common hall. Sounds of feasting and general merriment were issuing forth. Ulf joined the others as Hildegard followed close behind.

"Where to now?" he demanded.

"Let's get out of the courtyard, in case they manage to put their shoulders to their prison door and get out past those drunks in the guardhouse," Hildegard suggested. She looked round for somewhere safe where the runaway girl could be hidden.

"They won't open that door in a hurry. It opens inwards." Ulf twirled the key.

"We might not be noticed up top." Hamo pointed to the battlements. "The guards are only on duty on the landward side."

It was true. Where the battlements overlooked the ravine on two sides, nobody bothered to keep watch. Only on the causeway side of the castle was there a strong detail of guards and lookouts.

"Let's get up there without being noticed, then. Slowly and casually," murmured Hildegard. There were vaults supporting several arches along the walls, where the sentries could take shelter, and they could climb up and make use of one of those.

It was still snowing. It helped conceal them and kept most people indoors. They hurried across the yard to the nearest set of steps. The girl was shivering with cold, teeth chattering audibly by now. The thin linen shift she had been sleeping in was no protection against the cold.

Ulf noticed and removed his thick woollen riding cloak. "Take this, my lady." He draped it round her fragile body.

She was no more than sixteen, slim and pale, with a pretty face and long fair hair caught up in a silver crispinette, an expression of dazed joy on her face as it slowly sank in that she had been freed from the molestations of Earl Morcar. "You may call me Isabella," she smiled round at them, clearly not quite believing in the sudden turn of events.

"She needs something on her feet," Hildegard pointed out, preparing to take off her own boots.

The two masons muttered something to each other; then Matt made a small bow to the girl. "My lady, trust us. Hamo and I will make a chair of our hands and carry you until we find shelter."

Half collapsing with cold, the girl could only agree, and in this way she was carried up the steps to the battlements and was hurried along to the nearest recess under the stone groin halfway along the wall, where the snow had not penetrated.

Hildegard happened to glance out between the crenellations as they ran along. Towards the high moors that stretched on that side of the castle, something was moving. She gave an exclamation of surprise and stopped.

"Look, everybody, what is that?"

She had to say it twice to make them turn and look.

Through the driving snow appeared a chain of tiny lights moving along the horizon at a steady pace towards the castle.

"Hundreds of flaming bloody torches!" exclaimed Matt in stupefaction.

"It's a ferkin great cavalcade!" Hamo gripped the stone embrasure. "Is it this earl they're prating about?"

Hildegard peered through the driving snow. "It's the king of the north!" she exclaimed. "At last!"

CHAPTER 28

The vanguard of the earl of Northumberland's retinue had just started out onto the peninsula leading towards the castle. The cavalcade snaked back onto the ridge of moorland in the snow-driven night, stretching back as far as the eye could see onto the bleak track across the treeless barrens.

Hundred upon hundreds of blazing torches lit the way, jetting stars off the caparisons of the horses, glittering from the gold banners, and gilding the helmets of the earl's private bodyguard. As the numbers of those setting out across the narrow ridge towards Kilton swelled, in the rear the baggage trains hove into view. One after another, they rolled out of the blizzard, torchlight glimmering on the myriad body servants, pages, horsemen, kitcheners, bottlers, bakers, butchers, and no doubt candlestick makers of the earl's household. The blizzard drove against them, but they drove harder through it.

Soon the shout from the sentinel in his lookout above the gatehouse rang out in response to a command to open the portcullis. With a rumbling of winches, the huge metal gate was lifted to allow the earl to enter.

He was visible now, in full armour, balanced on the footboard of a gleaming char with gilded leather hood, his standard fluttering above him, bright in the driving snow. The first horsemen began to clatter over the drawbridge, the char rumbled after them, and the earl entered between the echoing walls of the bailey to the fanfare of trumpets.

The group on the battlements watched for some time as the procession roared in under the gatehouse. The shouts of the newcomers doubled in volume within the confines of the walls.

Ulf and the masons turned their attention back to the abducted Isabella long before the last straggler hurried in as the drawbridge started to lift and the portcullis crashed shut.

Driven into shelter by the blizzard, they huddled in the lee of the wall near an unmanned sentry tower.

"Thanks be to Saint Benet. The earl has arrived. It's obvious what we must do." Hildegard said. "We must put Lady Isabella's predicament before Northumberland." She turned to her. "You must trust him. Throw yourself on his mercy."

Countless sumpter wagons encircled the bailey. The luckier members of the earl's household poured out of the nooks and crannies where they had been able to get a ride. Others began to unwrap the sacking from their feet, shake out their cloaks, and rub frostbitten fingers.

A cart containing nothing but kindling was unloaded; logs were tossed from another one into the open space between the walls. Fires were started. Cooking pots filled with already prepared pottage were positioned over the flames and the alemaster directed the manhandling of the barrels before ordering the spigots opened.

The snow-blasted travellers began to hang out whatever they could to dry on makeshift lines over the fires. Lastly, the provisions were unloaded and carried off into the castle kitchens.

Most of the household would be bedding down under the wagons tonight, despite the snow, and there was a lot of hurrying about to claim the best places.

In the middle of all this, descending from his gold-covered char, appeared the earl, to be greeted by his chamberlain, already wielding his white stick of office and moving forth in a cloud of servants.

"Ordered chaos," remarked Ulf as he stood with the others on the wall and looked down. "And in all this there should be young Harry Summers, the earl's secretary."

Turning to Isabella, Hildegard said, "With Harry's help, it should be easier to get an audience. We believe Northumberland's here for important matters of state, but if anyone can persuade him to take time to consider your predicament, Harry can."

"I'm afraid I'll be sent back to Morcar," Isabella said, burying herself even deeper into Ulf's thick cloak.

"Did you make a legal promise to him?" asked Hildegard.

Isabella shook her head. "I met him only when I woke up here. After I was abducted, they kept me drugged. I was slipping in and out of nightmares all the time. I think they kept me in a tower somewhere deep in a wood, but I have only the most hazy memory of what happened. My warder was a stranger, a rough fellow, though he tried to put on airs. He had food sent up to me. I'd find it on the floor beside my mattress whenever the drug wore off."

"Did you ever see who brought it?"

"A girl brought it sometimes, but she seemed too frightened to come into the chamber and used to leave it outside the door. I caught sight of her once or twice as she scurried back down the stairs. I found it too much to go up and down the stairs. I felt so weak all the time. I doubt whether the girl ever saw me. Sometimes," she added, "the rough fellow brought food. Mostly, it simply appeared while I was sleeping."

Hildegard turned to Ulf. "Was the girl Alys?"

He nodded. "She told me she was ordered to go into the woods on errands, leaving bread and cheese for the men, she was told, although she said she hardly ever saw anybody. It was only when the scare over the dragon occurred that she was told not to go anymore. It was Fulke who always sent her."

"Thank heavens for the dragon, then." Hildegard gave a quick glance at the masons, but their faces gave nothing away. "Would they have abducted her as well, in time?"

"She's not a pawn in the game between the barons. This manor in dispute is unimportant in the greater battle for power. She was probably going to a different sort of buyer, like other novices who have passed through Handale."

The two masons were listening intently but added nothing. Hildegard felt they were holding something back.

Before she could say anything, Ulf turned to Isabella. "When did Morcar come into the picture, my lady?"

"I don't know. One day I was in the tower; the next I woke up here. Was that yesterday? I'm not sure. All I know is that filthy fellow was leering over me, touching me, and I scratched his face and then"—she frowned—"I'm not sure what happened next. I felt drowsy again and"—her frown deepened—"I feel bruised all over, as if—" She dipped her face out of sight inside the cloak and her shoulders began to shake.

Hildegard and Ulf exchanged glances.

"He'll pay," muttered Ulf through tight lips.

Northumberland had decided it was time to make his entrance by the time they descended from the battlements. The herald blew a fanfarade on his horn. The earl climbed down with great ceremony from his gleaming char. Snow was cleared to make a path through the crowd. Guards stood on both sides, holding aloft lighted torches, and, down this avenue of fire, the king of the north made his stately entrance into the inner court.

His men followed in order of precedence. It was somewhere in this crowd that Hildegard spotted Harry Summers.

Smarter than when she had last seen him—pulled from a game of skittles to answer to Mr. Medford, head of the king's Signet Office—it had been a year ago in the earl's London mansion. Harry had been the innocent key to unravelling a murder.

Now here he was, wrapped in a red cloak, his fair hair hanging in damp ringlets, his merry glance taking everything in with evident good humour.

Ulf waded through the throng, brushing aside one of the guards wielding a smoky torch, and gripped Harry by the arm.

Not so innocent these days, judged Hildegard when she saw the young man's hand go swiftly to his dagger.

As soon as he realised it was Ulf at his side, he threw his arms round him with a yell of delight.

"You old devil, Sir Ulf, of all people. Are you here with Earl Roger de Hutton?"

She saw Ulf shake his head and mutter something, and Harry clapped him on the back and gave him several rib-shaking thumps. "Lord of the manor of Langbrough and well deserved," he shouted. "And is your lady present?" He looked round, caught sight of Hildegard, did a double take, recognised her despite the absence of her white Cistercian habit, and exclaimed with further expressions of delight before going through the whole rigmarole of greeting again, although this time with less thumping and more close hugging.

As they began to drift towards the inner court with the rest of the household, Ulf told Harry about the boon they wanted to ask and the best way of going about it.

He turned to reach out for Isabella, who had been ushered along by the masons and now stood half hidden under her cloak behind him. As he stepped aside to reveal her, her hood fell back. Hildegard was close enough to observe Harry's change of colour. Isabella simply stood in the falling snow, staring at him, without speaking.

The silence lengthened as the crowd flowed around them.

Ulf looked nonplussed at Harry's reaction. None of them had seen him tongue-tied before. "It's an urgent matter, Harry," he prompted. "I wouldn't presume to ask a favour of you otherwise."

"No. That's quite all right," Harry responded. He stared at Isabella for another moment or two, then suddenly spun on his heel and marched into the thick of the crowd still surging in Northumberland's wake.

"Well, I hope he means it," remarked Ulf, gazing after him in dismay.

"I think he may well mean it," replied Hildegard slowly.

The two masons were silent.

Isabella had a look of alarm on her face. "What's going to happen to me if I come face-to-face with Morcar? I must get away!"

With a little cry, she slipped past Ulf and pushed on into the crowd. In a moment, she had vanished from sight.

"Go after her!" Hildegard exclaimed.

"Which way did she go?" Matt was peering over the heads of the crowd.

Ulf looked worried when, almost an hour later, Isabella had still not been found. "What the devil made her run off like that? Was it something to do with Harry Summers? They looked at each other as if they'd met before."

Hildegard could not work it out. "Here's Harry now," she said. Not waiting for Ulf, she went over to the earl's secretary as he left the feast hall and, taking him by the arm, pulled him to one side. "Have you seen Isabella?"

He turned scarlet. "What do you mean?"

"Simply that. Have you seen her? Shortly after meeting you, she ran off. We've no idea where she went."

"Ran off? But where to?"

"I had the feeling you already knew each other."

Harry shook his head. "Never seen her before in my life." He bit his bottom lip. It was as if he'd been felled by some catastrophe, and he stood gazing into the crowd, unseeing, with a dazed, desperate expression.

"Harry?" Ulf came up and put his arm round the young man's shoulders. "Is there something we can do? Are you all right? You look as if you're suffering in some way. It's not the ague from all this bad weather, is it?"

"Suffering, did you say? I surely am. You have no idea." He rubbed the back of a hand across his face, then raked his fingers through his tangled curls in a distracted fashion. "Earl Morcar's boasting that she's the heiress of Kilton Castle. Ownership has been in dispute for many years. Now it's resolved." He looked round at the soaring battlements and the three tall towers. "He intends to get his hands on this place for the balance of power it'll give him in the current battle between Gloucester and King Richard. Morcar doesn't give a tinker's cuss about her." Then he shook his hair back and said more alertly, "We have to find her. Where can she be?"

"Anywhere Morcar is not." Hildegard explained as much as she thought fit, but Harry was already ahead of her and filled in the details himself. His eyes hardened. She saw his fists clench. "It's worse than I thought."

Matt was standing by watching all this and he made a perfunctory and somewhat hostile bow to the earl's secretary. "If I may be permitted to speak?"

"Speak, then. Go on!" Harry was unusually irritable.

"I know we've already had a look on the battlements, but I still reckon she must have gone back there. It's the only place she knows that's far from where that old goat was keeping her." He gestured towards the steps. "Let's try up there again before that fiend gets to her."

Harry Summers was already moving off. "Show me!" he commanded in much the same tone as the earl would use to a vassal.

Matt was already at his heels, and after a moment the two older men, Hamo and Ulf, with Hildegard trailing behind, began to retrace their steps up to the high battlements.

They did manage to find her before Morcar did. It was not without some difficulty, as she must have heard footsteps and decided it was the earl and his men in pursuit. She had wedged herself between a stack of tiles left to repair the roof of one of the lookout towers, and it was only Matt's sharp eyes that managed to pick out her shape from the shadows.

"It's us," he whispered, talking softly, as if to a small animal. "Don't be scared. It's only us. Come out, Isabella. Come out."

Harry Summers pushed him aside. He extended his hand. "My lady," he said in a strong voice, "I beg you to come forth. You'll be safe with me. I give you my oath."

Shaking with her recent fright, Isabella was persuaded to get to her feet and, with the help of the two young men, was helped over the tiles. When she jumped to the ground, she turned at once to Harry Summers. She said nothing, merely looked up at him with large, clear eyes through the snow that mantled them.

Matt turned away.

Harry extended his hand. "My lady? Allow me to escort you to his grace, my lord Percy, earl of Northumberland." He led her back along the wall, the two of them looking at each other as if nobody else existed.

Left to follow, everyone trudged back, too. Hildegard noticed that Matt had held back. When the procession reached the step leading down into the courtyard, he gave Isabella a long, defeated stare, then bowed his head as he began to descend.

Hamo put his arms round the apprentice's shoulders when they reached ground level. "Your time will come, bonny lad. You're scarcely out of swaddling bands."

"That's that, then," remarked Hildegard with satisfaction as she and Ulf descended the steps into the bailey. "I suddenly feel very old."

He put an arm round her. "Mistress York, you'll never be old." He squeezed her against him and, with his arm round her waist, led her back towards the inner gate. "We need to have a talk ourselves," he murmured in her ear when they came to a stop.

"We do?" She met his glance. "Oh, I see."

"Don't look so alarmed," he teased, reading her expression as quickly as ever.

"I was just thinking about Fulke and whether he'll have gone to ground by the time we get back to Handale Priory."

CHAPTER 29

Events at Kilton were not yet concluded, however. A lavish feast was laid on for all the magnates summoned by Northumberland for the purpose of discussing the extent of their commitment to the king's personal quarrel with his uncles, Gloucester and Warwick.

"Personal quarrel? Is that how he wants us to see it?" asked Hildegard when she heard this from the earl's own lips. She was sitting in the feast hall with the others.

Ulf looked disgusted. "He's a slippery customer, I've always thought so. Now he's wriggling out of his oath of fealty to King Richard. He's waiting to see which way the dice will fall." He told her he had spoken earlier to Roger de Hutton, a strong supporter of the king. "He's the only friend Richard has in the north. I can't see him wanting to stick his neck out if there's no one to follow him."

"The Lancasters hold every major castle and town in Yorkshire," she remarked worriedly. "It's difficult for him. Gaunt and Bolingbroke are in accord. The only buffer between Northumberland's territory and Lancaster's is this swathe held by the inheritor of Kilton Castle. While it's in dispute, Northumberland's dilemma is plain to see." She turned to him. "Northumberland must feel he needs to tread with caution."

"Damn him to hell!" exclaimed Ulf. "He should support his

king without demur. What does an oath mean if it can be forgotten when it suits?"

"What do you think will happen next?"

"The king has the support of the City of London—"

"But the present mayor is in Gloucester's pocket. Everybody knows the elections were rigged. How long will the City think it worth their while to support poor Richard?"

"We'll have to wait and see."

They turned their attention back to Northumberland, who was still on his feet. Talking.

"And now," he bellowed in his northern accent, all flat vowels and ironstone consonants, "we deserve meat, drink, and merriment! Bring on the fool!"

His own fool came tumbling out of a box onto the table and proceeded to go through his repertoire of somersaults and cartwheels, along with some other ribald accomplishments that had the hall in an uproar of joy.

Things were rowdy when Hildegard tugged at Ulf's sleeve. "Look over there. It's Morcar. That steward must have let him out."

With a black velvet cloak over one shoulder, his elaborate wine-coloured capuchon, and a clipped beard, he looked languidly confident, a noble among northern peasants, and people automatically made way for him. Two henchmen in blue and green got up on either side as he rose from the long table where they had been eating. A way was cleared as he made his way to the foot of the dais.

To Hildegard's astonishment, he breached all the rules of etiquette and stepped up onto it and stalked over to accost Northumberland himself. It was obvious he had something urgent to say.

Northumberland's mouth dropped open as the earl tugged at his sleeve. He was holding a piece of dripping venison between his fingers and the grease ran down inside his cuff as he paused with it halfway to his mouth. They watched as Morcar said something and the earl cupped his free hand round his ear, the better to hear what was being said.

Northumberland glanced round the table. His guests were leaning forward to catch Morcar's words. His lips moved as he seemed to ask a question.

Hildegard said, "I wish I could lip-read."

Morcar bowed deeply. Northumberland's small, piggy eyes looked him over. His lips, just visible in his nest of red beard, were set in a grim line.

"It must be about Isabella."

Ulf put his hand on her arm. "Wait."

The earl said something to his chamberlain, who rose, grasped his stick, and managed to establish a modicum of silence among the revellers while the earl rose to his feet. He leaned heavily against the table with the piece of venison still clutched in one hand. He waved it to include everyone in his orbit.

"Not making a long speech, so stop your groaning, lads," he called affably to one or two knights who had started to give him a slow handclap. "It seems we have two lovers among us." There were cheers at this and one or two slanderous remarks about people known to everyone else. "They are," bellowed Northumberland, his voice rising in exaggerated disbelief, "so much in love, I'm told, that they wish to marry! Can you believe it!" He flapped the back of one pudgy hand at Morcar. "Be seated, man."

Looking mystified, Earl Morcar went back to his place and turned expectantly to listen to the rest of what the earl had to say.

"Harry Summers!" shouted the earl. "Call Harry Summers! Where are you, you dice-playing young wastrel?"

There was little refinement in the earl's manner. Harry emerged amid a sea of backslapping and a few cheers from those at the back of the hall who must have had little idea what was going on. No one does, for that matter, thought Hildegard, giving Ulf a glance.

"This"—the earl put an arm round Harry's shoulders and squeezed the breath from him—"is the young devil who pretends to be my secretary! Isn't that so, Harry?"

"It is, Your Grace. To my great honour."

"And are you married yet, Harry?"

"No, I'm not, Your Grace."

"No, he's not!" came a roar from those who knew him. They began to bang their ale mugs on the table, chanting the name Summers until the chamberlain fussed forward to quiet them.

"No, you're not married, you lucky young devil. But we've decided to rectify matters and put you in chains. Harry Summers, everybody!" The earl pushed him forward, to increasing cheers. "Your turn. Speak up," he shouted over the noise. The earl plumped down with a satisfied smile and the ale mugs clattered again.

Harry looked nervous. He was flushed. He stared out over the heads of the combined retinues of several households. Everyone fell silent. He took a deep breath.

"I, Harry Summers—"

"Get on with it!" somebody shouted, interrupting him.

"I'm trying to, you losel. Give me chance." He took another deep breath. "I, Harry Summers, say to you all, as my witnesses, and in good faith, to hear my oath—that if her guardian does not give me one penny and the lawmen find against her claim of inheritance, I hold myself satisfied by her to be my lawful wife." His lips trembled. He gazed over the heads of those nearby into the back of the hall. "My fair lady Isabella, I want you as my wife and shall cleave to no other from now until the end of time. And I give you this, my pledge, before witnesses and before God. Amen."

Morcar leaned forward with a frown.

Then a woman's voice spoke up from the back of the hall. "Hear this my oath. I take you, Harry Summers, as my man, to have and to hold, in poverty or riches, for fairer or grimmer, for the duration of my life. And to this I give you my pledge. I, Isabella of . . ."

She hesitated and glanced at Northumberland.

"Kilton," he roared. "I'll make sure of that!"

Morcar jerked to his feet. He glared at Northumberland and then he peered back into the recesses of the hall through the smoke of a dozen cressets to see who had spoken, and then he gave a terrible shout.

Walking between the crowded tables of feasting guests came Isabella. She was wearing a gown of pale green silk, her hair was loose, the silver filigree crispinette nestled on her head, and a smile of the utmost happiness was on her face.

Harry Summers started down from the dais to meet her, but before he could take her hands in his, Morcar, spitting like a cat, stepped between them.

"No! You can't do this! She is betrothed to me! This is invalid. I'll have the lawmen stop it!" He turned to the earl and asked peremptorily, "Where's your attorney?"

Northumberland's lip curled at being addressed like this. "Sit down, you old fool. We don't need an attorney. It was done according to the law and there are plenty who'll bear witness to it."

"Oh no, you don't cheat me like this. This is only a presumption of marriage, an intention; the law will bear me out. It's a formula *de presenti*. It means nothing!"

"I said, 'Sit down, you old fool.' In fact, don't sit down!" Northumberland gave him a ferocious glance. "I'll tell you what to do, Earl Morcar. Get back to the lands you used to hold in my name. Get back to the lands you lost. Wrest them back from the Scots who took them from you. Do that! Go on! Get out! And don't come beggin' to me again!"

Morcar stood, mouth opening and closing like a cod's. He

blinked once or twice. Seeing that there was nothing to be done, he gestured to his men to follow, then slunk away through the cheering ranks of Northumberland's supporters.

At the door, he turned as if to give a parting shot, but by then most had lost interest in him. Hildegard thought she must have been the only one to see his lips draw back in a vicious snarl as he made his exit.

"A satisfactory outcome," Ulf observed as he guided Hildegard outside.

"To most, yes." She mentioned Matt. "I think he was smitten, too."

"He'll get over it."

It had been tempting not to stay to eat and drink their fill in the feast hall, but Ulf had urgent business to attend to.

He looked down at her. "I'm going to search for Petronel before that devil rides off with him."

"I know. I'm coming with you."

He tucked her hand in his under his cloak as they crossed to the stables.

CHAPTER 30

Ulf's task was to find his stolen horse, then persuade the stable hands still on duty that Petronel belonged to him. While Morcar stood by waiting for his men to bring down his personal baggage and the pack ponies were being loaded up, Ulf was conducted by the prancing little page, Pippin, between the rows of stalls until he came to within a few feet of the last stall, where a horse was covered by a green-and-blue blanket.

Some attempt had been made to keep it out of sight behind a few bales of hay, but Pippin, dancing with delight, pulled Morcar's colours from her back.

Ulf said something to the stable hands, then gave a whistle. The horse poked its head round the bales, and when it saw Ulf, it started to pull and strain at its halter and snicker with pleasure.

"Let him loose," Ulf ordered. "See whether he comes to me or to that thief over there."

Morcar stepped forward, spurs jangling. "What the devil do you mean? Are you calling me a thief?"

Both men had their hands on the hilts of their swords.

The horsemaster came up. "I heard all that." He glanced at Ulf. "You're saying this here fellow stole your horse?"

"I am."

"When was this, like?"

Ulf told him. He also described the horse with the thoroughness of an owner.

"Go ahead, then. Call him. It's a fair test."

Morcar bristled forward. "It's ridiculous! I won't participate!"

"Go on," the horsemaster urged Ulf. "If he doesn't know you, you lose him. Can't say fairer than that."

Ulf whistled again. With a surge of rippling muscles, the great black horse lunged free of his restraints. His head moved above Ulf, sniffing the air, and then his muzzle came down with a whickering sound and nuzzled into Ulf's neck. He breathed softly through his nostrils, making sounds of delight, and Ulf flung his arms round the stallion's huge neck with a look of joy on his face.

"I reckon that proves it." The horsemaster nodded. "Take him." He turned to Morcar. "It's not up to me to bring charges. Horse thieving is a serious accusation."

"Leave it," murmured Ulf, still fondling Petronel. "He's got a hard task ahead of him. He'll need all his energy to get his land back from the Scots."

"Now we can safely say it's been a satisfactory outcome," Ulf said as he led Petronel out into the stable yard.

"Not quite," Hildegard objected. "I have one or two things to settle back at Handale Priory."

"You're not going back there?"

"As soon as possible. You don't have to come, Ulf. The masons will want to be getting back as soon as they can. I'll return with them."

When she left him to find her sleeping quarters in the visitors' tower, Ulf was standing in the falling snow with his arms round the neck of his great, beautiful beast of a horse, Petronel.

The visitors' accommodation was in the tower in the outer court, but she made her way past the gatehouse guards thankfully without being noticed. She was just crossing to the tower steps when a rider came tearing in at speed across the hastily lowered drawbridge. He dropped from his mount almost at her feet.

"Mistress, quick, be so kind as to direct me to his grace the earl of Northumberland."

"In the feast hall. Through there." She pointed. "What's happened?"

"Tragedy! A matter of major importance."

She noticed the royal crest on the leather satchel slung over his shoulder. "Is it the king's business?"

"It is. You may as well know, as it's being broadcast throughout the realm. It's Robert de Vere, marquess of Ireland. He's been defeated by Henry of Lancaster."

"By Bolingbroke?"

The man was about to rush on, but she detained him. "I beg you, tell me what's happened."

"De Vere was outmanoeuvred by the three armies riding against him. Bolingbroke caught him in a classic pincer grip at Radcot Bridge. They didn't even engage. The Welsh archers melted away and de Vere had to run for it. Nobody knows where he is. But the army he raised has disappeared. It's all over for the king."

So Bolingbroke had made his choice. Now it was up to Northumberland.

"He's in there!" She pointed again. "You'll know which one is the earl."

The courier ran on towards the inner courtyard, and Hildegard felt herself drawn reluctantly after him to witness for herself what effect his news would have. It was momentous. It must mean civil war. Now, surely, the north would rise up in defence of the king. Northumberland could not refuse to go to his aid.

Northumberland was on his feet when she returned to the hall.

Everyone looked poleaxed.

The earl was saying, "If the king had commanded us to raise an army on his behalf, we would have gone. But did he? No, he did not. No message was sent. No courier was despatched to seek our aid. No word came." He glared round at his followers.

"How were we to know he needed the help of our army?" he continued. "Are we necromancers? Do we read his desires in the lees of our wine cup?"

Northumberland, more verbose than usual, gave his men another baleful glance. He had already been swiftly into his answer to the courier's news by the time Hildegard had reached the hall. Now she stared at him in disbelief.

But he had not finished.

"I ask you again, my friends, why did the king not call on us? Are we out of favour? We northerners. We are already aware that he regards our continual sacrifice in defending the realm against the Scots in the Marches as of little account. He questions our honesty in deploying our militia. He does not recognise our victories. He starves me of gold to pay you, my men."

A snigger of disbelief from somewhere in the hall was quickly stifled. It was common knowledge that Northumberland received a chest of gold from the exchequer to cover his expenses every time the Scots attacked.

He did not hear this hint of disbelief and continued in the same vein.

"Our king demands more and then more still, without reward or recompense. He appoints new Wardens of the March on a whim, often fellows without a title among them. And now, when his quarrel with his uncles is too much for him to deal with, he sends this courier! He begs for help! From us! The men he otherwise ignores!

No offence to you, my friend." He lowered his voice and turned to the courier. "You are only doing your job, as must we all. Bringing the news from Radcot, wherever the hell that is. Some heathen place down south, I'm told. But it is we; we are the ones he now expects to sacrifice our Marcher privileges to the Scots and run to his aid! I ask, why us?"

Northumberland took a deep drink from a chased gold mazer, wiped his beard with the back of his hand, and continued. "I say, leave southern quarrels to the southerners. Leave it to those who reap the rewards. Leave it to the men who fight among themselves and notice us only when they need our help. Why should we put ourselves at risk in a petty family quarrel? Would they do the same for us if I fell out with my son, young Harry Hotspur?"

Hildegard did not wait to hear more. So that was it. Richard would be left to his fate.

Despite the fact that the north had been in uproar when, only last autumn, the dukes, led by Gloucester, had impeached King Richard's chancellor, Michael de la Pole, a wealthy merchant's son from Hull, on what everyone knew to be trumped-up charges of embezzlement, now, it seemed, their memories were short. Not one landowner had spoken in the king's defence.

Roger de Hutton, she noted, was absent.

She went out into the snow and looked up at the sky. It had cleared. Somewhere up there, King Richard's star shone, but among all the millions in the sky tonight, it was hard to see whether it was falling or not.

During the night, a howling easterly rocked the three towers of Kilton Castle. The sound kept everyone awake. By morning, the wind dropped and the sun glittered in the bluest of skies. Best of all for the travellers, snow on the moors road had been scoured away from all but the deepest dales.

The two masons were for taking the long route back to Handale Priory. As they could see from the battlements, where they went to make a survey of the terrain, frozen drifts lay deep and treacherous in the gullies between the tree-covered ridges of the woods.

"Be it so," Hildegard reluctantly agreed. She hoisted her bag onto her shoulder.

She had already said good-bye to Ulf. He intended to stay a few days to see if Northumberland would have a change of heart and to hear any further news from the south as soon as it was brought in.

He would, he told her, stop at the priory on his way back to Langbrough, when, no doubt, the bailiffs would have arrested Master Fulke on charges of abduction, theft of goods, and possibly murder.

As they neared the outer limits of the priory, the snow, unlike that on the high moor, lay deep and undisturbed. They had a hard walk of it, feet sliding from under them, despite taking the easier well-worn track from the moor. When they at last entered the woods, Hildegard was glad she had rejected Ulf's offer to hire a palfrey for her. Here it was easier on foot. They eventually emerged at the top of the slope midway between the tower and the masons' lodge.

"Now for it," muttered Hamo. "I wonder how poor old Dakin is getting on."

They trailed up to the still-locked and silent lodge.

"We'll get the key from Carola, then come back."

"To risk attack by the dragon of Handale?" Hildegard asked, giving them both a sideways look.

They exchanged glances with each other but made no comment.

There were no footprints of a clawlike nature anywhere, apart from the tiny scuttering prints of field mice and shrews and one or two winter birds.

But there was blood.

Over by the door into the enclosure was a mound of dark reddish brown. It had stained the snow where the hound had fallen, then spread like the blood on a butcher's chopping block.

"They've taken it away," observed Matt.

They stepped round the place where the hound had been brought down, opened the door, and went inside.

CHAPTER 31

Dakin greeted them outside the guest hall with both hands raised above his head.

"What, no shackles?" Hamo went up to him and punched him playfully on the chest. "Good on you, bonny lad. What happened?"

"The prioress decided she would not bring charges. The blame for the theft of the chalice, if it really was stolen, was put on the escaped novice. The prioress has washed her hands of the whole business."

I know why that is, thought Hildegard. She does not want to be associated with Fulke when he's charged with abduction and selling girls to the whoremasters. She said, "And as for Master Fulke? Still suffering from the ague?"

Dakin smirked. "He's hiding in his chamber. The prioress's attorney has been coming and going. He's staying with us now. Soon there'll be more seculars than nuns."

Carola was sitting inside the hall, drawing as usual. She greeted Hildegard somewhat cautiously. "Let's call for wine, mistress, and you can give us a full account. I can see it's mixed news from Kilton."

"Indeed." Hildegard sank down beside her and pulled off her wet boots with a sigh of relief. "But, tell us, has Fulke confessed?"

As soon as their story was out and the masons had been told about the king's defeat in the south, Carola told them that Fulke had so far made no confession but instead had denied everything. After that, Hildegard told them she had returned for a reason which she would divulge later.

She got up and picked up her boots. "I gave a promise of help and I must keep my word."

Her boots were still not dry, even though she had positioned them close to the hearth for the last hour. Still, they would get wet again in the garth. She pulled them on and opened the door. The garth was running with rapidly melting snow. Icicles hanging from the snouts of the gargoyles were dripping like noses. She bent underneath these waterspouts and crossed to the door into Basilda's private domain.

The prioress was sitting in her chair, looking out through the open door when Hildegard appeared, as if expecting a visitor. Her first words confirmed that it was Hildegard she expected. "Yes," she said, "I heard you were back from Kilton, Mistress York. A useful visit, I trust?"

"It was most eventful." She avoided all mention of Isabella, deciding to wait and see how much Basilda knew about Fulke's traffic. Instead, she told her the news from the south, about de Vere's defeat at Radcot Bridge.

Basilda frowned. "Will there be a rising against the king?"

"It depends on the depth of his uncle Gloucester's ambition."

"Or that of his cousin Bolingbroke," she remarked drily. "Now would be the time to strike to bring the king down, if only they have the gall. How shameless are they? I wonder. Will they find a way to justify moving against the Lord's anointed? If so, where does that leave us?"

Hildegard raised her brows.

"We depend on the acknowledged mystery of the Church for our safety," Basilda stated.

"Notwithstanding Arundel's treatment of those nuns on the south coast a few years ago?"

Basilda glowered. "That was iniquitous. Negligence in a commander most heinous and abhorrent to all decent folk. He will surely pay for such an outrage if there is any justice."

They referred to a horrific event when some of the duke's militia, billeted on a small priory on the coast near Southampton and held there for longer than planned, decided to enjoy more than the nuns willingly offered. About twenty nuns were abducted and forcibly taken out to sea, there to be raped, some to be thrown overboard.

The men had gone unpunished and Arundel had managed to wriggle out of any responsibility. At the time, the whole realm had been shocked, but now, with the passage of time, the guilty had got away with it. And, as with the wrongful impeachment of de la Pole, memories were short. Instead, more recent outrages were being shuddered over.

Hildegard stood in the doorway. "I've all but finished my work in the scriptorium, my lady. I trust I may go up in order to complete it?"

Basilda gave her a long, considering look. "Are you a friend of Handale?"

She wants to know what I have discovered, thought Hildegard. Remembering the penitents in the cells and the way the novices were treated, she could not answer straightaway.

Basilda's expression was enigmatic. "Friend or foe? I can read the answer on your face, madam. Perhaps you'll tell me what your purpose is? Why are you here?"

"I arrived, as I told you, with the intention of settling a personal dilemma—"

"And have you achieved this purpose?"

Honesty made Hildegard shake her head.

"You may go up." Basilda waved a hand in the direction of the scriptorium. "I doubt you'll find anything up there to help you resolve your dilemma."

So, no hint that she knew about Isabella and her importance as a pawn in the events to come if the dukes declared for war against the king. And no hint that she was afraid Hildegard might have discovered her own personal secret.

A formidable cardplayer.

Hildegard took the stairs two at a time.

There was already someone sitting at the desk by the window. It was Desiderata.

"Mistress York, how delightful." She rested a hand on the vellum unrolled across the desk and beamed a welcome.

"I'll come back." Hildegard began to back out of the door. "The prioress didn't tell me there was anyone else working in here."

"Please don't leave because of me." Desiderata gave her kitten smile, all sharp little teeth and sleepily narrowed eyes. "I'm copying the kitchen accounts. You may help if you wish."

Desiderata is certainly trusted, thought Hildegard.

With nothing she would like less than to have to sit and listen to Desiderata's simpering comments, she stifled a sigh. "I'd be honoured, domina." She used the title given to the more learned nuns in her own Order.

Desiderata acknowledged the compliment without irony and got up from her place. "Sit here, do. I'll go down and find another chair. I'm so glad our dear lady prioress asked you to lighten my task."

As soon as she had gone, Hildegard hurried over to the shelf containing the earlier records of the priory and reached up for the two or three rolls she had not yet inspected. They were untouched since she had last been here. Blowing dust off them, she quickly unrolled the first one. She had a good idea which set might contain information helpful to Mariana.

Down below, Desiderata's voice could be heard rising and falling. A door closed and the sound was cut off.

Quickly scanning the contents of the rolls, Hildegard was acutely aware that the nun would soon return, and she hurriedly searched through them to find the approximate year she wanted.

It was in the third roll that she hit on the one that related to the year of Mariana's entry into the priory.

Before she could read it, a sound from the floor below made her stuff the whole thing inside her sleeve. When the door opened and Desiderata walked in carrying a stool, Hildegard was at the desk, apparently reading the vellum that had been spread out for her.

"I was wondering, domina, do you wish them to be ordered by date or topic?" she asked, conscious of the bulge in her sleeve.

"Oh, I think date order might be best, don't you?"

Sweetness and light reigned for the rest of the afternoon until nones.

The bell began to toll. It sent the birds in the garth flying up with hungry squawking as their scavenging under the melting snow was disturbed. Black-robed figures began to file down from the *dortoir* and process silently into the cloister.

Desiderata went to the window. "Poor dears," she commented. "So sad."

"Their lives?" asked Hildegard in surprise.

"Their fate." The nun gave the familiar little smile. "Time for prayers, mistress. No slacking now."

Aware that she would have an hour's privacy in which to solve the mystery of Mariana's baby, Hildegard made some remark about following her down and after Desiderata left she quickly took the roll from her sleeve and spread it out.

It took some time to find what she was looking for. When she finished reading, she returned the roll to the shelf, pushing it in among the ones that had been examined already. It might lie there for some time without anyone ever bothering to read it. On balance, it might be the best thing that could happen.

She went out. Down. Into the garth.

Poor Mariana.

And that, she told herself, makes me sound as syrupy as Desiderata. The difference was compassion rose from the bottom of her heart.

"Did you hear the dragon roaring in the night when we were at Kilton?" Hildegard asked as they were drinking a warming beverage before going up to their beds.

Dakin jerked his head round. "No, but the conversi brought in that dead deerhound."

"Was it killed by the dragon, then?"

Dakin looked confused. "What do you think, Carola?" He bent his head and pretended to adjust the lacing on his boots.

Carola was leaning back in a chair, resting her eyes from too much close work that day. "I don't know. But I do know that if we can't get away from here and back to Durham, I'm going to be roaring, too."

Hamo had just come in. He must have been hanging round the kitchen again, talking to his dairymaid. He brought lumps of ewe's milk cheese for everyone. "It's still thawing," he said. "If the master doesn't show up, we may as well load our tackle and leave. Like as not we'll meet him on the Durham road."

"No one heard the dragon while we were away," cut in Hildegard pointedly.

Dakin got up. "I'm off. Good night, all."

Matt, carving a piece of wood, was giving all his concentration to his work.

That night, it rained so hard that almost every trace of snow had vanished by the time people began making their way over to the church for the first office. Shortly after the service was over, the bailiffs rode in from Whitby.

There was no doubt about their arrival. They could be heard all over the garth, voices booming along the cloisters, making them echo. Confident voices. Men with the authority to do and say what they pleased. Several heads appeared at the cell windows as the nuns looked out to see what was causing the commotion.

The man in charge took something out of an inner pocket with a flourish. "I have here a warrant. We seek a Master Fulke, a guest of this priory?" He looked round.

"Aye, we all know he's here," his companion agreed. "Fetch him forth."

They were accompanied by a couple of bodyguards. Nobody wanted to argue with them. The cellaress sent the nearest onlooker to rouse Fulke from his bed.

The servant came back almost straightaway. "Too sick to be moved, my lady."

"You'd better go inside and see him," suggested the cellaress. The same servant was delegated to show the bailiffs the way to Fulke's bedchamber.

Hildegard saw Josiana walk briskly off towards the prioress's parlour. She followed the bailiffs and stood at the door with the others. It would be interesting to see whether they dragged Fulke out in his nightshirt or merely set a guard at his door.

A few moments later, the two men reappeared. A command or

two was uttered. It was to be guards, then. Fulke must be profoundly sick, or a convincing mummer.

Desiderata went up to one of the men. "I wish to make it known that I have the duty to bring food and drink to the prisoner." She smiled sweetly up at the more imposing of the two guards.

"That's perfectly acceptable to us," replied the bailiff, having overheard her. "If we can't trust a nun, whom can we trust?" He smiled at the dimpling young woman, who now turned her attention to him.

"So kind, master," she said breathily. "Perhaps you would like to have something fetched from the kitchen for yourselves?"

"We'll go over there, if you'll be so kind as to show us the way?"

In an amicable group, they left the guard on duty and moved off across the garth.

Hildegard had not seen Mariana since her return to the priory, and not wishing to draw attention to the fact that she wanted to speak to her, she had not asked for her whereabouts. Now she decided to seek her out.

The *dortoir* was fairly busy with a lot of coming and going, the nuns unsettled, it seemed, by the appearance of men from the outside within their isolated community. Hildegard's presence caused far less comment than that of the men, even though she was entering forbidden quarters. Climbing to the first floor, she went unchallenged, peered in through the apertures in the doors, and found Mariana's cell with little difficulty.

The nun was on her knees in front of a wooden cross. Doubtful about disturbing her, Hildegard hung about in the corridor until impatience forced her to give a tentative knock on the door. Mariana's devotions were not so deep that she did not start up at once. Scrambling off her knees, she took two strides to the door. "What's happened? What do you want?"

"I made you a promise—"

Mariana gasped. "You have information?"

Hildegard nodded.

"Not here." She glanced furtively along the corridor. "Meet me—" She searched her mind for a convenient place. "Meet me at the priest's house. Nobody goes there now."

"When?"

"After vespers. We have a little freedom before compline. People usually stay in the cloister to while away the time."

"Very well."

She could not tell from Mariana's expression whether her information would be welcome or not.

A little while later, Fulke was persuaded to get out of bed. He made a shaky appearance in the refectory, sitting between the two guards, looking as if he lacked the strength to attempt an escape. He had been safe from the law as long as the snows lasted, but now that the roads were open, he could be dragged back to the nearest town to face his accusers.

An attorney appointed on behalf of the earl of Northumberland had sent word to the bailiffs in Whitby to the effect that the earl had evidence against a Master Fulke of Ruswarp. He stood accused of bringing goods into the port at Killingbeck without paying tolls. Other charges would be remitted at a later date. This one was enough to hold him for the time being. The accusation of abduction would no doubt come later. As for murder, burning on the tongues of the masons, it was up to them to accuse him. If they believed they had enough evidence.

Fulke must have suspected he was in for it. He looked like a defeated man.

It didn't stop him from sharing a stoup of ale with his captors. The men became more friendly after several drinks. With armed guards and two no-nonsense bailiffs beside him, it was, of course, impossible for Fulke to escape.

Hildegard left the masons to keep an eye on him. With luck, he would confess everything after a few drinks and they would not be obliged to offer any evidence against him. The badge Giles had lost close to where his body was found was no evidence of murder, despite the fact that it had obviously been torn off in a struggle, and a glib serjeant-at-law would dance rings round it.

Although the snow had vanished from the ground near the priest's house, some still remained like a scab on the thatch. Inside, the atmosphere was dank. It was like an ice cave. The hollow room echoed dismally to the sound of Hildegard's entrance. Water could be heard dripping in a melancholy way onto the floorboards in the upstairs chamber, where the priest had done his solitary writing.

She had arrived early, missing vespers on purpose to be sure to be present when Mariana arrived. Now she stood turned to the window, where a patch of sky could be seen.

Everything about the priory contributed to her feeling of unease. A strong sense of the tight bonds among the nuns suggested that much was going on under the surface, and it did not make her position easy. She was not trusted. She felt she was here on sufferance. Did they imagine someone had planted her here? If so, what was she not supposed to discover?

The only connection she had with anyone they might fear was with the archbishop of York, but Alexander Neville had major problems of his own at present. If the dukes were determined to go after the king himself, the archbishop would be in the firing line, too, as he had so movingly admitted to her in London last year when de la Pole was the first of the king's men to meet his nemesis.

It had been over a year since she had seen Archbishop Neville. If there was a network of spies put in place by the duke of Lancaster, with maybe Fulke as an informer, even he could not imagine she still took orders from Neville. She had served her purpose down in Westminster. Proud to have done so, indeed, despite the horror of that involvement.

She realised she had not thought of Rivera for some days, except once, falling asleep, when that insatiable longing for him had swept over her again like a black wave dragging her down into the depths of a seemingly endless grief. But she had surfaced. It was once only, in a week of nights. A victory of some sort—if forgetting the beloved can ever be seen as victory.

Pay attention, she warned herself when she heard a step outside.

Desiderata had followed her.

For some reason, she went cold.

The nun, her tight wimple framing her face as if it were in a vise, flitted past the window. A black wraith. Now there, now gone.

Hildegard went decisively to the door and flung it wide without waiting for her to open it. "Why, Desiderata!" she exclaimed. "I was just leaving. Have you come to clean the poor boy's house? I'm afraid he was like most men and it needs a thorough scrubbing." I can play her game, she thought when she saw the nun give a start and two pink spots appear on her cheeks.

"I believe the servants will be expected to clear up after him," she said, dithering. "I hope it's not too bad?"

"I'll leave it to your expert supervision!" Hildegard swept out before she could reply and was out of earshot before the nun could stop her.

As she turned the corner onto the garth, she nearly bumped into Mariana. "Someone is already at the house," she explained. "Let's go elsewhere to talk. Follow me."

CHAPTER 32

Mariana was white-faced.

"So what are you going to do?" Hildegard watched as the nun paced back and forth across the floor of the mortuary. She had sent the attendant nun at vigil to the main buildings on an invented errand so that no one would disturb them.

Mariana was aware of that. She made no answer. Instead, she began to tear in silence at her clothes. She ground her nails into the palms of her hands. She made no sound and her silent rage, slowly building, was worse than any ranting might have been. Her chest began to heave as she struggled for breath. Her mouth worked. Still no sound. Hildegard waited and watched, aware that her greatest kindness would be to allow Mariana to come to terms with the situation herself. And then be there for her.

The nun ripped off her head covering. She let the black fabric drop to the floor. Everything she did was in slow motion. After the head covering came the wimple. Her fingers groped behind her neck for the ties and she tore them loose. With a slow, dreamlike movement, she freed her hair from its constraints.

It was a gold colour, and it bristled due to the savage cut the Order demanded. She ran both hands over it, rubbed it hard, then put her head in her heads and began to weep.

Still she did not speak. Instead, she uttered a long, low moan and began to pull at her habit, tearing the tough fabric, wrenching it to free herself from its touch, as if it were contaminated with Venice poison. Kicking off her leather sandals, she fell suddenly to her knees in her shift and rocked back and forth, her arms clasped tightly around herself as she struggled for breath.

A word escaped her. Nothing more than a gasp.

Hildegard crouched beside her but did not interrupt her. She listened to the words that were now beginning to pour from the nun's lips. Obscenities, curses, and those two words, over and over, "My baby, my baby . . ." on and on.

Hildegard rose to her feet. It was an ironic choice of place in which to give the nun the information that had been denied her. A death house. The two corpses still lay shrouded on the trestles, waiting for the coroner and burial.

Its incongruity could not be helped. She had expected Mariana to react strongly, and this was the best place possible, a private place where she could freely express her grief. And the dead cannot hear.

Then the nun began to howl. Her words became a long, unbroken scream. A curse on the man who had betrayed her. Curse after curse. The roof hollow reverberated with his name. Even the candles seemed to flicker with the energy of her rage. It seemed as if the sound would never stop.

Hildegard went to the door and looked out. The grey buildings that had contained Mariana's anguish for so long were unchanged. She had half expected to see them crumble at this rage against the misery that had existed within their walls for so long.

When she turned back, Mariana was weeping without making a sound. The first instance of her grief had abated. Tears glistened on her eyelashes.

Hildegard went to kneel beside her again. "Is there anything you want to ask me, Mariana?"

Mariana raised a wet face towards her. "How could he lie about me? Why would he hate me so much?" She tightened her lips in bewilderment. "I gave him everything. Like a fool. Like a blind, trusting fool. And all the time I meant nothing to him—"

"I'm sure he did not plan it like that."

"Sure? How can you be sure? How can either of us know anything about the mind of a man like that? He used me for his own pleasure and cared not one whit for me. He consigned me to a living hell. I broke my vows because of him, because I believed his lies. I believed he loved me. I imagined I loved him. I allowed him to absolve me from sin, when all the time I knew he was wrong. So I'm as much to blame; I accept that. But it was he, older, with such authority, such power—"

"And you were just a young girl, no more than nineteen, knowing little of the world, and—"

"And trusting him to take care of me—because I thought he loved me—because of my vanity? It must have been my wickedness, my lewdness, that led him astray—"

"Don't shoulder all the blame yourself, Mariana. He was your superior, a man you were supposed to revere, and he seduced you, led you where he wanted you to go—"

"I thought he knew everything about Godliness, understood everything, loved everything. Loved me."

"When he was still lord bishop of the diocese—I mean still alive, available—then you might have asked him what had prompted him to forget his vows so completely, but even if he understood the darkest corners of his own mind, he still might have been unable or unwilling to explain. Everything comes down to speculation. It leads nowhere. It's best not to tread that path. He simply and weakly succumbed to desire."

Mariana nodded. She regained some vigour. Her eyes were beginning to clear. She leaned back on her heels. "Things must be arranged with gentleness. My . . ." She hesitated. "My son must be told the truth very carefully. And then a visit must be arranged." She clasped her hands to her breast. "I'll meet him! Hold him in my arms! A living, breathing creature! Is it a miracle? I cannot believe"—she held out one trembling hand—"I cannot believe that this blood flowing through my veins also flows through his. Flesh of my flesh, my beloved child."

Hildegard's first impression of Mariana had been of a fierce, cold woman, unbalanced by the harshness of the regimen at Handale, but now she saw a side that must have been hidden for years.

After some little time when they had knelt together and talked about her son, a three-year-old in the care of monks at Furness Abbey, her eyes shone with love for the little creature she had held once, briefly, after giving birth in the sordid conditions of a penitential cell.

She was already making plans when, rearranging her torn garments, they left the mortuary together.

Hildegard had promised to accompany Mariana to Basilda's parlour. To be an advocate if she needed one. Already, Mariana had made the big decision to leave the Order. To regain custody of her child. To plan a future that would be free of lies and punishment.

The prioress was in her chair, as usual. Mariana told her what had changed. She uttered no words of recrimination against Basilda. None would have been appropriate, as what had happened had been under the rule of the previous prioress, the one now enjoying a comfortable life as a corrodian at St. Mary's Abbey in York.

Basilda's small, sharp eyes flickered towards Hildegard and she nodded once as she took in what Mariana was saying.

The hawk on its perch danced back and forth and the prioress took it onto her wrist and began to stroke the bird's head with one finger. Hildegard was reminded of Archbishop Neville. In defeat, he had sought solace in the care bestowed on his hawk, too.

Eventually, Basilda gave a huge sigh that shook her jowls. "And you, Mistress York, with your useful facility in reading texts, will no doubt have read those other texts between Master Fulke and myself?" She rested a challenging glare on Hildegard, who nodded.

"But you have told no one?"

Hildegard shook her head.

"I trust this reticence will continue?" Basilda's expression had something of pleading in it, which Hildegard was astonished to see.

Hildegard replied, "I have no desire to rake up matters that can only discomfort the living."

Basilda turned to Mariana. "You may as well get out, then. Pack your things. Go to him. Praise God you have a son. There is no greater joy and duty than for a mother to care for her child." She blinked rapidly, as if her eyes were filling up, then said sharply to Mariana, "I'll write a letter to the abbot of Furness. You'll find he's a very different type to the man who fathered your child." She beckoned to Hildegard. "As you're so good with the pen, you can write what I dictate. Then we shall have only the matter of Northumberland to occupy us."

"Is that so? I mean—" Hildegard faltered as she recalled how she had suspected the prioress of murdering the priest, her own son, and how now, unequivocally, that was unlikely to be so. And yet someone had made him a target, she was convinced. It could not have been accidental. "The death of"—she faltered again, glancing at Mariana, who was innocent of the truth—"the death of your priest," she said tactfully, "is still unsolved."

"You mean you believe there is some puzzle attached to it?"

"I do."

"Was it not an accident?"

"Was it?"

"A careful boy. Difficult to believe he could ever be careless, the discipline of his upbringing—" Basilda looked confused. "And not death by his own hand, either. A great sin. Not to be countenanced. And he was looking forward to the fight over his inheritance."

Hildegard said, "I believe the manner of his death is open to question."

Basilda sent Mariana upstairs to fetch the writing implements. While she was out of hearing, the prioress turned to Hildegard.

"Tell me bluntly. You think he was murdered?"

"I believe it's a possibility."

"That's what Josiana, my cellaress, believes, too." Tears again came into her eyes and brimmed on the folds of flesh beneath. "He was harmless. He would never have won Kilton. He knew it. But he was looking forward to testing his mettle against the men of law. He thought to prove himself in order to delete the dishonour of his birth. He was no pawn in Northumberland's power games, no use to Bolingbroke. Fulke was aware of that. So why would anybody have wanted him dead?"

A note of determination came into Basilda's voice. "Do this one thing for me, Mistress York. Find his killer. And leave that person's punishment to me."

First impressions are often misleading, Hildegard thought, not for the first time, as she made her way outside after writing Mariana's letter for her. Even when the plain logic of expediency led to an obvious conclusion, it often failed to take into account the ambivalent nature of the human heart. To see someone as black or white was no more than to regard them as characters in a morality play. It was not true to the light and dark of human nature.

To think she had secretly suspected Mariana and the prioress of harming the priest.

The matter concerning Northumberland was explained by Basilda before they left.

The earl had decided to visit Handale that very day. It was his own priory, one his family had endowed generations ago. Until now, he had taken no interest in it. With the roads free from snow, it was an opportunity, then, to pay a visit before returning north to his stronghold at Alnwick Castle.

At the same time, he would use the priory church for the blessing of the marriage between Harry Summers and the heiress of the Kilton lands. And during this time, his chancellor and other relevant officials might as well give the accounts a casual once-over, nothing rigorous, of course, but an opportunity to get things straight should never be lost.

After Hildegard and Mariana left Basilda, and crossed to the refectory, they found the place in ferment.

There was some merriment among the masons when the news about the earl was recounted by Hamo's dairymaid, who had got it from the head kitchener shortly after the harbinger of the earl's retinue had put in an appearance.

Apparently, he had announced, "A few demands will make his grace's visit more tolerable," and then produced a list of requirements as long as his arm. The earl, the conversi were relieved to discover, would not expect to be housed overnight. It would be a short visit only. Even so, it involved a wholesale scrubbing down of the kitchens. Conversi were seen on their hands and knees in all the places the earl was likely to set foot. The church shone. Incense was thick in the air.

The turmoil increased when, unheralded, bedraggled, and out of temper, the masons' master, Sueno de Schockwynde, finally puffed in after his servant, leading a melancholy horse. Not much later, he was followed by his travel companions, the Durham coroner and his clerk.

They had set off a week ago, as soon as they had received the prioress's message about Giles's death, but then the snows had come and they had been halted halfway across the moors.

Schockwynde came across Hildegard in the warming room while everyone was at mass. He gave a double take. "Have you left the Order, domina—sister—I mean, mistress, is it?"

It showed how ruffled the master was after his journey, she thought, that he addressed her without the elaborate courtesies that so often brought him mockery from the rougher elements.

"My decision has not yet been made," she admitted. "It's a long story. For the time being, I'm known as Mistress York and would welcome your discretion."

"It's yours." He bowed.

"But tell me, master, how did you fare over the moors in this weather? I hear you had to take refuge for a few days?"

"It was utterly and completely abominable," he replied. "Not just because of the snow—that was trying enough—but also because of an event so vile that we are left with nerves shattered and our thoughts in disarray." He turned to the coroner, who had just entered. "You would not disagree, Rodrick?"

The coroner, a rotund, cheerful-looking man, belying his gruesome calling, went over to the hearth, rubbing his hands and holding them out to the warmth. "Mistress, I will not sully your sensibilities by detailing what befell us."

"Suffice to say it will have ramifications for our dear beleaguered sovereign," said Schockwynde, butting in.

"For King Richard!" exclaimed Hildegard with a sudden feeling of dread. "But what on earth's happened? You can speak plainly to me. You know me of old, master. My sensibilities have been tried and tempered. Tell me what happened."

"It's this." Schockwynde, eager to blurt it all out, lowered his voice. "A royal courier was sent from the king to his barons of the north, begging for assistance against the rebels, his uncle dukes. We know this from letters found in his bag. But"—he lowered his voice still further—"he did not reach the earl of Northumberland, King Richard's main hope, and why not?" He drew back, the look of horror on his face arousing Hildegard's impatience.

"Why? Tell us!"

"The courier left Archbishop Neville's palace near York in good order, but he never reached his destination. He was murdered at an inn on the moors."

"Murdered most horribly, though I say it myself," the coroner interjected. "One of the most vicious and obscene injuries a man can receive." His cheerful expression had become bleak. "I am continually surprised by the cruelty of one man to another, but this was particularly heinous."

"Its symbolic intention is clear," added Schockwynde. "Recall the rumours about the murder of the king's great-grandfather at Berkeley Castle? With the sword inserted . . ." He gestured.

"It stands as a clear message to the king," the coroner averred.

Hildegard stared in revulsion. "They're warning that what will befall him if he does not bow to his uncles' authority will be what happened to his great-grandfather, King Edward the Second?"

CHAPTER 33

The news stunned and alarmed the masons when they heard it. Their horrified response demonstrated, if proof were needed, their unshakable loyalty to the king. Hildegard saw the news as another piece in the puzzle. It explained Northumberland's lack of support for King Richard. The truth was that he had never, in fact, received Richard's request for help. Any one of the king's many enemies could have put a price on the courier.

The big question remained, of course: If the courier had arrived safely with his message, would the earl have mobilised his army and marched south to the king's aid or not?

By now, the defeat of the royal supporters at Radcot Bridge had also spread through the priory. It ran as fast as flames through thatch.

A mood of feverish uncertainty took hold. For the first time since the Rising in 1381, personal allegiance had again become a game of jeopardy. To be caught on the wrong side could be a serious business once more. It could mean the loss of rights and lands . . . and life.

Master Fulke was not forgotten in all this. The bailiffs had set a time for the charges to be read, after which, if everything went according to plan, Fulke would be escorted to a cell in Whitby jail-house.

The bailiff's men escorted him from his not-too-arduous imprisonment. Neatly attired in an expensive black cloak and velvet overmantle, with a jaunty capuchon tied into a stylish knot on his head, and his beard combed, he looked every inch the wealthy, respectable merchant he pretended to be. Signs of the ague had quite disappeared. By contrast, the masons looked a disreputable bunch in their work-stained leather jerkins and unkempt hair. The bailiff looked them over and Hildegard could tell where his natural sympathies lay at the start.

Fulke tried to take command of the situation at once. "Continue," he said as soon as the bailiff read the charges. "Let's get on with it. I need to see my attorney as soon as we leave here."

"How do you answer?" asked the bailiff, refusing to be hurried.

"Not guilty, of course. What do you expect? I had those goods for sale legally and aboveboard."

"Aboveboard? We have information that they were very much below board." The bailiff gave a nasty chuckle. "You brought a quantity of war feathers and bow poles into the country from Norway without paying duty. Where are your bills of lading?"

Fulke raised his shackled wrists. "If you'd release me, I'd show you."

"Back in Ruswarp, I suppose?"

"You suppose right. Where else would I keep my records of trade?"

"The earl's steward knows nothing about any records."

"Is he the one lodging this charge?"

"He is."

Fulke looked momentarily deflated; then he snarled, "And who informed him, I'd like to know."

"You will. By and by." The bailiff smirked. "We're getting somewhere, then. You admit there was something to inform him about?"

"I admit nothing!"

The bailiff's clerk was writing furiously. The bailiff had more to say. He gave Fulke a confident smile. "We'll send someone to fetch your records, Master Fulke. But first, there's another charge here. It concerns girls who have been passed on to a fellow in—"

"Save me!" Fulke raised his shackled wrists to heaven in a dramatic gesture of supplication. Then he turned to the bailiff. "This comes from that novice who absconded, doesn't it? That raving fantasist. She said she'd do this to me, the vindictive little bitch. Where is she? You must have found her to be able to—"

"What had she got to be vindictive about, Master Fulke?" The bailiff suddenly seemed to be enjoying himself.

Fulke threw back his head and gave a worldly smile. "Ask the prioress. She knows what she was like."

"We'll do that, so we'll soon have an answer to that one. We'll also be asking questions in the Whitby stews. And there's one lady Isabella, abducted and sold to the Earl Morcar as a prospective bride for a considerable sum, we're told and—"

"This is insanity. You can't tell me it's against the law to act as a marriage broker?" Fulke gave a disgusted look and turned away. "I've had enough of this. I'm not saying another word until my law clerk gets here."

"We'll go to him, so you needn't bother calling him yourself," replied the bailiff, indicating to his own clerk to put his writing desk away. "That's it for now—"

"Just a minute!" Dakin stepped forward. His fists were bunched. "I accuse this man of murder—"

Schockwynde pushed himself importantly forward. "Hold back, fella. There's a due process." He spoke to the bailiff as one professional man to another. "An apprentice of mine was done to death a week ago. Foul play is suspected. The coroner here has come to examine the body—"

"And you have evidence that it wasn't a natural death?"

"I'll say! The man's throat was ripped out." Dakin burst forward and had to be restrained by the guards.

The coroner spread his hands in a placating manner. "I must see the body first, before we go any further. I take it it's in the mortuary?" He turned to Dakin. "After that, you can accuse this fellow of murder if that's what it looks like."

"And you'll have to lay before us the evidence for your accusation," stated the bailiff sententiously, "otherwise, you'll be in trouble, making false accusations against an innocent man. Let's repair to the mortuary. Lead on!"

With a nod of the head, the bailiff indicated for the coroner and the master mason to follow him, but when Dakin infiltrated the group, he was not turned away. The rest of the masons trailed along a few yards behind, their faces grim. A muttered exchange between Hamo and Will was too quiet to be overheard.

It was clear they thought Fulke would wriggle out of the accusation if he could and, knowing that they had no evidence worth a tattle, they knew he would find it none too difficult. Dakin had also put himself in the wrong by making an accusation with nothing but blind grief to back it up.

Hildegard was frowning as she followed them.

They stood round the body in a silent group. The nun who had been keeping vigil pulled back the sheet. Even in the dim light, the sight of the wounds drew a gasp from everyone.

"He's certainly dead," observed the coroner, recovering first. "He's suffered a particularly frenzied attack, by the look of things." He bent closer to examine the striations of congealed blood in the wounds disfiguring the corpse. Everything was frozen by the snows, whose chill still lingered in the stone-built chamber.

Fulke was gazing in something like horror at the body. The bailiff stood eagerly at the coroner's elbow. Schockwynde turned away and looked likely to vomit. Dakin had a face of stone, as did the other two masons. Carola went hurriedly to the door.

"And the story is that this beast of Handale attacked him while he was walking in the woods?" murmured the coroner as he placed the tip of his dagger into one of the wounds. "A good three inches," he murmured, withdrawing the dagger and peering at the tip.

The bailiff was following his every move. "What did he use as a weapon?" he asked in an awed tone. "Those wounds are too wide to be from a knife or even a sword."

"Well, they were certainly not made by claws," murmured the coroner. He straightened. "But maybe by a claw-hammer?" He gave Dakin a stern glance. "You use claw-hammers in your work, I presume?"

"Of course we do." Dakin looked blank.

"Do you keep a close watch on them?"

At this, Dakin dropped his glance and stared at the ground for a moment. When he raised his head, he looked the coroner in the eye. "I'll not deny it. Working out here with nobody much coming by, we leave them where we use them. Someone could easily walk into the lodge and take one."

Hildegard bit her lip. She had done that very thing herself when she had needed something to prise the lock off the tower door.

The coroner bent over the body again. "May as well check that they're all there when we go back," he suggested in a mild tone.

"They are. I know for a fact. We moved all our belongings into the priory in the expectation of leaving. Nothing was missing."

"When did you do that?" asked the bailiff.

Dakin looked at him with an expression of growing astonishment on his face. "We did it," he said, "shortly after a deerhound was found outside the enclosure gate with its throat and belly ripped open and its entrails spilling onto the snow."

"We'll need to compare wounds if you're hinting both hound and man were killed by the same kind of implement."

Dakin looked from the coroner to the bailiff. "Where was Master Fulke when the hound was killed?"

Fulke had no alibi. The prioress was asked to invite the concerned parties into her parlour, where she could either corroborate or deny Fulke's claims.

"First, to go back to the illegal imports," announced the bailiff, digging his clerk in the ribs to prompt him to start writing. "Master Fulke has the right to be told how the earl's steward knew about them." He eyed the prioress with an invitation to proceed.

Her answer was short. She avoided Fulke's stare. "I told him," she replied.

Fulke swore. Then he lunged forward with the clear intention of inflicting harm on the prioress, who, seeing this, did not move a muscle but merely stared him down. Fulke was dragged halfway across the chamber by the bailiff's two bodyguards and slammed up against the wall. He was pinned there and his betrayed glance never left the prioress's face.

"Why, Basilda?" he croaked. "Why betray me? You got your cut!" He clearly intended to bring her down with him if he could.

Imperturbably, she told the bailiff, "Yes, it's true. I did receive money. I wanted to lure him in far enough to provide the earl with hard evidence." She gazed brazenly round the group, as if to challenge anyone to disagree. "If I'd acted too soon or called a halt to his activities, he would never have been caught, would he?"

"There's something in that," agreed the bailiff. "Did you know what he was smuggling?"

"I didn't. We suspected it was arms. We also suspected he intended them for the duke of Lancaster's son, Henry Bolingbroke. Knowing the accused's allegiance as I do."

"Why, you two-faced—" Words failed Fulke and his mouth dropped open.

The bailiff frowned. "Now, where were you, Master Fulke, two nights ago?"

Fulke recovered sufficiently to snap, "At home. In my bed."

"Can anybody back you up?"

He gave a resigned smile. "Not then, no. I slept alone."

"So what was to stop you coming back here and slaughtering the deerhound?"

"Why in bloody hell should I do a pointless thing like that?"

"Whose hound was it?" asked the bailiff with interest.

"We believe," replied the prioress, "that it was one of two belonging to our miller. He has been informed and, snow permitting, should arrive soon to identify the beast."

"No dragon," murmured Schockwynde. "Beast though it was. But it couldn't claw itself to death, so there has to be another creature at large."

"And I assume you have no alibi for the night the apprentice was murdered, either?" asked the bailiff, turning to the accused.

Dates were checked. Fulke gave a smirk. "I do have a witness to my whereabouts, as it happens."

"In bed again?"

"Just so." He nodded. "But not my own. I beg discretion, however, when ascertaining the fact from the lady concerned. Her husband has a reputation to uphold."

Encouraged to share his secret, he murmured a name to the bailiff, who raised his eyebrows at what was clearly a piece of juicy local scandal. He nudged his clerk. "No need to record that." Turning back to Fulke, he said, "I hope for your sake she backs you up."

The bailiff had done what he had set out to do. He had plenty to get to work on and enough to keep Fulke in custody. The latter gave Basilda a malevolent glare as he was led out.

When the others followed, they stood outside in some confusion.

"That's a turnup," observed Hamo. "So who did him in? We're back where we started."

"Unless the lady denies him." Dakin, for one, was still convinced Giles had been murdered by Fulke or one of his men because he had stumbled on their secret at the tower. He clenched his fists. "It's not ended yet."

Before everyone dispersed, a servant came up to announce the arrival of the miller. He was a tall, loose-limbed fellow, not unlike a grizzled version of Ulf, Hildegard decided. Saxon. Down-to-earth. Naturally pious. He was looking worried. He had been told about the dead animal in the woods. His favourite hound had gone missing.

He was taken to a lean-to near the animal pens in the outer garth and shown the mutilated deerhound.

He dropped to his knees in the straw and buried his face for a few moments in the gore of matted fur. When he stood up, he said, "That's her. What mad witch would do such a barbaric thing?"

He was taken off by the conversi for a sup of ale to sustain him before getting down to the melancholy task of burying the hound.

"She was an old lady," he kept saying as they escorted him away. "Retired from the kennels at Kilton. She wouldn't have harmed a fly. She delighted in walking these woods with me."

Hildegard followed with Hamo and Will, who had offered help with the shovels.

The conversi were sullen. "It wasn't one of us who did it,"

somebody was heard to mutter, "so it must be as the miller claims, a mad witch. And we all know the nuns are secret witches—"

"Aye," another agreed, interrupting, "dancing naked on the Sabbath by the light of the full moon."

When questioned as to which nun they suspected, they fell silent.

With everyone sombre of mood, even the arrival of the earl with a small retinue and the bridal couple could not raise anybody's spirits. Northumberland, glaring round in his usual belligerent fashion, clearly thought it was the last place on God's earth where anybody would wish to be, and he made it clear he was there only on sufferance, doing his duty. He was conducted to the prioress's private parlour. A bevy of guards stood outside the door and surveyed the priory with disdain.

While the masons were busy and everyone else was hanging round the cloister in the hope of getting another glimpse of his grace, Hildegard went across to the men's guest wing. The bailiff had joined the others waiting to see the earl pass by, but he had left his two guards outside the chamber where Fulke was incarcerated.

"He's just having his bread and cheese," one of them said when Hildegard appeared.

"It's not him I've come to see."

At that moment, Desiderata swept out of Fulke's chamber with an empty bowl of pottage in her hands. She narrowed her eyes when she noticed Hildegard talking to the guards. "Have they decided to move him?" she demanded.

The guards shrugged. "Not that we know of, sister."

With a searching glance at Hildegard as if to discern her business, she set off towards the kitchen.

Hildegard took the opportunity to slip inside the baggage room across the hall. It was a cell-like place lit only by one small window high up in the wall and piled with the masons' equipment.

Quickly, she began to search through it. There had usually been several claw-hammers of various sizes littered about the lodge. Racking her memory, she recalled how many and what size had been stored under the eaves as the masons were preparing to leave. She found the one she had used herself to pick the tower padlock. Then she pulled aside some sacking and stared. Something extremely strange was revealed.

It was not a weapon. It was a kind of mask like the ones used in mumming plays. A long leather-covered snout, a wild mane of string, a jaw that opened and closed to reveal two rows of wooden teeth painted white. Holes for eyes. The whole thing on a structure of wire mesh.

An object hideous and unnerving when sighted by moonlight in a haunted wood.

She lifted it up and was just turning it over in her hands when the door behind her slammed shut.

"Well, well, mistress, what have we here? I think this is where we came in. You. Me. An empty chamber."

It was Dakin.

CHAPTER 34

"This time there are no corpses present, only the dragon of Handale." She held the mask out.

"Beautifully crafted, don't you think? A joining of the skills of woodworker and metalworker, with the art of limning thrown in." Dakin was eyeing her closely. He didn't move, but kept his back against the door.

"Tell me," she said, "how did you manage to make that hideous roar?"

He took two paces across the room then. Swift. Determined. She became very conscious of the knife slotted in his belt, his towering strength, his strange manner.

He reached out a hand. "With this." She flinched back as he lunged forward. He reached inside the head and grasped a metal horn-shaped object with a mouthpiece. He swung it, and as she ducked out of the way, she saw him bring it to his lips. Then he blew.

The chamber was filled with the dread racket of the wild beast that had terrorised the nuns. He lowered it. The echoes dwindled to nothing. "Now you know."

"But you were in chains when it was running wild out there."

"Later on, yes. That's when the others took over. We thought it a good joke to go along with the idea of a dragon after Fulke tried to scare us into keeping away. We thought, we'll show you dragons, you losel. Nobody tells us what to do. We guessed he must have a secret reason for wanting to keep us out. We caught him roaming about one night and scared him so much, he ran off with his tail between his legs. That must have been the night he'd received his payment from Morcar. If we'd only known he had gold on him, we'd have made ourselves a profit."

"Did you guess what he was up to?"

Dakin shook his head. "Nor did we imagine he'd do Giles in for ignoring his warning."

"We don't know it was Fulke. It seems unlikely now."

Dakin looked savage for a moment. "Somebody did it."

"I have a plan," she told him. "But I must talk it over with the prioress before saying anything else. I came here to look for the claw-hammer used by the killer. There's one chisel missing from your set."

Now that the thaw had done away with the snow, another trial by weather came up. It was the wind. It howled in across the sea from the east, biting, bending, and breaking everything insubstantial in its path. The trees outside the enclosure roared like the ocean, and branches cracked and gnawed one another. An ancient beech fell onto the high wall and brought part of it crashing down. Nuns seemed to fly like crows across the garth, with their garments winging out around them.

The marriage party led by the earl entered the church for the blessing through Basilda's private entrance and appeared to the congregation from behind the altar.

In the massed light from the candles, the earl's expression was surprisingly genial, and turning to Harry Summers, he was seen to slap him on the back. "Let's get this done, young lad, and get back to the comfort of Kilton. You'll want to get to your bed, and

I've a whole hogshead of Guienne waiting for me, as well as a few sides of good red meat. These nuns live on moonbeams."

Summers, who had eyes only for Isabella, nodded vaguely, as if the words were in a foreign language. "Indeed, Your Grace." He briefly lifted his glance from Isabella's face and turned shining eyes to his lord. "She is most beautiful, you must agree. How should I ever need food when my love sustains me so?"

The earl's reply was drowned out by the wind as it howled and racketed round the building. His own priest offered up a blessing and intoned the words of a nuptial benediction. It was soon over.

"Very satisfactory," murmured the bailiff to Hildegard as they clustered under the porch and assessed the strength of the wind before leaving the shelter. "I do believe we'll have to claim an extra night's hospitality from our lady prioress. There's no going back to Whitby in this. Not over those cliffs. We'd be dashed into the ocean the minute we put our heads above the summit."

"True. But the earl is returning to Kilton."

"Not by the cliff top he isn't. Still, at least we've had the honour of seeing him and we've got our man. It's all been worthwhile." He nodded with satisfaction; then, clutching his hood to his head, he set off across the garth. His guards were just at that moment coming to meet him.

Dismay was audible as they shouted something to him against the wind. Hildegard turned at the sound and a phrase or two was blown her way.

"Gone!" she heard. "Shackles unlocked—how the blazes?"

She saw the bailiff swivel to the earl's group, which was on the verge of departure. Saw his moment of indecision. Then she watched as he urged his men back towards the erstwhile prison. All three disappeared inside.

———

The prioress was in her parlour, seated as usual. The blazing fire reached halfway up the chimney, as usual. But her expression was one Hildegard had never seen before. She listened to Hildegard as she outlined her plan for winkling out the priest's killer and she cocked her head to one side as she heard about Fulke's apparent escape.

"He won't get far, but I'd better watch my step, I suppose." She was unperturbed and changed the subject. "In my opinion, Mistress York, your plan is not unlike a wild clutching at straws. There must be a better one. But as we have so dismally failed to think of an alternative, then yes, let's do it."

She rang the small ceramic handbell Hildegard had noticed when she first arrived. It summoned a different novice, one in pattens.

"My lady?"

"Bring the cellaress to me. Then fetch my two strongest conversi."

Josiana, suspicious at first, then more eagerly, agreed to do as Basilda suggested.

"It's Mistress York we have to thank for this ruse, is it?" She eyed Hildegard with an expression bordering on approval.

"Yes. And this is how we'll go about it." Basilda could not stop her jowls from trembling. "You, Josiana, will keep 'em at vespers for a little longer than usual to give us time to lay the bait. Then make your announcement: A decisive clue to the murderer's identity has been uncovered in the priest's house. No one is to venture there this night, under pain of severe penance." Basilda beamed for the first time. "Make sure they understand that. We'll lure this rat into the trap if it's the last thing we do."

It was desolate in the cloister garth after the earl's retinue had left. His men had cut a swathe of woodland from the road to the main gate in order to make a path to the priory wide enough for the earl's horses, and now, with the wind raging, they had left the same way.

The sacristan scurried across to the bell tower with her head bent, robes flapping, to ring the bell for vespers.

The bailiff, morose at the disgrace of losing his prisoner, conducted a desultory search around the garth for the missing Fulke. Everything about him showed that neither he nor his men expected Fulke to be lingering about the place. He would have had the nous to make good use of the earl's new way through the woods and be long gone.

The moon began to rise. It was a baleful lamp behind the thrashing branches of the trees. The bell for vespers clanged. Its final sonorities were borne away more rapidly than usual on the wind. Everyone filed into church. Except, that is, for the prioress, detained in her room by an indisposition after the excitement of the earl's visit, and Hildegard, whom no one regarded anyway.

The cellaress's voice could be heard at once, and soon, no doubt, she would issue the appropriate warning. Meanwhile, the two strong and trusted conversi carried the prioress in her chair across the blustery garth to the house of the priest. Hildegard walked alongside and opened the door when they arrived. Battered by the gale, the old place creaked and groaned like a ship at sea. The conversi were dismissed but told to stand by after they had placed the chair in the shadow under the stairs with Basilda still in it.

After they left, Hildegard pulled the blind halfway down and remained beside the door, with a view onto the path. Out of the darkness, Basilda whispered across to her. "I'm going to try to stand. Do not be alarmed if you see me on my feet."

In moon shadow, as night descended to a deeper hue and enveloped the house, Hildegard saw a towering figure rise up. It was an alarming sight. Tremors of fear sent her hand to the hilt of her knife in the sudden thought that she had made a dreadful misjudgement.

She was here alone. Possibly the prioress was mad. Her faithful servants were the only people within shouting distance.

Basilda began to chuckle darkly. There was a loud wheezing as she proceeded across the floor. Her hoarse whisper came again. "I do believe I can make it up those stairs if I take my time. Can you tell whether they've finished vespers yet?"

Relieved at such a normal request, spoken in such normal tones, Hildegard lifted a corner of the blind. "There's no light in the garth. The doors are still closed."

"Then I'll do it. I'd like to see where he spent his time, see his few belongings, my poor boy."

A turmoil of shadows separated into one bulky shape rising little by little up the wall. The stairs creaked. After a long and painful progress, a scuffle at the top showed that the prioress had reached the summit. A voice whispered from above, "Now we wait, mistress. And trust that your ruse brings the killer into our trap."

Figures flitting across the garth some time later showed that the service was over. A cloud of dark winged shapes flew and scattered and eventually disappeared.

It was a shock to hear within the continuing roar of the wind a small scraping sound very close at hand. A mouse, perhaps?

A shift in the level of darkness showed that the door was being pushed open. A hooded figure stood on the threshold, then quickly melted into the darkness only a few feet away.

Outside, the full moon glittered coldly over the priory, its buildings, its garth.

Hildegard held her breath.

Without pausing, the shape began to ascend the stairs. Hildegard watched with mounting alarm. Who was it? Should she follow in case the prioress did anything foolish? Whoever this was would certainly be armed with a weapon of some sort. Her thoughts flew to the missing claw-hammer.

Before she had a chance to set one foot in front of the other, there was an exclamation from the floor above. Suddenly, a light blazed at the top of the stairs.

"Who are you?" It was the prioress. She sounded unafraid. "Remove your hood at once!"

There was a scuffle and a gasp, then a heavy crunch, as if someone had fallen heavily against the wooden stair rail.

"What are you doing here, you old bitch?" It was a voice Hildegard recognised, confirmed by the prioress.

"Desiderata! What are you doing here?"

"What do you think I'm doing? I'm here to find out what that spying York woman thinks she's found. I'll destroy it; then I'll destroy her!"

"I should have guessed it! You haven't changed. You murderous whore. It was you killed him, wasn't it?"

"So what, lady? The world's well rid of men like him. It was the easiest thing to slip his medicine into the holy wine. He was a no-good whoreson, preening himself among us nuns, listening to our confessions with that false, sad smile. He was like all the rest of them. A strutting cock of the walk. He deserved to die!"

"You vindictive little madam! I took you in because I believed you deserved a second chance."

"More fool you, my lady." Desiderata gave a cackling laugh. "And now you're at my mercy! You stupid, gullible old woman! Did you really think I was sorry for my righteous culling of sinners? Someone has to do it. I am the avenging angel, sent by the Lord to cleanse the foul sin of venery from this stinking hell pit. You should thank me for my mercy in sending the fouldoers to their doom. But my work isn't finished yet. You yourself are the fount of iniquity, and for once your bodyguard is absent. That cellaress, Josiana! She can't protect you now! And when she shows her worthless face again, I'll do for her what I'm going to do for you!"

Hildegard was already halfway up the stairs when she heard Desiderata give that uncanny cackling laugh again. There was a flash of light as something was ignited. She heard Basilda cry out. Then there was a roaring, louder than the gale outside, a weird and frightening sound. This time, it was not the dragon of Handale.

It was the roar of flames.

A bright glow came from inside the chamber. Basilda screamed, not in fear, but with rage. Desiderata's laughter rang out. By the time Hildegard reached the top, the place was turning into an inferno.

Basilda was on her hands and knees, heading through the smoke towards the door.

Desiderata, rushing madly from one side of the chamber to the other with a burning brand, kept thrusting it into the wattles between the timbers. Soon the timbers themselves were alight. Basilda, coughing, was crawling inch by inch towards the door.

Hildegard reached out to help her, but Desiderata caught sight of her through the smoke and let loose an insane shriek.

"You. Mistress York? I've been following you! I should have done for you in the woods when you were whoring with those masons. But it's your turn now, you fornicating bitch from hell!"

By now, Desiderata's clothes were on fire. She seemed not to notice. Instead, she stumbled across the floor towards Hildegard, the brand raised aloft. Hildegard hesitated. With the apparent intention of bringing the burning brand down across the prioress's back, Desiderata lunged.

In the nick of time, Basilda reached the lip of the stair and threw herself over the edge and began to slither down.

A sound came from below. Then a figure raced up the stairs two at a time, and as Hildegard tried to break the slow tumbling of the prioress, this second figure held out its arms, and together the two of them struggled with the great weight bearing down upon them in an attempt to break its headlong fall.

Basilda's robes were alight.

Through the smoke, Hildegard recognised Josiana. Her large hands smothered the flames. She was shouting to Basilda to get out of the burning house, but the prioress was wedged halfway down the narrow stairs, while behind her the inferno took hold with a furious and deadly certainty. The thatch was by now a mass of flames.

Coughing and spluttering, the two women managed to drag the prioress down the stairs. They could still hear Desiderata's insane laughter above them, interspersed with a list of names.

Hildegard started back up the stairs. Desiderata stood at the top. Her hair was alight. Her black robes were a mass of flames. She did not attempt to descend, just stood there, burning, declaiming with a rapt expression the list of names as the flames devoured her.

As she slithered to the bottom of the stairs, Basilda panted, "That's the litany of souls she has cast into hell! God bless them all!"

Basilda was on her knees, shouting, "Murderous, insane child of God. My own fault. Mea culpa! Mea culpa! I should never have taken her in. God forgive me." She broke off in a fit of coughing.

"Come outside into the fresh air," Josiana barked. "Come on now, move!"

"I'm doing my best. Don't bully me, Josiana." The prioress crawled toward the door and the cellaress hauled her with difficulty to her feet.

"What is that in your hand, Basilda?"

For the first time, Hildegard noticed that the prioress was clutching a small object. It was her son's leather-bound missal, the one she had seen lying on his desk, where he had last used it. Basilda held it close to her heart and said nothing as she allowed the two women to help her outside.

Once far enough away, they turned to look back at the burning house. It shone brighter than the moon. They saw the roof cave in with a huge roar, and from the heart of the conflagration they could hear the exultant screams of the nun in her death throes.

It was not over. The danger of fire increased as gusts of wind carried the raging flames across the priory roofs, settling them on thatch and tiles indiscriminately. The thatch of the *dortoir* caught fire. For a moment, there was a lull. It was damp from the snows, but then billows of smoke rose up. Hildegard started to run towards the building as flames began to shoot upwards.

"Get out, everyone! Get out!" she shouted.

Faces appeared at the windows as she banged on the door to rouse them. Face black with smoke, she was a warning of what had happened. The garth was illuminated by the lurid light from the priest's house. By now, the nuns were beginning to understand. One by one, they came tumbling out of their cells and down the stairs into the garth.

"Free the penitents!" shouted Hildegard, remembering how they were locked in their cells. Everything was confusion. Some nuns tried to go back upstairs to the upper floor to where the penitents were trapped. Others were still running down in bewilderment. Shouting to them to release the penitents, Hildegard forced her way inside. Mariana was standing at the top of the stairs.

"Open the doors. Let them get out. The roof's on fire!" Hildegard shouted to her.

Quickly, the nun ran two at a time to the second floor. When Hildegard reached the top soon after, she could hear her shouting at the penitents to get out. She was heaving the wooden beams off the doors and dragging the occupants out into the corridor. Flames were already beginning to sputter along the ceiling. She worked her way rapidly towards the far end of the corridor. Hildegard screamed at her to get outside. Saw her hesitate. Then watched as she went on to open other doors.

Driven by a need to rescue the woman from her own foolhardiness, Hildegard ran along the corridor, colliding with the penitents, who were now streaming down the corridor. She managed to grab Mariana by the sleeve. "Enough, now. Come away!"

"One more," she replied in a hoarse, smoke-dried voice. She wrenched the bar away to release the last of the imprisoned nuns; then together, all three fled down the corridor, hands touching both sides to guide them through the thickening smoke towards the stairs.

Face blackened, reeking of charred wood and straw, coughing now and then, but otherwise alive, Basilda had collapsed on the ground in the garth. She raised a hand towards Hildegard. "You saved my life, mistress. I hope you think it worth it."

Still her usual self after all that, thought Hildegard, going over to her.

Basilda added, "We certainly flushed out the rat we were after. I should never have given her a second chance. It went against my nature to do so. But compassion won. I suppose you know her story?"

Hildegard admitted that she had glimpsed something of the details in the priory rolls but had not been able to believe it was the same woman.

"That was only the half of it. She was a murderess from childhood, her first victims her own baby brother and younger sister. The boy was found headfirst in a water butt. She locked the latter in the pigpen with a farrow known for its ill temper. Cleverly done. Children are always dying in such ways." Basilda drew a rattling breath and Josiana slapped her on the back until she got her breath back.

"No one thought to doubt they were accidents," the prioress continued. "She must have become mad with the knowledge that she held the power of death in her hands. She pushed another child into a cooking fire, another into a river. I know this because she confessed to my son and he came to me in great distress, wondering what to do. Josiana here kept an eye on her as best she could."

"I was her jailer. I kept her close to us with duties that made her feel trusted. I bear as much blame as you, Basilda. It's not all yours to shoulder alone. We were fools."

"But knowing all that, how did she escape the law? Why was she brought here?" Hildegard asked in astonishment.

"She had a wealthy and doting father. He paid for her to be hidden, first at Rosedale, and when they found her too much, then here at Handale. He believed she could do no wrong." Basilda rubbed the back of one smoke-blackened hand across her face. "She was his daughter and he loved her despite everything. She had a way of beguiling men. She used her power to lure them to sin, and then she felt justified in killing them because, in her insane view, they proved themselves servants of the devil. My poor son." Basilda blinked. "Despite what he knew about her, he fell for that beguiling smile. He thought he could help her."

"Don't, Basilda." Josiana rested a hand on her shoulder.

The cellaress took up the story. "Her father believed the devils could be knocked out of her by prayer. She'd be better here rather than on the gibbet she deserved, with the flames of hell to follow. He believed she was not at fault for the murder that brought her to the notice of the law. She told him she'd been raped by the young man she later stabbed and mutilated. It was not true, of course. The youth's only sin was to fall in love with a pretty face. Her mind was so twisted by her consciousness of her own guilty desires, she turned her hatred on him. Blaming men when they succumbed to her witchcraft and believing it her duty to rid the world of them— revenge of a devilish kind."

"It's God's work, she told me when that apprentice Giles was found. I prayed she had had nothing to do with it," Basilda said.

Hildegard nodded. "She used a claw-hammer to attack him, one she stole from the masons' lodge. I believed she used it to attack the miller's deerhound, as well. And then she worked on its body with a knife." Hildegard recalled the conversation in the cloisters on the subject of whether animals had souls.

"Go and make sure everyone got out in time, Josiana." Basilda gestured towards the burning building.

The thatched roof of the *dortoir* was well ablaze. Nuns stood around in the garth and watched it burn with dazed expressions. The wind seemed to lift the flames and deposit them with a loud *whoosh,* as if from a giant hand, onto different parts of the brittle straw.

Basilda surveyed the destruction of her priory with suppressed rage. She had not given up on it. Soon she was ordering the nuns to bring water from the overflowing butts to douse the flames. Conversi scrambled to fetch ladders so they could pour water on the more distant buildings on the opposite side of the garth, which so far had escaped the flames. Constructed of stone and slate, they were less vulnerable than the buildings in the outer garth made of wattle, daub, and thatch. Belatedly, the sacristan went to the tower and swung the bell in a racketing alarm.

Everyone was out now: the bailiff and his two men; Master Schockwynde in a long nightgown; the coroner, shrugging on a fur-lined cloak over his long undershirt; the masons, rubbing their eyes in the smoke and gazing with dismay at the destruction.

"Everyone accounted for?" It was a miracle no one had been

injured. Hildegard could see no one missing, except, of course, for Fulke, who would be in some safe house by now.

Basilda's hand was still closed round her son's missal. Something pathetic in her smoke-smeared face touched Hildegard's heart for a moment before she turned away, saying, "Let's get those who need it to the infirmary and call your herberer with salve for burns."

"No need, mistress. She's already approaching."

Indeed, the old herberer, spry and upright, was marching across the garth with a large leather scrip over her shoulder, which Hildegard guessed would contain all that was needed to treat the wounded. She went over to see what she could do to help.

CHAPTER 35

It was much later, when the bell began to toll for the night office, that someone exclaimed, "Still only matins! It seems as if a full twenty-four hours have gone by. What a time!"

Fortunately, there had been few injuries. Smoke was the main problem, and everyone was instructed to clear their lungs for themselves. With the wind beginning to drop, voices had become lowered, as well.

It was into this relative silence that a shout came from the outer garth.

It turned out to be the sacristan on her way back from the bell tower. She ran up, breathless with alarm. "I can hear noises coming from the dovecote!" Superstitious enough to believe it was the murderess's trapped soul risen from the dead, she called out for somebody to go and see what it was.

As Hildegard was within earshot, she made her way over. "The dovecote?" she asked.

The sacristan pointed but would not go any nearer.

Accompanied by the masons, Hildegard and a few others went over to investigate. They could all hear it: a man's voice, his shouts fading for a moment before being vigorously renewed.

They stood outside.

"Somebody's locked in!" stated Hamo with a sudden grin. "Guess who!"

Not locked in, as they discovered when they looked for the key; it was more that they were locked out. Hamo banged on the door.

"Come out, Fulke!"

He must have recognised their voices, because suddenly the door flew open and he came tumbling outside, covered in bird droppings, gasping, "Has she gone?"

He stared wildly round. His hair was awry and a gash on his forehead puckered and leaked blood into his normally dapper beard. He was trembling from head to foot. His clothes were a mess.

"Where is she? Don't let that murdering bitch near me! For God's sake, protect me!" He stumbled forward into their midst, as if they could make a shield to keep him safe.

He soon admitted that Desiderata, all the while flirting with him when she brought food to his prison, had lured him into one of the store sheds with the promise of what he could not resist. As soon as they were alone, she had produced a claw-hammer from her sleeve and attempted to smash it into his face. Thanks only to his quick reflexes, he had dodged and suffered only a glancing blow. He had taken to his heels and locked himself in the first safe place he found.

"She's mad. What have I ever done to her?" he moaned. "Don't let her anywhere near me, for Benet's sake."

"She won't come near you," Hildegard told him. "She's dead."

When all the confusion was over, with the conversi busy putting things to rights next morning, Ulf and his men turned up at the priory on their way back home from Kilton Castle. He was conducted to the refectory, where he found Hildegard sitting with the masons, having a farewell drink. He knew the master mason already. Schock-wynde, still looking shaken, told Ulf the entire story, what he knew of it, from beginning to end.

The masons were ready to leave for Durham, and their pleasure showed. Schockwynde had promised to send some men back when the weather improved to finish the prioress's building works. One aspect of the plans had bothered Carola. It was about a small cell built within one of the walls, with only a small opening through which food might be passed. When the master took this up with the prioress, she blandly agreed it would no longer be required.

Carola also told Hildegard about her suspicions over Dakin's apparent involvement with Fulke. Now she knew his only concern was to find Giles's killer.

"I thought he had decided to go in with Fulke to make some money," she admitted. "We knew Fulke was up to something, and Dakin believed he could turn it to his own advantage. We are hand-fast." She smiled somewhat shyly at Hildegard. "My own mother approved, but Master Schockwynde told me I could do better for myself. Dakin thought he would win the master's approval if he had wealth of his own."

"I wondered about that," admitted Hildegard. "But have you changed Schockwynde's mind?"

Carola nodded. "I pointed out to the master that he had fallen in love with my mother and some would say he could have done better for himself, too, and married a duchess. Given his lineage." She smiled. "He admitted he had loved mother from afar for many years when she was married and would go on doing so even if she became a kitchen maid." She smiled again. "He's pompous at times but as soft as a brush at heart."

After they left, Hildegard went up to get her bag. She had already packed and was ready to leave, and as Ulf loaded her things onto a pony, he grinned at her in disbelief. "I thought you came here for peace and quiet so you could make up your mind about what to do next?"

"That's what I was hoping for!" She smiled across the animal's back. "One thing's sure: I won't be joining the Benedictines."

He came round to help her into the saddle of the palfrey he had brought along for her. When she was astride, she said, "I suppose I'd better return to Swyne."

"It's the feast of Saint Nicholas the day after tomorrow," he reminded her. "Come with me to Langbrough. Let's give little Alys a Christmas to remember. We'll lock the doors against the world's madness, and you can put off all decisions about your future until the twelve days of Christmas are over."

She gave a sigh of happiness. "That sounds wonderful."

Just then, a courier came trotting through the gate. He was beaming. "Thank Saint Benet, they've cut a track through those woods at last. I'm looking for a Mistress York?"

"You've found me," Hildegard replied.

He didn't dismount. "Good. That means I can get straight on to Durham in time for the winter feast. Here." He pulled a vellum out of his bag with the great seal of Meaux attached and thrust it into her hands. "No reply requested." He saluted and in a moment had set off into the woods again, back towards the moors road.

With sudden misgivings, Hildegard tore off the seal. Aware of Ulf's eyes on her, she hurriedly scanned the page that opened out.

The message was short. To the point. No greeting.

I understand you are back from pilgrimage to St. James's Compostela. Attend me at Meaux. Signed *Abbot Hubert de Courcy.*

Ulf was staring at her intently. He had recognised the abbey's seal. "What does he say?"

"You can guess."

He turned his head. "Yes, I suppose I can. That's that, then."

Without a word, he went over to Petronel and hoisted himself into the saddle. Turning the horse's head towards the gates, he urged him on and his men began to follow. Hildegard watched him leave.

The group was almost out of sight down the opened woodland avenue when she stuffed the summons to return to Meaux into her bag and pressed her heels into the flanks of the mare.

"Wait for me, Ulf!"

He turned at the sound of her voice. When he saw her following him, the smile he gave lit up his face. "Home, then?"

She nodded. "And good-bye to Handale!"

EPILOGUE

December 29, 1386, the Tower of London

King Richard was invited to remain in the Tower of London after the defeat at Radcot Bridge. In effect, he was a prisoner. He is said to have spent one full night in the company of his cousin Henry Bolingbroke, eldest son of the duke of Lancaster, and Thomas Mowbray, Henry's shadow and hereditary marshall of England.

King Richard's twentieth birthday was only days ahead, on the Feast of the Epiphany, January 6. His cousin was nine months the younger. They were not here to celebrate birthdays.

Bolingbroke: "You think we daren't touch you because of your anointing."

Richard: "And because of my sword."

He draws the sword. Bolingbroke draws his. Richard is an elegant swordsman. He practises every day, as his tutor, a veteran of Poitiers, Sir Simon Burley, recommends, and but for the fact that Mowbray sidles up behind him and grabs him by both elbows, he would easily have defeated Bolingbroke's swaggering, boorish sword thrusts. Thus his cousin, ever the opportunist, and with Richard's arms safely pinioned, is able to stroll up and force his sword from his grasp.

Bolingbroke: "Now what are you going to do?" He touches him under the chin with the point of his sword.

"Kill me. Be a regicide. See how England loves you then. You'll be dead men."

"We won't be so crass." He presses the point of his sword against Richard's chin again.

Mowbray looks pale now Richard is at their mercy. Suddenly, there is no limit to what might happen. But Bolingbroke has no qualms. He has proved a bully in the lists, and now that he has his victim in his power, he wants to make the most of it.

"Kneel, you piece of effeminate filth."

"Kneel to you?" Richard laughs.

Bolingbroke goes closer and says into his face, "Kneel, or I'll put my sword up your perfumed arse."

Such is the venom in his bloodshot eyes, his face red, carroty beard bristling, Richard's mouth drops open.

"Have you forgotten what they did to our great-grandfather Edward?" Bolingbroke smirks.

"It's not true. No man in this realm could be so vile as to do that to their king."

Now it is Bolingbroke who laughs out loud. "Couldn't they? Do you want to try me? What do you say, Thomas?"

Mowbray stutters a reply.

"See?" Bolingbroke pokes Richard under the chin with the point of his sword again. It is razored steel. Even a scratch brings a dribble of blood onto Richard's clean white shirt. "Imagine this up your fundament, O King!"

"You filthy animal, Harry."

"Kneel when you address me, coz. C'mon. Down!" To encourage his cousin's obedience, he waves the sword in Richard's face. "Or shall I give you a quick haircut? How many slashes will it take to shear your golden locks? This is good steel here. Good steel, isn't it, Thomas?"

"It is indeed. Very good."

"Hear that, you white-arsed sot wit?"

"You seem very interested in my backside. Isn't your wife enough for you?"

"Kneel!"

Slowly, Richard kneels to his cousin. His glance is fixed on Bolingbroke's boots. Fury is in his heart. He will kneel now because it is expedient to do so. But later he will make Bolingbroke do more than kneel.

He raises his chin. "Is this how you mean, Harry?"

When Bolingbroke looks down into the fair and noble face, he feels an urge to smash it. Even now, on his knees, Richard is still king.